Nightmare Series Box Set

Books 1 - 3

Written by David Longhorn
Edited by Emma Salam

Thank You!

Hi there! I'd like to take this opportunity to thank you for purchasing this book. I really appreciate it, and to show how grateful I am to you, I'd like to give you **a full length horror novel in 3 formats (MOBI, EPUB and PDF) absolutely free!**

Download your full length horror novel, get free short stories, and receive future discounts by visiting www.ScareStreet.com/DavidLonghorn

See you in the shadows,
David Longhorn

Nightmare Abbey
Nightmare Series Book 1

Nightmare Abbey

Prologue: England 1792

"What is evil?" asked Lord George Blaisdell. "Seriously, you fellows – what is evil, truly?"

The two other men seated at the great dining table exchanged significant glances. They and their host had drunk a sufficient amount of port wine to remove all inhibitions, but not quite enough to hopelessly fuddle the brain. Fortunately, much of the alcohol had been mopped up by the feast the lord had laid out for them.

"Evil is surely the rejection of Christian principles?" suggested Donald Montrose, a young Scottish writer of satirical verses.

The two older men laughed.

I've made a fool of myself, thought Montrose. *Well, it was inevitable. I should not have accepted an invitation from such a man. I wish I was back in London among my fellow hacks. But I need a wealthy patron, and they are not easy to come by.*

"A very Presbyterian answer," rumbled Blaisdell, raising his wine to Montrose in mock salute. "Your chapel-creeping, Bible-thumping Scotch ministers certainly spend a lot of time condemning sin. Especially sins of the flesh, eh? Never stop thinking about flesh, your average holy man."

The lord snapped his fingers and a serving girl came forward to refill his goblet. She was completely naked except for a generous layer of gold paint, as were the other two girls waiting at the table. At first, Donald had thought they were statues standing in alcoves along the walls of the great dining room. He tried to avert his eyes from the girl pouring wine for Blaisdell, but could not help glancing at her obvious charms. She smiled at him, and he felt himself blush hotly.

"Simple lust, fornication, or any of your so-called deadly sins," continued the lord, running his free hand along the breasts and thighs of the girl. "None of them are really more than animal desires, impulses shared by all living things. Evil? I think not. Off you go, Sukie!"

Blaisdell gave the girl a playful slap on the rear and she retreated to her alcove. The lord turned to his guests and slapped his palm on the table to win back their attention.

"No, my friends!" he declared. "Evil is not merely a falling short, a failure to observe some code or other. It is an active force in the world, a darkness at least as powerful as that of light."

Donald was puzzled by the question, and disturbed.

"Do you mean to suggest, my lord," he asked, "that the revolution currently underway in France is an upsurge in this force you speak of?"

Blaisdell looked at the young man for a moment, then gave a dismissive snort.

"Peasants banding together to chop the heads off their betters? Pah! Such uprisings are nothing new. But you have a point, Donald. Because if this revolution spreads, brings chaos to the whole of Europe – well, perhaps that will prove me right. Darkness will indeed triumph."

"Stop dancing around the subject, George," said Sir Lionel Kilmain, the older of the two guests. "What do you mean by evil? Devil worship, perhaps, like that damn fool Wilkes and his friends of the Hellfire Club?"

The lord mulled this over, staring into the blazing coal fire for a moment before replying.

"You are right, Kilmain," he said finally. "Now may be the Devil's time. And yes, a few short years ago the Hellfire Club made great play of toasting the Prince of Darkness and such. It was claimed that the infernal dignitary did put in an appearance at one of their gatherings. But there is nothing new in such practices."

Silly talk, thought Donald. *Perhaps designed to get a rise out of me.*

"Surely," he began, battling the alcohol to choose his words with tact, "only the ignorant peasantry believes in a literal Devil these day? Old Nick with horns, cloven hooves, a stink of sulfur?

For a moment, Blaisdell looked as if he might take offense and Donald tensed. He had heard that the notoriously wayward lord sometimes had his serving men pitch annoying houseguests into his ornamental fountain. But then Blaisdell's broad face relaxed into a grin.

"Scoff away, Donald," the lord said. "I, for one, would not be surprised if Old Nick did not put in an appearance this very evening."

Kilmain gave a half smile, pointed a pale, bony finger at his host.

"I suspect you have a surprise in store, my friend. But please, toy with us no longer."

Blaisdell stood up, swaying slightly, and rested his large, flabby hands on the tabletop.

"What if I were to tell you," he said slowly, "that the monks of the old abbey were in thrall to Satan? According to the locals, they made sacrifices. My tenants still whisper darkly about blood rituals. Chickens, lambs. And even, on occasion, an orphan child. All slaughtered in a solemn ritual on a pagan altar. An altar that my workmen discovered lately while draining an old, mill pond."

Nonsense, thought Donald, *the man is merely showing off.* But he felt an undeniable chill despite the roaring coal fire in the hearth.

"Nothing would surprise me about a bunch of Papists," observed Kilmain, who Montrose knew owned extensive lands in Ireland. "Superstition and shenanigans all the way with your Catholics, I've found – an absurd mix of the Christian and pagan. I've lost count of the number of times some old biddy has put the evil eye on me for turning her family out of their hovel. But what of it? The monks of Malpas were driven out in the days of Henry Vlll. And good riddance."

"Yes," agreed Blaisdell, "and my ancestors acquired their lands at a very fair price. But the altar they used for their unholy rituals still exists, as I say, although a little worse for wear. It is, in fact, the centerpiece of a little temple I have had built, dedicated to the gods of pleasure and debauchery."

Kilmain frowned.

"A temple? I saw no new buildings in your splendid grounds," he mused. "And no sign of building work in the abbey ruins. So this temple must be–"

"Underground!" exclaimed Montrose, then felt himself blush again.

"Quite right," said the lord. "Beneath our feet, in fact.

Come, my friends, let us descend into the ancient cellars of long-defunct Malpas Abbey! I have been quite busy. See what you think of my – my very personal conception of an unholy temple."

Montrose, unused to wine of any sort, wobbled slightly as he followed his social superiors out of the room. As he left, he caught the eye of the brazen Sukie, who gave a distinctive wink as well as a smile. Montrose had a sudden, vivid image of her slipping into his bed that night. He shook his head, trying to clear his thoughts.

I must not have lustful thoughts, he told himself, and made an effort to recall his toothless grandmother eating porridge.

Blaisdell led his guests through what seemed to Montrose, in his wine-befuddled state, to be a maze of corridors. Eventually they arrived at a doorway decorated with a Grecian lintel. Kilmain remarked on this, asking if the stonework was genuine.

"Marble, taken from the Sibyl's Temple at Cumae," Blaisdell explained, as he unlocked an obviously new set of double doors. "But there's a stone down here that's far older than the most ancient Greek carving, if I'm any judge."

Which you're probably not, thought Donald, tiring of his host's pretensions to scholarship. So far as he knew, Blaisdell had been thrown out of Oxford University in his first semester for beating up one of his lecturers.

They waited for a few moments inside the doorway while Blaisdell lighted torches from a tinder box. With each man bearing a light, they began to descend into the cellars of the medieval abbey.

"Quite the Gothic atmosphere, Blaisdell," remarked Kilmain. "Very much in fashion."

"Fashion?" snorted the lord. "Perhaps. But I like to think it reflects my own unique taste, uninfluenced by the pulling milksops they call artists these days."

The temple was an opulent display of wealth, a circular chamber fringed with marble columns that – Blaisdell explained – had been imported from Sicily at great cost. The walls were decorated with friezes showing various scenes from mythology. Montrose noted that all of them depicted depravity and violence, invariably sexual in nature.

"Not bad, eh?" shouted Blaisdell. "Your classical mythology is full to the brim with amusing filth."

"I fear our young friend is not so keen on the classics," Kilmain observed dryly.

Donald followed Kilmain's example and placed his torches in a sconce at head height. Meanwhile, Blaisdell walked around the circumference of the room lighting more torches. In a couple of minutes, the room was filled with flickering orange-red light, plus the inevitable smoke. Donald's eyes began to tear up, and he took out a handkerchief to wipe them. As he did so, he thought he saw a small, spindly shadow appear in an alcove where there was no one to cast it. But once his eyes were clear nothing was visible.

"Behold!" roared Blaisdell, making a theatrical gesture. "The altar of evil! Imagine what monstrous deeds those wicked monks performed in this hidden chamber, eh? Let us hope we can live down to their standards, Kilmain."

While the gentry bantered, Donald observed the prize exhibit, which stood in the exact center of the circular space. The supposed Satanic altar was disappointing after all Blaisdell's boasting. Donald had expected something brutally imposing, but it looked like a nondescript lump of limestone or some other pale substance, about four feet high and roughly as wide. The upper surface was flat, certainly, but the rest of it seemed like outworked stone. It was only when he stepped a little nearer that Donald could make out some worn – but still discernible carvings – that looked nothing like the classical Greek and Roman sculpture he was familiar with.

"Celtic," he mused. "Or pre-Celtic –Turanian, perhaps. Certainly dating from well before the Romans arrived in these parts."

"Good!" said Blaisdell, "Very good. It seems we do have a man of learning, Kilmain. I had wondered. Well observed, lad. But do you have the stomach to put these antique artifacts to its original purpose, eh?"

Donald gave what he hoped was a worldly smile.

"I am sure such pagan relics have no real power, my lord,

whatever superstitious villagers may say. The days of the old gods are long past."

Blaisdell and Kilmain exchanged another one of their glances. Donald, suspecting that he was excluded from some joke or prank, tried to look dignified.

"You may be right, Montrose," said Blaisdell. "But let us see."

The lord looked up toward the top of the stairs, and Donald turned to see a stout serving man descending with a bundle in his arms. It was an object about a foot long and swaddled in a white blanket. Suddenly it wriggled and for a horrible moment, Donald thought that it was a baby.

"What is this?" he demanded. "Surely that cannot be—"

Then the bundle emitted a squeal, and he laughed in relief.

"A piglet!" he exclaimed.

"Yes," said Kilmain. "At the very least we'll dine on fresh pork tomorrow. You can't conduct human sacrifices in England nowadays, lad. Too many busybodies around, too much officialdom."

Donald gave a hesitant laugh, unsure if his host was joking. He and Kilmain watched as the servant crossed the room and laid his burden on the altar, then withdrew to a respectful distance. Blaisdell, meanwhile, had donned a black robe like that of an old-time monk and stood over the wriggling animal.

"Surely, my lord," Donald began, "you are not going to actually kill—"

"Silence!" hissed Kilmain, drawing the Scotsman aside. "He may seem playful now, but if thwarted he can turn very nasty. Let him have his fun."

Donald nodded, watching as Blaisdell produced a dagger with an ornate handle from his robe. Raising the weapon over his head, he began to chant in a resonant voice.

"I conjure thee, Lucifer, Lord of Light! Look favorably upon our devotions, O Prince of Powers, and reveal yourself to us!"

Then he stabbed the piglet. There was a final squeal, and bright, arterial blood seeped out of the swaddling and pooled on the altar. Donald, having grown up on a farm, could not help but feel a pang of sympathy for the young animal. And, for the first time, the pure contempt he felt for decadent aristocrats like Blaisdell and Kilmain rose to the surface of his mind.

How typical of the idle rich, he thought. *To take the life of a defenseless beast for fun. I despise these people. I would not accept this man's patronage if he offered it.*

Time passed. The blood that had spread over the altar began to darken. Kilmain gave a quiet chuckle. It seemed apparent that nothing was going to happen, and Donald had to suppress a desire to laugh. Then he gave a yelp and clapped his hands over his ears. The air was torn by a high-pitched sound, somewhere between a shriek and a whistle. A few months earlier, Montrose had witnessed a sudden escape of steam from one of the new engines used to pump water out of mines. The intense, piercing sound now assailing his ears was even worse.

The sound ended as suddenly as it had begun. Donald felt a ringing in his ears, removed his hands from the sides in a gingerly fashion in case the noise resumed. Looking around he saw that Blaisdell was trying to say something to Kilmain, but the Irish landowner shook his head. They were all clearly all deafened. But after half a minute or so, their hearing began to return.

"What the hell was that?" demanded Kilmain, sounding annoyed. "One of your tricks, Blaisdell?"

"Shush, man!" returned the lord, holding up a finger. "No tricks! Do you hear? What is that?"

A quiet, barely-audible sound was becoming perceptible over the crackling of the torches. It was a gentle rustling, like someone trying to walk stealthily over dry leaves. Donald looked around the room, but saw no sign of movement. Then he glimpsed a dark form appear for a split second around the side of the altar, on the same side where Blaisdell stood. He got the impression of something that might have been a head.

But there were no eyes, he thought, starting back towards the stone steps. *Can't have a head without eyes.*

"What is it, lad?" asked Blaisdell, glancing at the floor

around him, his voice betraying nervousness. "What did you see?"

"There was something, perhaps an animal," Donald replied. "It looked at me around the side of the altar. It must have been around your feet, my lord."

"Nothing here now," Blaisdell said, but he moved quickly away from the altar.

"Ghost of the piglet, perhaps," suggested Kilmain. But despite the sarcastic remark, he sounded unsure of himself.

"That sound," Donald said. "Has it happened before?"

"We never done this before, sir," replied the servant, who had backed halfway up the stairs. "Never should have meddled."

"Oh, shut up man!" bellowed Blaisdell. "You're as bad as the villagers. Clearly we have failed to conjure the Evil One, but perhaps we heard a soul screaming in purgatory, eh?"

Kilmain's eyes widened at the suggestion.

"It reminds me of the Irish tales of the banshee," he said. "A screeching spirit. Invisible, some of the time."

"And what does this banshee do?" asked Donald, timidly.

"Portends the death of a person of note," Kilmain replied. "The peasants love stories in which the banshee heralds the demise of a cruel landlord. But that is in Ireland, of course. No reason for it to manifest itself here in England."

Again, thought Donald, *your tone is less confident than your choice of words. Perhaps you fear the cruel landlord's fate?*

"Oh, come in," said Blaisdell, starting to climb the cellar stairs. "Enough of these fireside tales for infants and addle-pates. We can finish another bottle or two of port, eh? What do you say, gentlemen?"

"I fear I must retire for the night, my lord," said Donald. "I am not as used to strong drink as you."

"Pah! What about you, Lionel?" demanded the host.

"Lead on, George," replied Kilmain, apparently recovering his good spirits. "I will help you demolish a bottle – or a cask, if you like!"

Donald was the last to leave the cellar, and felt a disturbing sense of being watched as he reached the doorway.

It was a chill sensation in the back of his neck, causing the small hairs to rise.

Don't look back, he told himself. *No need, nothing there.*

He glanced back, unable to stop himself, and saw only the circle of guttering, smoking torches and the crudely worked slab of stone in the center. It was as he turned his gaze away from the so-called temple that he glimpsed a movement near the altar. He paused in the doorway, twisting his head around to stare directly. There was nothing there, of course. The altar was bare.

Did the servant remove the piglet's body? He must have.

"Come on, lad, your bed-warmer will be getting cold," roared Blaisdell from up ahead.

Donald hurried through the door, resolved not to ask about the dead piglet.

***

"What do you think of our young friend?" Blaisdell asked.

"He can't take his drink, that's for sure," replied Kilmain. "He looked distinctly green about the gills when he went off to bed."

Blaisdell laughed, and held up his glass for a refill. It was well after midnight. The gilded serving girls were stifling yawns and shivering a little. The candles on the dining table had long since burned down, leaving pools of wax smearing the silver candelabra. The only light now came from the great fireplace. But the two gentlemen continued to drink and talk.

"Did you really expect the Devil to appear, George?" Kilmain asked. "It seems most improbable."

Blaisdell shrugged, and pulled Sukie down onto his lap after she had poured his wine. Gold theatrical paint smeared over his velvet waistcoat.

Too drunk to notice, thought Kilmain. *Or too rich to care.*

"To tell you the truth, Lionel," said the English lord, running a hand over Sukie's thigh, "I was not quite sure. I was raised by religious tutors. Fear of hell-fire, eternal damnation, was beaten into me from my toddling days. One never quite escapes that, no matter how fiercely a man may rebel against

9

his upbringing."

Kilmain raised an eyebrow in genuine surprise.

"Quite an admission, George. You implored Lucifer to materialize so that he wouldn't? So you could convince yourself that he does not exist?"

Blaisdell nodded thoughtfully, staring into the fire. Then he pinched the chin of the girl on his lap.

"What do you say, Sukie? Is there a Devil?"

Sukie gave a slightly nervous laugh, clearly unsure how to respond.

"If there is such a one," she said finally, "he is more likely at work in France nowadays, like the Scottish gentleman said."

"A good answer," commented Kilmain, holding up his own glass for his own attendant. "Here, Lizzie, move your arse – I'm dying of thirst."

Kilmain waited for a few moments, but no serving girl appeared. He twisted in his seat and looked round. Lizzie was standing just behind his chair, pitcher of wine in hand, but showed no sign of responding to his order.

Taking the living statue thing too seriously, Kilmain thought. *Silly girl seems to be daydreaming.*

Before he could rebuke her, Lizzie dropped her pitcher, the earthenware vessel shattering on the floor. Wine splashed around Kilmain's shoes, and he leaped up, cursing the girl for her clumsiness. Instead of responding, she started to back away, raising her hands, eyes wide and staring.

"God preserve us!" said Blaisdell in a small voice. He, too, along with Sukie, was now staring past Kilmain towards the entrance of the room. Kilmain turned, and saw the Devil. Framed in the doorway was a reddish-brown figure, crouching to allow its curved goat horns to pass under the lintel. It was reddish-brown, cloven-footed, shaggy with clumps of black hair. It was the Devil of a thousand medieval pictures and carvings, the Satan of Dante and Milton. Its face was goat-like, smiling evilly, the eyes slits of orange fire. At the end of hugely muscled arms, its hands sported wicked black talons.

The Devil took a step forward, bringing it closer to the fire, illuminating every warped and obscene detail of its anatomy. The women screamed. Sukie began to mutter to herself, her eyes shut tight. Kilmain caught snatches of the Lord's Prayer. The hideous apparition took another step forward, evidently unhindered by holy phrases.

Impossible, Kilmain thought, anger rising. *A stupid joke. It must be.*

"Did you hire this fellow from the same theater where you got these girls?" he demanded, turning on his host. "You insult me, George. This is crude beyond—"

Kilmain paused, seeing his host's pale face. Blaisdell looked utterly terrified. A pool of dark fluid was spreading over the fabric of the chair between the lord's hefty thighs.

If he's feigning fear, he's the finest actor in England.

"You summoned me. I have come to take you to Hell!"

The voice was bestial, mocking. Kilmain hesitated, looked again at the monstrous figure that was now just a few strides away, reaching for him. He glanced at a plain wooden box on the mantel above the fireplace, knowing it contained Blaisdell's dueling pistols. He grabbed Lizzie, shoved her towards the nightmarish intruder, then made a dash for the guns.

***

Donald had forgotten to wind his watch, so when he arose to answer a call of nature he could only be sure that it was well after three in the morning. He vaguely recalled climbing the grand stairway to his room, very much the worse for drink. The effects of the port wine were still apparent. He untangled himself from the heavy cotton sheets and flinched slightly as his feet touched the cold, wooden floor. The fire in his bedroom had died down, so that the room was barely visible in the faint glow of coals. He could hear muffled noises from downstairs – shouts, raucous laughter.

Drunken revelry.

Donald used the commode and then, rather than go straight back to bed, went to the window. It was a cloudy, rain-swept April night. He could make out nothing but a wedge of light cast from the dining room window onto the lawn. It was clear that his host and probably Kilmain were still carousing.

As Donald watched he saw a shadow appear, evidently cast by someone moving close by the great French windows.

Now, whose shadow is that? They must be very drunk, whoever they are, prancing around like that. Or perhaps Blaisdell is forcing one of his girls to perform? Kilmain said they were actresses or dancers.

The person casting the shadow seemed to crouch, then leaped with remarkable agility. At the same moment, there was a crash of breaking crockery and an outburst of shouting. More shouting, followed by a scream, presumably that of a woman but Donald was not entirely sure.

Decadence and debauchery, Donald thought. *All the rumors are true. Blaisdell is just another silly lord squandering his inheritance on drinking, whoring, and a little amateurish Satanism.*

Another shadow appeared, this one evidently cast by a man walking backwards, arms raised up in front of him. A smaller figure leaped onto the man's back. There was a yell, another crash, more yells and screams. Donald became concerned.

Perhaps things are getting out of hand. But what can I do? Other than take notes for another satire on the idle rich?

He made for the bedroom door but then stopped, gripped by indecision. He imagined himself walking in on a full-blown orgy, clad in his cheap nightshirt, every inch the impoverished scribbler come to gawp at his social betters. As he hesitated, the alarming cacophony from below died away. Donald went to the door and opened it a half-inch, straining to hear. His bedroom opened onto a balcony that in turn looked out over the central atrium of the great house, with the entry to the dining room one floor below. There was no sound. It was pitch black, not a single candle to cast light on the scene.

"Oh, to hell with the lot of them," he muttered to himself. Then he started back. The door was being pushed open. In the waning glow of the fire, he could just make out a small, lithe form as it came noiselessly into the room. His unexpected visitor was naked, undeniably feminine in form, but a thick fall of dark hair almost concealed the face. He could just make out a snub nose and a broad, full-lipped mouth.

"Sukie?" he asked.

By way of reply, the interloper raised a slender hand and placed her fingers on his lips. Her other hand ran over his chest, down toward his loins. Donald made a feeble effort to retreat, but she pressed herself even closer. Confusion reigned in the young man's mind, not helped by a collision with a bedside table. A pitcher of water fell onto the floor and Donald slipped, landed heavily on the bed. The intruder sprang on top of him. The great mass of hair dangled in his face.

"This is – this is most improper," he said feebly.

In reply, the visitor gave an odd, dry cackle.

"Most improper. But it's what you want!"

The voice was rasping, as if the throat repeating his words was devoid of moisture. Donald wondered if Sukie had some kind of ailment. She certainly did not sound like a healthy young woman.

She might have the French pox, he thought. *What if I caught syphilis? You go blind and insane!*

Donald had a sudden, terrifying vision of lunatics on display at Bedlam in London, many of them covered in syphilitic sores. No early morning tumble, even with Sukie, was worth that degree of risk. He tried to shove the girl away, but she simply clung to him all the tighter and began to lift his nightshirt. Her strength startled him, scared him a little. Bizarrely he felt the seductress had become an assailant.

"Get off me, Sukie!" Donald shouted. "I'll have none of you!"

For a moment, it seemed as if his words had succeeded where physical force had failed. The figure above him became unnaturally still. Then the unpleasant cackling laugh came again.

"But I'll have some of you!" said the rasping voice.

Panic seized Donald and, with a huge effort, he managed to free himself. As Sukie lunged at him, he grabbed her by the hair, planning to hold her at bay. But great swathes of hair simply came off in his hand, along with what looked like a layer of scalp.

"Oh my God!" Donald yelled, trying to retreat, only to fall onto the floor, winding himself.

With much of her hair gone, the being that leaped onto him could be seen for what it was – a close facsimile of a young woman, one that could pass for human in the dark. The face that pushed into Donald's had the look of a waxen mask, with a rudimentary lump of nose, gaping holes where its eyes should have been. Its mouth was no longer that of a voluptuous young woman but a round, funnel-like protuberance. The sober, rational part of Donald's mind wondered how such a thing could speak at all.

"What are you?" he screamed, struggling vainly in the monster's grip. He struggled to recall passages from a Scripture concerned with banishing evil spirits. "Are you a demon? I abjure you depart in the name of our Lord Jesus Christ! Begone, foul thing!"

The weird mouth parts extended, tentacle-like, roaming over his face before settling over his left eye socket. There was a vile sucking noise, and Donald screamed out in pain as blood gushed over his cheek. Then it tore out his other eye. The pain was so excruciating that he felt sure he would pass out, but somehow the agony continued.

Donald was aware of his inhuman attacker releasing its grip, and put his hands to his face. His fingertips found the empty sockets. He cried out not just in pain but also at the insanity of it all. He howled until he found himself gasping for breath and sobbing, half-choked on his own blood.

"Yes! It is what you most feared!"

Donald froze at the words, his terror almost driving the pain from his mind. He felt his grip on sanity start to fray.

It's still here! Oh Jesus it's going to kill me now. Let it be quick at least, let it be quick.

But instead of finishing him off, it whispered a few words in his ear. What was left of Donald's rational mind, just before it was submerged in a dark ocean of mental chaos, recognized the phrase as a kind of self-fulfilling prophecy.

"You will be blind and mad in Bedlam!"

Chapter 1: A Paranormal Partnership

"Naturally the foundation will cover all your expenses," said Ted Gould, as a discreet waiter seated them at a corner table. "We're very keen on this partnership."

Matt McKay looked around the restaurant. It was classier than what he was used to, even before you took into account higher British prices. When he glanced at the menu, he felt relieved that Gould's employers were paying. They made small talk, ordered, then got down to business while waiting for the first course.

"I'm grateful for this opportunity, of course," said Matt, choosing his words carefully. "But I'm still not clear as why the Romola Foundation wants to team up with a show like ours?"

Gould, a plump, bald Englishman in his mid-fifties, raised an eyebrow.

"Don't we both investigate the same phenomena, albeit in different ways?"

And on very different budgets, Matt thought, glancing at the prices again.

"True," he said, "but 'America's Weirdest Places' is an entertainment show. Clue's in the title. Sure, we make a professional product, but it's basically about going to haunted houses and getting some footage that gives people a thrill."

"Quite," returned Gould, taking a sip of mineral water. "But what makes your show different from a dozen others is that you seek out the less obvious, the more bizarre. That derelict funfair in Utah, for instance. Excellent episode. Atmospheric, well-paced – I'm surprised you didn't win some kind of award."

"But nothing really happened," Matt pointed out. "We gave our audience the back-story – in this case, the fatal accident on the roller coaster – and then our psychics experienced stuff. There were noises at night, shadows, like you said, lots of atmospheric shots. But that's it. Don't get me wrong, I loved the show like my own child, but we're not scientists, we're entertainers."

"Which is precisely why we scientific investigators need you," Gould said. "For a long time we've been sniffy about show business, and popular conceptions of the paranormal. And a fat lot of good it's done us! Some of us think the time has come to stop being so poo-faced about it, and get ourselves a much higher profile. The Romola Foundation was set up in 1865, Matt, and still hasn't found conclusive evidence of psychic phenomena."

But you've certainly spent a ton of money looking, thought Matt. *And I need some of that action.*

"You don't need to persuade me to bring my team over here, Ted," he said. "But why not use a home-grown outfit? Every country has ghost hunting shows, stuff like that? Especially here – isn't England the most haunted country on earth?"

Gould's amiable features froze for a split-second before he smiled again and waved away the suggestion.

"We've looked into it, believe me," he said, "but none of our British production companies were interested in Malpas Abbey. It's not really on anyone's radar as a haunted house, you see. Nobody has stayed there in decades."

Not exactly a lie, Matt thought. *But not strictly true, either. You can't kid a kidder. What are you hiding, Ted?*

The waiter returned with fashionably small portions of food on square plates. During the lull in conversation, Matt noticed Gould absentmindedly rubbing his right wrist. He caught a brief glimpse of a white streak before the older man's shirt cuff fell back into place.

An old scar, and a bad one, Matt thought. *Another little mystery. But here I am in one of the most expensive restaurants in London being offered a ton of cash. Am I going to argue?*

"So, Ted," the American said, picking up an elegant silver fork, "shall we talk dates?"

***

"Seriously?" asked Benson. "People spend their time and money on this – this half-baked nonsense?"

"All good clean fun," responded Gould, picking up the remote to stop the recording. "And these are just the edited

16

highlights. The cases in which we have found – well, enough to arouse our interest."

Benson, chairman of the Romola Foundation's board, grunted noncommittally. He was a spare, silver-haired man of around seventy, well-preserved and sharp-witted. He and Gould were seated in a small theater at the organization's London headquarters. The lights were dimmed, but they did not sit in darkness. Absolute darkness was never permitted anywhere in the building. The walls of the room were decorated with pictures of paranormal phenomena, all photographs or stills from amateur movies. All had been verified as fakes, mute reminders of the importance of skepticism.

"I see shadows, flickers of movement, shapes – some suggestive," he conceded. "But wouldn't we see the same phenomena in any of these absurd shows?"

Gould shook his head.

"Not according to our analysts."

He began to fast forward, stopped, froze a scene. It had been taken with a night-vision filter, the whole screen was black or garish, fluorescent green. A pretty, fair-haired woman was in the foreground, facing to one side, evidently speaking to someone out of earshot. In the background was a circular aperture, perhaps a drain. Gould fiddled with the remote, zooming in clumsily on the opening. Benson leaned forward.

"Hard to judge the height," he murmured. "But that is possibly a child?"

Gould began to move the clip on, one frame at a time. The shadowy figure in the opening seemed to change shape, unfolding to become taller, more spindly. As it emerged, it moved so quickly that it left blur lines. Then it vanished.

"No doubt about that, I think," Gould said flatly. "It's one of them. And it keeps happening. At least three times, with several more possible occurrences. Nothing like this has been seen in any similar series."

"And you really can't say which member of the team is triggering the crossover?" asked Benson. "After all, one could cross-reference the personnel on a given episode—"

"Of course we thought of that," said Gould, a little testily.

"They have had the same core team for two years, made dozens of episodes. It's one of them, but we don't know which."

"That woman," Benson said, referring to a printed sheet. "She's the presenter, Denise Purcell? And there are two others who regularly appear. Both self-proclaimed psychics?"

Gould nodded.

"I think at least one member of that team triggers intrusions without realizing it. They're all focused on more conventional ideas – apparitions, poltergeists. Nothing I've seen suggests they are aware of the Interlopers, let alone how dangerous they can be."

Benson looked from his subordinate to the screen, then back again.

"Very well, Edward," he said. "I will sign off on this one, and keep the board off your back. Dangle your bait as you please. Let's hope that nothing too dangerous takes a bite at it."

The informal meeting was adjourned, no records having been kept, as was customary. Officially, Benson was a hands-off chief executive, never intervening in the work of investigators like Gould. In reality, Gould knew that Benson knew everything and watched everyone.

***

"Why are British freeways so bendy?" asked Frankie Dupont. "We keep kind of swooping to the right and left, instead of going straight ahead."

"Probably because they had to avoid so many stately homes, historic sites," suggested Marvin Belsky, leaning forward from the back seat. "Can't just put a road through Stonehenge or Windsor Castle, right Jim?"

Jim Davison, the foundation's driver and general helper, laughed and shook his head.

"Good try, Marvin, but no," he said. "These motorways were deliberately built with curves to stop drivers falling asleep at the wheel. You have to keep moving your hands, just a little, see? Otherwise you'd go straight off into the landscape.

They'd spotted the problem with your freeways. And German autobahns, of course."

Marvin looked slightly peeved at being corrected and Denny felt a twinge of satisfaction. Ever since the team had arrived in England, Marvin had been delivering impromptu lectures about what he called 'the old country'. He claimed some kind of aristocratic heritage. Frankie had already annoyed him by asking if he was related to the Yorkshire Belskys.

"Are we there yet?" demanded Brie Brownlee, the younger of the psychics currently appearing on 'America's Weirdest Places', "We've been driving, like, forever. And the cell signal keeps dropping out."

"Shouldn't you know that already, darling?" Jim shot back, with a mischievous grin at Frankie. "Or are your powers intermittent?"

Brie sighed.

"I sense spirits, I don't read minds," she said with heavy emphasis. "If you want all that Vegas stuff, try Mister Belsky."

Sandwiched as she was between Brie and Marvin, Denny felt the latter take in a deep breath. Wanting to avoid another pointless dispute over all things paranormal, she started to fire-off questions about their destination at Jim.

"So how big is this place? Is it very run down? Is the power on, or will we be using lamps? And can we shower when we get there?"

"Whoa, Nellie!" exclaimed Jim. "I've never even been there. I'm relying on GPS to find the way. But from what I hear, the place is a bit decrepit. Nobody lives there, just a caretaker who's based in the village, because–"

"Because nobody dares spend the night," completed Marvin. "We know."

The GPS system told Jim to turn off the motorway, and sure enough a moment later a sign appeared. Arrows pointed to the city of Chester, plus a variety of more obscure place names. Malpas was not among them. When Brie pointed this out Jim explained that the village was simply too small.

"But it's not that remote," he said. "You're about ten miles outside Chester, which is a nice enough place. When you're finished at the Abbey you could do a bit of shopping, see the sights."

"Sounds cool!" said Brie. "I love buying knick-knacks, little gifts for my boys. Maybe they'll have some Harry Potter stuff! Did they make the movies around here?"

"Not that I know of," said Jim. "How old are your boys?"

"Well," Brie replied, "one's just turned six, and the other's forty-three – my husband's the immature one."

As the two chatted, Frankie took out a lightweight camera and started to film the old city. Chester was picturesque, Denny thought. But after the flight plus a two-hour drive from Manchester airport, she was ready for rest, not sightseeing. She hoped Malpas Abbey would not be too Spartan. Matt had not been very specific about facilities.

"Getting closer," muttered Marvin. "I can feel it. Kind of pressure building up. The way some people sense a storm coming."

Aha, thought Denny, *we've reached the ambiguous remark stage. He's limbering up for the performance.*

"I feel fine," chirped Brie. "The sun's shining, and we're on an adventure. I only hope we can help some poor souls move on from the earthly plane."

"You're clearly one of life's optimists," remarked Jim. "They've tried to exorcise the house. Twice. Once in the nineteenth century, again just after the First World War when they wanted to use it as an infirmary for disabled soldiers."

"What happened?" asked Brie, as Frankie swung her camera round to focus on Jim.

"Not sure about the Victorian exorcism," he admitted. "But they say the priest ended up in an asylum. The one in 1919 was worse. Two people died. The police concluded that the third man, who escaped, had killed the other two and then – well, entertained himself by rearranging various parts into a kind of collage. The bloke was deemed unfit to stand trial, though – totally insane."

They drove on in silence for a while.

***

"They'll be pissed," said Matt, looking around the archaic kitchen. "They're used to hotels, or motels at least. Not doing their own cooking."

Gould ran a hand along a work surface, frowned at his fingers.

"Could be a lot worse," he pointed out. "There's electricity, a gas range, showers. The previous owners tried to turn it into a high-toned hotel, but–"

Matt paused in his examination of cans and packets.

"But the evil spirits drove them out?"

Gould shook his head, gave a thin smile.

"Not exactly, but things did keep going wrong. And that's all I can say."

"Sure, I get it," said Matt, resuming his scrutiny of the supplies. "You don't want to taint the experiment by putting ideas in our heads. That's the bit I don't get. People can look stuff up online now, you know?"

"True," the Englishman conceded. "But there are a lot of things that don't make it to Wikipedia. Eyewitness statements, recorded interviews. The Foundation has a lot of material in its archives about this place."

Matt stood up, closing the doors of the cupboard, and leaned against the edge of the sink.

"Okay," he said, "it's not quite Buckingham Palace, but it's still an impressive place. I just wonder if–"

Matt paused, frowning, then pointed up above Gould's head. The Englishman, puzzled, turned to look up into the shadowy corner of the kitchen ceiling.

"What?" asked Gould.

"Those marks on the wall," Matt said. "You can just make them out. Parallel scratches."

"Oh," said Gould. "Just the wear and tear you get in an old building. Settling of the foundation caused cracks to appear in the plaster work. Nothing unusual. Parts of this house are over five hundred years old."

"Right," said Matt.

They left the kitchen to continue their tour. As Gould led him out of the kitchen door, Matt looked back at the parallel lines. They were faded, obviously not fresh.

21

Probably nothing, he thought as Gould led him along a dimly-lit corridor. *But might be worth mentioning to the team. Could look pretty spooky in the right light.*

"This is probably the area you should focus on," said Gould, turning a corner. "It's supposed to be the most troubled part of the house."

Matt stood for a moment, looking from Gould to the wall in front of them.

"Troubled by what?" he asked. "The curse of sloppy workmanship?"

***

The Mercedes SUV was almost too big for the country lanes that led to Malpas. On a couple of occasions Jim had to pull over to let a tractor pass, scraping the side of the vehicle against overgrown hedges. Denny dozed off a couple of times, having been unable to get much sleep on their flight. She tried to focus on the passing scenery, but there was little to see but farmland and the occasional cottage. Finally, they arrived at a set of impressive marble columns that marked the gateway to Malpas Abbey.

"On the home stretch," said Jim encouragingly as he got out to open the huge, cast-iron gates.

"My butt will be DOA," complained Marvin. "I'm paralyzed from the waist down."

"Aw, quit moaning," said Brie. "Think of it as a free vacation."

Denny stared out at the spacious grounds of the Abbey. They showed signs of long-term neglect. There were straggling clumps of trees, an ornamental pond that was covered in slimy green weed, statues clad in dark green moss. Then the house itself came into view. Denny gasped. Everything about Malpas Abbey was distorted, out of proportion, and supremely ugly.

It's the vilest place I've ever seen, she thought. *I can't do this. I can't go in there.*

The house did not so much stand as squat amid a straggling array of shrubs.

"Wow," said Frankie. "That is amazing – like Dracula's

castle. Cool."

"You think so?" asked Brie. "I think it looks kind of like Hogwarts. Old, dignified. I can imagine lots of venerable wizards giving lessons on spells and stuff in those upstairs rooms."

"Cold and inconvenient," added Marvin. "But I must admit, it's a very fine building. If I have to stay in a mausoleum, let it be a handsome one."

Can none of them see how evil it is? Denny wondered.

Jim stopped the SUV by the main entrance, and within seconds, the team – minus Denny – was approaching the huge ornate doorway. It was gaping open, and Denny was sure she could hear breathing from inside. Long, slow, deep breaths, like those of a huge animal.

The house is alive, she thought. *It knows we're here.*

She scrambled out of the car and started to run after the others.

"Stop!" she shouted. "Don't go in there!"

Frankie was already across the threshold, glancing back at Denny with a puckish grin as she entered the house. The others were close behind, despite the breathing sounds that were now much louder.

"Can't you hear that?" Denny shouted. "It's alive"

Marvin gave her a disdainful glance as he stepped inside.

"It's not a live show, honey," he said, his voice growing faint as he receded into darkness. "Everything is edited."

Denny tried to run, but she was frozen to the spot. Then a monstrous tongue unrolled from the house's doorway, a living carpet of dark red, glistening meat. The tongue wrapped itself around her, lifted her effortlessly, then began to draw her into the maw of the house. She tried to scream, but had no breath in her lungs. The doorway grew closer as she made futile efforts to break free.

"Wake up sleepyhead! We're here!"

Denny jolted upright, realizing that she had been leaning on Brie's shoulder. The SUV had stopped. Frankie was already unloading gear and Marvin was standing with Jim looking up at the front of the house.

"Whoa, sorry," Denny said, rubbing her eyes. "I had this

weird dream. The house – well, let's just say it was surreal. It seemed like a monster, like it was alive. And hungry."

"Well, if it is alive, it's having a nap," said Brie cheerfully as she unbuckled and got out, stretching her arms and legs with exaggerated pleasure. Frankie was still filming, of course. *And I look like an idiot,* Denny thought, fixing a smile as she followed Brie into the autumn sunlight.

The real Malpas Abbey was nothing like the grotesque structure of her daydream. It was a large, red brick house with two floors. It reminded her of some of the fine old houses they had passed in Chester, only wrought on a larger scale. The windows were tall and narrow, and a small bell tower stood at one corner. There was little decoration on the outside, and as she looked closer, Denny could see signs of weathering and general neglect. Old mortar had fallen away, chimney pots were missing, and there were small cracks and flaws everywhere.

Maybe it's not an evil place, she thought. *But nobody's loved it for a long time.*

"Okay guys!" she said brightly. "Frankie, we need some reactions from the team. Nothing fancy, just first impressions."

Predictably, Marvin repeated his 'gathering storm' remarks almost word for word. Denny knew it would play well with their audience – the two psychics had been chosen precisely because they were opposites in almost every way. Marvin's snarky pessimism provided the perfect contrast to Brie's positive but humorless, and somewhat preachy, take on the paranormal. Or, as Frankie had once put it, each made the other more bearable.

Denny was surprised, therefore, when Brie's turn came, the normally ebullient woman seemed almost lost for words.

"I guess we'll find out if it deserves its evil reputation," said Brie. "I hope we haven't had a wasted journey, of course, but – well, I guess I'll just wait and see."

Over their years of working together, Denny had worked out a series of hand gestures for the team. From behind Frankie, she signaled Brie to 'jazz it up', but the psychic's only response was a slight shake of the head. Brie gave a brief smile, then looked up at the house with an uncertain expression.

"Yep, just wait and see."

Denny shrugged, and Frankie swung her camera round to point at the front door as it began to open. Matt appeared along with a bald, pleasant-looking man introduced as Ted Gould. The team was used to staged introductions, pretending to meet local experts for the first time for the benefit of the show. Frankie gave Denny a questioning look, and received a nod in return.

Keep filming, we'll do it live, re-shoot later if it's clunky.

Gould turned out to be a natural, every inch the English gentleman with a wonderful accent. Denny could imagine him as the lord of Malpas, graciously welcoming his guests. Or she could up to the point when he led them inside and through the house's murky interior, and showed them what he termed 'the dark heart of the house'.

"So, this old doorway was bricked up at some point?" Denny asked.

"It's been sealed more than once," corrected Gould, stooping to point out details. "See? The brickwork down here is centuries old, Georgian or Regency, while up here you see twentieth century work."

"Okay," said Marvin. "So what's on the other side? What did people wall up? Torture chamber?"

Gould shook his head.

"Close, but in fact it's a staircase down to a cellar. It's commonly believed to be the Satanic temple of Lord George Blaisdell."

"Wooh, that's creepy!" said Denny, looking to Brie for a similar reaction. Again, though, Brie seemed subdued, staring vacantly at the wall.

"Getting anything?" Denny prompted. "Sensing a presence?"

Brie looked startled by the formulaic question, and shook her head wordlessly.

Crap, thought Denny, *this is not exactly fizzing.*

"Okay," she said, "is the plan to actually bust through this wall? See what's on the other side?"

Gould nodded gravely.

"I hope so. A good swing with a sledgehammer should bring this old stuff down. Then we'll see if there's anything unusual there. It could just be an empty space."

"Let's hope not!" Denny said brightly, turning to the camera. "Because we didn't fly three thousand miles to look at an old-time broom closet!"

She was about to signal Frankie to stop filming when Matt's voice echoed down the corridor.

"Hey, guys? There's something here. Something on the wall."

Denny saw the flicker of a flashlight, made out Matt's face peering up. The group parted to allow Frankie through, followed by Denny and Gould. When Denny saw what Matt was looking at she felt her heart sink.

Aw come on, she thought. *This is so fake.*

YOU LET HER DIE

At first glance, the writing on the wall looked as if it had been daubed in some kind of dark paint. But as the beams from Matt's torch and Frankie's camera light played on them, it became clear that the words had been gouged out, maybe half an inch deep.

"This wasn't here when we passed by earlier," said Gould. "I would take an oath on that."

Denny gave him a hard stare, but could see no sign of embarrassment. She looked up at the wall again, wondering which of the two men had created the message and how they had done it.

Quite effective, she thought. *Though it's a bit pretentious. Still, now it's here we've gotta use it.*

Chapter 2: Who You Really Are

"Blaisdell had a reputation for hiring actresses, dancers and the like, and getting them to take part in kinky – well, I guess you'd call it role-play nowadays. Orgies on a classical theme – Antony and Cleopatra, Zeus abducting a nymph, stuff like that."

"Gross," said Denny. "So he was a bad guy?"

"Not exactly evil," Gould pointed out. "A lot of aristocrats were very depraved in those days, but had no paranormal encounters. Blaisdell, however, seemed to have gone too far."

The team was seated in the great dining room on furniture that, as Marvin had observed, had apparently given up on life some years before. However, the elaborately decorated chamber made a good backdrop for the routine Q&A, included in every episode of the series.

"So what happened to this sleazy person?" asked Marvin.

"Well, that's where the story gets murky," Gould said. "One dark night in November, 1792, Blaisdell is thought to have held some kind of black magic ceremony."

"Thought to have?" Denny put in. "You mean nobody really knows?"

Gould, smiling slightly, shook his head.

"The morning after, the entire household was either killed, or vanished. The only survivor was a Scottish journalist called Donald Montrose. But he did not tell a very coherent tale. However, a gamekeeper was out chasing poachers in the grounds on the night in question. He said nothing at the time. But that man did claim – many years later – that the Devil had come to claim Lord George Blaisdell."

"In person?" asked Denny.

"The gamekeeper – who was apparently on his deathbed – said he actually saw the Devil, horns and all, through the windows of the Abbey. It was dismissed as local gossip, of course. Illiterate commoners were not given much credence in those days."

"But we are talking about the literal Devil, with horns, a tail, all that?" Denny persisted.

Gould paused, then spoke more seriously than before.

"Perhaps everyone encounters the Devil they deserve," he suggested. "In olden times, most people really did believe in Hell, Satan, as literal concepts, not metaphors. Even cynics like Blaisdell, who mocked religion, could not have been free of the idea of damnation, eternal punishment."

"So we won't encounter Lucifer ourselves, unless we believe in him?" asked Marvin.

"Personal demons," said Brie, suddenly. It was her first contribution to the discussion.

Non-sequitur, thought Denny. *Let's get back on track.*

"Was Blaisdell the first person to summon up dark forces, Ted?"

"By no means," replied Gould, clearly relishing the opportunity to lecture some more. "From ancient times, Malpas was known as a troubled place. The Abbey was supposedly built on the site of a pagan temple – some standing stones were apparently torn down by the monks. However, it's still rumored locally that a kind of altar was kept in a secret room by the monks."

"Devil worshipping monks!" exclaimed Denny. "I saw that movie!"

"Possibly," Gould said, laughing. "Opinions vary as to what the altar was for, though. Some did indeed say it was for raising demons, devils, evil forces. But one writer claimed the monks used the hidden chamber as a 'place of trial by ordeal'. A monk accused of impurity was locked in there, and if he survived, he was deemed good. But a black-hearted individual would invariably be driven mad, or killed, or whisked away."

"And ever since then, Malpas Abbey has been a troubled place?" Denny put in.

Gould nodded.

"The house has been occupied without incident – or reported incident – for decades at a time. But inevitably, sooner or later, something happens. Some disturbance occurs, and the residents move out. Sometimes it's just glimpses of what may be generally classed as ghosts. Sometimes – well, it's a lot more drastic than that."

After half an hour, Matt decided that they had enough material, and they moved on to filming the team settling into their rooms.

"We all need to get our heads down, people, get some sleep," said Denny as they trooped up the grand staircase. "Because we're going to stay up tonight, looking for – well, whatever haunts this place."

She had hoped for an enthusiastic response, maybe even a whoop from Brie. Instead, Brie said nothing and Marvin muttered something about 'getting it over with'.

"The team seems kind of subdued," Denny told the camera, moving close to Frankie's microphone so she could speak quietly. "Maybe that message – whoever or whatever wrote it – knocked them off-kilter. But let's hope they're back to their usual selves by sundown!"

***

Brie sat on the huge, four-poster bed and stared at the pattern on the worn carpet.

Gotta keep busy, she told herself. *Don't think about it.*

She stood up, walked mechanically into the antiquated bathroom, turned on the hot tap in the sink. There was a rumbling from somewhere below, and a gout of brownish water shot out, swirled down the plughole. Brie waited for the water to clear, which it did eventually, then washed her face. She did not feel like tackling the shower.

Brie dried her face, looked at her reflection in the speckled mirror. She saw a reasonably attractive woman, maybe a little heavy-set, jowly, but with a kind face.

A good person, she thought. *Caring. Wife and mother. Church-goer. Supporter of worthy causes.*

"I didn't let her die," she said. "I was young, I didn't know. I never told her to–"

A shadow flickered behind her, cutting off the light from the bedroom. Brie spun around, heart racing, wondering if the intruder might be Frankie.

She wouldn't sneak around, she told herself. *She doesn't like me much, but she wouldn't act like that.*

Brie emerged tentatively from the bathroom, looked behind the door, then checked under the bed. There was nobody else in the room. Her alarm subsided, then she jumped as a fast moving shadow shot across the floor. It was a bird flying past the window. Brie laughed in relief, went to look out at the grounds of Malpas Abbey. Black shapes hopped on the ill-kempt lawn. She could just make out the cawing of crows.

Or maybe ravens. Aren't they birds of ill-omen?

Brie shook her head, trying to dislodge the dark thoughts that had surged up when she had seen the writing gouged into the wall. She drew the curtains not quite closed, letting some of the September light spill into the dark-paneled room. Then she walked back to the bed, said a short prayer, took off her shoes, and curled up on top of the covers.

Sleep, she told herself. *Got a job to do. People relying on me. The Lord will not forsake me if I am sincere and humble.*

The plumbing began to rumble again, louder this time, and did not let up. She guessed someone had decided to try their shower. She got up and opened a secret pocket in her flight bag. She took two powerful tranquilizers from a small packet, replaced the rest of her stash, and sealed the pouch. Then she climbed onto the bed and drew the four-posters curtains around her. It was oddly comforting.

Like being out camping with the boys, she told herself. *Good memories. Positive thinking.*

When she lay down again the familiar effects of the prescription meds kicked in. The rumbling gradually dwindled as sleep claimed Brie.

***

"You big jerk!" Denny snapped. "How did you do it? Did you cover it up, with a sheet of paper or something? Then pull it off just before we arrived?"

"What are you talking about? And for Christ's sake, not so loud!"

Matt was defensive but angry, holding up his hands in front her. Denny had slapped him a couple times before, during their brief relationship. They were supposedly over the breakup, but every now and again, the bitterness would surge up. Now they were in his bedroom having a fight. It was too familiar, something Denny had experienced far too often.

"That dumb message!" she hissed, jabbing a finger into his chest. "I'm supposed to believe it just appeared?"

Matt held up his hands in a helpless gesture.

"You think I'd be that dumb?" he asked. "With so much riding on this?"

"I *know* you can be that dumb!" she almost shouted. "What about Akron, that creepy doll we so conveniently found in a tire factory that was pretty much the most boring place on earth?"

"Oh, come on, I just moved it into plain sight!" he protested. "I never faked anything, just did some stage dressing."

"That wall was not stage dressing, it was just fraud!" she said, struggling to control her anger.

"I didn't do it! Jesus!" Matt shouted. He was pacing up and down, now, and Denny recognized his martyred air.

"Okay," she said, trying to stifle her doubts. "If you didn't, who did? Gould?"

"I don't see how he could have done it," Matt said, and stopped pacing. "I was with him the whole time since he drove us here. And that wall was blank when he showed me the blocked doorway."

They looked at one another.

"So it's a genuine mystery?" she asked. "There's nobody else here who could have done it?"

Matt shook his head.

"Some caretaker comes in every morning, but he wasn't here when we arrived. I suppose–"

"What?" she asked, as he Matt paused for thought.

"Somebody could be hiding," he pointed out. "It's a big house, none of us knows it, whereas Gould might have set something up."

Denny turned that idea over in her mind.

"Let's see if anything else happens," she decided. "I'm sorry I unloaded on you like that. Maybe I'm more tired than I thought."

"Yeah," he said. "Let's get some shuteye."

He padded the bed. Denny smiled wearily.

"Yeah, we both sleep a lot better alone," she said, adding from the doorway.

***

"You let me die."

Brie sat upright, confused by the unfamiliar surroundings, disturbed by the dream that was already fading. It took her a few seconds to recall where she was. When she did remember, she sighed. She checked her watch and found she had only slept for two hours. The sun was lower, though, and its autumn light was streaming through a gap in the curtains. She got up to draw them fully closed.

"You let me die."

This time she could not dismiss the words as part of some half-remembered nightmare. The voice, though low pitched and whispering, was disturbingly familiar. It was a girl's voice, that of a teenager on the brink of maturity. Brie felt sure that it was the voice of her own conscience.

She never did grow up. Never got the chance.

Unwelcome memories swarmed in her head. Facts Brie had not considered for years suddenly demanded her attention. Guilt began to take possession of her, a corrosive and all-embracing guilt that she could do nothing to assuage.

"I was too young," she said as she drew the curtains closed. "I didn't know what I was doing."

Brie remembered her awkward sixteen-year-old self, raised in a tight rural community, dominated by the pastor of her church. Brother Charles had declared Brie to be especially blessed, someone who could commune with angels, a child gifted with prophecy. From her childish talk of auras and spirits, he had woven a small-town cult, with Brie as the figurehead. And then things had gotten too serious, too soon, and her parents had taken her away, burned that bridge behind them.

"I know who you really are."

The simple statement sounded like a threat of the direct kind. And this time Brie could not convince herself that the voice was in her head. The room was still not totally dark, since the old curtains were threadbare and still admitted a wan light. In the colorless radiance, Brie saw the faded drapes around the four-poster bed move, just a touch. But still far more than could be explained by a rogue breeze in the old house.

"Who am I?" she asked, surprised by her own courage. "I'm not that naive kid any more. I've tried to make amends."

"But I'm still a naive kid. I had no choice."

The figure that emerged from the curtained four-poster was almost, but not quite, Marybeth Carson. Of course it couldn't be. Marybeth had died from a rare kind of leukemia nearly twenty years ago. Died not quite a year after her friend and neighbor Brie had told Marybeth to fear nothing, that God would cure her, that all she had to do was put her trust in Brother Charles. Everyone in their little town knew that the pastor channeled the healing power of the Lord. Everybody in town said so, gave examples, spoke of miracles. But it turned out that Brother Charles had had his limitations, and the doctors had been right all along.

"I believed in him," Brie whimpered. "Everybody did. I just went along with the rest."

The apparition slowly, painfully, disentangled itself from the bed's draperies and stood upright. Even in the poor light Brie could see that Marybeth was naked, painfully thin, and terribly sick. The wasted body was hairless as the girl's skull, and Brie recalled the doses of chemotherapy and radiation that had been too late.

Someone looking that bad could not really stand, she told herself. *This is an apparition sent by the Devil, a trick to make me despair. To make me lose my faith.*

Brie began to recite the Lord's Prayer, rushing through the familiar words as the Marybeth-thing advanced on her. As it grew closer, the revolting creature began to lose much of its semblance of humanity. Great tumors began to erupt from the parchment-like skin, until the entity was a walking cancer, a horrific mass of diseased tissue creeping toward her on spindly, malformed legs.

It reached out for her, and Brie stumbled back until she felt the window sill in the small of her back. Reaching for her with bony arms, the being's bloated face seemed to smile. Tears streamed from tiny black eyes while the huge mouth drooled.

"I've been lonely, Brie. You were so nice when you visited me, read the Good Book to me, prayed with me. I just want to give you a great big hug."

***

Ted Gould made his way out of the kitchen door and into what had been a Victorian herb garden. He looked around making sure nobody was overlooking him from one of the house's back windows. All of the guests had been carefully allocated rooms at the front, south facing. When he was satisfied, he took out his phone and called Benson to report on the new development.

"Is there any chance the Americans are faking a phenomenon?" Benson asked at once.

"I don't see how," Gould replied patiently. "I was watching the producer the whole time. None of the others had the opportunity, let alone the time. So it seems that there has already been a response."

"In broad daylight?" Benson still sounded skeptical.

"There are a few examples," Gould pointed out. "If conditions are dark enough. Remember, we don't know if they're strictly nocturnal, or simply taking advantage of the fact that we are visually-oriented beings."

A pause, then Benson asked what he planned to do next.

"Go through with the plan, as outlined," Gould replied. "What else is there? This response supports my hypothesis that at least one of them can trigger a PD event. That means we will at least gather some data, perhaps more."

Another pause, then Benson spoke emphatically.

"Very well, Gould, you are free to use your own judgment. But keep me informed. And if there is any serious risk to the team, I will insist on extraction. Do you understand?"

Gould ran his left hand over the pale scars on his right wrist.

"I understand, sir."

***

The scream cut through the gloomy interior of the house and set Denny racing along the landing. She almost collided with Frankie, who was emerging from her own bedroom, camera at the ready as usual.

"I'm assuming that was Brie," Denny said.

"Could have been Marvin," Frankie shot back, with a wry grin.

A second later, they almost collided with Brie, who was running barefoot towards the staircase. For a moment, Denny wondered if this was part of some conspiracy involving the wall graffiti. But then Brie collapsed against the wall sobbing, and Frankie stopped filming. It took them a while to get Brie to explain what had happened, by which time, Matt, Marvin, and Jim had arrived.

"Something in your room?" asked Denny, not quite sure what Brie was saying.

"I've tried to make amends!" Brie babbled. "I never hurt anyone, just tell them good things, help them feel better about themselves!"

She's in a hell of a state, Denny thought. *God, I hope she doesn't have to bail on us.*

"What did you see?" Matt asked.

"You mean you don't know?" Denny asked him.

"I've no time for your BS!" Matt replied, striding off along the passage. He stopped at Brie's door, looking back at the rest of them, then went inside. Jim got up and started to follow, but Matt emerged from the room after just a few moments.

"Nobody in there," he said. "She must have had a nightmare."

"It was real!" the psychic protested. "I saw her. She was – God, she was dying, still dying after all these years."

"Must have been a bloody realistic nightmare," commented Jim, crouching down by Brie. "Hey, let me help you downstairs? We can have a nice cup of coffee in the kitchen."

Brie stared at him as she blew her nose on a tissue, then

nodded.

"I'd like that," she said in a small voice.

"Hey," said Denny, feeling she had not been sufficiently sympathetic, "we can swap rooms if you'd rather not go back in there?"

"Thanks," Brie replied, sniffling.

As Jim and Frankie helped Brie to her feet, Denny caught Matt's eye. He made a motion with his hands.

Pill-popping, Denny thought. *She's still on that prescription garbage. I guess he found her stash. Again. God, this could be a mess.*

Brie might have caught the expression on Denny's face. She looked the young woman in the eye and said simply, "I know what I saw. And it knows what you really are."

Frankie, Jim, and Matt led Brie downstairs while Denny stood watching them go with Marvin. Marvin, who had looked on saying nothing while the drama unfolded, solemnly tapped the side of his head with a forefinger.

"These upbeat religious types – they're often unstable," he remarked, and set off back to his room.

***

"So, Ted, tell us a little about the Romola Foundation."

After the incident, Denny had given up on getting some sleep for now. Jim and Matt were keeping the still-shaken Brie, company in the kitchen. So Denny asked Gould to give some background on the case. Before they began, she explained that the footage might not be used, but would probably furnish a few useful clips. Now they were standing outside Malpas Abbey, in what Frankie pronounced perfect daylight.

"The Foundation was set up by Sir Algernon Romola," explained Gould, "a very wealthy gentleman whose beloved wife died in childbirth. Spiritualism was very much in vogue at the time, and Romola – perhaps understandably – seized upon the notion that he could speak to his wife again."

"And how did that pan out?" Denny asked.

"Sadly, Romola was a very intelligent skeptic, and quickly

realized that a lot of spiritualist mediums were simply frauds. Long before Houdini, Romola began exposing common tricks – usually some basic conjuring that was only possible because séances were held in pitch darkness."

"So he became disillusioned pretty quickly?" Denny put in.

"Yes," said Gould, "but there were just a few instances where Romola, for all his perspicacity, could not find any evidence of fraud. Things moved, presences were felt, and in some cases, actual injuries were inflicted, allegedly by poltergeist activity. Romola was fascinated but also frustrated by these few instances of genuine paranormal events."

"So he set up a charitable foundation to settle the question?" she asked.

"Indeed," Gould replied, "and over one hundred and fifty years later, we are still grappling with the paranormal."

Not bad, thought Denny, *but a bit ordinary. It needs a personal touch.*

"And how did you become involved with the foundation, Ted? Were you always interested in the paranormal?"

For a moment, Denny thought Gould would give an evasive answer. But then he looked past her, gazing into the distance, and began to talk.

"When I was a boy, seven years old, most Saturdays I used to go out with a group of friends to what we called the forest. Actually, it was a small copse of trees just a few dozen yards across. But it was pretty big to us. It was about a fifteen or twenty-minute walk from the village where we lived. We used to play soldiers, climb trees, turn over stones, and see what crawled out. Anyway, on the weekend in question, some kind of mix-up must have occurred, because when I turned up, there was nobody else there. The forest was deserted. I spent some time mooching around, waiting for the gang to materialize. No dice. So I decided to go home after eating the packed lunch my mum had made. I sat down on a fallen tree and started unwrapping some sandwiches. Then – and I remember this very clearly – I became aware of the silence. It was autumn, the leaves had started to fall, but there were normally plenty of birds around, plus squirrels, other small animals. But now, there was total silence, not even a breath of wind. The sound of the grease-proof paper was really loud as I opened my little packet of sandwiches. So loud, in fact, that I stopped, worried that I would attract attention. That something would know I was there."

He shrugged, smiling, but Denny noticed that the smile did not reach his eyes.

This could be good, she thought. *It might even be the real deal.*

"Right after the silence hit me like a wave, I was suddenly sure I was being watched," Gould went on. "I could feel the hairs standing up on the back of my neck. And nothing could have made me turn around and look to see who or what was behind me. Then I heard a crackling sound, like someone walking very stealthily through the leaf litter. I put my lunch back in my little satchel and got up, moving slowly."

"Oh my God," breathed Denny.

"Of course, I'd been given all the usual warnings by my parents," Gould went on. "Don't talk to strange men, don't accept candy or get into a car ... all that stuff. But I just knew, at a visceral level, that this was different. That if I turned around, it wouldn't just be a stranger's face I'd see. Or at least, not a human stranger."

Gould paused, and Denny – for the first time in years – found herself unable to come up with an instant question. Frankie swung round to capture Denny's hesitation, waiting for the next question.

"So, what happened next?" she managed to ask, after missing a beat.

Gould looked away, then back at Denny.

"I ran. All the pent-up fear just burst out in panic. I ran like a maniac, and by the time I got home, I had a terrible stitch in my side. My mother was there, surprised to see me back so soon. Then she saw my face and realized something was wrong. But I could never really explain it to her. The silence, the watcher, that creeping sound."

"But you didn't actually see any evidence of the paranormal?" asked Denny, feeling the first stirrings of disappointment.

Gould looked away again.

"I didn't, no – I just felt a presence. But the day after my scare, a little girl who lived on the other side of the forest disappeared. She was a little younger than I was. She'd gone out gathering blackberries with friends. They were just on the edge of the forest and they noticed she had gone. Vanished into thin air, that was what the newspapers said. The police found the jar she had been using, but nothing else. Not at first."

"But they found something later?" Denny asked, trying to keep her voice level.

"Weeks later, after search parties had gone over the whole area a dozen times, they found her. What was left of her. She was dead. Desiccated, as if all the moisture had been sucked out of her. The coroner returned an open verdict – that's usual when there's no obvious cause of death. To this day, there's no convincing explanation as to where she went, what happened. What took her."

Again, Frankie swung the camera around to capture Denny's expression.

"Thanks for sharing that with us, Ted," said Denny. "So that's what got you interested in the paranormal?"

Gould shrugged.

"I had almost forgotten it, or perhaps the trauma had induced a kind of amnesia. Then years later, it came back to haunt me. The feeling of being alone in the woods. I was working as a research physicist at Cambridge when I happened to hear about the Romola Foundation. I'd become frustrated with mainstream science, so here I am. And here we are."

Gould turned to look up at the front of Malpas Abbey. Denny knew, without turning to look, that Frankie was now shooting past the Englishman, focusing on the old-fashioned windows, the climbing vines, the worn brickwork.

"I think that's a wrap," she said. "Thanks, Ted. That was great."

"Glad it was okay," said Gould, then turned to walk back inside.

Denny and Frankie discussed the segment, agreeing that it would work with minimal editing. Then they decided to film the house and grounds, including the old abbey ruins. As they moved from one spot to the next they chatted, and inevitably the future of the show came up.

"So Matt thinks this can revive our ratings?" asked Frankie.

"The big question, the one you never answer – why do you keep doing this crummy job?"

"Because I can't get another one," said Frankie simply. "Newsflash – times are tough for everyone."

"No, no, no!" insisted Denny. "No way. You're a damn good camerawoman, cameraperson, whatever. You make a cheap show look classy. And you know how to edit properly, for God's sake. Why not go for it, get yourself a job with a proper outfit?"

Frankie shook her head.

"Guess I just love working with you guys," she said, taking a sip from her water bottle. "It's the glamor of it all."

Chapter 3: Nightmare on a Sunny Afternoon

After they had finished filming, Denny went back upstairs and switched rooms with Brie. The psychic was now dozing on a sofa in the dining room, covered by Jim's coat, and Denny didn't want to wake her. As she moved Brie's things, she resisted the temptation to search her colleague's luggage for pills, preferring to keep an open mind. But she also resolved to ask Matt if he had found anything when she got the chance.

"Kind of spooky, I guess," she said to herself, standing in the middle of the big guest bedroom. "But not that bad."

Brie, consistently the team's most popular member with their audience, had naturally been given the best room. Denny opened the curtains wide, let what remained of the afternoon light dispel most of the gloom. There was nothing to see but old furnishings, a few faded pictures, and a dark red carpet that had seen better days.

Matt checked the room, she told herself. *He didn't see anyone, so there's nobody here.*

Despite this, she found herself holding her breath as she opened closets and drawers, only to find them empty. The *en suite* bathroom was far too small to furnish a hiding place. But still something bothered her, a nagging doubt. She felt she was missing something obvious about the room, no matter how closely she scrutinized its contents.

I need to rest. Just stop thinking and sleep.

Denny lay down on the bed without drawing the curtains around her. Predictably, despite her tiredness, sleep would not come. Instead, she found herself remembering all the strange beds she had slept in down the years. There had been dozens during the making of each season of the show. Before that, had been the life of an army brat, traveling between bases. Vague memories of her childhood fears began to form, not quite well-defined enough to grasp details.

The dark, she thought. *Everyone's scared of that when they're kids. No biggie.*

Then she sat upright, listening intently. A faint scratching, just barely audible.

Could be rats?

One thing about Matt she had learned. Like a lot of arrogant, men, he could sometimes overlook the obvious.

He looked around the room, sure. But he was awfully quick about it. Did he look under the bed?

Denny began to creep slowly towards the edge of the mattress. But she had only been moving for a couple of seconds when she felt a sudden bump. One of the wooden pillars gave a creak, a furled curtain swayed. She froze. All her childhood terrors were suddenly with her again. Killer clowns, boogeymen, aliens, vampires all merged into a formless, faceless monster lurking in the dark.

None of those are real, she thought. *But there could be some jerk hiding under the bed. Some jerk in a mask, maybe.*

Denny estimated the distance to the door as no more than four yards. It was unlocked. But it was also a big, cumbersome slab of oak, with a clunky knob. Again, Denny suppressed her fears as best she could. She stood up on the mattress, crouching to avoid hiding her head in the four-poster's stiff canopy. Then she took a flying leap, landing just short of the door. She slammed a hand against the door panels, feeling a pain in her wrist as it absorbed her momentum, then grabbed the knob.

Denny had yanked the door open and was already halfway out of the room when she risked a look behind her. There was nothing crawling out from under the bed, no childhood monster reaching out for her, no creep Matt had paid to create some cheap scares. She heaved a sigh of relief, leaned against the door frame. Then she bent down to peer under the four-poster, and saw nothing but daylight.

"God, I am such an idiot," she breathed.

Then the frame of the four-poster shook again, and a pale, half-formed face appeared. Its features were incomplete, like a mask of wax in process of melting. It looked down on her from on top of the bed's broad canopy. Killer clown, movie vampire, alien – its features flowed and rippled as it tried out one horrific visage after another, apparently unable to settle on one. A hand waved lazily at her, then the creature withdrew out of sight.

Denny rushed into the corridor, slammed the door behind

her, then leaned against it. It took her a few minutes to summon the willpower to run downstairs and call for help. This time she made a point of ushering everyone into the room, hoping that if some trickery had been played Frankie or maybe Jim would spot it.

"Nothing there now," said Gould, standing on a chair to look on top of the canopy. "Here, take a look."

Denny reluctantly accepted the offer. Gould was right, she saw. But then she looked more closely and saw that there was a dent in the canopy that was roughly the size of a small person – a woman or a child. She also noted that the dust had been disturbed.

"So there might have been something up there," said Frankie, taking Denny's place to film the area. "Cool."

"Not cool," retorted Denny. "Scared the crap out of me!"

She gave Matt an accusing look, still unwilling to absolve him.

"What?" he asked. "You think I'm faking all this? You got crazy ex-girlfriend syndrome, hun."

Gould looked from one to the other, realization dawning on his face.

"You two have a more than professional history, I take it?"

"Got it in one, Sherlock," Frankie called down. "But don't worry, it never leads to social awkwardness."

She jumped gracefully down from the chair.

"So, we done here?"

***

Jim had prepared a basic meal for the team, arguing that pasta might induce sleep more effectively than willpower. When Denny knocked at his door Marvin protested that he had been sleeping perfectly well already, but the offer of food brought him downstairs. Gould, who had eaten earlier, decided to take a walk before sunset. After they had eaten, Jim went to check on the boiler, which was still making ominous sounds.

The team – minus the still-sleeping Brie – was left to review the small amount of footage shot so far. Nothing out of the ordinary happened until they came to Gould's interview.

"He's lying," said Marvin bluntly.

Matt chimed in with an 'Uh-huh'.

"How do you know?" Denny demanded, stopping the recording. "He seemed totally sincere to me."

"Which is how a good liar sounds," retorted Marvin, sarcastically. "Okay, so the guy may not be making it all up, but it's mostly BS. Now, I must go back to my splendid suite. If you want me, I'll be trying to get my shower to work. It looks like it was designed by Edison or one of those guys."

The medium got up and left the room.

"To be fair," said Matt, seeing Denny's annoyance, "I think he's telling the truth as best he can. But he's lying by omission – there's something else."

"Why?" demanded Frankie, showing signs of genuine annoyance. "He could've just said he was always interested in ghosts and stuff. Hell, that's what most people say."

"Why does anyone make up grandiose lies?" Matt said, with a helpless gesture. "But, like I said, this guy has a secret. If Brie was here, she'd say he's got a troubled aura, poor man."

"Okay, maybe Gould is not completely on the level, but what about all the other stuff that's happened?" demanded Denny. "No way was what I saw fake. Or am I a big fat liar, too?"

"No, but you were on that boundary between sleep and wakefulness," Matt pointed out. "In a place where someone said they saw something. Your imagination was working overtime, an exhausted brain."

"Oh, bullshit!"

Denny got up and took the dirty plates over to the sink. Frankie joined her while Matt, wearing a martyred look he had long since perfected, left.

"You wash, I'll dry," offered Frankie. "And he's still a complete asshole, in my humble opinion. Seriously, what did you ever see in him?""

"Looks," admitted Denny. "I'm kind of superficial."

"That way lies heartbreak," sighed Frankie. "It's character that counts."

"Open your eyes, girlfriend," Denny said. "The beautiful

ones can get away with anything."

After a few moments, Frankie asked, "So what happened? I mean, what did you see?"

Denny gazed thoughtfully at her friend before answering.

"Would you believe, the boogeyman?"

Frankie raised a quizzical eyebrow, and Denny tried to explain the way so many childhood fears had merged into one bizarre form.

"But they didn't quite work," she added. "I mean, there were traces of all the things I was scared of as a kid. But the face kept flowing, as if it couldn't make up its mind what it wanted to be. Does that make sense?"

Frankie shrugged, meditatively drying a plate while looking out at the sunlight garden. Finally, she spoke.

"A shrink would say you went to sleep in a strange place, just after having a disturbing experience thanks to Brie. So your subconscious dredged up a whole lot of boogeymen, basically because everyone's subconscious is a total jerk."

Denny couldn't help laughing at Frankie's analysis, but felt herself agreeing with the gist of it.

"Maybe I should talk to Brie?" she suggested, as they finished putting away the crockery. "She can't sleep all day; we need to get ready for the big opening."

Frankie looked dubious.

"I reckon the big opening will be a bust," she said. "These things always are. The bigger the buildup, the bigger the letdown. Remember that old lumber mill in Maine?"

"Don't remind me!" replied Denny, shaking her head. "Believe me, I don't want to fall flat on my ass again. But we've got to have some gimmick for the show. 'Hey, we're spending the night in a haunted house' just won't cut it. Even if the house happens to be in England. We need to open that doorway."

They agreed to meet up outside the temple entrance later, then Frankie went to start setting up small cameras around the house. Activated by motion sensors, the cameras were standard equipment for the show.

Denny took a breath and paused outside the door of the dining room, listening. There was no sound from inside. She knocked gently on the dark wood panels, but there was no response from Brie. It occurred to Denny that the psychic might have simply gone upstairs to her new bedroom, while the rest of them were elsewhere. The kitchen was in back of the house, well away from the entrance hall.

"Brie?" she said quietly, opening the door a couple of inches. "You in there? Is it okay if I come in?"

There was a vague noise, somewhere between a moan and a grunt. The heavy curtains of the grand chamber had been drawn. A little light made it through chinks at the edges of the drapes. Denny crept inside, closing the door behind her, and waited for her eyes to adjust to the gloom. When she could see more clearly, Denny could make out a humped form on the sofa. Brie was evidently still asleep, covered with a tartan blanket. Denny went to stand over her colleague, unwilling to wake her.

"Brie?" she said.

When there was still no response Denny turned to leave. "What?"

The voice was low, rasping, and Denny felt a pang of compassion for Brie. Looking closer, she saw that nothing of the woman's head showed except a few strands of fair hair.

She's been crying, maybe lost her voice. Not good for the show.

"Brie, I just wanted to check if you're okay?"

"I'm okay."

Again, the words were at a level just above a whisper. Denny bent down so she could hear Brie clearly.

"Can I get you anything? Coffee, or maybe a sandwich?"

"No," came the reply.

After hesitating a moment, Denny perched on the arm of the sofa and thought about how to discuss her own experience without alarming the other woman. They had never become friends, despite working together. Their relationship was purely work-based.

Partly my fault, Denny thought. *I focus on the job too much.*

"Brie," she said. "I had this – thing happen. In my room. I mean, in your old room. I saw something."

There was no response from the huddled figure below her. Then came a slight movement of the chunk of hair.

"What did you see?"

Denny tried to explain, recounting her experience as she recalled it, aware that she sounded very much like a child confusing a nightmare with reality.

"So," she concluded, "they searched the room but nobody found anything. I guess that means there was nothing there? Right?"

"Could go somewhere else," came the croaky response. "Big house."

It was a simple point, but one that Denny had not really considered. If what she had seen was a living entity – as opposed to an apparition – it could indeed have left the bedroom and gone into hiding elsewhere. There were dozens of empty rooms in Malpas Abbey. The weird being could be in any one of them, or in the attic.

"Good point, yeah," she breathed, not feeling very grateful to Brie for the worrying notion. Then, remembering what her colleague had been through, she went on, "Oh, I nearly forgot! Will you be able to take part? In the doorway sequence? Because we can only do it once."

Another pause, and Denny was about to repeat her question when the tress of hair moved again.

"I'll be there."

"Okay," said Denny, trying to sound bright and positive. "Looking forward to it. Remember, if you need anything, just holler."

She reached down to pat Brie's shoulder, but when her fingers brushed the woolen blanket, the body underneath jerked. Denny snatched her hand back.

"Sorry," she said.

As she left the dining room, she recalled how into hugs Brie had always been, sometimes to the point of annoyance.

Now she can't bear to be touched, thought Denny. *Whatever it was, it shook her up very badly.*

***

"All I'm saying is, if you're doing this, stop it."

Matt McKay stood, arms crossed, blocking Ted Gould's way out of the walled herb garden. The Englishman held out his hands in a placatory gesture.

"I'm not *doing* anything, Matt," Gould insisted. "I couldn't concoct an apparition of the sort those young ladies said they saw, even if I wanted to."

Matt looked skeptical.

"I don't like people on my team getting terrified, especially if it's happening off camera," he said. "And you and Jim – you've had plenty of time to prepare a few little tricks, right?

"Interesting that you would be happier if your people were terrified on camera," commented Gould. "But we're not here to scare anyone. We're here to conduct an investigation. Jim is as honest as the day is long, incidentally. That's why he was chosen to help out. He's reliable. Now, if you'll excuse me–"

Gould tried to step around Matt, but the younger man blocked his way back into the house.

"An investigation?" said Matt. "One your fancy foundation could easily have done without our help. So what's the real motive, here? Why us?"

Gould sighed.

"Because, despite whatever you may think, I believe that your team contains at least one genuine psychic. Someone who can somehow connect with–"

"With what?" Matt demanded. "Why do you never just spit it out and say ghosts, the afterlife, spirits of the dead? Isn't that what you're all about?"

Gould shook his head, then pointed down at the rich growth of weeds around them.

"No, Matt, that's not what I'm about. It's not death I'm interested in ... it's life. Life as real in its way as any of those wild plants. A form of life that, like a weed, takes root where it can in our world. But not life as we know it."

Genuinely puzzled, Matt could only stare as Gould stepped around him.

"Do you mean aliens?" asked Matt, belatedly.

"Oh no," Gould replied. "If only it were that simple. But we are talking about beings from another world, if that's any help."

Matt was left staring at the door as it closed behind the Englishman.

***

Despite her earlier scare, Denny managed to get a couple of hours sleep in the big master bedroom. She was woken by her cell phone's alarm just as the September sun was nearing the horizon, turning the sky myriad shades of red, orange, and gold.

This really is a beautiful place, she thought, as she freshened up. *Guess I'm lucky to be a part of this – whatever it is. Adventure? Yeah, let's call it an adventure.*

When she went downstairs, the others had already assembled in the main hall, apart from Frankie and Matt, who were setting up the shot outside the sealed doorway. Denny was pleased to see that Brie was looking much better. The color had returned to her face, and she was chatting happily with Jim. Gould, now wearing a bulging backpack, was exchanging banter with Marvin. The two seemed to have hit it off, surprising Denny.

"Hi!" Denny said, approaching Brie and Jim. To Brie she added, "So, did you finally manage to get some sleep?"

"Yes," the medium replied with a smile. Denny was pleased to hear that Brie's voice showed no sign of hoarseness. "It was okay in your old room. Cozy. And I didn't really feel comfortable on that couch."

"Aw, sorry, I shouldn't have disturbed you," Denny said. "But hey, you bounced back, good for you!"

Brie looked puzzled at that remark. Denny was about to say that Brie had seemed pretty washed out when they had talked earlier. But Gould interrupted, clapping his hands.

"Are we ready to go, team?"

As they followed the Englishman Brie asked, "Did you disturb me? I really don't recall. As soon as I got into a proper bed I was out like a light, believe me!"

"No, I meant when we talked downstairs," Denny explained, but the puzzlement on the other woman's face left her floundering. "In the dining room?"

Maybe she was half asleep and just forgot our conversation, Denny thought as Brie continued to look vacant. Then a more worrying thought struck her. *Maybe it's the pills. Best not push it.*

"So, Jim," Denny said, changing the subject. "Our handyman ready to work up a sweat? Gonna take your shirt off, give us gals a thrill?"

"Oh God, don't," replied Jim in mock anguish. "If this goes wrong I'm going to be a prize berk."

"Berk? Is that a British curse word?" asked Denny, saying with a joshing tone. "Should I avoid it if I get to meet royalty one day?"

"Erm, well, it's a bit naughty, but nothing compared to what some of them say, allegedly–" Jim began, clearly unwilling to explain.

"Can we get on, people? Time's wasting," shouted Matt as the group rounded a corner. They walked past the peculiar graffiti on the wall. Denny noticed that Brie did not look up at the words, hurrying ahead with her gaze fixed on the floor in front of her.

"I'm ready to go, guys," Denny said. Frankie, wearing huge noise-canceling headphones, swung the camera around and gave Denny a thumbs up.

"Ready when you are," Matt said from behind Frankie.

Like we need a director, Denny thought.

"Well, this is it," she said to the camera. "For the first time in decades someone is going to enter the secret temple of Lord George Blaisdell. What will we find inside? Evidence of Satanic rituals? Who knows! That's all part of the fun. But guys, if there's a sacrificial dagger, it's mine. I called it."

Denny stepped back, then raising her voice a little, said, "Take it away, Jim!"

Jim hefted the sledgehammer, and Denny realized that it was an awkward tool to swing in the narrow corridor. Fortunately, Jim managed to take a proper swing and hit the bricked-up doorway dead center. There was a loud crash, echoing through the house, and an eruption of dust. A couple of bricks had been knocked out. Everyone else retreated, covering their mouths, as the Englishman took a second swing. This time a dozen bricks gave way, and a dark hole, big enough for a man to squeeze through, appeared in the doorway.

Jim stepped back and they waited for the dust to settle. Then Frankie moved forward, shining her camera light into the gaping void.

"What can you see?" asked Denny.

"A whole lot of doodly squat," replied Frankie, cheerfully. Then she put a hand to her headphones. "Whoa! Got a lot of feedback, there. Probably not a ghost, though."

"Okay, guys," said Denny, "pick up your flashlights. Jim, if you'd do the honors."

"My pleasure," replied Jim, and stepped forward again to knock away the remaining brickwork. When the dust had cleared a second time, Frankie stepped back into the aperture to get first shots of the interior. The others picked up flashlights, provided by Gould, and prepared to enter.

As usual, Denny led the way. She picked her way over the small heap of rubble. She was standing at the top of a flight of stairs that led down into a circular chamber about thirty feet across. The stone roof was low, no more than eight feet high. Her flashlight was just powerful enough to show that the walls were decorated with murals of some kind. She could also see a bulky object in the middle of the room.

"I think we found the altar that naughty old lord used, guys," she said over her shoulder. "Looks pretty creepy."

Denny went down the stairs, making her way carefully. Frankie followed, then the rest, the beams of flashlights flickering over walls and the floor. There were a few scraps of debris on the stairs. Denny bent down to pick up an old, yellowed sheet of newsprint. It was dated 1919.

"Hey guys," she said, holding the front page up for the camera, "apparently the US government's going to outlaw alcohol. You think that may have some unexpected consequences?"

This produced a ripple of slightly nervous laughter. The group descended to the chamber floor, then stood hesitantly around the base of the stone stairway. Nobody seemed to want to venture into the middle of the room. Denny decided to take the initiative and went to examine the murals on the circular wall.

It only took her a few moments to realize that they couldn't show the acts depicted by Blaisdell's artist. The violence might have been acceptable on TV, but the explicit sexual acts certainly were not. She found herself struggling, in the poor light, to imagine just how some of the debauchery depicted could have been achieved in real life. Then, when she saw a particularly horrific scene, she found herself hoping they had never been tried.

"Whoa," Denny breathed, "those old-time aristocrats were something else. Gonna have to blur out a lot of this stuff, Frankie."

"What is all this junk?" asked Marvin, who had gone in the opposite direction to Denny. He crouched down, rummaged through a small heap of cardboard boxes, then held up a rectangular object. "Hey, look! I found a camera! Kind of dusty, but it's neat."

"You found an antique," put in Frankie. "That thing runs on clockwork. It's an old cine camera, sixteen millimeter, looks like. My grandpa had one, they're cool."

There was a brief discussion as to whether the camera had film in it. After examining it, Frankie pronounced that it did and Gould offered to get it processed if possible. He made a big deal of the Romola Foundation's 'excellent facilities'.

That would make a nice extra, thought Denny. *Assuming the film shows anything interesting. And not just close-ups of those murals. Or a crazy guy murdering two other guys and arranging their body parts around the place.*

"Ted?" Denny asked, focusing on the audience. "The last time this place was opened some real bad things happened, right?"

Gould nodded.

"They bricked it up again after the incident," he said. "Though whether that worked is a moot point. After all, two of us had paranormal experiences before we broke through."

"Yeah, if the altar is the source of whatever goes on here, bricking it up clearly doesn't work," said Marvin, gazing at the lump of stone with obvious distaste. "What a comforting thought!"

"Hey," Brie put in, pointing. "What are you up to, Ted? That's not a camera?"

The Englishman had produced a small box from his backpack. Attached to it by a cable was a plastic tube, which he began to wave around in front of him.

"It's just a basic Geiger counter," explained Gould, with a smile at the others' obvious puzzlement. "You've seen 'em in the movies. Well, in real life they're much the same. Point at things, wait for the clicking noise. If it makes a very loud sound, step away from the object."

The Englishman frowned, then, and jabbed at a button on the control box.

"Well, it *should* be making a slight clicking noise, except that today it doesn't seem to be working. Odd. It was fine when I tested it earlier. And this chamber is lined and floored with stone, which always has some trace levels of radioactive isotopes."

Frankie made a sad trombone sound. Denny, suppressing a giggle, asked Gould why radiation was an issue in any case.

"It's basic science to take as many measurements as possible, get plenty of data," he replied, waving the detector back and forth. "When the Victorians started looking into the paranormal, they were quick to use photography. It makes sense to employ more advanced detection equipment now that we have it, yes?"

"Maybe," chipped in Marvin, "but I can't imagine a ghost being radioactive – or are you seeking the spirit of Robert Oppenheimer?"

Gould gave a thin smile and set off back up the flight of stairs. Near the top, he stopped, held up the Geiger counter, and then operated a control. A series of clicks came from the gadget.

"Getting anything, Ted?" asked Denny.

"Yes, it started working," he said, and began to walk down into the cellar again. Then he stopped, frowning. "But now the damn thing's not registering at all."

"Piece of junk," remarked Frankie, "you should get a

refund."

Gould nodded absently, peering at the device's controls.

"Or," he said, "there really is no background radiation at all in this chamber."

"Hey, that's a good thing, right?" said Denny. "I mean, 'cause radiation's generally a bad thing?"

"But it is a universal thing," said Frankie. "It's everywhere on earth, or under it, right?"

Gould said nothing, but began to walk around the room, still frowning at his gadget. Frankie, meanwhile, moved forward and began to film the supposed altar. Examining the stone more closely, Denny could see that it had been carved quite elaborately at some remote time. The images had almost worn away over the centuries, but she could still make out the rudimentary forms.

"Faces," she said. "This thing's covered in weird faces."

Behind her, someone was trying to stifle a scream.

"What is it, Brie?" asked Jim.

"Footprints!" Brie said, as Frankie swung round to focus on her. Brie was pointing at the floor, and Denny could make out some tracks in the dust. "These footprints aren't ours!"

"Do ghosts usually wear Nikes?" asked Denny.

She was hunkered down next to the supposed ghostly footprints, which seemed to go all the way round the altar stone.

"Those tracks do look awful familiar," Frankie said. "And there's no way they were made back in 1919."

Denny stood up, turning to face the others.

"So either it's ghosts with questionable fashion sense, or somebody here is messing with us."

Brie and Marvin looked startled, while Gould and Jim looked shifty. Matt, Denny noticed, was trying to move out of camera shot behind the bulk of Marvin.

"So three of us were here first," Denny went on. "Preparing the ground, so to speak. Am I right, guys? What do you say, Ted?"

Gould folded his arms, trying to look unabashed.

"Yes, we did enter this chamber a few days ago," he said. "Just to make sure there was something here. It would have been embarrassing if it had been empty, after all."

Then Jim took a breath and spoke.

"We faked it," he said. "I knocked that wall down a couple of days ago. We had a look around, then I rebuilt it."

"It was part of our arrangement," put in Matt quickly. He looked around at his team defiantly. "Like Ted says, we had to be sure there was something to find! We couldn't come all this way for an empty cellar and a house that may be haunted."

"You jerks," said Frankie. "So that was all faked?"

Jim nodded.

"It's easy to dirty up the mortar," he explained. "In the poor light it looked like it hadn't been disturbed for years."

"But in fact," Gould said slowly, "there was a gap of around two hours when nobody was nearby and that doorway was open."

"Plenty of time for a whole army of little spooks to sneak out," remarked Marvin, with deceptive mildness. "Good job, guys."

"Frankie," said Matt, "please stop filming."

"Sure thing boss!" Frankie's tone was fake-cheery.

"I'm sorry," said Brie, heading for the stairs. "I just can't go on with this – it's too much! I signed up for an entertainment show. All this fraud, on top of what I experienced. I quit! I need Jim to drive me back to town, whatever it's called."

"You're contracted to appear in the show," Matt pointed out, trying to head her off. "I sympathize, I really do. But a deal's a deal. Maybe you could just, you know, take another little rest? See how you feel later on?"

Crappy behavior, even for you, Denny thought. *You're not taking this place seriously enough.*

The team followed Brie up out of the cellar. The psychic was still demanding to leave and stay in a hotel or B&B in Chester. In the past, when Brie had had a bad reaction to a location, Denny and Frankie worked to talk her down. Now neither of them even tried.

"I'm sorry," repeated Brie. "It's just those faces on that altar reminded me of the thing I saw – the proportions were wrong, it looked inhuman. And this whole place, it's evil. I can sense it. And something else. Can't any of you feel it?"

"We've all seen the murals, honey," Marvin said, in his usual supercilious tone. "Clearly we are not in Disney World."

Brie shot him a hurt look, at which Marvin rolled his eyes.

"That's not what I meant!" Brie snapped. "I get this crawling sensation, like you get when someone's looking at you from behind. It's always there. Something's paying attention."

"It's only Jim looking at your ass," Marvin muttered. Denny quickly intervened to try and head off any pointless bickering.

"Maybe you could tell us what scared you when you were upstairs?" she asked Brie, gesturing at Frankie to get a medium close-up. "If you feel capable, that is. Talking about it some more might help. "

Brie glanced at the camera for a moment, then back at the entrance to the underground chamber.

"I ... I saw something scary in my room," she said after a moment's hesitation. "I'm not sure what it was. It had a weird face, deformed, freakish. I don't want to think about it at all. I just want to leave this place. Now. Please."

"Brie," said Gould, "would it help if I told you the whole truth about my own experience? The one I ... I glossed over earlier?"

Brie looked uncertain, but did not reject the idea out of hand.

"I knew it was bullshit!" exclaimed Marvin, triumphantly.

"True, I lied earlier when I was interviewed," Gould admitted. "Or rather, I told a heavily-edited version of the truth. That story about getting lost in the woods. It wasn't that straightforward. Maybe it will put things in perspective if I tell you what really happened – and what I discovered much later."

He paused, then looked Brie in the eye.

"We call what you saw an *Interloper*."

Nightmare Abbey

Chapter 4: Little Girl Lost

"Okay, so what did happen in that forest?" asked Denny.

Around the big kitchen table, the various team members looked on expectantly. Matt seemed angry at Gould for jeopardizing the show. Marvin had his characteristic half-smile of superiority. Brie was jittery, a mess of disordered hair and streaked mascara. Even Jim had lost his composure and glowered at his boss.

"If I tell you, promise you won't interrupt? I'm happy for Frankie to record this," he added. "People should know."

There were nods, noises of agreement. Frankie took out a small digital camera, began to film across the table. Gould sat back, looked into his coffee mug for a couple of seconds, then took a gulp. Another sigh, then he looked over at Denny and began to talk.

"She was called Lucy," he said. "She was my little sister, a couple of years younger than me. Of course, when you're an eight-year-old boy, that age difference can seem enormous. And my friends and I found her to be a terrific nuisance, always following us around. We had what we considered to be a gang, you see. We were the cool kids, and she was spoiling it, a little girl following boys around and wanting to join in with our games. It was particularly galling for me, of course – I was responsible for her. My parents made clear that I should always look out for Lucy. And naturally I didn't want to."

Gould paused then looked away, out of the kitchen window into the pitch darkness.

"And then one day I decided to play a nasty little prank."

***

"We've never come this far before," said Martin. "There's supposed to be an old well."

"My uncle said it's an abandoned mine shaft," interrupted Paul. "He said it's all overgrown and not properly fenced off."

"The point is," said Martin, sounding peeved, "that we're not supposed to go out of sight of the village."

Edward felt rising anger. His friends had complained

57

incessantly about Lucy following them around. Now he had a plan to deal with it, and instead of doing as they were told, they were whining.

"I thought we didn't want girls in the gang?" Edward said, putting as much sarcasm into his tone as he could manage. "You two should be wearing frocks. With ribbons in your hair."

Martin's freckled face reddened, while Paul started to stammer – sure signs that Edward's insult had struck home. He pointed back along the forest trail at the tiny figure in red that was scampering through the autumn leaves. He could just make out Lucy's voice, plaintively shouting.

"Slow down, Edward! I'll tell Mummy!"

Always whining, he thought. *She never shuts up. Never leaves me alone.*

"Guys, you want to play with Lucy every weekend?" Edward demanded.

The other two shook their heads.

"Right," Edward went on. "So let's give her a scare. Operation Little Red Riding Hood is under way."

Edward signaled to Paul, who nodded and stepped off the trail and behind a gnarled old elm. As he moved out of Lucy's line of sight, Paul opened his backpack and took out a Halloween mask. It was Dracula, complete with dripping fangs. Edward would have preferred something more disturbing, but they had had to work with what they could get in the village shop.

Besides, he thought, *Lucy is a real scaredy-cat.*

While Paul moved off into the undergrowth, Edward and Martin stood waiting for the little girl. Lucy was almost out of breath by the time she reached them, but she still had sufficient energy to pound her little fists on Edward's chest.

"I'm telling Mummy on you!" she exclaimed, in an irate squeak.

Grabbing his sister's wrists, Edward made placatory noises.

"Calm down, Luce! We were just messing around."

Lucy did not show any signs of letting her big brother off the hook, and resorted to kicking him in the shins. Edward gave Martin a significant look. Martin rolled his eyes, then stepped forward and patted Lucy gently on the shoulder of her red duffel coat.

"There, there," said Martin, awkwardly. "We're both sorry."

Lucy snorted, but stopped kicking Edward, who made a mental note to call Martin 'Lucy's boyfriend' for the rest of the weekend. The little girl pouted up at Martin, who was notoriously soft-hearted and an easy target for Lucy.

"Hey," said Edward, trying to deflect her attention, "we're playing a game of hide and seek. Do you want to join in?"

Lucy looked dubious.

"We shouldn't be in the forest," she said sulkily. "You know Mummy said we shouldn't go inside."

"Oh, rules are made to be broken," said Edward breezily. He had just learned the phrase and liked to use it whenever he could. "We can have more fun playing hide and seek where there are lots of places to hide. Can't we?"

Lucy looked from her brother to Martin, who nodded encouragingly.

"All right," she said. "At least hide and seek is better than pretending to be soldiers. That's so boring."

Typical girl, thought Edward. *No idea how to have fun.*

"Paul's already gone to hide," explained Martin, pointing in the direction their friend had gone. "All we have to do is go and look for him."

Lucy nodded solemnly, but made no move to step off the trail.

"We have to split up to search better," added Edward.

At that, Lucy began to pout again. She clearly suspected something, and for a second Edward thought their scheme was going fail before it had properly begun. But then Martin rescued the situation.

"And there's a special prize for the first person to find Paul," he said. "Chocolate! Just catch Paul and he'll give you a bar of Cadbury's Fruit and Nuts."

Lucy's eyes widened. She had a well-defined set of values, with candy of all kinds very near the top. After a moment's contemplation she smiled, and with a cheerful 'Okay!' set off into the undergrowth. As the little red figure vanished into the

wild greenery, Martin and Edward took out their own masks –
Frankenstein and a Mummy – and set off slowly after Lucy.

***

"Wow!" exclaimed Frankie. "You were a real Grade A
douche, Ted!"

Denny silently concurred, but then felt guilty. The
expression on Gould's face told its own story. The pain he felt
was that of a raw wound, not some half-forgotten trauma he
had come to terms with. Again, the Englishman scratched at
the pale scar, half-hidden by his shirt sleeve.

"Kids don't always think about consequences," said Brie
quietly. "We all did dumb stuff when we were small."

Gould gave Brie a faint smile.

"I tell myself that," he murmured. "But it's a flimsy excuse.
I knew we were doing something bad, but I did it just the
same. Organized it, persuaded the others to carry it through. I
was quite simply a cruel, selfish little turd."

That silenced the rest of the group. Gould folded his hands
and, again gazing out into the night, resumed his story.

"It was a stupid idea and it all went wrong, of course," he
said. "But not in the way any of us could have predicted."

***

Edward realized the flaw in his plan half a minute after
they had set off in pursuit of Lucy. The girl was too small and
the woods too dense. Sneaking up on her and giving her a
scare necessitated knowing where she was. Edward and
Martin had spread out until they were about twenty yards
apart. They tried to signal with gestures, but it was getting
harder to see each other. It was mid-afternoon in October, and
there was still enough foliage on the trees to block much of the
slanting sunlight. Also, they were trying to move stealthily,
and that slowed them down. There was no sign of Lucy and no
sounds. Edward had expected his sister to thrash her way
noisily through the under-brush. But everything was silent
except for the occasional bird call.

What if she has an accident?

The thought struck Edward like a blow in the pit of his stomach. He had never taken his parents' warnings about the forest seriously. It was just a big clump of trees between his house and the village. The grown-ups were close-mouthed and vague about why the area was shunned. But the more he thought about Lucy picking her way through the darkening forest floor, the more he wondered about the mine shaft, or the well, or whatever danger might be hidden amid the greenery.

The scream was shocking, cutting through the cool air and making Edward jump. It was so piercing that for a moment he doubted if it could be Lucy. Then he sighed with relief.

Paul found her. He jumped out at her, gave her a scare. She's probably wet her knickers!

Edward smiled at the thought and started to move more quickly. The scream had come from somewhere ahead of him. He took off his mask, hid it in his bag, and began to shout Lucy's name. The plan was to make her believe there were monsters in the forest so that she would never come back. The scream, Edward reflected, sounded promising.

She'll be having nightmares until Christmas, he thought, with grim satisfaction. *If it keeps her away from us, it'll be worth a punishment from Dad.*

The second scream was fainter, but drawn out for longer. It was worse, somehow. The first time had sounded right to Edward – the reaction of a silly girl surprised by a plastic mask. But why would Paul continue to torment Lucy?

Unless it's someone else.

Again, assorted grown-ups' warnings came to mind, swirling around his head as he began to stumble in a half run over the uneven ground. This time it was not the risk of accidents in the forest, but something even worse. The sort of thing that parents talk about in low voices after they've switched over in the middle of the news.

Don't talk to strangers. Never go anywhere with somebody you don't know. Never accept sweets. Even if someone says they know your mother or father, don't go with them.

"Oh God, please don't let it–" he gasped in an attempt at a prayer. "Please God, let her be all right. I'm sorry I did it, I didn't mean–"

Lucy's voice, plaintive now, sounded from somewhere ahead of him.

"Edward! Help!"

The brushwood grew denser, fallen branches, drifts of dead leaves, and dense clumps of weed all hindering his progress. It seemed to grow darker with each passing moment, now, and he told himself it was because a cloud had passed in front of the sun. Then he burst out of the undergrowth into a circular area about twenty yards across. It was thick with weeds but there were no trees, not even saplings. In the center of the clearing was a lightcolored stone about five feet tall. It was lumpy, squat, somehow menacing.

Edward stopped in surprise. He had had no idea the clearing existed. The stone looked as if it had once been a statue of some kind, but almost all the carving had worn away, reminding him of the ancient gargoyles on the village church. It was, he realized, in the heart of the forest. He did not need to think about its significance. Edward knew, with terrible finality, that this was what people really feared about the forest. He felt a sudden urge to run away.

"Leave me alone!"

Lucy's voice came from the other side of the pale stone. Edward dashed around the stone and stopped, more astonished than scared by what he saw. Lucy was being dragged into a hole in the air. He saw her legs kicking out. One of her little black shoes was missing. The lower part of her red coat was visible, but not the rest of her. Lucy's upper body was invisible. But Edward could still hear her voice, screaming for help, but faintly as if she was at a great distance.

"Lucy!"

He ran forward and grabbed her legs, began to pull her out of the impossible aperture. As he struggled to save Lucy, part of Edward's mind registered that the 'hole' was a kind of foggy sphere, a region of air that shimmered like a heat-haze despite the cool October day. It was about four feet across, but its edges were hard to make out.

Edward did not try to make sense of it all. All he simply knew was that Lucy was vanishing, that it was somehow his fault for being mean to her, and that he had to save her. He dug in his heels and pulled harder. After a couple of seconds, Lucy came unstuck and was released, then he fell backwards. He fell against the white stone, and it winded him. Lucy dropped out of the air into a patch of wildflowers, her face pale, eyes staring, but apparently unhurt.

As soon as she focused on Edward, she jumped up and flung herself on him. She did not cry, simply clung to him. Her utter stillness scared him even more than her screams had done. He saw red welts on her arm, felt terrible shame at his part in what was happening.

"It's all right," he said, trying to convince them both. "It's all right, we're going home now, Lucy."

He staggered to his feet, tried to set his sister down, but she was determined to cling to him with arms and legs. Rather than argue with the terrified girl he turned to leave the clearing via the rough trail he had forged.

"Hurry," he heard her say into his shoulder. "She's coming!"

Edward wanted to ask who 'she' meant, but before he could ask he felt a blow in the middle of his back. He fell forward, heavily, crushing Lucy underneath him. The girl's screams blended with another sound, a kind of low snarling and hissing. Sudden, intense pain shot through his back. He felt his shirt rip, and his flesh. Edward screamed, rolled over, punched and kicked blindly at his assailant. His fist connected with a face that he could just make out in the gloom. The figure crouching above them jumped up, making a kind of mewing noise.

I hurt it, he thought. *And it's not very big.*

Then another figure appeared, and a third. They leaped at him, their hands making the slashing motions he had seen in fighting cats. They were all child-sized, but fast-moving and disturbingly strong. Their faces were hard to make out, especially as they darted and lunged at him. Edward raised his hands in front of his face, and a burning pain shot through one forearm.

Two of the creatures were keeping him occupied, while the third dragged the screaming Lucy back towards the shimmering, cloudy sphere. No matter how much Edward tried, he couldn't get to her. Then the sky must have cleared, and a shaft of sunlight lit up the clearing. The golden glow caught one of the monsters on the face, and Edward reeled back, almost falling, hands raised now not to ward off attack but to block a horrific, impossible sight.

The thing had Lucy's face, but the features were not quite finished. The snub nose seemed half-melted, like candle wax, the mouth was little more than a crude slit, the eyes small and beady. Yet the resemblance was still there in the shape of the face, the proportions of the small body. The hair that straggled from the nightmare being's head was the exact color of Lucy's auburn.

"You shouldn't be so nasty to me, Edward," lisped the half-formed mouth. "We're family, after all."

***

"The next thing I remember," said Gould, after a pause, "was running through the forest, shouting for help. Martin and Paul found me, and tried to calm me down, get me to explain. But I couldn't – I couldn't make sense out of what had happened. I just kept saying 'Lucy's gone, they stole her face'."

"Oh my Lord," whispered Brie, eyes bugging. "The thing's face – like the one I saw. Not quite human, but so close it was horrible."

"I saw one, too," murmured Denny. "Complete with unfinished features. Maybe mine couldn't decide on a face."

Gould nodded, then reached into the jacket that he had hung on the back of his chair. He took out a flask and poured amber liquid into his coffee. He offered the flask around. Only Frankie took a mouthful, coughed. Denny caught the distinct odor of Scotch whiskey.

"Wow, that's the good stuff all right," she spluttered.

This prompted nervous laughter, and everyone started talking at once. Matt seemed to think the entire experience was a kind of false memory covering a more disturbing, but entirely natural, incident. Marvin dismissed that idea, while Denny tried to mediate. Frankie continued to film what became a heated discussion, while Gould sat looking into the distance, evidently wrapped up in his memories.

"Okay," said Matt loudly, holding up his hands for silence, "the stone in the forest, whatever it was. If people knew it was there, warned their kids not to go near it, why didn't they do something about it? Smash the stone, maybe concrete over the whole clearing. Hell, why not tell the police, MI5, whatever?"

"Good question," Gould conceded, absentmindedly running a finger along the scar on his forearm. "But many years later when I asked local people, including my parents, about the forest, none of them could say why it was reputedly a bad place. It just was. Nobody went there. That was the key fact. Stories about a well, or an old mine, or lurking perverts were concocted after the fact. As for the stone, well, it was just a bit of old rock. For the authorities, there was nothing to connect it to a little girl vanishing."

Matt gave a noncommittal grunt.

"But you're right," Gould went on. "The police did investigate the whole area, and they did the clearing. There was no sign of a struggle, not a trace of Lucy. None of her clothes, or her shoes, were found. Not that day, at least. It was a mystery – made the national papers. The place was swarming with reporters."

The story isn't over, thought Denny. *That's why he needed a slug of whiskey. There's even worse to come.*

"I heard the story in fragments, down the years," Gould went on. "They sent me away to my grandparents for a fortnight after the disappearance. My physical injuries were treated, blamed on broken glass or wood splinters. I had no therapy, of course – I told you this happened a long time ago. Just a little holiday. So I wasn't there when they found the body two days later. It was on the edge of the forest, the side nearest our house, not the village side. She was in her red coat, with her dress, socks, shoes – all readily identified. The only strange thing was that the dress was wrongly buttoned. And her shoes were on the wrong feet."

"You mean," gasped Brie, "someone had undressed her,

then – Oh Lord."

Gould stared into his coffee for a long moment before resuming.

"In those days, of course, they did not have very advanced forensic techniques. Certain tests were made, and I later found out that an autopsy was carried out. The results were described as inconclusive, but heart failure during an assault was settled upon as the cause of death."

"And that was it?" asked Matt. "You were all very British about it, I guess?"

"I never talked to my father about it, if that's what you mean," replied Gould. "After we lost Lucy, something in him died. He carried on working, but everything else – he would just sit in front of the telly, only spoke if you talked to him. Eventually they separated, and my mother raised me. Sometimes bereavement does that – smashes a family apart."

There were sympathetic nods, and Matt seemed about to speak, then thought better of it. Denny recalled how needy and clingy he had been when they'd had their brief, unwise fling. Matt had lost his mother when he was young, she remembered. *I'm not here to psychoanalyze my co-workers, or ex-lovers,* she thought. Denny focused once more on what Gould was saying.

"I could almost have written off everything that happened in that clearing, if it had not been for my mother's attitude. My mother was stronger than us menfolk, I suppose. That's often the case. But she never discussed it, either. Once I caught her crying on Lucy's birthday, but that was it. Then my father died, still quite young, and at his funeral, my mother told me something. At first, I didn't understand what she had said, it was so unexpected."

Gould looked up at Denny, then at the others around the table.

"It wasn't her. That's what my mother said."

For a moment Denny was puzzled, then realized what Gould meant, given the context.

"It wasn't Lucy?" asked Brie, frowning. Then understanding dawned. "You mean they found – that creature?"

Gould nodded.

"It took a while for me to get the rest of the story out of her. She and my father had had to identify the body, you see. But when she saw it, she became convinced that it was not her daughter lying on the slab in the county mortuary. My father, at first, thought she was merely in shock. Then, as she continued to insist that Lucy was still alive, he became angry, confused, and unable to talk to her at all. From then on, they only communicated about mundane things, never really talked. And because I was a child they didn't tell me."

"But isn't that called Impostor Syndrome?" asked Marvin. "When people get the idea a loved one has been replaced by a lookalike, somehow? It's a mental disorder."

"True," said Gould. "But in Impostor Syndrome it's always a living relative, never a dead one. And there's more. Many years later, when I first became involved with the foundation, I sought out the doctor who had performed the post mortem examination. Turned out he'd retired."

***

"Dr. Beddows gets a bit confused," the nurse explained, leading Gould into the day room. It was a pleasant July morning and the residents of the Bide-a-Wee Home for Retired Gentlefolk were enjoying the sunshine. Two elderly men were playing chess, while a white-haired old lady was busy with the Times crossword. But about a dozen other old folk were simply basking in the golden light.

The nurse gestured at a man with a mop of gray hair and a straggling goatee sitting on his own in a wing-backed armchair. Gould went over and introduced himself, then tried to explain why he was there. But Beddows gave no sign that he recognized Lucy's name, staring up at Gould with watery, pale blue eyes.

"Michael?" the old man asked. "Is that you?"

"He thinks you're his son," the crossword lady explained. "Lives abroad, never visits. This often happens, I'm afraid. He has good days, but this might not be one of them."

Gould introduced himself and offered to shake Beddows'

hand, but the old man just looked blankly up at him.

"I'm here to ask about Lucy, my sister," Gould said, speaking slowly. "She was found dead, and you examined her body. Do you remember that?"

"Lucy? No, no," said Beddows, shaking his head emphatically so that a cowlick of white hair flopped over his forehead. "No, you told me that your lady friend is called Carla. Or was it Martha?"

Gould pulled up a chair and tried to explain again, but Beddows just asked a series of questions about Michael's work and family life. They talked at cross-purposes for a couple of minutes, but it was clear that the old doctor was just becoming more agitated. Gould stood up, frustrated at hitting a blank wall in his investigation. At the same time, he felt sorry for Beddows, left to vegetate by his only close relative.

"I'm sorry, doctor," Gould said, offering his hand to the old man again. "I shouldn't have bothered you. I just wanted to know about Lucy."

"At first I felt bad because it was a child," murmured Beddows. "Then I felt frightened, because it was all wrong."

Gould stopped, and tried to process what he had just heard.

"The Lucy Gould autopsy?" he asked, sitting down again. "There was something wrong, something strange about it?"

"Everything was wrong – it was so disconcerting!"

Beddows was staring intently up at him now, his eyes focused, his manner showing no hint of confusion. The old man's gnarled hand fastened on Gould's arm, gripped it with surprising strength.

"It was almost a child, you see," he hissed. "Almost, but not quite. The organs weren't right, and the skeletal structure – everything was simplified, as if someone had taken tissue, bone, and cartilage to make a living doll, a passable facsimile. I remember thinking how awful if that creature had lived, passing for human, but not. Going to school, sitting at the dinner table, being tucked in bed. The brain was outlandish. What thoughts might such a thing have had?"

The old man shuddered. Gould struggled to process what he had just heard. The pleasant, sunlit room seemed impossibly calm and ordinary. Not a place for such revelations.

"You're sure it wasn't my sister?" he demanded, struggling to keep his voice low as the other residents looked on. "It wasn't Lucy at all?"

Beddows nodded gravely, then looked around.

"These people can't imagine it," he whispered. "The things I saw. Beneath the skin, so much that wasn't right. Monstrous! But who could I tell? I had a career, a position in the community. The newspapers had already reported the death of a child. The police had it all typed and filed. Terrible thing. Grieving parents. So I signed the forms, wrote what they wanted, kept my nose clean. Oh yes. It had already begun to decay, you see. Disintegration accelerated rapidly once it set in. Soon there would be nothing identifiable!"

"You did what they wanted?" asked Gould, taking the old man's hand in his. "Who do you mean? Did someone pressure you?"

Beddows frowned. His expression of intense concentration faded, facial muscles slackening. The old man leaned back in his chair, which creaked.

"Pressure? No, no pressure at all – it's very relaxing here. Everyone is very kind. But I do get lonely, sometimes, Michael. I wish you'd come more often."

***

"Oh my God," said Denny. "That's horrible."

It's also ratings gold, she could not help thinking. *The guy's a natural storyteller.*

"It has the ring of truth," added Marvin, again surprising Denny.

He's given up on his trademark cynicism, she thought.

"But what are these things?" demanded Matt. "Where do they come from? Do you know, Ted? Don't hold out on us, not in this situation"

Gould rubbed his chin, glanced around at his listeners.

He's wondering how much more to reveal, thought Denny. *I'll bet our audience gets that.*

69

"Okay," Gould said. "The scientists I work with think the Interlopers come from what they've dubbed the Phantom Dimension. PD for short. A real, physical realm, like our own universe, but existing parallel to it. Obviously one world is closed off from the other, but there are weak spots where energy and matter can pass through. Gateways, if you like. Our ancestors knew about them, and placed those odd marker stones to show where they could sometimes be found. I'm sure that some stones were simply warnings, like a buoy marking a wreck."

It took the others a few moments to process these ideas.

"So the stones aren't sacrificial altars?" asked Marvin.

"Some might have been," admitted Gould. "We don't know, despite many decades of research. All over the world, you find stones carved with strange faces, not quite human visages. It's conventional to say the prehistoric cultures that produced them were depicting their gods, or demons. And that is what the Interlopers must have seemed, for a long time. Beings that could change their shape, appearance, and drag people into some strange realm. The Trickster of Native American myth, the Little People of Celtic folklore. There are lots of variations on the theme."

"These things are intelligent?" Denny asked.

Gould nodded emphatically.

"Intelligent, aggressive, cunning. And not bound by the same physical laws as ourselves. That's why they can read our thoughts, to some extent, and change their appearance accordingly. In the Phantom Dimension, what we call magic seems to prevail – willpower alters reality. It might be that that is where we get all our magical beliefs – half remembered stories about the PD and its denizens."

"Hang on," interrupted Matt. "If they enter our world, surely our laws apply?"

"That's a good point," agreed Gould. "Some believe there's a kind of conservation of energy involved – they can survive here for a while because they bring their own weird reality with them. But this power they have dwindles, is diluted by our reality, so that they must return to the PD or suffer dissolution. Like the Interloper that took Lucy's form –

something went wrong, it died, and disintegrated."

"So it decayed because it ran out of paranormal juice?" asked Marvin.

"You have a knack for making the most serious matter seem frivolous," replied Gould.

Soon everyone was talking at once, throwing questions at Gould, interrupting one another. Then Jim banged the flat of his hand down on the table. For the first time since Denny had met him, the stocky man looked angry. And scared.

"This is all very nice," Jim said. "But what I've heard only convinces me that we're in immediate danger. We should go. Now."

This triggered more argument, as the group split along predictable lines. Jim and Brie were keen to get out at once, while Gould and Matt both wanted to stay and finish filming. Marvin, Frankie and Denny were caught in the middle.

It's a great opportunity to get rock-solid evidence of the paranormal, Denny thought. *But only if we live through it.*

"If we stick together," Gould was saying, "they can't do us any harm. Remember, they prey on our weaknesses; fears, hopes, deep emotions. A group is too diverse to attack in that way."

Jim began to protest, but Gould shut him down with a single remark.

"Are you quitting your job, Davison? Because I hear you ex-army types have poor employment prospects these days."

It's a stalemate, Denny thought. *But we came here to make a show.*

"Ted," she said, "if we filmed the gateway to this other dimension that would be the clincher. So far we've got nothing useful on tape."

"If we got that, we could leave," conceded Matt. "So we go back into that temple, see what happens, right?"

"No," said Brie. "Everything Ted has said just convinces me I need to get far away from this place. I still want to leave!"

Chapter 5: Little Boy Lost

"Okay," said Denny, trying to salvage something before they had to stop filming. "Maybe you guys could tell us something about the psychic aura of this – whatever it is, altar?"

Marvin snorted in derision.

"Down there is just some dirty minded old lord's rumpus room," he said, gesturing at the doorway. "I sense a lot of tension, fear, confusion – but only from the living people standing right here. There are no spirits, evil or otherwise."

"But Brie says she can sense evil," Denny objected. "So who's right? Ted? Do you feel anything?"

Gould shook his head.

"Apart from a chill, no. And I don't claim to be psychic. Anyway, the cold is what you'd expect in an unheated cellar in autumn."

"I want to go now," Brie insisted. "I will not spend the night here. Will somebody call me a taxi? Or should I do it myself?"

"Okay," Denny sighed, looking into the camera. "For the first time in the history of 'America's Weirdest Hauntings', one of the team has – let's say – withdrawn from the field of battle."

Brie really is freaking out, she thought. *And I don't blame her. If what she experienced was worse than my encounter, she's right to draw the line.*

After Frankie had stopped filming, Gould arranged for Jim to take Brie into Chester and find her someplace to stay. Brie also insisted that Jim come upstairs with her so she wouldn't be alone while she packed. The rest of the team adjourned to the kitchen, where an old kitchen range provided much needed warmth.

"Guess we can film them driving away," Matt said, sulkily. "Or can we simply edit Brie out?"

Denny began to protest, but Frankie settled the issue by pointing out that they already had several hours of footage that included Brie.

"Crap," said Matt. "We'd have to miss out all the

preparations back in the States, the flight, arriving in England."

"Can't be done," Frankie said, with finality. "Make a virtue of necessity, play up why she's leaving."

"Prescription meds?" Marvin asked in his all-too-familiar bitchy tone.

Gould looked startled at this, but said nothing. Matt shot Marvin a 'cut it out!' look.

"Okay, I'm not on any kind of pills, and I'm still pretty sure I saw something," insisted Denny. "Maybe not a ghost, or the devil, but something scary and weird. This house is haunted in some way."

"But we've got nothing on tape!" said Matt, frustration clear in his voice. "Two of the team are confronted by God-knows-what, and they're alone with no camera running."

"Maybe that's it," said Denny. "Whatever we're dealing with doesn't show itself to more than one person. Perhaps it preys on *individual* fears somehow? What do you think, Ted?"

Gould looked cagey, then shook his head.

"In the past, more than one person has been involved in manifestations," he pointed out. "And in 1919, something supposedly killed or wounded several people."

"Or they went crazy and attacked each other," Matt said. "That was the official verdict, wasn't it?"

"Yes," Gould admitted. "But when you consider the evidence ..."

The debate went to and fro until they were interrupted by a text message from Brie to Denny, 'Ready to go!' When they got to the main hall, she was descending the stairs, followed by Jim, who was loaded down with her luggage. Denny again tried to persuade Brie to stay, but failed. When Jim opened the front door, a gust of chill, damp night air blew in. It was now pitch dark outside.

No streetlights, thought Denny, with a shiver. *We're a long way from help.*

"Well, if you have to go, good luck," she told Brie. "And don't keep Jim to yourself, we need him here."

Brie said her slightly awkward farewells then left, clutching Jim's arm as he struggled with her bags. Matt shut the front door behind them and as he did, the hall lights flickered, died, then came on again.

"Looks like she left just in time," observed Marvin, wryly.

"It's probably just the old wiring," said Gould, but without much conviction.

"First that thing with the Geiger counter, now this," Denny said. "Any connection, Ted?"

"Electrical equipment sometimes becomes unreliable in these situations," replied the Englishman. "But you all knew that already, I'm sure?"

True, Denny thought, *but why do I get the feeling you know a lot more than you're letting on?*

Matt, Denny, and Frankie began to discuss how they would cope if the power failed. They had batteries for most of their equipment, but recharging might become an issue if they had no power for the whole night. Frankie decided to start the raw editing process, beginning with footage from the various automatic cameras.

"So I put one camera in the hall," she said, "looking down from above the doorway, right? So here's Brie after her panic, going into the dining room for a lie down, Jim and me take her inside, then you see us come out."

"Okay," said Denny, "you know the motion sensor thingy works. So what?"

"So this," Frankie said, as the others gathered around the kitchen table to look at the laptop screen. "See, this is Brie leaving the dining room to go upstairs, just a few minutes later. Now we jump forward about ten minutes and this is you, see?"

Denny stared, confounded by what she was seeing. She watched herself knock gently on the dining room door, then go inside. Frankie skipped forward a few minutes and Denny emerged, closing the door gently behind her. Another fast forward and the team gathered in the hall, Brie descending the stairs, followed a couple of minutes later by Denny.

"Oh my God," Denny breathed.

"I don't get it," said Matt. "So you went into an empty room and came out again? We're not making art-house movies, guys."

74

"I talked to Brie in there," Denny said, looking at Matt, then Gould, then back at Frankie. "She was curled up on the couch under a rug. I heard her speak!"

But I never saw her face, she thought. *Or even the slightest bit of her skin. Just that hunk of hair.*

"But nobody else went into the room," Gould pointed out. "Or left it. Did they?"

"Good point!" Frankie murmured. "Let's just check."

She reversed the video slowly. It jumped from the point when the camera detected Denny to Brie going upstairs. Frankie slowed things down even more and began to inspect the movie one frame at a time.

"There," she said, freezing the image and pointing at the screen. "See? Something there."

Brie was just vanishing upstairs. Behind her, a blurred shape was emerging from one of the many anonymous corridors of Malpas Abbey. It was out of focus, so that Denny could only just make out a form that was vaguely human in shape. The next frame was time-stamped much later, and showed Denny coming from the kitchen into the hall.

"The motion sensor had trouble with it," Frankie said. "Like your Geiger counter, maybe, Ted? Something about these boogeymen screws up our tech. But it's there. The little gadget that caught something."

Open-mouthed, Denny looked up from the screen to see Matt giving her a mirthless grin, while Gould looked more thoughtful.

"It seems you actually conversed with some kind of entity," said Gould.

"And you didn't notice," added Marvin, stroking his chin. "Not sure what that says about you. Or Brie, for that matter."

"Close encounter, girlfriend," said Frankie.

***

"I'm so grateful," said Brie, as Jim helped load her bags into the SUV. "I just want to get home to my boys, you know? I've never been so far away from Tommy – that's my son. I never thought I could miss someone so much."

She's yearning for familiar surroundings, Jim thought. *Figures. If I was half a world away from home and terrified out of my wits I suppose I'd be the same.*

"No problem," the Englishman replied. He could just make her out in the light spilling from the round window above the front door. Rain was falling, and Jim wished he had put on a thicker coat. But he had assumed he would be spending most of this assignment indoors.

"Okay, Brie," he said cheerfully, as he slammed the rear door of the Mercedes. "Let's get you back to civilization. Well, Chester at least. Near as; makes no difference!"

They got into the car and buckled up. Jim was about to start the engine when he paused. He had glimpsed movement through the rain-spattered windshield. A pale object, low on the ground.

Furtive, Jim thought. *Skulking. Lurking on the edge of visibility.*

"Is something wrong?" Brie asked, her voice betraying jangled nerves.

Get a grip, he told himself. *This woman is on edge, she doesn't need any more scares.*

"No, nothing!" he said. "Thought I saw a deer, that's all. Or maybe it was a badger. Lots of wildlife out here."

Jim started the engine and began to maneuver the vehicle carefully down the rutted driveway towards the main gate. The wipers and headlights seemed oddly ineffective, and he struggled to make out anything ahead of them. Then the white pillars loomed up and he heaved a sigh of relief.

"Not far to the main road," he said. "Then it's a straight drive into Chester and we can—"

A sudden shock ran through the car, which lurched to one side. Brie screamed as Jim struggled to control the big Mercedes, but it slewed off the road and collided with a granite gatepost. There was a sickening crunch, and the engine died.

"Damn it! We blew a tire!"

"Oh, God," said Brie. "This damned place! It's not going to let me get away!"

Jim reassured her that it was just an accident, probably down to a piece of broken glass, and he could change the tire easily enough. He tried to speak with more confidence than he felt. He had checked out the driveway himself a couple of days earlier. It had been in poor condition, but there had been no glass or other hazards.

"Okay, you stay here with the heating on," he said, restarting the engine. "I'll get out and fix the tire. If I can't fix it, we can just walk back up to the house and take Ted's car, see? No problem."

Brie whimpered a little, but did not protest as Jim got out a flashlight. When he stepped out into the darkness, the chill struck him again. The rain had already turned the dirt underfoot to mud, and for good measure, he had driven them into a patch of waist-high nettles that stung his hands as he worked. Cursing under his breath, Jim got the tools and began to jack up the vehicle. When he removed the front wheel, he gave the blown tire a cursory examination. It was hard to tell in the poor light what had caused it to fail.

Looks like it was slashed, he thought, running a finger along a tear in the rubber. *Cut deep, but not right through. Just enough so it would run for a few minutes before blowing. Is someone pranking us?*

Jim glanced around, swinging his flashlight. The beam showed raindrops, damp nettles, muddy ground, and gravel. He shone the flashlight up at the gatepost, squinting as it illuminated a grotesque statue squatting on top of the pillar. It was gargoyle-like, a grotesque diminutive figure squatting above him. Lit from below, it seemed doubly uncanny.

Like a gargoyle on an old church. But at least a carving can't hurt you, he thought. *Whoever or whatever cut that tire, on the other hand ...*

Shrugging off the thought, Jim resolved to be practical. He put the flashlight down and began to attach the spare wheel. More stings added to his frustration, and he wished he had some thick gloves. Still, he was making good progress. But as he worked, a nagging doubt began to worry at the back of his mind.

The gateposts, he thought. *Details are wrong, somehow.*

When he finished, he got the flashlight and shone it up at the gatepost again. There was nothing on top of the pillar. He shone the flashlight over at the other gatepost. It was topped by a granite ball. Jim began to work frantically, kicking the jack away and not bothering to collect the tools. He snatched open the SUV's door. Brie stared into the flashlight beam, her eyes huge with fear.

"Okay," said Jim, trying not to sound overly concerned. "We're good to go."

"What's wrong?" Brie asked.

"Nothing," he said firmly, fumbling with his safety belt. "Got the wheel fixed, no problem."

He clashed the gears putting the Mercedes into reverse, then spun the wheels in the mud. The SUV backed up a few inches then slid forward, hitting the granite gatepost again. Jim took his foot off the gas, tried to gulp down his nervousness, tried again. This time the big car struggled back onto the furrowed driveway, slewing from side to side as Jim revved the motor.

"Right," he said, changing gear. "Let's get out of this godforsaken–"

The sound of the rain and wind grew suddenly louder. A chill blew through the interior of the SUV. In the rearview mirror, Jim saw a pale shape moving swiftly in the gloom as he heard one of the rear doors close. He lifted the flashlight as high as he could in the confined space, prepared to bring it down hard.

"What is it?" asked Brie, twisting around in her seat. "Did that thing get inside?"

"Don't worry," he said. "I'll sort it out. Just get ready to run if–"

"Mommy?"

The voice was that of a child. Jim hesitated, lifted himself in the seat to look into the back of the Mercedes. He could just make out a pale face looking up at him. It was apparently that of a small boy, small features topped by a mop of brown hair. Definitely not the leering gargoyle figure he had seen earlier.

"What are you doing here?" he asked, turning the flashlight to illuminate the newcomer. Small, skinny hands quickly covered the face.

"Mommy! The light's too bright!"

An American accent, Jim thought, brain racing.

"Tommy?" said Brie, unfastening her seat belt. "Is that you?"

"Mommy!"

The small figure flung itself forward between the seats, and wrapped pale, skinny arms around Brie. Jim saw then that the diminutive figure was clad in some kind of grayish-brown, ragged garment, more like some kind of medieval robe than regular clothes.

"Who is this?" Jim demanded. "Brie?"

"It's Tommy! Can't you see?" Brie looked at him over the small head she was clutching to her. "Jim, this is my son!"

"It can't be!" Jim protested. "How did he get here all the way from America?"

"The bad people brought me," said the boy, speaking in muffled tones. His head turned, and he looked at Jim. In the beam from the flashlight, the being Brie insisted was Tommy did look like a normal child.

There's definitely a family resemblance, Jim thought. *The nose, and the eyes.*

"Who brought you?" he asked. "Who are the bad people?"

"You are!" yelled 'Tommy', then buried his face in the front of Brie's coat again. Jim hesitated, wondering if he should continue with their journey or turn back.

This is just the sort of thing Gould needs to know about, he thought.

"Does it matter how he got here?" Brie demanded, her voice quavering with emotion. "He's scared! We've got to go! Get him to safety!"

"Okay," said Jim, shrugging. He put the Mercedes into gear, and nosed it through the gate. But as the road came into view in the headlights, Tommy began to thrash around and whine.

"No, no, don't take me away!" he cried. "Take me back to the big house!"

For the first time since the newcomer had appeared, Brie looked uncertain.

"No, honey," she said, "that's a bad place."

"That's not your son!" Jim shouted, his mind suddenly

clear of all doubt. "It makes no sense, Brie!"

"Tommy?" breathed Brie. Jim pulled up and again raised the heavy flashlight, but hesitated to bring it down on what still looked very much like a child's head. Tommy had become very still, his arms still wrapped around Brie. Then he emitted a growling noise that sounded more like a vicious dog than a child.

"No!" Brie shouted, trying to push the creature away. In a matter of seconds, Tommy had started to change, limbs growing longer and thinner, head losing its human-like roundness, hair becoming more sparse. The creature suddenly darted its head up and fastened onto Brie's face. Jim heard a sickening sound, part biting, part suction. Brie screamed and thrashed, trying to break free of the monstrous embrace, as Jim brought the flashlight down hard on the back of the elongated head. The being emitted a snarl, twisted its head around a hundred and eighty degrees, revealing a blood-stained muzzle.

Part-wolf, part-baboon, thought Jim, as he aimed another blow. Even as he brought his improvised club down, the creature was lunging toward him and the blow barely connected with the white, bare shoulder. The creature shoved its inhuman face towards Jim's, and he glimpsed an array of needle-like, blood-stained teeth. Impeded by his safety belt, Jim tried to grab his assailant by its long neck, but it was too fast and too strong. He flinched, closing his eyes, trying to protect his face with his free hand. He felt pain and the hot gush of blood.

"Get out Brie!" he shouted. "Run!"

***

"Okay," said Matt. "So, what have we learned from this?"

"These things are way out of our league," said Denny. "I vote we quit."

"Seconded," said Frankie.

Matt and Gould both began to protest at the same time.

"Seriously?" Denny said, hands on hips. "This is not listening for things that go bump in the night, guys. We've never encountered anything this extreme."

"No," said Gould, "but you've come close to them a few times."

"What?" exclaimed Matt. "You never told me that!"

Denny and the rest of the 'America's Weirdest' team listened while Gould explained why the Romola Foundation had invited them to England. By the time he had finished, Matt was even madder about the information withheld, and other team members were not far behind.

"And you chose now to tell us?" shouted Denny. "Jesus!"

"I'm sorry," Gould said. "But if we had told you that one of your team has an affinity with these beings it would have tainted the experiment."

"Well, we wouldn't want that," said Marvin. "Anyone else feel like a rat in a maze?"

"Rest assured," Gould went on, "that anyone who wants to join Brie can do so. I'll drive you back to Chester myself."

"What if we all want to quit?" demanded Denny, angrily. "Because I've had enough of your bullshit, Ted."

"Hey, let's not be hasty!" Matt began, but hesitated at a sound in the distance. "What was that?"

"The front door?" suggested Frankie. "Jim can't be back already?"

They had just reached the door into the hall when it was yanked open and Brie rushed through, colliding with Denny. Brie was bleeding from a cut on her cheek. Gould and Marvin held the psychic upright while she babbled about 'Tommy' and 'monsters'. Denny wrinkled her nose. Along with Brie came a stench, like rotting meat. Then Denny saw Jim coming through the front door, carrying something in his arms. It was a gray-brown, nondescript object wrapped in Jim's jacket. Denny saw that it was dripping an oily black fluid onto the floor tiles.

"It just died," said Jim flatly, throwing his burden down.

The stench grew stronger when the rotting creature hit the floor. The impact sounded to Denny like wet laundry being dropped. The group formed a semi-circle around the disparate jumble of organic debris, exclaiming at the foul odor. There was little to see apart from a spreading puddle of putrefaction.

A few traces of what might have been bones, organs and tendons were rapidly disintegrating.

"What the hell is that?" asked Marvin, stepping away.

"It's an Interloper," said Gould, covering his mouth with a scarf. "I've never seen one this close. Not in a long while, anyway."

"You've even got a name for these things?" Jim said resentfully. "You might have given me a heads up, boss! It scared the crap out of us. It could have killed us both if it hadn't suddenly fallen apart. Brie's wound isn't too bad but it will need cleaning, can somebody see to that?"

"I'll do it," said Marvin.

To Denny's surprise, Marvin took Brie gently by the arm and led her to the kitchen, where they'd stowed their First-Aid kit.

"I'm sorry, everyone," said Gould, "but I never expected them to be so aggressive all at once. Normally they lurk on the margins of perception, observing. When they decide to meddle, though—"

"They kill people, or try to," said Jim. "Ted, I vote we all get out of here."

"Same here," Denny and Frankie said simultaneously.

"What I said earlier stands," Matt insisted. "We can't just walk away from here with nothing. We can't afford it."

Matt looked around at his team.

"If we don't get a usable show out of this, it's game over," he went on. "Ratings have not been great for the last season. If we go back empty handed, the network drops us, and we've got nothing."

"You kept this quiet!" objected Denny. "What happened to all that stuff about us being one big happy team?"

Chapter 6: The Exchange

After much bickering, it was decided that Jim would remain with Brie while the rest of the team filmed for an hour in the cellar. If nothing happened, they would leave. Matt was grumpy about the last point, arguing that they had nothing of value in the can.

"We've had real paranormal experiences," Denny pointed out. "And two of us were attacked, could have been killed. What more do you want?"

Gould tried and failed to persuade Marvin to come with them, arguing that a psychic would be useful.

"I'm happy here," Marvin said. "I communicate with human spirits, not monsters from some hell dimension. But hey, knock yourselves out!"

As the depleted team walked back along the dim-lit corridors towards Blaisdell's temple, Frankie filmed Denny firing questions at Gould.

"Okay, let's accept your theory of the Interlopers," she said. "But why do they only turn up sometimes? Like, when a crazy, old lord tried devil worship? Or in 1919, when those guys were killed? Why then, but not the hundreds of other years that people lived here?"

"Some people have an affinity for them," said Gould. "Quite unintentionally, some people trigger the PD gateways just by their proximity. Perhaps in ancient times such people were shamans, witches. They could call up the Interlopers, bargain with them."

"Bargain for what?" Denny shot back.

Here, Gould looked uncertain.

"Perhaps persuade them to kill enemies – they would make ideal assassins, able to shape themselves into seductive or terrifying forms. Also, there are numerous legends about good or bad fortune following people who have dealings with supernatural beings. The familiar deal with the Devil is just one variant of a very old idea. These beings may have powers over luck, fate, destiny – there's still so much we don't know. But we're keen on finding out."

"But what do they want?" she persisted. "Why do they

kidnap people, kill people? Or try to replace them?"

"What are we doing here?" Gould riposted. "Research, experiment."

"You mean they're scientists, too?" asked Matt.

"I think they're trying to understand us better," replied Gould. "And I don't think they're doing their research out of a love of abstract knowledge. I think they have a higher purpose. A goal in mind."

"Bet it doesn't end in hugs and puppies," commented Frankie, sourly.

They arrived at the temple doorway. The interior was pitch black. Gould took a handful of small flares from his backpack. He explained, as they worked by chemical reaction, they should not be affected by any fluctuations in electrical power. He lit the first flare then threw the small metal tube onto the floor at the bottom of the staircase.

"Okay, who goes first?" asked Matt, standing at the back of the group.

"Not you, apparently," Denny replied, and stepped inside. Gould's flare emitted a bright pinkish glow that made the circular chamber look even more unworldly. The murals, in the flickering light, almost seemed alive. She clicked on her flashlight and picked her way carefully down the stairs, keeping her attention focused on the mass of stone in the center of the room. Behind her Frankie followed, filming the screen while keeping Denny's head and shoulders just in shot.

"I got that screech in my cans again, like feedback only worse," Frankie said, lifting her headphones with a grimace. "Could be a sign of something wicked coming this way."

Denny reached the cellar floor and paused for a moment, taking in the scene. So far as she could tell, nothing had changed. She swept the flashlight beam across the floor, picked out their own footprints in the dust. Then she paused, swung the light back to the altar. Shadows danced, but so far as she could see, they were all cast by her light.

"Heads up," warned Frankie, "I'm getting visual interference now. Snow on the screen."

At the same moment, Denny's flashlight began to flicker then faded to a dull orange glow. Gould struck another flare, threw it over by the altar past Denny.

"Hey you guys, I need help!"

Everyone turned to look up at the top of the stairs. Denny could just make out a stocky figure staring down at them.

"Jim!" she shouted. "Did something happen?"

"It's Brie," came the reply. "Hurry!"

Frankie swung around and pointed her camera up at the doorway just in time to see Jim look to one side then run off along the corridor out of sight.

"What's wrong with Brie?" Denny called, dashing up the stairs. "Jim?"

She heard Gould shouting something but could not make out the words. She rounded the corner, hesitated. A figure was standing about ten yards away, just outside the feeble glow of the light in the corridor.

"Jim?" she said, suddenly doubtful.

The being that had mimicked Jim crouched, its pale limbs elongating, and bounded towards Denny. She saw small, black eyes, a face that was flowing even as the creature hurled itself forward. It snarled, held up claws that now only bore a vague resemblance to human hands. Denny screamed and ran back into the cellar. In her panic, she stumbled halfway down the stairs, fell, and landed hard. Piercing pain shot through her right ankle.

"Jesus Christ," exclaimed Matt, who was halfway up the stone stairway. "What is it?"

"One of them!" shouted Gould. "Get it on film!"

"Still running," Frankie said, aiming her camera up at the doorway. "Poor quality, better than nothing."

They waited for the Interloper to appear in the doorway, but the portal remained empty. Denny glanced round, seeing puzzlement vying with anxiety on her colleagues' faces. Then she saw something else. The air behind Frankie was starting to shimmer. Denny remembered Gould's description, and opened her mouth to shout a warning. Before she could make a sound, however, a pale, elongated figure materialized. The Interloper wrapped long, thin arms around Frankie, who yelled out in alarm and let go of her camera. Denny was struggling to stand when the first creature appeared, bounding

85

down the stairs. It shot past Gould and Matt before the men could respond and joined its companion. Between them they easily lifted the struggling Frankie off her feet.

"Help her!"

Gould and Matt were both frozen with shock, and by the time Denny had staggered upright, Frankie had been dragged into the shimmering sphere. The abduction had taken seconds. Denny fell to her knees, starting to weep with anger and confusion.

"It was her all along," said Gould, in a stunned voice. "They sensed her. I thought it was one of the psychics, but it was her."

"What are you talking about?" shouted Denny. "We need to do something!"

"You gonna go into that thing?" demanded Matt, pointing at the sphere of turbulent air as he backed towards the stairs. "Because I'm outta here!"

"Sure, run away!" Denny cried. "That's your specialty!"

She stood again, sobbing at the pain, and started to limp forward. Gould grabbed her arm, refused to be shaken off. She began to beat at him with her free hand.

"You can't," he said firmly. "Believe me, it's pointless. It's been tried. If you knew what–"

Gould stopped, staring past Denny, who turned to look into the weird gateway to an unimaginable reality. The shimmering globe was darker, pulsing, growing. It turned almost opaque, and then a hand appeared, clawing at the air. Denny stopped struggling, fell back against Gould.

"Don't just stand there, you assholes!" Matt shouted from the doorway. "They're coming for us all!"

"No!" Denny shouted, hoping against hope. "It's Frankie, she's trying to get back!"

She staggered forward and made a grab for the hand, only realizing as she grasped the fingers that it was way too large to be Frankie's. She tried to pull free but now she was gripped tight. A vague bulk was materializing in the air in front of her, forming three feet above the floor.

"Get away!" Denny shouted, breaking free with a tremendous effort. She fell backwards just as the stranger emerged fully from the weird portal and collapsed onto the cellar floor. A wave of the now-familiar stench washed over Denny then the shimmering globe vanished.

"What is it?" Matt yelled.

Good question, thought Denny, as she pushed herself on her behind away from the grotesque figure that had appeared. *Is this a human or not?*

At first, she thought the figure might be an Interloper taking the form of a Halloween scarecrow. But then she saw the tell-tale marks of old wounds on the head and hands, and a few strands of gray hair on the head. Denny decided that she was looking at a tall, painfully thin man clad in ragged clothes that – she realized – must once have been expensive finery. The newcomer wore a long coat, now mostly black with dirt, but she glimpsed of a lining of red silk. A single, tarnished, silver button still clung to the coat, which had lost most of one sleeve.

But the man's face was far more ravaged than his garments. It was much-lined, deathly white, with dark staring eyes that showed white all around. Denny's flashlight, dropped in the confusion, suddenly flared brightly, restored to full power. At the sudden illumination, the stranger gave a choking cry and covered his face with his hands. His fingernails were long and ragged, but again they looked distinctly human. Then the stranger croaked out a single word.

"Light!"

"Is it one of them?" Matt asked, his voice revealing uncertainty. "It doesn't look too dangerous."

No, he's not nearly agile enough, thought Denny, as the stranger huddled on the floor, quivering. *This looks like a regular human.*

"Who are you?" she managed to ask, trying to sound nonthreatening.

The stranger uncovered his face, gazed at her open-mouthed.

"Who," he said, as if sounding out the simple English word. "Who?"

The ravaged face contorted in bafflement, as if Denny had posed an immensely difficult problem. Gould stepped forward, bent over the prone figure.

"Is it George?" Gould asked, in a coaxing tone, as if speaking to a small child. "George, yes?"

The ragged man uncovered his face, gazed up at Gould.

"George?" he gasped, then gave a crazy grin. "Yes. Yes!"

"Ladies and gentlemen," he said. "I think this is our host. Lord George Blaisdell."

"Aw, you're crazy!" scoffed Matt, who had paused halfway up the stairway. "That guy vanished, what, two hundred years ago. Right? How could he be here now?"

"George," the stranger repeated. "Lord, yes. Was a lord."

The newcomer accepted Gould's offer of a hand and got slowly to his feet. Denny stepped forward and took the man's other arm, helped lead him to the steps, where he sat down. As she helped George hobble slowly across the chamber, she saw that the back of his coat had been torn open lengthwise, as had the garments underneath.

"Gould," she said. "There's something on his back."

The object sticking between Blaisdell's shoulders was like a huge cyst. A little larger than a baseball, it was dull brown and pulsed like a beating heart. From it radiated black strands that vanished under the man's skin.

"Don't touch it!" Gould warned. "It might be dangerous!"

"I wasn't going to touch it," replied Denny. "I'm not crazy! But what the hell is it?"

The growth on the man's back looked something like a fungus, but its pulsation reminded her of documentaries about weird deep-sea creatures.

Could it be some kind of disease, she wondered. *Or a parasite from the Phantom Dimension?*

Gould began to fire questions at the man, repeatedly calling him George, trying to establish his identity for certain. But the stranger just stared, open-mouthed, at Gould. Denny raised her hand for silence and drew on her own journalistic experience.

Okay, never ask a question with a simple Yes or No answer. Always get the person to tell their story.

"George," she said gently, "where have you been?"

The thin, shabby man looked up at her, and for a moment

Denny feared that he might be too far gone to tell them anything. She thought of traumatized veterans, accident victims, and the abused and damaged who struggled to face their pasts. But then the stranger put his hands to the sides of his head and screamed.

"Hell! I have been in Hell!"

***

Matt ran along the hallway, fuming silently at the idiocy of Denny and Gould, determined to get out of Malpas Abbey as soon as possible.

Screw the goddamn show, he thought. *To hell with them all. Captain Matt's not gonna go down with this ship.*

He reached the main hall and was about to head back toward the kitchen when he stopped, struck by a simple idea. The Mercedes was, according to Jim, still at the gates. The keys would be in the ignition. Even if they weren't, Matt could hot-wire a car. It was one of many skills he had acquired in his adolescent years.

They'll still have Gould's car, he reasoned. *It's not like I'm actually abandoning them.*

Smiling to himself, he went to the front door and opened it. As the chill night air blew in a spray of rain, he hesitated.

What if there are more of those things outside?

Matt looked around, gazed for a moment at the jumbled heap of rotten remains that Jim had dropped onto the hall floor. That Interloper was safely dead, and he had seen two others drag Frankie through the gateway. He hefted his flashlight. The large, rubber-encased torch made a decent club.

How many of the sneaky little bastards can there be? Maybe they're all gone now.

Rather than dwell on possible answers, Matt set off into the night, slamming the door behind him. The noise was so loud that he flinched slightly. Anyone nearby would have heard it. Or anything. He set off at a steady jog along the driveway, the flashlight flickering between full power and near-failure. As he got further from the house, though, the

89

light from the torch became steadier.

Gould was right about his weird physics stuff, Matt thought. *A lot of good it will do him if more of those things come through after that George character.*

Now he could see the bulk of the Mercedes ahead, gleaming in the rain. The driver's door was open, and as he climbed in, he saw Jim's keys dangling from the ignition. Slamming the door, he started the engine, flicked on the headlights. The beams illuminated the way to safety. Matt felt himself grow even more tense as he saw how little separated him from freedom and safety.

Put that pedal to the metal, he thought. *And in five seconds, I'm on the road back to the sane world. Back to reality.*

"Were you really going to leave me, baby?"

Denny's face, her eyes huge and dark, appeared in the driving mirror. At the sight of her, Matt felt his all-too-familiar emotions wash over him. There was confusion and guilt at his decision to run out on her, his intense desire to possess her again, but above all, resentment at the way she had ended their relationship.

"Denny?" he said. "How did you—"

"I ran after you," she said simply. "Remember, I was a track star? You always said I had great legs. Among other attributes."

She reached over and ruffled his hair, and he saw that she was naked.

No, he thought, with a sudden stab of fear. *No way is this really her. This is one of them.*

"Get out," he snapped, picking up the heavy flashlight. "Get away from me you freak!"

"Aw, you got me," said the Interloper, leaning forward to put her face a few inches from his. "But I had you fooled for a second, right? You really wanted it to be her. For her to come crawling back to you."

Matt did not bother to reply, but instead brought the torch down on the creature's head. There was a sickening crunch, and the monster emitted a pathetic yelp, and fell backwards.

"Oh, you really hurt me, Matt!" it whined, holding its pale

hands over the wound. Dark fluid oozed between its long fingers. "No wonder they always end up leaving you!"

"Shut up," he grunted, trying to land another blow. But this time the Interloper was too quick for him. Sharp-clawed talons grabbed his wrist, and they began to struggle for the flashlight. Matt punched at the creature's face but it dodged, moving with alarming speed. Its limbs seemed to be elongating during the fight, the pale body that had been so like Denny's became distorted, a caricature of humanity. And as it lost its seductive form, it became stronger.

Gotta kill it quick, he thought desperately. *Beat its goddam brains out.*

"Should have played along, baby," the Interloper hissed through its hideous, needle-like teeth. "Now there's gonna be none of the pleasure, just all of the pain."

***

"Calm down, George," Denny said, patting his shoulder. "You're safe now."

"What do you mean, George?" Gould asked. "Why do you say you were in Hell?"

"Because the Devil took me there, you silly girl!" replied George, his British accent now very obvious. "I taunted him, took his name in vain, and he came for me. He killed the others, I saw him do it – but me, he took. He chose me to torment for all eternity. Or so I thought."

Denny detected a hint of pride in the way George talked of his abduction. The man was pleased, even after his horrendous ordeal, to have been singled out by the Prince of Darkness – as he undoubtedly saw the Interloper that had taken him.

Maybe he is an old-time aristocrat, she thought. *He gives off that kind of vibe. But could someone live for over two hundred years in the Phantom Dimension?*

"What was it like?" Gould demanded, leaning over George. "Is it a world like ours?"

"Like?" said George, quietly. "There are black stars in a pale sky, living stars that watch you. The sky hurts your eyes, the stars mock you! Cruel stars, hungry stars! And there are things like trees, but with eyes, and mouths, and they walk on their roots. The demons that took me can change their shape, strange beasts. Some squirm, some burrow! They took me into their vile catacombs to be tortured, humiliated, starved. But everywhere is in a great turmoil, a fierce wind blows down from the black stars, sears the skin, scours the mind of reason ..."

The monologue trailed off and George stared vacantly. A thin trickle of drool fell from one side of his mouth.

"How long were you there?" Denny asked.

The pale, withered face turned up toward her again.

"No days or nights in Hell," George mumbled. "No way to tell the time. An eternity, a moment, who can tell?"

"A night under the hill," murmured Gould, eyes wide. "That fits."

Denny frowned at her colleague, but before she could ask him what he meant, he went on, "We have to get this man some medical help."

Gould helped the stranger to his feet.

"Come on, George," he said, "let's get you to the kitchen, at least it's warm there."

Denny joined Gould and between them they aided the limping, wheezing George up the stairway. At the door, they paused for a moment to look back. There was no sign of the spherical disturbance that marked the gateway to the Phantom Dimension.

"What if it's closed for good?" she asked.

"It always opens again, eventually," Gould replied. "Come on, let's get him to the others. That First-Aid kit will come in handy again."

***

"Did you hear a scream?" asked Jim.

"Maybe," whimpered Brie. "They shouldn't have gone back to that evil place!"

Jim was changing the dressing on Brie's cheek while Marvin paced back and forth in the kitchen. The single light bulb that lit the room faded again, flickered, then returned to full strength.

"Hold still," warned Jim. "I need to swab it with antiseptic. Then I'll put on a fresh dressing."

"Does it look real bad?" asked Brie. "It feels numb. Frozen. What if it's infected with something – something alien, something nobody can cure?"

"It's fine," Jim insisted, finishing up. "Just a nasty scratch. You'll be good as new after a few days."

The hell she will, Marvin thought, looking at Brie's face. *That's a festering wound. If she looks in a mirror, she will lose it big time.*

Even in the weak light, he could see that the injury had turned black and seemed to be spreading via dark filaments under Brie's skin.

"God, you people are idiots," snorted Marvin, resuming his pacing. "We should just leave."

"If you want to help," said Jim, "you could go and get the Mercedes. The keys are still in the ignition. I might even have left the engine running. Take my flashlight."

Now you're taunting me, Marvin thought. *Calling me a coward. They're always mocking me, trivializing my contribution.*

"Maybe I will," he replied, pleased at the surprised expression on Jim's face. "Way you tell it, these things play on fear. Well, I'm a grown-up, so no boogeyman's going to scare me."

Jim's face now showed concern, and some irritation.

"It would be stupid to go alone," he said, standing up. "I'll go with you."

Marvin felt relieved, but Jim's offer prompted Brie to have a full-on panic attack. Jim had to sit back down and speak soothingly to her to stop her hyperventilating. As Brie would not come outside with them, the Englishman concluded that they had no choice but to stay with her.

"Nah, I'll go anyway," Marvin said, trying to sound casual. "End of the driveway, right?"

"At least take a weapon of some kind," Jim said, looking around the kitchen. "There must be something you could use."

Marvin glanced around the stark kitchen, then picked up a

93

small saucepan, hefted it. He felt slightly ridiculous, but it was a kind of metal club. He gave what he hoped was a jauntily ironic salute to the others and left. When he reached the hallway and saw the heap of foul remains where Jim had dropped them, he hesitated. The creatures were unearthly, disturbing. But the Interloper had nonetheless been killed in a fight with Jim.

A smack in the head with a cheap saucepan might just be enough, he reasoned. *I'll show them who's the real man of action here. Cool, decisive. Gets the job done.*

As he stepped outside and slammed the door behind him, Marvin was already visualizing his success. He would walk back into the kitchen, throw the dented pan into the sink, then casually remark that everyone's ride was ready.

With his free hand, he flicked on the flashlight, played the beam around the area just outside the house. There was nothing to see but gravel, weeds, mud. A gust of wind blew a spray of rain into his face

Nothing to be scared of, he thought. *These Interlopers are just glorified vermin, when you think about it. Stand up to them and they'll run, or get their heads smashed in.*

Marvin set off down the driveway. He began to whistle a jaunty tune, then thought better of it and stopped.

Chapter 7: Night Moves

"Who the hell is this?" demanded Jim, jumping up from the table.

"Good question," Denny replied, as she and Gould helped George to a chair.

By now, the stranger had recovered some composure and was staring around him with obvious curiosity. He still seemed confused and afraid, though. George allowed himself to be seated, leaning forward so that the bizarre growth on his back did not touch the back of the chair.

"Jim, I think this is Lord George Blaisdell himself," Gould began. "But before we talk about that, let's try and help him. Perhaps some water?"

Jim offered George a plastic bottle of spring water. The stranger stared at the container, took it gingerly, then poured a little of its contents onto his hand. Then George drank, sipping cautiously at first before greedily gulping down the entire bottle. Brie, who had been gazing in puzzlement at the newcomer, got up and offered him a candy bar. Again he seemed puzzled, and Brie had to show him how to unwrap it, and then mime taking a bite.

If he's never seen a Snickers, Denny thought, *maybe he is from a bygone age.*

"What about that parasite, or whatever it is?" she asked Gould. "Will it die eventually, in our world?"

Gould looked startled at her suggestion, then frowned.

"You know, that's a very sensible notion, based on what we know," he said, drawing her aside and speaking in a low voice. "I'm impressed by how cool you are about all this. But if that strange organism is somehow part of his circulatory system, its death – for whatever reason – could harm him. Trying to remove it would be very risky, of course."

Gould glanced over to where Jim and Brie were tentatively speaking to George, who was not making much sense.

"To be honest, I've no idea how to proceed. This seems to combine the paranormal with the medical in a grim way."

"Guess doctors at a regular hospital would be as baffled as we are," Denny mused. "But we can't just leave him here.

We've got to take him to safety!"

Gould nodded.

"The foundation has its own medical division," he said. "I'll call them in. It's time they sent help anyway. Things have gone much farther than I imagined."

"That's quite the understatement," murmured Denny.

While Gould stepped outside to use his phone, Denny brought the others up to speed on what had happened. Brie and Jim were both stunned to learn that Frankie had simply vanished. Denny, for her part, was amazed to learn that Marvin had gone alone to help the group.

"And Gould thinks this bloke is Blaisdell?" Jim said, staring at George, who was now sitting with a vacant expression, chin smeared with chocolate. "Really? We're talking about time travel?"

"Gould said something about a 'night under the hill'," Denny recalled. "Does that mean anything?"

"Fairies," said Brie, surprising Denny. "In the old days they said a night under the hill with the Little People was a kind of time-twisting event. A man who went away with them would return, not having aged. But he'd find his family all dead and gone, his home in ruins, and himself a forgotten man. Time just flows differently there."

Jim was shaking his head as Brie put her theory across.

"That thing we saw was nothing like Tinkerbell," he pointed out. "If we're looking for fantasy creatures, the Interlopers are like demons. Or Morlocks."

"No, I get that," Brie said, becoming more animated. "But the Victorians prettified the way we see all our folklore! The term 'Fairie' once meant another world, a weird, scary place where our laws don't apply. It was only applied to cute little people with wings much later."

"Some medieval scholars called them 'longaevi'," Gould put in. "It means 'the long-lived ones'. As Brie says, they were not originally seen as sweet-natured, but capricious and often destructive. Creatures to placate or avoid, for whom time works differently."

Denny thought about the idea. If Gould and Brie were right, then over two centuries could pass in the human world, while much less than a human lifespan could pass in the Phantom Dimension. She tried to recall how old Blaisdell had been when he had vanished, but could only summon the vague idea that he had been middle-aged.

"George," she said, leaning over the stranger, "can you tell me how old you are?"

The man gawped up at her, then gave a mirthless laugh.

"My dear young lady," he said, again with a touch of aristocratic superiority, "I have not had occasion to celebrate my birthday for some time."

Denny had to smile at that.

You may have been a reprobate, she thought, *but you've got guts – they obviously didn't break you.*

"You're thinking that Frankie has really only been over there for a few seconds?" Jim asked. "Weird notion. But if it's true–"

Denny nodded.

"It means she might not have moved far from the gateway on the other side. Or been moved. If someone went through, they could grab her back. They wouldn't be expecting that."

Realization dawned on Jim's face. He shook his head emphatically.

"Oh, come on," he protested, "you're not proposing that I actually go and look for her!"

Denny felt a surge of anger. Jim had fallen short of her expectations.

"No, I want to go," she retorted. "But I need somebody with your background on my side. Think of it as rescuing a hostage from enemy territory,

Jim still looked doubtful.

"Okay, suppose you throw yourself through that – that hole in the air. How could you be sure you'll find your way back?"

"I could be secured with a tow rope," said Denny. "You must have one in your car, or Gould's?"

"Well, yeah, there is one," Jim began, clearly not convinced. "But it seems a bit crude as a way of exploration in another dimension."

"Needs must," she replied. "Better a crude way than do

nothing at all."

Denny turned to George again.

"How did you escape?" she asked. "What did you do?"

George's eyes seemed to lose focus as he struggled to recall. His forehead corrugated in a frown.

"I – I can't remember clearly," he said. "I was in their cursed burrow one minute, the next I was falling back into God's true creation."

"Did they let you go?" Denny asked.

"Let him go?" put in Jim, incredulous. "Why would they?"

"No, no, she may be right!" exclaimed George. "I was a captive, then I was free. All else is a blur of pain and confusion. I simply remember the black globe, I knew it offered escape ..."

As George trailed off again, Jim stood up and stepped back from the table.

"That sounds fishy. Maybe he's not human, now," he said. "Maybe they've changed him."

Brie, alarmed, got up to cling to Jim, eyes wide with fear.

"No need to get paranoid, guys," said Denny, moving closer to George and gripping the ragged shoulder of the man's coat. "Whatever they did to him, he's still a human being. One of us. We can't turn against each other. That's probably what they want. They seem to thrive on negative emotions in some way."

Jim seemed set to argue, but was interrupted when Gould re-entered the kitchen from the old walled garden. He was damp from the rain, and looked frustrated.

"I can't get a signal," he said. "Maybe one of you could–"

Then Gould paused, puzzled, and looked around the kitchen.

"Hang on – where's Matt?" he asked. "Didn't he come back here?"

"Maybe he met up with Marvin," Jim suggested.

"Shouldn't they both be back by now?" Denny asked.

***

The keys were still in the Mercedes, though the engine had stopped. Feeling pleased with himself, Marvin got into the vehicle and slammed both front doors. He was quickly aware of the foul stench that had come from the corpse of the Interloper.

"Guess I can live with that," he said, starting the engine, then twisting around to reverse up the driveway. But then he eased his foot off the gas and smiled to himself.

I could just drive into that city, whatever it's called, and get a bed for the night. Why take risks? I owe them nothing.

The thought tempted him for a couple of moments, but then he rejected it.

"I may be a selfish asshole," he said firmly, "but I am not a monster."

Besides, he thought, *I can't abandon him—*

Marvin suppressed the thought, squirming in discomfort. He revved the engine and then commenced reversing the big SUV, squinting into the darkness. He had to move very slowly, and toyed with the notion of turning around, but was not prepared to risk going off the track. He was concentrating so hard that the knock on a side window took him by surprise. In the gloom, peering through the rain-spattered glass, he could just make out Matt's leather jacket.

"Jesus Christ!" he shouted, stopping the car. "Matt, what the hell are you doing?"

"Sorry!" came the reply, as Matt lugged the door open and climbed inside.

"What's going on?" demanded Marvin. "I thought you were filming in the cellar?"

"That's finished," the other man replied, staring out of the windshield. "Hey, I got an idea. Let's just go."

Marvin stared for a moment, wondering if he really had heard Matt suggest they ditch the others. Matt's face, smiling brightly now, turned to face him.

"Yeah, I mean it, Marv. Just you and me, let's blow this joint. There are too many of those freak things around. I killed one just now, threw its corpse into the bushes. So, what do you say, big fella?"

Marvin felt a hand on his knee, and looked down to see slender, pale fingers kneading his plump thigh.

Oh God, no, this is too much.

"Matt," he said, trying to sound composed. "This is hardly the time–"

"Aw come on, big guy," said Matt, his tone playful. "We both know it. I could see how broken up you were when I was with Denny, that little surge of hope when we broke up."

Matt's almost too-handsome face leaned closer in the dim light.

"I saw it all. I know just how you feel."

Can't be happening, Marvin thought. *But it is, oh God, I never believed–*

"You never believed I could fall for a selfish old queen with a hairpiece and a big ol' belly like yours?" asked Matt, his tone more teasing now. "Oh ye of little faith."

"What? Marvin exclaimed. "I don't understand. You said–
"

He stopped, feeling a terrible chill run through him. He could see the collar of Matt's pale blue shirt, now, and it was stained with an irregular patch of black. The face that was looking into his was, he realized, a brilliant facsimile of Matt's. But it was a little too good-looking, devoid of any blemish or line. A kind of mask.

"Yeah," said the Interloper, "actually Matt always thought you were a big joke. Guess the joke's on him now, though, huh? What's left of him."

Oh, shit, shit, shit!

Marvin began to fumble at the fastening of his seat-belt. Matt's hand suddenly gripped his flesh so hard that Marvin cried out in pain. The belt came free and he tried to open the driver's door, but the creature was fast and way too strong. It pinned him against his seat and straddled him. It gripped his face in long, inhumanly strong fingers.

"You don't want to run away with me after all!" wailed the Interloper. "Is that any way to treat a regular guy? Maybe I can change your mind."

"Let me go!" Marvin screamed, all self-control gone. "I've done nothing wrong, I don't deserve this!"

"Oh, Marvin," said the creature, shaking its head. "That's not how it works. You make us what we are. Don't you get that?"

It leaned closer, and he saw that what had been a well-defined mouth and chin had bulged out into a weird snout. The being nuzzled at this neck as he whimpered in terror.

"You make us what we are," it repeated. "We are the captives of your wildest hopes, your darkest fears. And if you're kind of pretentious, so are we!"

"Leave me alone!" Marvin yelled, struggling in vain to free himself from the Interloper's grip.

"Can't do that," replied the entity. "There's only two ways this can end. You get away and reveal a bit too much, or you don't. And as we've already got ourselves a fine, young specimen ..."

Marvin felt sharp teeth bite into the side of his neck. A gush of warmth spread over his shoulder. With a tremendous effort, he shoved the creature away, and roared with pain as the Interloper tore away a chunk of his flesh while falling backwards. Marvin opened the car door and, clutching at his wound, fell out onto the driveway.

"Don't leave me, Marv! We've got a good thing going here!"

Even in his abject terror, Marvin still recognized lines from the fantasies he had rehearsed so often in his mind. The monster that was not Matt was, he dimly realized, picking ideas and phrases from his mind.

They're emotional vampires, he thought, staggering upright and starting to stumble towards Malpas Abbey. *They feed on our emotions.*

"Close, but no cigar!" the creature snarled, as it landed on his shoulders and bore him to the ground. "We don't feed on your feelings, we suffer from them. That's why we have to end you. All of you."

Even if Marvin had had the presence of mind to ask what that meant, he was soon unable to say anything at all.

***

"Nobody's got a signal?" asked Gould.

Jim, Denny, and Brie all shook their heads. George looked on, clearly baffled as to why four people were staring forlornly at small, glowing rectangles.

"Could be the signal drops off at night," Gould went on. "Maybe if we were nearer to the village."

"What village?" Denny asked.

"You dozed off," Brie explained. "We passed through one on the way."

"Malpas Village is just a dozen houses and a church," Jim explained. "I noticed a cell mast on the church tower. It's about half a mile away."

"Okay," said Brie, with a touch of her normal perkiness, "let's all go there! Go to the village, get help."

"No!" Denny found herself standing between the others and the door, holding up a hand. "We don't leave anyone behind if we can help it. Jim, I need that rope."

A predictable argument ensued, with Brie insisting on leaving and Jim tending to agree with her. Gould seemed undecided, almost furtive. But they all fell silent when George stood up and walked over to Denny.

"You are more courageous than the men here, lass," he said. "Has manliness fallen out of favor in England? I see women wear breeches, now."

Jim guffawed out loud, but Denny felt oddly moved.

"At least he gets it!" she shouted. "Are we going to try and help Frankie or just run away?"

"I'll help," said Gould simply.

"We'll give it a go, and we'll all stick together," added Jim. "Nobody goes off alone."

***

In the village pub, two men drinking at a corner table received simultaneous text messages.

"Benson?" said the older man, looking at his phone.

The younger man nodded.

"Looks like Gould hasn't reported in on schedule."

The two rose and, leaving their pints unfinished, went out into the rainy night. Behind them, a handful of locals watched them leave without staring, then began talking about the Abbey, and what might be going on there.

The two men got into an unmarked white van, then the older man took out his phone again. He held it midway between them before making the call.

"Control, what's up?"

"What is up," came Benson's voice, "is that Gould has been out of touch for over two hours. You and Davenport get up there and reconnoiter. Do not intervene, merely check the lie of the land."

"What if they're in trouble?" said Davenport.

"Report that they're in trouble, and try to establish the nature of said trouble and how much there is of it," Benson's voice responded. "That is all."

The call ended. The two agents exchanged a look.

"He's a cold-blooded bastard," said Davenport. "Like a reptile in a two thousand quid suit."

"And he's the boss," replied Forster, starting the engine. "Never forget that."

They did not speak again until they reached the turn-off to Malpas Abbey. As the van climbed the shallow gradient towards the estate, a light mist appeared. It gradually grew denser until it was thick enough to cut visibility to about ten yards.

"Foggy all of a sudden," remarked Davenport.

"We're in the countryside in autumn," said Forster. "Not exactly surprising."

"Doesn't mist tend to lie in the valleys? We're going uphill," the younger man pointed out.

"Here we are," said Forster.

The van's headlights showed the stone pillars marking the main gates. The fog inside the gateway was so dense that it formed a silver-gray wall.

"We can always get out and walk up to the house," Davenport said slowly. "Though of course we might just fall into an ornamental pond in this muck."

Forster grunted noncommittally, then took out his phone. He tried to call Benson, and failed.

"This is not normal," insisted Davenport. "We should go back."

"No," said Forster, firmly. "I'm in charge. We can't ask for new orders, so I say we go in. Get the gear out."

"Can't we at least drive up the doorway?" whined Davenport.

"Oh yeah," said the older man, sarcastically. "Why not hire a brass band to march along behind us, just so everyone knows we're coming? Stealth recon, you nitwit."

The two men climbed out into the damp night air, walked around the van, and opened the rear doors. Forster took out a double-barreled shotgun, handed it to Davenport, then picked up an identical weapon. Davenport frowned at the gun.

"You'd think the boss could run to something more effective than this," he grumbled. "The world's awash with assault rifles, and we're equipped to shoot bloody pheasants."

"Benson draws the line at illegal handguns, apparently," said Forster. "Here, take a taser and a baton. You never know."

Forster got himself a First-Aid kit and two sets of night vision goggles.

"Right," he said. "Now we're suitably equipped, let's go and visit one of the stately homes of England."

***

"Here's how we do this," said Denny. "We stick together, look after our wounded, get them to the vehicle. Then Jim drives them into Chester for medical treatment, right?"

Jim and Gould exchanged a glance, then nodded.

"Seems like the right thing," Jim said.

"Ted," Denny went on, "will you stay and be my backup?"

Gould hesitated.

"If I stay, there has to be some kind of time limit," he said finally. "I can't just wait for you to come back. Can it be half an hour?"

"Make it at least an hour," Denny insisted. "Because that won't be very long on the other side. Just a few minutes, in fact."

"True," Gould conceded.

Jim and Gould armed themselves with kitchen knives, while Denny selected a glass rolling pin. Then the three of them ushered Brie and George out to the hallway. The group skirted the Interloper's remains, but George hung back to peer more closely at the mess of rotted tissue and pale bones.

"A dead demon!" he exclaimed. "I never saw a dead one before. Surely such things are invulnerable by divine ordnance?"

"They're not demons," said Gould. "They're as mortal as you or I."

George looked puzzled at that, and fell silent as they left the hall. They were confronted by a wall of fog. Taken aback, they paused, then Gould and Jim switched on flashlights that shone dimly and flickered.

"When did that roll in?" asked Brie.

"It was clear enough outside a few minutes ago," Gould said. "So ..."

"It might not be natural," Denny finished. "Big deal. Let's get to your car, Ted."

Gould's Ford sedan had just come into view when Brie shrieked and fell. In the weak torchlight, Denny saw the woman scrabbling to get up in what looked like a mud puddle. Then she noticed the dark red stains on Brie's hands, the black patches on her denims. Gould's flashlight picked out a heap of wet, sausage-like objects around Brie's feet. Then the flickering radiance fell onto a pale body. The face was distorted in pain, but still recognizable.

"Matt!" Brie screamed, hurling herself away from the horrific scene and colliding with Denny.

Matt's entrails had been torn out and flung across the pathway. His undershorts were still on the body but his shirt, jacket and pants were gone.

It took his clothes, Denny thought, numb with horror, and trying to fight down her rising gorge. *Like they did with Lucy Gould, to make a more convincing fake.*

She turned away from the unbearable sight. Denny felt herself start to grow faint with shock, and staggered across to the car.

"You okay?" asked Jim.

She could only shake her head at first, then managed to say, "Give me a minute."

"Sorry, but time's pressing – do you still want to stay

behind?" asked Gould.

Denny looked up at his anxious face, and guessed that he was conflicted, hoping to draw courage from her.

"Nobody's going to judge you for leaving," Jim added. "None of us signed up for this."

Matt's dead, she thought. *I can't help him. Frankie might still be alive. I have to believe that.*

"Ted, I'm still willing to try if you'll back me up," she said.

"Right, I'll get the tow rope," said Gould, unlocking the car and then throwing the keys to Jim. "We'll keep two of the flashlights, you take everything else."

While Jim and Brie tried to persuade the confused George to get into the Ford, Gould and Denny got the rope out of the trunk. As an afterthought, Denny tossed her rolling pin and picked up a heavy wrench.

"This still strikes me as bonkers," grumbled Jim. "You've no idea how to open the way through and even if—"

They all stared around them to see a figure had appeared in the fog, back towards the house. It was barely visible, but Denny could see it was dressed in Matt's clothes.

"A demon!" cried George, scrambling into the car and curling up on the back seat.

The Interloper raised its hand in an ironic salute, then turned and vanished. A couple of seconds later, they heard the sound of the house's great front door opening, then slamming shut.

"It's going back!" breathed Denny. "Come on, Ted!"

Chapter 8: The Phantom Dimension

"Should we have left them?" asked Brie.

"No choice," Jim replied, peering ahead into the fog.

The Ford's headlights seemed to have little impact on the gray murk. Jim nosed ahead in low gear, but still almost collided with the SUV, which suddenly loomed into view. The big Mercedes was blocking the driveway. Rather than get out, Jim nudged it out of the way.

"That'll piss of Gould," he remarked, with forced jollity. "Still, it's a company car."

"Horseless carriages," said George, from the back seat. "An age of wonders. Are they powered by steam?"

"He's perking up," observed Jim, with a wry smile at Brie. "Want to give him a lecture on internal combustion engines? Maybe move to aviation, the internet?"

Brie managed a weak smile at that, and they set off again.

"Soon, we'll be at the gates," said Jim confidently. "Then it's a clear road to Chester, a nice clean hospital, and for me, a hotel, and a hot shower."

But as they progressed slowly down the fog-bound driveway, the familiar gateposts failed to appear.

"Could we be on the wrong road somehow?" asked Brie, tentatively.

Jim shook his head.

"The house had only one driveway, and we are still on it. If we'd somehow passed the gates without seeing them we'd be on tarmac, not gravel, so I can only assume–"

Suddenly Jim hit the brakes, and the Ford slewed to one side.

"What the hell?"

"Oh my God," cried Brie.

The SUV was in front of them again, its bulky shape unmistakable despite the fog.

"How did we come around in a circle?" Brie asked.

Jim looked at her, then back at the Mercedes he had shoved out of the way three minutes earlier.

"I'm sure we did not circle round," he said in a monotone. "We were going in a straight line, I'd swear it on a stack of

Bibles."

From the back seat, George spoke quietly.

"They will not let us go unless their purpose is served."

***

"Sorry," said Gould breathlessly, catching up with Denny at the entrance to the temple. "I've never been very athletic."

"All the more reason for me to go through while you hold the fort," she replied. "Let's see if our little friend has gone through."

There was no sign of the Interloper in the cellar. But their flashlight revealed the now familiar shimmering sphere in the air, just to the side of the altar. Gould lit another couple of caving flares and threw them down. Then they descended and started their simple preparations.

"Okay," said Denny, "I'm going straight through. You give me an hour, right? Then pull my string, see what happens."

After fastening the rope around her waist, Denny climbed onto the altar and prepared to pitch herself through the gateway. After a moment's thought, she threw her flashlight and the wrench into the portal first. They vanished.

"What if it's a hundred foot drop on the other side?" asked Gould.

"Then get ready to haul me up, big guy," she replied, and executed a swan dive into what looked like an empty space.

Gould braced himself but the rope did not run out at speed, as he had feared. Instead, it gradually played through his hands in spurts, a few inches at a time, then stopping for several minutes. He checked his watch every few minutes, wondering what would happen if he pulled on the rope and it snapped. Or if, instead of Denny, what came through was an inhuman monster.

Don't imagine the worst, he told himself. *That might make it more likely, given the way these things operate.*

"Fear is the mind killer," he said aloud, then wondered where he had dredged up the quotation. He began to obsess over trivia, trying to remember the names of the current England cricket squad, filling his mind with irrelevant data to suppress any memories or feelings the Interlopers might exploit.

Does Denny have no deep, dark fears? he wondered. *Is that why all she saw was a mish-mash of commonplace childish fears?*

An hour had passed, and he gave a gentle pull on the rope. It yielded an inch or two. He wondered if this meant Denny was standing up, or if he was pulling at her inert – maybe dead – body. Gould gave another tug on the rope and felt it give, then become slack. Anxiety mounted as he began to reel it in, hand over hand, wondering whether the slight resistance he felt was from Denny or the strange portal itself.

The question was settled when the end of the tow-rope appeared and fell to the floor.

"Oh Jesus. What do I do now?"

As in reply, the gateway darkened, swelled, pulsed with strange energy. Gould took a step back as something came through. It was not Denny or an Interloper, but a compact, boxy object. Frankie's camera fell to the floor with a crash, fragments of plastic and glass scattering over the stone slabs.

***

Denny rolled when she landed but the impact still winded her. She felt a stab of pain in her thigh as she landed on something hard. *Flashlight or wrench,* she thought. *Either way I'll have quite a bruise.*

She lay curled up and opened her eyes tentatively. At first, she could see nothing but a swirl of garish colors, the buffeting of a strong wind that was burning hot. She remembered standing in front of a huge industrial oven on an assignment. She squeezed her eyelids shut again, took a tentative breath of the scorching air. There was a smell of burning vying with faint tang of decay in the air, something like a match struck in a moldy bathroom

Opening her eyes again, she looked down and saw that she had fallen onto an uneven surface. It felt rubbery, and looked like dimpled reddish clay. By one of her hands, a pale creature like a centipede writhed then made a dart for her fingers.

Denny quickly pulled her hand away, scrambled upright. She picked up her flashlight and wrench, holding the latter ready as a club. But nothing else appeared to threaten her.

At least I can breathe the air, she thought. *I'd look pretty dumb if I was poisoned or suffocated in the first ten seconds.*

In front of Denny, the reddish ground extended away in all directions. It seemed utterly featureless as first. But as her eyes adjusted to the peculiar light, Denny saw that she was at the top of a shallow rise. Ahead of her was a bleak plain, dotted by black blotches that might have been clumps of trees. There were also some more regular shapes, straight lines that might have been walls. It was hard to get a sense of size or distance, however. The light was dim yet also oddly painful, a purplish radiance that made her think of ultraviolet.

Denny looked behind her at the gateway. Instead of a rippling sphere of disturbed air, the gateway on this side was a pitch-black globe, roughly a yard across. It hovered about four feet above the ground. Beneath the sphere, she saw smoke rising from an area of blackened soil, yet she felt no radiant heat on her face and hands. Unable to make sense of the phenomenon, she filed the observation away for future reference. Then she looked up.

"Oh my God!"

The sky was a shimmering, silvery color. There were a few ragged shreds of reddish cloud. There was no sun or moon, just a general luminosity streaming down onto the wasteland below. Above the clouds were the black stars George had ranted about. They were star-like in that they twinkled, throwing out flashes of green and orange light. But there the resemblance ended. These stars were, she felt sure, living creatures of some sort. They moved relative to one another. They looked like huge black starfish, their arms waving lazily. But at the center of each black star was a gleaming disk.

Eyes. They have eyes, just like George said. These stars really do look down.

Shuddering, she turned her attention back to the landscape of the Phantom Dimension. There was no sign of any thing living other than dozens of the centipede-like bugs. Then she saw something out of place nearby, a dark object with straight edges. It seemed familiar, even in the deceptive light. Denny walked toward it, feeling her feet sink into the ground, hearing a squelching over the howling of the wind.

It was Frankie's camera. Already some strange process had half-buried the bulky piece of equipment in the reddish earth. As she squatted to look closer, Denny saw that the ground itself was heaving and sucking at the camera. She looked down at her feet. What she had taken for a kind of dirt was acting like a living thing, and throwing eager tendrils up and over her shoes.

If I don't keep moving, I'm dead.

Denny wrenched her feet free of the hungry ground and tried to remember how to work the camera. As she tinkered she flicked on the built-in light, and a pool of blue-white radiance revealed the dirt to be bright ocher. A pale, sinuous creature writhed in apparent discomfort, then scuttled for the shadows. She followed the worm-like animal with the beam, watching its intense reaction as it tried to escape. Then, feeling slightly guilty, she turned off the light.

Maybe what we think of as normal light is painful to some of the things that live here.

Denny filed the idea away as potentially useful and started to circle the camera, looking for footprints. Then she told herself not to be so dumb, as it was clear that the nature of this alien dirt would have erased any tracks. She raised the viewfinder to the horizon, hoping to see a structure, some sign of intelligence. A tall, tapering shape might have been an obelisk of some kind.

But that's way too far to walk, so long as I'm tethered by this rope.

Denny lowered the camera, focused on details that were maybe a hundred yards away. Now she could see that what she had taken for a wall seemed to be the remains of a collapsed building. As she swung the camera around, more apparent ruins appeared peeking out of the ruddy earth. It occurred to Denny that she was standing in the middle of what had been a settlement of some sort. But it had long since been abandoned.

Why? Something to do with the gateway to our world?

Now a dark blur that resembled a clump of trees came into

view. It consisted of dark, thick trunks supporting a canopy of oval, fleshy leaves. Then one 'trunk' lifted itself out of the ground, moved toward her, replanted itself. The supposed clump was walking, coming her way. She recalled that George had said something about trees with eyes. Denny lowered the camera, scanned her surroundings with the naked eye. She wondered if the half dozen or so dark blurs were nearer than when she had arrived.

She focused again on the distant, pylon-like object. She could see now that it was in fact one of many, as other more-or-less conical forms were just visible on the horizon. Denny reasoned that she might be looking at a city, the Interloper equivalent of Manhattan. The things might be the skyscrapers of the Phantom Dimension. But it seemed improbable, given the apparent ruins around her. She felt strongly that this was a world in an advanced stage of decay.

This was a dumb, desperate idea. They were right. But I had to try.

"Frankie!" she yelled. "Where are you?"

Her voice sounded oddly flat, and she could not believe it would carry far. The wind increased to a gale and almost knocked her down.

"Help!"

The voice was almost inaudible over the howling gale. She could not make out the direction it had come from. But it sounded like a woman's voice, high-pitched, desperate.

Did I imagine it?

There was a tremendous yank on the rope, so hard that she fell backwards onto her behind and dropped the camera. Cursing, Denny scrambled to her feet, trying to minimize contact between her skin and the strange, living dirt.

That's already an hour? I've only been here three or four minutes. That's a big time shift.

Another tug on the rope made her stumble. She hesitated, then heard a faint, plaintive cry. Again, there was no sense of direction, and she looked around, desperately seeking some clue. There were no buildings, but if Frankie could be heard despite the gale she must be nearby. Almost anything seemed possible, including some kind of kind of invisibility cloak.

Underground, Denny thought. *If my world looked like this, I would not live on the surface of it.*

Then she remembered that George had used the word 'burrow'. She pivoted slowly, shielding her eyes, looking for anything that might be an entrance. A dark smear in a low ridge caught her eye. She picked up the camera and zoomed in on it. There was movement in the entrance, a glimpse of what might have been a pallid face. She took a deep breath.

Sorry Ted, she thought. *Only way I can get there is without a safety line.*

She had just dropped the end of the rope to the ground when another jerk pulled it right through the black, pulsating sphere. The only material link to her reality was gone. Denny turned the camera round and looked into the dark lens.

Better make it good. Might be my last words. If anybody ever hears them.

"I'm going underground," she said. "Don't wait for me."

***

"What do you mean?" Jim asked, stopping the car and turning to face George. "Are you saying the Interlopers have got us going around in circles somehow?"

"They are deceivers," George replied, looking from Jim to Brie, as if seeking understanding. "Like all the Devil's minions."

"You mean they created this fog to keep us trapped here?" Brie asked, her voice unsteady. *"They can do that?"*

Great, thought Jim, *she might have a total meltdown if she thinks we can't get away.*

"Just shut up, George," he snapped. "We're safe so long as we're in the vehicle. The worst that can happen is we wait until the fog lifts. Then we'll be able to see the way to the main road."

"But what if it doesn't lift?" demanded Brie, again on the edge of panic.

Jim reached over and took her hand in his.

"I know you've been through a lot," he said. "But think of your son, your husband. You'll see them again if you just–"

Brie, who had been looking out through the windshield, gave a scream and pointed. Looking ahead, Jim could make out two figures emerging from the fog. They were carrying guns, which they pointed at the Ford.

"Crap!" exclaimed Jim, and slammed the car into reverse. Then he paused, staring at the two men as they came closer. "No, hang on, it's all right! I know these guys!"

A couple of minutes later, Forster and Davenport had been brought up to speed on the situation, insofar as Jim could explain things.

"I don't get it," Forster said. "We got in all right, but you can't get out?"

"It's like a force-field, or something," said Davenport. "A one-way portal."

Forster rolled his eyes at Jim.

"The main thing," Forster pointed out, "is that we don't know how many of these Interlopers are still at large, if any. We should go back and check on Gould and the girl, rather than muck around out here."

Brie began to protest at that, but Jim managed to soothe her by pointing out how well-armed the newcomers were.

"These are my old mates from the army," he said. "They're good blokes, they won't let anything happen to you."

"And we've got guns," Davenport added. "Can be useful things, guns."

Jim turned the Ford carefully and they set off back the way they had come. It was only after they had driven a few hundred yards that Jim began to wonder if they could get back to Malpas Abbey, any more than they could reach the main gate.

***

Distances were deceptive. It took Denny far less time than she had expected to reach the burrow, despite the vicious battering from the unceasing wind. She paused at the entrance, which was a roughly circular tunnel about five feet high, sloping sharply downward.

"Hello?" she shouted, but heard nothing over the gale.

Peering into the dark, she tried to discern movement, but saw nothing other than blackness.

Okay, let's go for it.

She switched on the flashlight, which flickered worryingly and then produced a steady, if weak, beam. Denny began to climb down.

Maybe it was an Interloper, trying to lure me in, she thought. *But why go to so much trouble? Why not just jump me as soon as I arrived?*

Frustration vied with fear as she reflected, once again, about how little she knew about the enemy she was hoping to defy. Creatures that defied natural laws, that could change their appearance, and that drew on people's thoughts and memories. Monsters. How could she defeat a whole world of monsters?

"One at a time," she murmured. "If that's what it takes."

It soon proved impossible to keep upright without using at least one hand for support. Denny shoved the wrench into the waistband of her jeans, reasoning that the flashlight might double as a club.

Also, she thought, *they don't seem to like bright light much. Maybe they're real sensitive to it?*

She continued down until she the tunnel divided. As she hesitated, shining the flashlight into each aperture, she noticed a gleam of metal. Something was half-buried in the dirt floor. When she bent down to examine it, she realized it was the wooden grip of an antique pistol.

"Flintlock. One of George's, maybe?"

She took a moment to examine the area more closely and saw other items from her world. A couple of bottles, a maimed plastic doll, and a badly damaged paperback book all lay around her. She reached down and picked up the book. The covers were missing but a contents page told her it was a collection of stories entitled *The Adventures of Mister Bunnykins*.

"Cute," she said, tossing down the paperback. She noticed then that the mundane debris all seemed to lie at the entrance to the left hand tunnel. She decided to follow it, and discovered more discarded everyday items as she went. As she rounded a corner, she heard a very human-sounding phrase echoing around her.

"Help me!"

This time the sound was clearer, and it was definitely coming from ahead. What's more, the tunnel was leveling off. Ahead of her, the flashlight revealed an opening into a large chamber of some kind.

"Frankie?" she shouted, hoping to hear her name in response. But there was only an inarticulate cry.

Denny entered the cavern, which was about eight feet high and thirty across. Three other tunnels opened into it. There was a figure sprawled against the far wall, legs and arms fastened to the reddish dirt by a network of pale strands. As Denny approached, she could see the fibers were alive, tensing and flexing as the prisoner struggled against their grip. The captive's face and body were almost totally covered by a pale, living web.

"Frankie?"

A moment of intense joy ended when Denny stepped nearer. A few strands of long hair escaped the web-work, while Frankie always cut her hair short. Now Denny could see that the prisoner must be a child, only a shade over four feet tall. A stifled squeal came from the material covering the face.

"Help me, I'm scared!"

It was a little girl's voice, the accent British, the fear in it spurring Denny to frantic action. She shoved her flashlight right up against the white fibers, and they jerked spasmodically in evident discomfort. She dropped the wrench and with her free hand tried to tear the strands away from the head. After a few moments, she had revealed a small, heart-shaped face. The girl gazed up at her, eyes huge with fear.

"Don't be scared, I'm here to help you!" Denny said.

"Are you – are you a real person?" asked the girl.

"Yep," Denny replied, ripping away more of the pale strands to free the girl's right arm. "And we're going to get you home. Help me get this stuff off if you can."

The girl was still for a moment, then began tearing at the living bindings with her small fingers. Soon most of the restraints had been ripped away, though a network of white fibers remained clinging to the girl's body. Beneath the unpleasant web of tissue, she seemed to be wearing badly stained pajamas. The garments were mismatched, the top covered in teddy bears while the pants were pink with green polka dots.

Like they just put her in whatever kids' clothes they could grab when they were in our world, Denny thought.

The webbing gave way and the child fell forward, away from the wall. Denny caught her. Looking down at the thin, fragile body she saw that the pajama top had been ripped open, just like George's shirt. A dark brown nodule, two inches across, clung to the skin between the girl's shoulder blades. Like the one attached to George, it pulsed with alien life.

"Guess that makes both of us human," she murmured. Then she knelt down and put her hands on the girl's shoulders.

"Okay," she said. "I'm Denny, what's your name?"

The girl's blank expression made Denny wonder if she had lost her memory, through trauma or perhaps some stranger process. But then the child seemed to remember.

"My name is Lucy."

***

It had taken Gould a while but he had finally figured out how to work the replay system on the damaged camera. He watched, awe struck, the footage of the transition to the Phantom Dimension during Frankie's abduction. Then he saw Denny appear, shared her reactions to the strange other world, and heard her final message.

Don't wait for me.

Gould felt a sudden pang of guilt. He had allowed someone to venture into the Phantom Dimension with nothing but a can-do attitude. Now he had to decide whether to wait, knowing Denny might never return. He checked the time. It was now just over an hour and a half since Denny had gone through the portal. The longer he left it, the more chance there was of Interlopers coming through and attacking him. He felt a strong desire to cut his losses and run. He sat on the cellar steps, gazing into the shimmering globe.

Am I a coward?

A door slamming in the distance jolted him from his reverie. The sound of voices followed. Gould ran up, back into the house, just in time to encounter Forster and Davenport. The newcomers gave a quick, if slightly garbled, description of the situation outside. Gould updated them on the Denny situation.

"Okay," said Davenport, hefting his gun. "We go through and get her back. In fact, we save both of 'em, right?"

Forster shook his head.

"Not part of the mission, lad," he growled. "And you never go into hostile territory without orders, and then only with preliminary recon. We're staying firmly in this reality."

"Well, give me a bloody weapon and I'll do it!" shouted Gould, angrier with his own indecision than their hesitation.

"Let's not be hasty," soothed Forster. "Why don't we go and see this mysterious gateway of yours?"

***

It took a second to register, then Denny gasped.

"Lucy? Do you have a brother called Edward?"

The child nodded, but before Denny could ask her anything else, there was a screeching sound from one of the other tunnels.

"The monsters are coming back!" hissed Lucy. "They do bad things!"

"You're telling me," Denny replied, taking the girl's hand. "Right, we're gonna run up that tunnel. When we get outside where there's room, I'll carry you. Okay?"

Lucy gazed solemnly up at her new-found friend.

"Okay."

Another screech, louder this time, spurred the two on. Lucy ran stiffly at first, but managed to keep up with Denny's brisk pace. As they reached the fork in the tunnels, Denny glanced back and saw several white figures bounding after them.

"Faster!" she urged breathlessly, pushing Lucy ahead of her.

She turned the flashlight back on the Interlopers, but its feeble radiance seemed to have no effect. The pursuers were gaining. Denny hurled the flashlight in frustration and had the satisfaction of seeing it hit one enemy squarely in the face. The Interloper fell squealing into the dirt, but the others were not deterred. By the time the fugitives reached the opening onto the surface, the nearest creature was just ten feet behind.

Denny took out the wrench, preparing to make a last-ditch stand and give Lucy the chance to escape. She gestured towards the black globe, barely visible in the distance.

"Run to that sphere, that's the way out! Go Lucy! Lucy, you gotta run!"

Instead of obeying Denny, the child was standing still. Lucy was looking up at the sky rather than back at their pursuers. The pursuit had stopped, the Interlopers huddled in the entrance to their burrow. And they, too, were looking up.

Denny raised her eyes and saw a vast, black star blotting out much of the sky. The monstrous entity had descended and was now lowering dark, rope-like tendrils towards the two humans. The single, enormous eye swiveled, seemed to focus on Denny. She felt a chill run through her.

"Don't move!" hissed Lucy. "If you move, they see you."

Vague memories of dinosaur movies flashed through Denny's mind.

Predators sense motion, she thought. *Makes sense.*

A black tendril, thick as her thumb, brushed against her shoulder. Denny gave a small scream, but remained motionless. The black star was, she now saw, drifting slowly across the sky, gaining height. The prevailing wind was moving it away from them. Already they were out of reach of the trailing tendrils. The Interlopers saw this too, and began to edge toward the mouth of the tunnel. The movement, albeit slight, seemed to alert the vast, floating entity. The black star stopped drifting, started to descend, its vast eye scanning the ground. But it was moving at a leisurely pace.

"Now or never," said Denny. "When I say run—"

"We run," replied Lucy, smiling for the first time. "Like in 'Doctor Who'."

Chapter 9: Showdown

"How long has it been?" asked Brie.

"Eight hours, forty-seven minutes since she went through," said Jim, wearily. "Or about ten minutes since you last asked."

The group had been gathered in the great dining room since the early hours of the morning. They had broken up some old furniture to make a fire. Brie's wound had been dressed again, while George had been given a proper meal and tea, which he gulped down with relish. George had also been found some of Matt's clothes, including a shirt that fitted loosely over the parasite on his back.

Arguments over what to do next had given way to sullen silence, broken by occasional remarks. Between them, the four Romola Foundation men had worked out a rota, with two of them always on watch in the cellar. At the moment, Gould and Forster were on guard at the gateway.

"Is it getting lighter?" Davenport asked. "Hard to tell in this murk."

"What if we never get out?" Brie moaned. "What if we – just starve?"

"No way can this go on forever!" protested Jim. "Whatever those creatures are doing, they've got to run out of energy eventually. Right?"

Jim looked at Davenport for support. The latter nodded, cleared his throat.

"You obviously know the folk tales, Brie," he said. "Beings from the other world can influence space, time, perception – but their powers are strictly limited. They can be killed, they can be outwitted, they can only visit our world for brief spells. All the stories say so."

"But why keep us trapped here at all?" Brie demanded, looking around at the men. "What is it they want?"

George, who was sitting in an armchair nearest the fire, shrugged.

"How can we understand the motives of demons? Tormenting us, that is their delight!"

"You're a ray of sunshine and no mistake," said Davenport

sourly.

"It is clearing!" Brie shrieked, jumping up and running to look out the French windows.

The mist, previously a dark gray wall, was definitely growing paler. As they watched, a bright blur in the sky gradually resolved itself into the sun's disc. It was soon so bright they could not look at it directly. In less than a minute, all that remained of the unnatural fog was a ground mist then there was nothing but a crisp, pleasant autumn morning.

"We can get away!" exclaimed Brie, jumping up and actually clapping her hands with joy.

"Okay, everyone outside to the vehicles," said Jim. "I'll go and get Gould and Forster."

***

Forster had lined up some Molotov cocktails by the foot of the staircase. He had taken gasoline from a spare can in the Mercedes, which they had recovered earlier and parked outside the main entrance. Everything was set for a quick getaway. Now Forster was sitting on the bottom step while Gould leaned against the ancient altar stone.

"Sorry, Gould," said Forster. "But I reckon she's dead by now."

As Gould began to protest, Forster raised his hands to placate his colleague.

"I know, time flows differently there. But even if you're right about that George bloke having spent, say, ten years there for two hundred here – that means Denny's been in the PD for, what? Half an hour, thereabouts? With no special equipment. No air support, no bio-hazard suit, no effective weapons, no back up."

Gould shook his head.

"We don't know how dangerous the PD is in small doses," he pointed out. "If it's as vast as the earth we know, she could be in no more danger than someone spending half an hour in the Sahara, or Tibet."

"Or at the South Pole in their undershorts," Forster riposted. "Be realistic–"

Both men suddenly sprang upright as the gateway darkened and a pale, spindly figure materialized. Forster raised his shotgun, but Gould warned him to hold his fire. A diminutive form fell sprawling to the stone floor with a yelp of dismay.

"Is it one of them?" demanded Forster, circling to one side of the newcomer as Gould moved closer.

Then the sphere of shimmering air became a gray blur, and Denny fell through, almost landing on top of the stranger.

"It's her!" Gould reassured Forster, then reached to help Denny to her feet. "What happened?"

"Long story, they're close behind," Denny gasped. "Help Lucy."

Gould froze, then stared down at the huddled figure on the floor by his feet. He saw now that it was a girl with long hair, wrapped in spirals of white fiber. Dark eyes looked up at his. The child was clearly terrified. There was no hint of recognition. But her face was so familiar that for a moment Gould wondered if he was dreaming.

"What?" he demanded, unsure that he had heard correctly. "Lucy?"

"It is," said Denny. "But we're going to have company in a second."

She stooped down and grabbed Lucy by the hand, then pulled her towards the staircase. Forster shouted something, taking aim at the gateway. A lithe creature appeared, materializing in the act of leaping forward, clawed hands outstretched. It was not remotely human. Gould glimpsed a nightmarish face with a circular funnel-like muzzle containing a ring of teeth.

Forster fired, catching the Interloper in the thigh. It screeched and fell, black blood spraying over Gould. He fired both barrels into the hideous face, watched its monstrous features explode into a massive gout of foul liquid and torn tissue. The Interloper writhed, limbs twitching, then grew still.

They were both reloading when the second Interloper appeared. Behind, a third was coming into view. Denny and Lucy were clambering up the stairs. The two creatures were focused on catching the fugitives. Gould shot one in the back, while Forster knocked the other down with the butt of his gun, then finished it off.

"Too many," Forster said, jerking his head at the gateway. "Retreat."

By the time the fourth Interloper had fallen into their world, Forster had lit one of his firebombs. Raising it above his head, he smashed it onto the cellar floor, directly below the portal to the Phantom Dimension. The Interloper squealed as burning gasoline sprayed over it, but still bounded forward. Gould shot it in the face. Two more bombs covered the whole area around the altar with burning liquid. The stench of burning flesh mingled with gasoline, the roar of flames not quite masking the screeches of Interlopers in their death-agony.

Gould and Forster waited at the top of the stairs until the smoke and fumes drove them out into the corridor. It was clear that nothing else would be coming through for a while.

"What the hell?" asked Jim.

"Close enough," replied Denny. "Guys, this young lady is called Lucy."

She looked at Gould, who was clearly puzzled.

"Ted," Denny said gently, "maybe now isn't the time ..."

"Lucy!" Gould said, falling to his knees in front of the little girl. Tears blurred his vision as he tried to take hold of her. Lucy wriggled, began to shout in panic. Denny gently disengaged Gould's arms from the child. Lucy's eyes were wide with fear, now, and she clung to her rescuer.

"Think about it, Ted," Denny said quietly. "She hasn't seen you grow old. She still remembers the little boy who teased her."

"All fascinating and maybe heartbreaking," Forster said, not turning his gaze from the doorway. "But we have a problem when that fire burns out. Which will be soon."

"We can leave," said Jim. "The fog's lifted."

"Fog?" asked Denny.

"Tell you on the way," Jim replied.

***

"You'll be okay with Brie while I go and get you some great new clothes," said Denny. "You don't want to wear those raggedy pajamas forever, right?"

Lucy had finally stopped clinging to Denny when they had arrived in Chester. The sight of a normality, an English town bustling with shoppers, tourists, and commuters, had seemed to calm the child. Now they were in the apartment rented by Forster and Davenport, who had discreetly left 'the girls' to use it and gone with the rest of the party to find a hotel.

"I don't want you to go," Lucy pleaded, tugging at Denny's hand.

"You'll be okay with me, sweetie," said Brie, smiling down at the girl. "We can make sandwiches for lunch – or you can just watch TV. Denny will be back real soon and then we can get you dressed nicely"

Lucy looked skeptical. Denny scooped up the child and deposited her carefully on the sofa. The Phantom Dimension organism attached to her back still pulsed with alien life. The black filaments spread under the girl's skin were much more apparent in normal light. Lucy curled up, careful not to let the nodule touch the back of the sofa.

How the hell will they get that thing off her? Denny wondered, then pushed the thought aside.

"Brie's right," she said soothingly, stroking Lucy's hair. "I'll get you some cool new clothes and in the meantime, you can get something to eat. It's a win-win situation. So you be good, now, and do what Brie says?"

Lucy managed to smile along with Denny.

"All right," she said. "I promise."

Lucy picked up the remote and switched on the TV. The screen filled with a vista of burning buildings. At the bottom of the screen words crawled by detailing bombing raids, diplomatic overtures, stalled peace talks. Denny took the remote and searched for a cartoon channel, found something bright, noisy, and innocuous.

"I'll try not to be too long," she said, kissing the top of Lucy's head.

***

"This is a very seedy hotel," grumbled Davenport, running a finger along a picture frame. "Our expenses can't be this pathetic?"

"Nice hotels don't let you smuggle smelly, half-naked old nutters past reception, as a rule," Forster said, nodding at Lord George Blaisdell. The old nobleman was sitting on the hotel bed, enjoying a triple-decker cheeseburger and fries. An empty coffee cup stood on the bedside table.

"I know he's not had real food for a while," Davenport observed. "But still, they must have had bloody awful table manners in those old times, don't you reckon?"

"And he smells a bit," Forster added. "But I daresay they didn't bathe too often, either. Think we can persuade him to shower at some point?"

"So what's the plan, boss?" Davenport asked, raising his voice to speak to Gould, who was standing by the window gazing out at Chester's rooftops.

"Hmm?" Gould looked round. "We need to get both victims to London. The foundation's doctors might be able to figure out how to remove those – symbiotes, or whatever they are."

At that, George looked up from his meal in alarm.

"Doctors?" he exclaimed. "Barber-surgeons and apothecaries, quacks the lot of 'em! I will not let a sawbones near me. I would rather be hag-ridden by this demonic leech to my dying day, sir!"

"With all due respect, your lordship," said Davenport. "You're talking a load of bollocks. That thing might have kept you alive in the PD – in Hell, if you like – but it can't survive in our world."

"Then let it wither away of its own accord, lad!" thundered the old man. "Why tinker with it? Doctors – charlatans all."

"Now might be the time to wrong foot him," Davenport whispered to his colleague.

"You never did tell us, your lordship," said Forster, in a friendly voice, "how you managed to make such a remarkable escape. After all, it's no mean feat to get out of Hell, is it?"

George looked blank for a moment, then gave a broad,

yellow-toothed smile.

"They were distracted," he said. "Moved me to a spot close to one of their magical doorways – why, I was not even a dozen yards from it! Then they left me alone, went off about other business. I managed to reach a shard of bottle glass and cut my bonds, and voila! Thus, I returned to the world of men!"

Gould turned from the window to stare at George, then exchanged glances with the other two.

"So, my lord," Gould said slowly, "you certainly enjoyed tremendous good luck."

"Fortune favors the brave," said George smugly, dipping his last curly fry in a puddle of ketchup.

"Excuse me, gents," said Gould. "I just need to step outside and make a phone call."

***

Denny went into the first store she found that sold children's clothing and headed for the section marked Girls. She made a guess at Lucy's size and bought sneakers, pants, several shirts, a jacket, and a variety of socks and underclothes. The store was busy, and Denny found herself in a long queue. In front of her a mother was trying to tell her daughter, who looked around six, that going to feed ducks in the park would be fun.

"I want to play on your iPad!" the girl kept repeating.

"We didn't have iPads in my day," the mother eventually said.

Like that's gonna work, lady, Denny thought. She smiled wryly at the way children so quickly seized on new gadgets, and how quickly adults forget that they had been just as obsessed with novelty.

Denny frowned. A thought had nearly crystallized in her mind, a nagging doubt that – she realized – had been with her for some time. Something did not quite fit. Something about the little girl and her mom's iPad. The way kids pick up new tech, new trends.

"Can I help you?" said the assistant.

Denny realized she was holding up the line, and rushed forward to pay for Lucy's new things. She was just leaving the store when her phone rang. It was Gould.

"Denny," he said, in a voice that was pitched higher than usual, "how is Lucy? Is she well? Does she seem okay?"

"Yeah," Denny replied. "She seemed fine when I left her with Brie. I went out to get some clothes."

"Right," Gould said, "Jim went out to get some for George. It's about George, I'm calling, in a way. It seems like his escape was – you could call it a set-up. Contrived."

Denny felt confused, impatient, all the stress she had suffered conspiring to fog her mind. She nearly bumped into a young couple, frowned at them, stopped walking.

"Why would they do that?" she asked.

"To prepare us for Lucy's return," Gould said. "To prime our expectations. Make it seem more likely. Just as all the terror and killing was designed to confuse us, make us more susceptible to tricks."

Denny's head span with the implications.

"But that would mean they took Frankie to lure me through, simply so I would rescue Lucy – no, come on!" she protested, ignoring odd looks from passersby. "How could they possibly know–"

She paused, reflecting on the way the Interlopers understood people's deepest hopes and fears. And then the thought that had been worrying at the back of her mind sprang into the foreground, clear as daylight.

"Oh my God!" she yelled. "Lucy knew how to work the TV remote! Nobody showed her – Ted, did you have a remote, when she was still with you? Did they have those in England then?"

"No," said Gould. "Or at least, I don't think so. God, I can't remember! It was so long ago, I–"

"If it's not Lucy, she could have picked the knowledge straight out of my mind," Denny said, starting to run. "But Ted, try and remember!"

**

"Hey guys!" said Denny, trying to sound cheerful as she dumped the bags of new clothes onto the dining room table.

Lucy was still curled up on the sofa watching TV, the nodule on her back pulsing steadily. Denny could hear the low rush of water from the small bathroom.

"Hey!" Denny said. "Got you new clothes. Where's Brie?"

Lucy looked round and gave a perfect, angelic smile. She picked up the remote and muted the TV sound.

Kids are just quick learners, Denny thought. *Proves nothing. Anyway, Brie could have helped.*

"Brie's taking a shower," she said, uncurling and jumping up. "Can I try my clothes on now?"

"Of course," said Denny, resisting the urge to back away as Lucy ran over to her and grabbed her around the waist. Denny looked down at the tangled mass of chestnut hair, forced herself to pat Lucy on the shoulder.

"Okay," said Denny, "let's take the things into the bedroom."

Lucy cheerfully picked up two large bags and scampered ahead. The bedroom was dark, its curtains drawn. Denny hesitated in the doorway.

"Lucy, you're big enough to dress yourself, now? Right?"

Lucy turned to look up at Brie, and now her face was in shadow it was impossible to read.

"Of course I am!" she said, and closed the bedroom door.

Denny let out a sigh of relief, looked over at the sofa, and the black oblong box of the remote. Then she re-crossed the room and stopped at the bathroom door.

"Brie?" she shouted. "I'm back!"

There was no reply. Denny tried the door handle, and it opened, releasing a wave of heat and steam. The shower was of the old-fashioned type, with a curtain enclosing a bathtub rather than a glass cubicle. Denny stepped forward and pulled the gaily-colored plastic sheet aside. Brie lay in the tub fully clothed, mouth open in a silent scream. Torrents of boiling hot water were parboiling her face. The dressing on her face had been washed away, revealing the dark patch where she had been wounded the day before. A bread-knife protruded from her chest.

128

Denny stifled a scream, staggered back into the living room. The TV screen was still radiant with the bright, colorful images of kids' cartoons. In the bedroom, Lucy stood, dressed now like a typical small girl.

Innocence in pastel shades. The thought swam into Denny mind, and as it appeared, the diminutive Interloper tilted its head to one side.

"You're very easy to read," said the entity. "But hard to scare. No real demons. Brie was much easier. I frightened her with the girl she helped to kill, so she didn't put up much of a fight."

"What do you mean?" Denny asked, partly to play for time, partly out of genuine fascination with the weird being in front of her. "No real demons?"

The thing with Lucy's face tilted its head to one side, and smiled.

"Most people have a deep-rooted fear," said the Interloper. "But you are almost a blank slate. No fear to draw upon. And no frustrated dreams, either. Nothing to exploit."

Denny began to edge toward the apartment door. Lucy made a sudden leap, scarily fast like a jumping spider. It blocked Denny's escape route.

"I did make a mistake with the remote control," the Interloper said, in a flat, emotionless voice. "It was stupid. As I said, you're easy to read, so I picked the knowledge out of your head. And now look what's happened."

It took a pace forward, crouched, its face starting to elongate, while its forehead seemed to shrink.

"Now, I have to go back," said the Interloper. "And leave no loose ends. I still have plenty to report. I've seen your world first-hand, not in fragments, not distorted through your strange minds."

"Why?" asked Denny, backing away. "Why do all this? Why try to fool us?"

"To find out more about you," Lucy said, its voice growing harsher, the syllables less clearly formed. "To spy on you. It took a long time to make me. I'm very special. I can survive for weeks, months maybe. But now I won't get to see inside the foundation."

Denny still struggled to understand the lengths of scheming the Interlopers had gone to. The question 'Why' kept circling in her head, even as she glanced about for possible weapons.

"Why?" it grunted. "Because we don't like you."

It made another sudden, terrifying leap and landed squarely on Denny's chest, knocking her back against the table, which collapsed under them. Denny screamed, but the entity that was no longer anything like Lucy Gould, and put a powerful hand to her mouth.

"We don't like the way you are now," it hissed. "We don't like your machines, your cities, your science. We liked you before, when you were weak and scattered, and scared of the forests, of all the shadowed places. Then you showed us respect, you gave us nice things to leave you alone! Now you think you're gods, but you're greedy and cruel and stupid and you're spoiling everything!"

It reared up, its transformation complete, an unearthly beast brandishing vicious claws. It lowered the weirdly prehensile funnel of its muzzle towards Denny's face. It half-hissed, half-slobbered words at her that she could barely understand.

"You're killing us!"

Amid her terror, Denny felt something alien probing her mind. It was like a dark tendril, touching memories and emotions, sending a chill through her. Then the invading force stabbed deep into the roots of her identity, trying to tear apart her very essence.

"Stop!" she gasped. "Get out of my mind!"

"No," Lucy gurgled. "I need to know more before you die! You are a strange one. Mysteries!"

"No!" Denny screamed, battling Lucy with her mind and body. For all its power, the Interloper was still no heavier than a small child. Denny visualized all her anger as a glowing ball of fire, erupting from the core of her being. She hurled it at the questing black tendril. Lucy flinched at the psychic impact, startled by an impulse so immediate and primal that she could not have predicted it. Denny seized her chance, broke the creature's grip, bringing up both knees to hurl it across the room. Lucy crashed into the TV screen. But even as Denny was scrambling upright, the Interloper had recovered, and knocked her down again.

"Simpler to kill you," it said.

The muzzle-mouth opened revealing a circle of long, thin teeth that turned outward. Denny struggled frantically but this time the grip of the Interloper's wiry arms and legs had immobilized her. She closed her eyes and twisted her head to the side, feeling the creature's hot breath on her face. But the pain that came next was not the kind she had expected. A jolt shot through her, and she arched her back in a spasm. The grip of the Interloper relaxed, and Denny heard a bestial screech followed by a sickening blow.

When she opened her eyes, Gould and Forster was standing over her. Gould was holding a taser, while the other man was putting down a shotgun with a bloodied butt. The creature had collapsed, and Denny easily heaved the Interloper off her and scrambled away from it.

"I didn't think it would be wise to blow her head off," remarked Forster, almost casually. "Besides, taking them alive might get me a bonus."

Gould bent over the tiny figure. The body was face down. He turned it over cautiously with his foot, taser at the ready, but the Interloper did not move. The eyes, now tiny black beads in deep, pale sockets, gazed blankly upward. A yellowish froth had formed around the mouth. Gould looked up at Denny.

"I think she's dead,"

"You mean *it's* dead," corrected Forster.

"Yeah," said Gould, looking down at the body in its incongruous child's outfit. "Yeah, that's what I meant."

"I'll get something from the van to wrap it in," Forster said. "Best keep clear of it, just in case."

After he left, Gould sat down and buried his face in his hands.

"I'm sorry," said Denny. "It must have been so hard to admit that it wasn't her."

Gould looked up, tears streaming down his face.

"I so wanted to believe," he said. "Right up to the moment

we came through that door. I wanted to see her there. An innocent child."

He covered his face again, giving a great, heaving sob.

"We'll find her," Denny said firmly, sitting by him and putting an arm around his shoulders. "We'll find them both."

Epilogue: The Romola Foundation

"I hate clearing up, it's so boring," said Davenport, climbing out of the van and surveying the house with distaste. "You sure the police are finished?"

"Yeah," replied Forster. "Property is now back in the hands of our lovely foundation."

"Will bricking up that doorway do the job?" asked Davenport, gesturing at a group of builders standing by a truck.

"That's not the plan," the older man corrected. "This time they're going to fill the cellar with concrete. Right up to the ceiling."

This gave Davenport pause for thought.

"So the little buggers won't be able to get out, into our world, ever again?"

Forster gave a weak smile, gestured at the great house. They started to walk up the steps to the palatial front door.

"Look, son, this is just one site. The foundation's identified dozens around the country, and dozens more overseas. We can't shut them out completely. But it sends a message."

Davenport muttered a few colorful versions of what that message might be. Inside they found that the police had removed all the investigators' belongings. The Interloper remains had been dealt with before the police had been called in. The two men went over the house room by room, looking for anything significant, but drew a blank.

"So," said Davenport, looking around him. "Is that it? Are we done?"

"Not quite," Forster said, leading him back to the cellar entrance. "Just a picture to take. I almost forgot, but you know how Benson likes everything strange documented."

In the corridor near the doorway, Forster pointed up at the wall. The message to Brie that had been scratched into the plaster was still legible.

"Oh, that," Davenport said, dismissively. "I got a shot of that the first time. And the other one."

Forster nodded absently, then frowned.

"What other one?"

This time it was the younger man's turn to lead his superior. Just outside the kitchen, there was a similar array of deep scars in the plaster-work, just above head height. The light was poor, and even using a flashlight Forster struggled to make out the words.

"I reckon it's a threat, kind of," said Davenport.

"Or just an observation," Forster mused, raising his camera to take the image. "Right, let's pack up and get out of this dump."

On the way back to headquarters, the two chatted about trivial matters, as always, rather than the grimmer aspects of their unusual work. But that night, when he was back at home with his family, Forster found it hard to focus on his kid's chatter about school or his wife's complaints about her boss. His thoughts kept returning to the enigmatic message scored deep into the fabric of Malpas Abbey.

THERE ARE WORSE THINGS THAN US

***

"The film from the obsolete camera you recovered has been processed," said Benson.

"So I gathered," replied Gould.

Benson raised a hand, and the lights dimmed. A low-grade, black and white film flickered on the screen. A group of men in old-fashioned British army uniforms were shown in front of a bricked up doorway.

"Medical orderlies, I take it?" asked Benson.

"Yes," agreed Gould. "Members of the Royal Army Medical Corps. The house was earmarked as an infirmary for wounded officers immediately after World War One."

"Hmm," said Benson. "Hence the desire to put the cellar to use."

"For storage space, probably," said Gould. "An unwise decision."

A couple of them raised hammers, knocked a way through. The film then cut to a scene in the cellar of Malpas Abbey, with two of the orderlies horsing around by the altar. A close-up followed, showing one man pulling a funny face next to the carvings on the pale stone.

"All good clean fun," observed Benson. "But I'm assuming the entire establishment, at this point, was full of men who had suffered considerable trauma on the Western Front?"

"Yes," said Gould. "Each with his personal demons."

The film suddenly became jerky as the man who had been fooling around stood up and looked at something out of camera shot. The point of view veered wildly, then came to rest on what looked like a ball of mist, hovering in the air. A dark shape formed inside the sphere, then leaped forward. The picture span, then the camera must have struck the floor and ended up on its side. A struggle was under way, but those involved were out of focus. Then a figure came into view, for a brief moment.

"They enhanced this image," said Benson. "Quite graphic."

The Interloper was a conventional image of Death, a skeletal figure with a skull-like visage. Much of the detail was lost in a blur of movement, but it was clear that one of the creature's claws was in the act of scooping the innards out of a still-living man. The soldier's face was frozen in a scream of agony.

"The terrifying death they had escaped in the trenches of Flanders came to claim them in England," Benson commented. "Almost poetic. But of no real practical value for our research."

"No," agreed Gould, his mouth suddenly dry. "I suppose not. Though ..."

Gould hesitated, glanced at the man in the dark suit.

"You have one of your theories, perhaps?" asked Benson quietly.

"We assume they deliberately draw on our emotions and memories," said Gould carefully. "But what if it's a two-way process? What if our obsessions, nightmares, fantasies, shape their appearance and behavior regardless of what they might want?"

Benson looked at Gould for a moment, gave a slight nod.

"And some people would be more influential than others. Your friend Ms. Purcell, for instance, seems to have no personal demons to evoke. But you may be barking up the wrong tree, Gould. Not for the first time."

"It's just a hypothesis," murmured Gould.

"Quite – and now for something completely different," Benson said, raising his hand again so that his long fingers were illuminated by the projector beam.

The black and white image was replaced by modern digital video. Gould saw himself, Denny, Matt, all in a state of confusion as an Interloper bounded down the steps into Blaisdell's temple. There was confused shouting. The field up vision spun, swung upwards as Frankie struggled with the creature that grabbed her from behind, then the second Interloper blocked the view as it leaped at her. There was a whirl of chaotic motion, a screeching sound, then blackness and silence.

"The transition is, as always, impossible to record with any clarity," murmured Benson, with a trace of frustration. "Perhaps with specialized equipment."

"Quite," agreed Gould.

Now the screen showed a bleak, outlandish scene, one Gould recognized from Denny's description. The camera fell to the ground, and pairs of feet – some human, some not – appeared briefly. There was a howling that suggested a strong wind, plus scuffling and the faint sound of Frankie's voice. Her cries dwindled quickly, then were gone. A couple of seconds ticked by on the digital readout in the corner of the screen. Then the camera was lifted and Denny's face, huge and distorted by proximity, appeared for a moment.

"The young woman showed great courage and initiative at this juncture," said Benson. "I agree that she may be an asset. Intriguing that she might be able to block the enemy's psychic powers. Training could help with that. And of course, it is better to have her inside the organization, rather than out in the world telling her story. She is impulsive, though. You'll have to watch that."

The viewpoint swung around as Denny panned around the unearthly vista, then settled on a vague object on the horizon. The camera zoomed in, but the peculiar light and the sheer distance meant the image remained blurred.

"Again," Benson said, "our people managed to remove much of the noise from one frame and get a clear picture."

The still image came up on the screen. Gould gave an involuntary gasp of horror.

"Despite its size, this object is, our experts think, a living thing rather than a machine. But whatever it is, it is most certainly heading for the gateway," Benson remarked. "And moving quite fast, considering its size. We must be thankful that it will take a good while to get there. Years, one hopes."

"But," Gould began. "There are so many other gateways!"

"Indeed," Benson said. "We must, as usual, hope for the best while we prepare for the worst. These – colossal entities could be emerging all over the world in the very near future. The human race would find it difficult to deal with them given our present state of chronic disorganization."

***

After parting company with Benson, Gould went to the Knightsbridge Hilton, where Denny had been booked at the foundation's expense. They had used a false name, as the killings of three people and the disappearance of a fourth had embroiled them in a media feeding frenzy. The loss of almost all of its personnel had, ironically, made 'America's Weirdest Hauntings' a ratings success again.

"What about the cops?" asked Denny, as they sat down for coffee in a quiet corner of the bar. "They thought I was crazy when I started talking about monsters. Eventually I just clammed up and they got some doctor to say I was suffering from PTSD."

"Which is why I didn't talk about monsters," said Gould gently. "Jim and I worked out a version of events that makes it seem – without saying it in so many words – that Frankie is a deranged serial killer, currently on the run."

"That's ludicrous!" Denny protested. "How can they be dumb enough to buy that?"

"Because their dumb theory doesn't involve monsters," Gould riposted. "Do you want to try telling them the truth again? Or maybe go to our wonderful British newspaper with your story?"

Denny shrugged.

"I might have to sell my story. No show, no job."

Gould looked around the bar, then leaned closer.

"The Romola Foundation would like to offer you a job," he said. "As part of my team of investigators."

Denny sat open-mouthed, coffee half-raised to her lips. She put the cup down carefully, then asked, "Does that mean I might get to go after Frankie again?"

Gould nodded.

"And you're still hoping to find Lucy," she went on. "Right?"

Gould looked out of the window at the skyline of London. It was a pleasant autumn day, sunshine glinting on the capital's tower blocks.

"I have to hope," he said. "We both do. And you've proven yourself. More than proved. If there's such a thing as a natural at this game, you're it."

Denny paused for a moment, then smiled up at Gould.

"Okay, you got a deal," she said, holding out her hand. "Say, did you get anything useful from Frankie's camera? I saw some crazy shit over there."

"No – no, we didn't," said Gould, shaking her hand firmly. "I'm afraid the memory was wholly corrupted. The physics team thinks it was a side-effect of the transition – something to do with quantum entanglement. Or so they tell me."

"Oh, crap," moaned Denny. "Better luck next time, I guess."

***

In a white, windowless room, Lord George Blaisdell lay strapped to a metal couch. The unusually-shaped frame supported his weight without crushing the organism fastened between his shoulder blades.

"He is still conscious, Wickes?" asked Benson, observing Blaisdell through a narrow slit in a padded door.

"Yes, sir," said Doctor Wickes. "Though he drifts in an out of delirium. His grasp on reality is somewhat fragile."

"Not surprising," Benson said. "And the PD entity? Is it simply a parasite?"

Wickes shook her head.

"Definitely not, sir. As far as we can tell, it is symbiotic. We assume it was affixed to his body specifically to allow him to survive for a prolonged period in the PD. Much as we might keep an animal specimen alive in an artificial environment."

Benson peered through the slit for a few seconds, then turned to face his chief biologist.

"In other words, that strange lump of tissue feeds him?"

"Quite right, sir," said Wickes, with a slightly nervous smile. "It has altered his biophysical structure so that it can somehow process compounds from the PD into nutrients."

"Fascinating," said Benson, firmly. "But can it be transferred to one of our operatives?"

Wickes looked more nervous, her eyes wide.

"Sir, it is part of his body now. We think that removing the symbiote would cause massive metabolic shock, possibly fatal."

Benson looked levelly at Wickes until the latter lowered her eyes.

"Get on with it. And do not use anesthetic. You don't know what effect such chemicals might have on that thing."

"But–" Wickes began. "If we kill him?"

"He's been legally dead for a long time," Benson replied. "Think of it as a kind of post-mortem."

Wickes signaled to a pair of orderlies standing nearby. Then she went to a long table that stood against the wall. Surgical instruments and a box of latex gloves were laid out ready.

When they opened the door, Blaisdell began to shout and writhe in his bonds.

"Turn him over, quickly," ordered Wickes.

The orderlies rotated the metal frame until the captive's back was facing upwards. Wickes took a deep breath and raised a scalpel. She began to cut away the flesh around the unearthly organism. The brown hemisphere pulsed and quivered as black fluid spurted from severed vessels. Blaisdell screamed.

"I thought I had escaped from Hell, but I was wrong!"

***

"Classic case of overkill, if you ask me," said the guard, checking Forster's pass. "Waste of my time. But hey, I'm getting paid."

Forster looked the man up and down, then stepped past him to the cell door. He opened the viewing slit and stood peering inside for half a minute. Then he closed the aperture and stood in silence for a few moments.

"Overkill," said Forster eventually. "Interesting term. Very applicable in this particular case."

The guard looked uncertain as Forster looked him over.

"If anything," Forster said, "I think it's a case of underkill to have just one bloke on guard outside this particular door. You know the procedure, right?"

"Of course, chief," the guard replied, sounding slightly aggrieved. "If our guest starts getting lively, I report it at once."

"You hit the panic button," corrected Forster. "Grade One alert. Your first priority is to get help down here. Don't try to do anything on your own."

The guard nodded, and Forster started to walk away towards the security checkpoint at the end of the corridor.

"Er, chief," said the guard.

Forster stopped and turned, raised an eyebrow at the young man.

"Yes? Something not clear?"

The guard shuffled his feet, reddened slightly.

"It's just," he said. "Well, it just seems a bit weird. I mean, why's that thing dressed like a little girl?"

* * *

Nightmare Valley
Nightmare Series Book 2

Prologue: England, Autumn 1914

"It will all be over by Christmas, mark my words," said the barman of the Black Swan as he finished pouring a pint of dark beer. "There you go sir, a nice pint of Burton's Best Ale to wet your whistle."

"Ta very much, and your good health," replied Bewick, raising the glass. "I wish I had your confidence about this war, though. Seems to me the Kaiser, the Tsar, the French, Turks, and all the rest of 'em have been spoiling for a fight for years. Now they've got one. This time they get to settle all their old scores. And we're being dragged into the sorry mess! Very disturbing."

Bewick took a mouthful of ale, wiped the froth from around his mouth with the sleeve of his well-worn coat.

"Yes," the barman said, nodding sagely, "but the way I see it, all these countries can't afford a long war, can they? What with trade being held up and all. No, all them daft kings and emperors will have their bit of fun and then it'll be back to the conference table, drawing more lines on maps. Our brave boys will be back in time to celebrate the New Year. You wait and see."

Bewick was not inclined to argue the point. As a commercial traveler, it was second nature for him to get along with strangers. He had come to the small town of Machen in the hope that, because it was an out of the way place, he would find fresh customers. So far, however, his efforts to interest local ladies in his hosiery and related products had failed miserably.

"Not much money about, I take it?" Bewick said, wiping beer froth from around his mouth.

"Don't quite get your meaning, sir?" the barman replied, with a tilt of the head.

"I must have called on two dozen houses today," Bewick explained. "Not a nibble. Not one person interested in my products."

He nodded at the samples case he had placed on the bar earlier.

"Oh, that," the barman said. "It's not so much lack of

money as people are—"

Then the man stopped talking and glanced over Bewick's shoulder. The salesman knew better than to turn around. But he did glance at the huge mirror behind the bar and saw a group of locals, huddled around a corner table. They were apparently not listening to the conversation. But Bewick had the distinct feeling they were noting every word.

"People are what?" he asked. "Not very trusting of outsiders? I get that a lot in these little places, off the beaten track."

"Yes sir, that's right," the barman said, in a very clear voice. "Bit wary of strangers, that's all! Don't get many visitors here in Machen."

Rather than press the point, Bewick drank the rest of his pint in silence. After finishing, he went upstairs to his cramped little attic room. It was the only accommodation in town and its general air of neglect proved the barman's point.

Strangers not welcome round here, Bewick thought. *Bloody yokels. Well, I'll just cross it off the list and move on down the valley tomorrow.*

Bewick stood looking out of the dirty window over the little town. Machen lay on the river Wye, a meandering watercourse crossed by an ancient stone bridge. To the west, the sun was sinking towards the hills on the Welsh border. Bewick frowned, looking more intently at a small wood land that lay above the town. He saw movement under the trees. But it was hard to tell from over a mile away whether the pale shapes were people or animals.

Deer, probably, he thought. *Or sheep? But sheep don't go into forests. Do they?*

Shrugging off the trivial mystery, he sat down on the bed to check his railway timetable. Then he lit the small oil lamp and started to write some letters. Bewick had lost all track of time when there was a stealthy knock at the door.

"Yes?"

The barman was standing outside holding a glass tumbler full of amber liquid.

"I thought you might like a hot toddy, sir," the man explained. "The nights are getting chillier, now, and it might help you sleep."

The salesman smiled, began to reach out, then hesitated.

"Oh, it's on the house, sir," the barman added.

"Well, that's very kind of you," Bewick replied, taking the warm tumbler. "Most considerate."

"Don't want you going away thinking all us country folk as inhospitable," the barman said, with a grin that looked a little forced.

Maybe he wants a big tip, thought Bewick. *Oh well, he's going to be disappointed. But it's a nice gesture, I suppose.*

Bewick sat down on the bed again and took a mouthful of the toddy, then nearly choked. It was very strong, definitely more whiskey than water. Bewick, a beer-drinker by inclination, only managed to consume a third of the glass before feeling distinctly woozy. He took off his boots and lay down, still fully clothed, and was soon out like a light.

When he woke up it was just after nine, according to his watch. The oil lamp was still burning, and he decided to change into his pajamas. As he got up, he glanced out of the window again, and stopped. Something was not quite right. His mind was still far from clear, thanks to the whiskey, but he forced himself to focus.

The little town of Machen was almost entirely dark. There were no streetlights, and only a few houses showed lights in their windows. The railway station and post office were long since closed and shuttered. Only the glow of the familiar blue lamp outside the tiny police station was visible. But outside the town, on the hillside below the woods, there was a sinuous line of flickering yellow lights.

Lanterns, Bewick guessed. *Dozens of lanterns. Looks like half the town is going up that hill. What the hell is going on?*

Bewick thought of a friend who worked as a junior reporter for a London newspaper. Whatever was happening in Machen might be of interest to the press, who often ran amusing little stories about rural folk and their bizarre customs. And that could mean a payment in cash. Bewick opened his door slowly. The Black Swan seemed quiet enough. He began to put on his boots then decided to carry them down, as he would make less noise that way.

So, my host thought a tumbler full of cheap spirit would keep me quiet, he thought. *Well, think again, my friend.*

Bewick felt a boyish excitement as he tiptoed down the steep staircase.

***

Sir Reginald Pelham stood with his back to Branksholme Woods looking down over the valley. He was twenty-four years old and had returned to England from India three months earlier to take over his late father's lands. His wife and six-month-old son had come with him. As the chill night breeze blew up, Pelham wished he could be back home in front his own fire with his family.

But apparently, he thought, *I have to be here, because of some absurd medieval tradition. I wish this old fool would tell me what I have to do, and when it will be over.*

Beside him stood the Reverend Arthur Stainforth, vicar of the only church in Machen. The clergyman was in his sixties, slow and unsteady thanks to rheumatism, but vastly more confident than the landowner in his dealings with the valley folk.

"You still have not explained this – what d'you call it? – this agreement to me," grumbled Pelham to the priest. "I don't understand why all this is happening. My father mentioned no such tradition. And it seems preposterous, on the face of it."

Stainforth shook his head.

"Your father," said the priest, "had no knowledge of the Covenant. That is the proper term, used since ancient times. That is because it has not been invoked since the war with Napoleon. It worked then, it may still work now."

"All right, it's a Covenant," snapped Pelham. "What does it involve? Because if they want me to raise wages or lower rents, I'll ..."

The squire hesitated as the priest hobbled a couple of paces forward and stared up into Pelham's face. The younger man raised a lantern and saw that Stainforth was trembling.

Anger? No, fear, thought Pelham. *The old boy's terrified.*

"You own all this land," the priest said. "Therefore you are

145

bound to keep the Covenant for all those who live in this part of the valley."

"And what does that entail?" demanded Pelham.

"Your mere presence should be enough, Sir Reginald," replied Stainforth. "But it's vital that, whatever happens, you allow the ritual to take place. Then the men will be protected."

Pelham felt frustration rising again. As an imperial army officer, he had been used to having his questions answered clearly and at once by British and native subordinates alike. And yet the priest had been a good friend of his father.

"I would be obliged, your Reverend," he began slowly, "if you would not treat me like a slow-witted child who–"

Pelham broke off when he realized Stainforth was no longer paying him attention, but had turned to stare into the trees. Looking around, the younger man saw nothing at first. Then he noticed a barely perceptible shifting of shadows, a hint of gray shapes moving stealthily in the darkness.

"Bloody poachers!" he exclaimed. "In my woods?"

The priest blinked up at the young squire.

"They are only your woods by day, Reginald," he said. "Best not to look too closely. Those are not poachers."

Pelham snorted, and bent down to tinker with the lantern he had brought. By the time it was lit, the first of the townsfolk had arrived at the summit of the hill. Pelham looked in vain for a familiar face, then recognized the postmaster, the town constable, two of his gamekeepers, and the barman of the Black Swan. Then a more imposing figure appeared and stepped out in front of the others. It was a tall, thin-faced woman in a black gown and shawl. Pelham recalled his father pointing the woman out to him many years earlier.

The wise woman, he called her, but I felt sure she was a witch. Father warned me never to cross her sort in my dealings.

"Is that old Ma Wakefield?" Pelham hissed to the priest.

"Aye, Sir Reginald," the woman said, in a voice that carried across the clearing. "It is I. What of it?"

"Is this a pagan affair, then?" Pelham asked Stainforth, deciding not to exchange words with the woman.

"This is a matter for all of us," the priest said in a

quavering voice, again glancing behind him.

"Aye, vicar, they be coming," Ma Wakefield said. "We should be ready."

There were noises of agreement from the crowd, now about fifty in number. The townsfolk formed a semi-circle around the landowner and priest, but Pelham noted that none of them strayed into Branksholme Woods.

"Sing the old verse," said the woman in black. "They need to know we are ready."

On cue, the townsfolk began to sing, most hesitantly, but gradually gaining volume as Ma Wakefield bellowed out the song.

> 'As before, it must be so
> Fair exchange and Covenant
> Good folk accept our gift and go
> Fair exchange and Covenant
>
> Let the men come home again
> From fields of blood or foaming main
> All will bear the lesser pain
> Of fair exchange and Covenant'

The townsfolk fell silent. There was a shuffling of feet, some coughing, a few whispered asides.

"Is that it?" asked Pelham. "Do we just go home now after a good old sing-along?"

"That is just the beginning of the ritual," said the priest, taking the landowner gently by the arm. "Please, sir, step to one side."

Pelham allowed the old man to lead him to one end of the ragged semicircle. Everyone else seemed to be staring into the gloom of the forest. A branch broke with a loud crack, and the crowd seemed to flinch. After the rousing chorus, there was an eerie silence, a sense of expectation.

"There's one!" shouted a young, male voice. The exclamation was followed by frantic shushing.

Pelham peered into the darkness under the trees and saw faint gray shapes moving, as they had before. He was sure there were more than three, perhaps as many as half a dozen, but it was hard to tell. They were at the limits of vision. But something about the way the figures moved struck him as more bestial than human.

Probably just a few locals in silly costumes, he told himself. *God knows these people love dressing up for their festivals.*

"Bring the tribute," said Ma Wakefield, taking up position on the edge of the woods.

The crowd parted and in the lamplight, Pelham saw a petite young woman walking forward. As she got closer he noted that she was very young indeed – surely still in her teens. Beside her walked an older man, and Pelham recognized the village blacksmith. The man was a widower with an unmarried daughter. The young woman was crying, while the man murmured in her ear. His tone was comforting, cajoling. As they passed close by him, Pelham saw that the woman was carrying a baby, bundled in a tartan blanket. He had a sudden, sickening conviction that this was no quaint village custom.

"Here, girl," said Ma Wakefield, holding out her hands. "Give the little one to me."

No, thought Pelham. *Whatever this is, I cannot permit it. It has a stink of evil about it.*

He started forward, but again the priest gripped his arm. When Pelham tried to shake off the old man, Stainforth clung to him with surprising tenacity.

"The child was born out of wedlock," said the priest. "They cannot afford to keep it. This is better."

"How can you sanction this, as a man of God?" demanded Pelham. "What did Christ have to say about cruelty to children?"

"This is a place of older gods, Sir Reginald," Ma Wakefield said. "Best face that and be prepared."

The wise woman had come up behind the two men and was holding the swaddled baby. She looked Pelham boldly in the face, showing none of the deference he was used to seeing from his tenants.

"And this dear child will not be harmed," she went on, in a gentler voice. "He will merely go away with the good folk to live with them in a better place than some English hovel. You should be grateful, because this will help you, too, Sir Reginald. Help you survive the storm that gathers over all the world."

Ma Wakefield's words elicited another murmur of approval from the assembly. Pelham looked around at the faces, illuminated by the yellow lamplight. He felt his outrage ebbing away, a sense of resignation replacing it. Resignation, and fear. He thought of his time in India, and the way he had seen the mood of crowds change when ancient rites were interrupted by the British authorities. He stifled a rebuke to Ma Wakefield and stood aside as the woman in black walked forward to the edge of Branksholme Woods. She knelt, and gently placed the baby at the foot of an ancient oak. Then she stood, raised her arms, and spoke in a loud, ringing voice.

"Good folk, wise folk, the long-livers, the far-seers! Behold this infant, our gift to you, unblemished, pure of body and soul! In return, we ask that the Covenant be upheld."

Ma Wakefield retreated, rejoined the townsfolk.

"What happens now?" hissed Pelham.

"Watch!" said the priest, his voice barely audible.

For the third time, pale shapes flitted among the ancient trees. Gradually they came nearer, darting from trunk to trunk, seemingly unwilling to linger in the light.

"Douse all your lights!" ordered the wise woman. "They do not like to be seen!"

Within seconds, the lanterns' butter-yellow radiance had dwindled to nothing. Pelham's eyes slowly adjusted to the night. A fine harvest moon had risen, casting a faint, colorless light over the scene. Pelham held his breath, knowing that the next act in the weird drama was about to begin. Sure enough, several pale figures emerged from behind the trees, and crept through the undergrowth towards where the baby lay. A querulous crying came from the small bundle.

This is horrible, Pelham thought. *I cannot allow this! A good man would stop this!*

Despite the urging of his conscience, he found himself unable to move, staring in fascination as the strange creatures bowed over the infant. The baby started to cry more loudly, and Pelham heard the mother sobbing quietly. Then one of the pallid creatures snatched up the pathetic bundle and bounded, with incredible speed, back into the woods. There was an audible sigh from the onlookers.

"What are those things?" Pelham whispered to Stainforth. "Apes or devils or what?"

The priest raised a finger to his lips.

"They must be referred to as the good folk," he replied. "Never call them anything else. They hate disrespect and are believed to hear everything said of them."

The rest of the strange creatures were staring at the priest and the landowner. At about ten yards' distance, Pelham could just make out small, pale eyes glinting in deep sockets. Their faces reminded him of the monkeys he had seen in Hindu temples, with low foreheads and long muzzles. One of the entities bounded forward a few paces and seemed to peer more closely at Pelham. Then it raised a long, spindly arm and pointed.

Oh my God, Pelham thought. *Do they want me as a sacrifice too?*

But before he could react, Ma Wakefield was striding past him, pushing through the crowd. She, too, was pointing. Now Pelham realized that the weird creature had been indicating someone at the back of the group.

"An outsider!" the wise woman bellowed. "One who should not be here!"

"How on earth can she see anyone?" wondered Pelham aloud, peering into the darkness.

"They can see very well in the dark, and she speaks to them with her mind," whispered Stainforth. "Oh, dear me, this is very bad! We should have been more careful."

Pelham looked back at the trees to see that the pale creatures had all vanished.

"We will wait here a while," Ma Wakefield said. "I will be told when it is safe to return to Machen."

The barman of the Black Swan hurried forward and said something to the wise woman. He seemed to be pleading. Ma Wakefield shook her head.

"There is no appeal, no pardon," she insisted. "All you can

do now is help clear up after it's done."

***

At first, Bewick was disappointed. He had trudged up the hill without a light, stepping in sheep droppings and falling over several times. Now he was at the back of the crowd, and as far as he could make out, all they were doing was singing some sort of folk song.

Silly buggers, he thought. *Why couldn't they just have a party in the Black Swan?*

But then he saw the baby being carried into the clearing, and felt the tension in the air. The appearance of the pale beings from the forest sent a chill down his spine. Bewick had witnessed violence and cruelty in his travels, but felt sure that this was something way beyond run-of-the-mill law-breaking. Ma Wakefield's involvement led him to dredge up some half-forgotten history.

Black magic, he thought. *Devil worship. It's a coven of witches, like in olden times!*

Bewick had already begun to slink away through the townsfolk when the cry went up. He began to run despite the darkness, and pelted down the hill towards the town. He could just make out the glow of the blue lamp outside the police station. He took a tumble, got up, and fell again. Then he paused, listening for sounds of pursuit. He saw no lights on the hillside above him, none of the shouting one might expect.

Bewick got up again and jogged towards the town at a less frantic pace, crossing the bridge and reaching the police station without incident. He shoved open the door and staggered inside. Behind the desk, a blue-uniformed constable looked up with a quizzical expression.

"Dear me, sir," said the young officer, "what have we been up to?"

Bewick was so winded that it took him a few seconds before he could get out a few words.

"Up – on the hill – a baby – witchcraft! Call for help – whole town involved."

The policeman opened a big ledger and picked up a pencil.

"Now then, sir, I really need a more detailed statement than that," he said. "Witchcraft? You do know this is the twentieth century, don't you?"

Bewick took several deep breaths and tried to give a more coherent account of what he had seen. The constable wrote swiftly in the ledger as the story unfolded. Then, when the salesman had finished, the officer gave a tolerant smile and leaned over the desk.

"Just between you and me, sir," he said, "what you've described is just a bit of traditional nonsense."

"Nonsense?" erupted Bewick. "Those creatures – those monsters, they were real! And so was that poor infant!"

"Yes, sir," the officer went on, his voice low and soothing. "But if you'd stayed to the end you'd have seen that these creatures were just lads dressed up in home-made costumes. The whole thing is a, what do you call it? A re-enactment of some medieval shenanigans that were, no doubt, bad at the time. But now it's just a bit of fun. That's why the squire and the vicar were there. You don't believe respectable gentlemen like them would take part in anything truly wicked? Do you?"

The explanation was so sensible, so commonsense, that for a moment Bewick felt like a fool. He had seen no actual violence done. Perhaps the shadowy forms flitting under the trees had been costumed performers.

"Well, now that you put it that way ..." he began, prompting another smile from the police officer. But then a thought struck him.

"But the child's mother," Bewick protested. "She was weeping, really broken up about it! Why would she do that if it was just a play or something? And don't tell me she was acting!"

The smile on the constable's face vanished. He tilted his head to one side, then slowly put his pencil down on the ledger, all the while staring at Bewick. The unblinking gaze was so intense that Bewick could not help but look away. He found himself gazing at the ledger. The pages were covered not with words taken as a statement, but a meaningless scribble of jagged lines.

"No, we can't write," said the constable, his voice growing

more guttural. "But we have other talents. Pity you would not be persuaded."

Bewick reeled back from the reception desk as the human-looking face changed, becoming elongated. His eyes retreated until they became glittering pinpoints in deep sockets. At the same time the inhuman creature's limbs extended, as did its fingers, while nails transmuted into vicious claws.

Bewick tried to run but before he even reached the door, the monster had leaped onto his back, talons reaching for his throat.

***

After the ritual, Pelham returned to his manor house on the far side of the valley. He found it impossible to sleep. It was only when the gray light of dawn appeared that he fell into a fitful doze. He was awoken at eight by his valet bringing his breakfast tray.

"What is it, Milligan?" he asked irritably, as the man hesitated by his bedside.

"I thought I should inform you sir," said the valet, putting the tray down on the covers by his master. "A rather peculiar woman called earlier. She was most insistent that I give you something."

Pelham looked at the silver tray. On top of the morning paper, that lay beside his plate of scrambled eggs, was a purplish stone hanging from a length of slick, brown cord that might have been leather. The stone was about two inches long, irregularly shaped. A hole had been bored at one end for the cord, creating a crude pendant.

"Did this woman say anything?" asked Pelham.

"Yes, sir," replied Milligan. "She said that if you wear it at all times you will enjoy good fortune. She said that it was a talisman."

"Is that all? Sounds like something a gypsy fortuneteller might come up with."

"Quite, sir," said the valet. "But the woman was most insistent and ..."

Milligan hesitated.

"You found her intimidating?" finished Pelham.

The valet looked shamefaced but said nothing in return.

"I don't blame you," Pelham said with a wan smile. "You can go now."

After Milligan left, Pelham picked up the odd stone. Knowing nothing of minerals, he could not tell if it was local or foreign, costly or cheap. He was tempted to toss it aside, but instead found himself placing the cord around his neck. The stone felt oddly warm on his flesh as it lay on his chest. He remembered a book he had read as a boy called *The Talisman*. He vaguely recalled it was about some kind of holy relic that protected a brave knight in battle.

"Perhaps all that business last night was just for show," he mused. "A clever charade to intimidate the new landlord."

After he finished his eggs and coffee, he lay back and pondered the night's events, wondering what he should do next. Despite the coffee, his eyelids grew heavy and he settled back for a pleasant doze. Instead, he was beset by troubling dreams. He was standing on a hill above a deep, dark valley. The landscape was like another world, with the remains of shattered trees and ruined buildings. The slopes of the valley were studded with blocks of concrete and crisscrossed with coils of rusting barbed wire. No blade of grass could be seen, and no birds sang.

A column of men in steel helmets, dressed in mud-spattered khaki uniforms, were marching past under a sunless sky. Their faces were wan, their eyes were cast down at the muddy road as they trudged along. Pelham looked for the beginning of the column, but it seemed to stretch all the way to the horizon. There were hundreds of thousands of soldiers, all mutely marching by. Looking the other way, he tried to make out their destination. All he could see at the far end of the valley was mist. The snaking column vanished into silvery grayness.

"Poor sods," said a voice at his side.

Pelham looked around to see the barman from the Black Swan. He, too, wore the khaki uniform and steel helmet. But he also wore a pendant, and the purple stone seemed to glow, offering the only real color in the dismal vista. Beyond the landlord were other familiar faces – Pelham's gamekeepers, his valet, the blacksmith. All wore a pendant.

A talisman, thought Pelham, looking down to see the same glowing stone on the breast of his khaki jacket. *That's what she meant.*

He picked up the newspaper from his breakfast tray and scanned the headlines. The great powers were mobilizing. Fighting had already broken out on several fronts. A British Expeditionary Force was being prepared to stop a German advance through neutral Belgium.

Putting down the paper, Pelham clutched the talisman. Again, he felt an odd sensation of warmth course through his fingertips.

I can take it off any time I choose, he thought. *Just a lot of superstitious nonsense. I'll take it off. Of course I will.*

And over four years later, he did.

Chapter 1: Mind Games

"She's been a bit quiet, doctor," said Mel Bavistock. "Not eating much. Doesn't seem to want to watch television, either – not like her at all."

"I think shunning TV is not, in itself, a symptom of illness," smiled Doctor Wakefield. "I've never written out a prescription for more telly, so far as I can recall."

Mel smiled at the attempted joke. She liked the doctor, a kindly man who had been widowed a few years back. She had even toyed with the idea of asking him out on a date herself, but never quite plucked up the confidence.

"Perhaps you've grown out of some of those TV shows, eh Isobel?" the doctor asked, looking down at the little girl sitting quietly by his desk. "Perhaps some of the programs you used to like are a bit babyish for you, now?"

Isobel looked up at Wakefield, then nodded.

"Fairy princesses are a bit silly," she said, then looked down at her folded hands. "I like stories about dinosaurs and spaceships now."

"Excellent!" exclaimed the doctor. "You can't go far wrong with dinosaurs and spaceships, I feel. Central to any good story."

"It's just – what with that business in the woods–" Mel began, then stopped, made a helpless gesture. "I know she wasn't hurt or nothing, but–"

"It was very traumatic for you, Mel," said Wakefield, sitting on the edge of his desk. "Like any mother, when your daughter got lost you were very upset. Now you're anxious, don't want to let her out of your sight. So that anxiety communicates itself to Isobel. And that, in turn, makes you even more anxious. See?"

He's so sensible, Mel thought. *And so kind. I just wish I could be sure he's right.*

"Put it this way, Mel," the doctor went on. "When Isobel and the other children were found, I examined them straight away. Just like the police, I concluded that they had experienced a few scratches and bumps from wandering in the woods, and that was it. It was a bit of an adventure, really –

isn't that right?"

Isobel looked up at the doctor again, her clear blue eyes unblinking.

"Yes," she said, "we had an adventure."

The grown-ups chatted some more, and then Wakefield offered to prescribe something to help Mel sleep. It was, he stressed, a short course of pills to get her back on track. After a brief hesitation, she accepted. Then they left the clinic and began to walk down the main street back to the Black Swan. A few spots of rain fell from the autumn sky, and Mel glanced up at the clouds, then found her eyes drawn to the looming presence of Branksholme Woods.

"It's not the trees' fault," said Isobel. "We just got lost."

"I know, poppet," said Mel quickly. "And I don't blame you or your friends. I was just worried, is all."

"Doctor Wakefield says I'm all right," said Isobel. "He must know, it's his job."

Mel laughed at the remark, its child-like bluntness.

That's like the Isobel I knew, she thought. *Perhaps she's getting back to her old gabby self.*

As they neared the pub, their neighbor opposite emerged from her shabby cottage. Mrs. Molesworth was known to most townsfolk as the Mad Cat Lady. Mel had always tried to be kind to her, giving her leftover food for her dozen or so pets and regularly passing the time of day. But recently the eccentric, old woman had taken against the Bavistocks. Today she seemed especially grouchy, giving Isobel and her mother a sour look.

"Looks like rain again!" Mel shouted across the road.

Mrs. Molesworth said nothing audible, but stumped off towards the local Safeway muttering under her breath.

Old bag, Mel thought, then felt ashamed. I *might end up like her, I shouldn't judge.*

"Well," she said to Isobel, "now you've got a clean bill of health I suppose you can help me with tonight's meals."

Isobel nodded, she waited for her mother to unlock the pub door.

"How can a person be a bag?" she asked.

Oh God, thought Mel, *did I say it aloud? Kids pick up on everything.*

***

Denny Purcell tried to focus on mental images. In her ears was a steady hiss of white noise delivered by headphones. Over her eyes, special goggles cut off all light.

"Next target," said Ted Gould's voice in her ear.

Denny struggled to make something meaningful of the fluorescent green and orange shapes drifting in her field of vision. Her mind, refusing to behave itself, conjured up an image of a large pepperoni pizza. It had been a while since breakfast and her last few answers had tended to focus on food.

I can't say pizza again, she thought. *Say something else that's round, think of anything round.*

"Giant chocolate chip cookie," she blurted out.

There was a pause.

"Okay," said Gould's voice. "At this point I think we should take the hint and break for lunch."

Denny heaved a sigh of relief as Doctor Zoffany removed the blinders, then the headphones. Gould tapped a key on a laptop, curtailing a series of supposedly random images. The theory was that he would strive to project them to Denny. She noticed that the last image had been the Empire State Building.

Guess imagining pizza counts as a near miss, she thought.

"How did I do this time?" she asked, looking from Gould to the scientist and back.

"I think we've established," said Gould, "that you're about as psychic as most people. Which is to say, not at all."

"Aw!" Denny said, in a tone of mock-complaint. "I was hoping for a new career in the carnival."

Zoffany, a dark-haired woman in her mid-forties, shook her head emphatically.

"We seldom find any paranormal characteristics in test subjects," she said. "But, given that you survived close encounters with the Interlopers, we thought you might have some unusual mental abilities. However–"

"I'm as psychic as the average tree stump?" Denny put in.

"That's a somewhat negative take on the data," Zoffany smiled. "You're just perfectly normal, is all."

Still sounds like an insult, Denny thought. *Who the hell wants to be normal?*

"So when I thought I was having some kind of psychic battle with Lucy ..." she began, then noticed Gould's expression. "Sorry, Ted, I meant the creature that impersonated her."

"I know," he said, with a faint smile. "It's convenient to refer to that particular Interloper as Lucy. Go on."

"Well," she continued, "I thought I was kind of battling her for control of my mind, that she was trying to tear me apart from the inside? And then I sort of hurled this ball of mental energy at her, put her off balance for a second. But maybe that was more imagination than anything else?"

Doctor Zoffany leaned back against a bench laden with elaborate testing equipment.

"We're reduced to guesswork when it comes to the mental powers of the Interlopers," she said. "As with so many other matters. They can read minds, to some extent – that much we know. And they use this to manipulate humans, through fear primarily. But also in other ways, like playing on hope, even love, which is quite remarkable–"

"I think we're all aware of that," interrupted Gould. "I desperately wanted to believe my little sister had come back from the Phantom Dimension. It was clever of them to exploit that – it very nearly worked."

Denny shuddered at the memory of the unearthly creature that had so closely mimicked a human child. Gould had repeatedly reassured her that the being that had taken on Lucy's form had been killed and the body 'disposed of discreetly'. She had not asked for details.

"So," she said, "if I'm not psychic, does that mean I'm no use to the esteemed Romola Foundation?"

"Not at all!" Gould said quickly. "You're the only person we know of who has ventured into the Phantom Dimension and survived."

"Yeah," Denny said somberly. "Pity about old George."

Lord George Blaisdell, an eighteenth century aristocrat, had been abducted and tortured by the Interlopers, then allowed to escape. Thanks to the weird disparity in time-flow between parallel worlds, he had only aged a small fraction of the two centuries that had passed on earth. But his captors had fixed a strange symbiotic creature to his body to keep him alive. Gould had explained to Denny that trying to remove the symbiote had killed the old man.

"Do you think the next time they remove one of those things," Denny said carefully, "they'll be able to keep the victim alive?"

"Surgery is not my field," Zoffany said slowly, not meeting Denny's eye. "But it could be that the amount of time that the symbiote is attached to a host determines how hard it is to remove. Blaisdell had been in the PD for a very long time. Your friend Frankie, by contrast, was only abducted a few weeks ago."

"There's every reason to hope, Denny," Gould said. "Time flows differently there, we know that much. So she's really been in the PD for a day or less."

"But time is passing for her," Denny said. "However slowly. I can't forget that."

A couple of minutes later, Gould was escorting Denny down to the ground floor of the Romola Foundation's headquarters. Simply walking through the palatial building in central London never failed to impress Denny. She knew how high property values had become in the capital, and yet the foundation – supposedly an obscure scientific research charity – occupied a grandiose Victorian town house.

"So," Denny asked. "It's been a while since we got away from Malpas Abbey. When do I get to meet the mysterious Mister Benson?"

Gould shrugged.

"Possibly never. He seldom talks to anyone outside his inner circle of scientists, money-men, and senior field operatives. Like me."

"But the guy is offering me a permanent job with this outfit?" Denny persisted. "Because I can't go back to working in TV. I'll always be 'the woman whose colleagues were taken out by a serial killer'."

The official police explanation for the 'Malpas Massacre', as the British press had dubbed it, was murder by an unknown person. Suspicion had fallen on the survivors, including Denny. But with zero forensic evidence and no motives, the investigation had stalled. The media, as usual, had enjoyed a brief feeding frenzy. But with none of the survivors willing to give interviews they, too, had moved on.

"Yes, you can have a job," Gould said, showing her into his office. "But first there's a probationary period."

Gould explained that all field operatives with the foundation had to undertake a basic investigation to prove their competence. As a professional journalist, Denny should not find going undercover and asking questions too difficult.

"I agree," she said. "So what mission are you sending me on? Let me guess – a remote lighthouse on a rocky crag, where the keepers have a habit of disappearing on dark, stormy nights."

Gould, who had seemed preoccupied all morning, managed to laugh at that.

"No, for two reasons," he replied. "One, it's a massive cliché, and two, lighthouses are obsolete in these days of satellite navigation."

He opened a drawer in his desk and pulled out a buff-colored folder.

"I'll email you all this, of course, but I thought you'd like hard copy," he said, handing it over. "Basically, you have to go for a holiday in a nice little town about a hundred miles west of here. And while you're there, check out some local folklore."

"Where is this town, exactly?" Denny asked.

"Machen – it's a small market town on the Welsh border."

"Okay," she said, opening the folder. "Why is it on the foundation's radar?"

"Could be a case of Impostor Syndrome," said Gould. "Or maybe something strange has happened with local children."

"Tell me more," she said carefully. "Is it anything like – what happened with Lucy?"

"That's what struck me as interesting," said Gould, his

voice level.

"Okay, it's the only town in England without a war memorial. Because they never needed one. That is kind of weird, but–"

"You don't see how it relates to the Interlopers?" finished Gould. "Me neither, but it's an odd coincidence. Keep reading."

Denny kept reading, and eventually came to a news item from a paper called 'The Machen Advertiser'.

THREE LOCAL CHILDREN IN 'ABDUCTION PANIC'

At first, it seemed like a trivial matter – some kids had gotten lost in the woods, adults were concerned, then the children turned up safe and sound. Then she realized how closely it resembled the disappearance of Gould's sister, Lucy, decades earlier. The difference was that Lucy had not returned.

But something inhuman returned in her place.

One part of the news report struck her as significant. She read it aloud.

"'The brother of one of the girls
was so traumatized by the incident
that he has been given special
counseling. According to a family
friend he 'doesn't believe his sister
is really his sister anymore'."

When she looked up at Gould again, he nodded gravely.

"It might be nothing more than what it seems," he said. "But given what we've both been through so far, Benson and I agree that it's well worth checking out."

Denny closed the folder.

"Okay, I'll go undercover. You said something about lunch?"

"I did indeed," said Gould, smiling. "There's a little Italian place near here that we have an account with. But before we go, one point about Machen. If Interlopers are involved and you get the chance to cross over again, don't take it."

"But Frankie," Denny began, only for Gould to hold up his hand.

"No," he insisted. "I'm sorry, but any attempt to rescue your friend – or my sister – has to be done by a properly-equipped security team. If you don't feel you can abide by that policy–"

"I get it," Denny said, resignedly. "No heroics, just check things out. Well, at least it'll be a break from Zoffany poking about in my mind."

***

"Okay," said Forster. "We've got three blokes on leave, and one down with food poisoning. You're up."

Noel Barrett looked around the foyer of the Romola Foundation, half-expecting to see another security guard. But no, he was the only one on duty. Paul Forster, formerly of the Parachute Regiment and now head of security for the entire operation, wanted him.

"Yes, you," Forster snapped, impatiently. "Come on. We're going down to the sub-basement."

Barrett had heard about the sub-basement level at the Romola Foundation, but had never expected to see it. It was reserved for teams of scientists and personnel like Forster, who had top security clearance.

And now I'm being assigned there, he thought, with a mixture of pride and trepidation. *This is the big time, Noel – don't screw it up.*

Five minutes later, after taking the special elevator reserved for senior personnel, Forster led Barrett along a brightly-lit corridor. They stopped outside a cell door. The security chief had already issued Barrett with a Taser to go with his usual telescopic baton. Now he stood aside and pointed at the door, which bore the number 101. There was a viewing slit in the door with a sliding cover. A utilitarian steel-framed chair stood by the door. Barrett's heart sank. He had seen chairs like that before, designed to make sure the person sitting on them never got comfortable enough to doze off.

"This door never opens, right?"

"Right, sir!" replied Barrett.

"You never open that slit to look inside, clear?" Forster went on.

"I'm not to open the slit, sir!"

"If you hear anything from inside that room, anything at all, you report using that phone," Forster went on, gesturing at an internal telephone mounted on the wall. "You dial 222 and that gets me and a special squad down here pronto, get it?"

"Yes, sir!" said Barrett, resisting the urge to salute. Forster had that effect on him.

"You've got an eight-hour shift, Barrett. During that time, nobody goes into that room without my personal say so."

"Understood sir," said Barrett.

Christ, he thought, *it's just guarding a friggin' door. How hard can it be?*

Forster looked him up and down and gave a slight grunt.

"You're new to the foundation, son," he said, in a gentler voice. "This is a bigger responsibility than you could possibly realize at the moment. If anything – and I mean anything – strikes you as in any way unusual, make that call. Get it?"

"I get it, chief! I won't let you down."

Forster made another noncommittal noise, then stalked off saying nothing else. For the next three hours, Barrett struggled with a newspaper crossword. Eventually he gave up, re-read the football pages, and then started daydreaming. It was then, when his mind was unfocused, that he felt the hairs on the back of his neck stand on end.

A veteran of tours in Afghanistan and Iraq, he instantly looked both ways, but the corridor was empty. At one end was a blank wall. At the other was a locked security door that could only be opened with a key card plus a numerical code.

No way anybody can be looking at me, he thought.

Yet he still felt the uneasy sensation. His instincts were telling him that he was being scrutinized. He had seen men ignore similar intuition and have their brains or guts blown out by snipers, or their bodies mutilated by IEDs.

But I'm in the heart of London, underground, behind half a dozen layers of top-quality security. I'm not on the front line.

As suddenly as it had appeared, the uneasy sensation vanished. Barrett shrugged, puzzled but not overly concerned, now. *Men get the willies in difficult situations,* he knew that.

No need to get spooked. It's just the mind playing tricks when it's got nothing to do.

Barrett picked up his newspaper and tried the crossword again. Frowning, he chewed the end of his biro as he struggled with the clues for several minutes. Then he stopped, dismayed at the mess he had made of the puzzle.

HELP ME.

He had filled in a six-letter answer with the words, and yet they did not fit the clue at all. He wondered where the phrase had come from. He scanned the rest of the crossword and realized that for the last few minutes he had been putting in a series of blatantly incorrect answers.

PRISONER.

AFRAID.

EXPERIMENT.

Some of his botched 'answers' did not even have the right number of letters.

"Idiot," he said aloud, throwing the newspaper to the floor.

For a moment, he toyed with the idea of calling Forster, then dismissed the notion. He could imagine his boss's reply if Barrett tried to explain that his failure to complete a basic crossword was a strange occurrence. But as he sat staring at the white-painted wall of the corridor, Barrett found it impossible to stop thinking about the weird answers he had put down.

Subconscious, he thought. *The subconscious mind at work. That's the explanation. So why did mine pick those particular words?*

Barrett did not think of himself as particularly bright or imaginative. But as he sat stiffly upright on his uncomfortable chair, fragmentary images surfaced in his mind. They were unpleasant images. Some came from movies, some from news reports, others from books and magazines. But they had a common theme. Innocent people confined in cells. Men in uniform guarding them. Scientists taking out the prisoners to perform cruel experiments.

It was as if his mind was a still pond and someone had taken a stick to stir up all the mud at the bottom. He tried to think of positive things, of his girlfriend, the holiday they planned to take next summer. He was going to ask her to marry him, pick out a ring. But the bleak, terrible thoughts kept swirling up to blot out happy images. And along with the horrific images of torture and misery came questions.

Who is in that cell? What have they done to deserve it? What is going to happen to them?

Barrett had not dared ask Forster the obvious questions. After eight years in the army, he was used to obeying orders without question. But there was no way he was getting paid to guard an empty room. Forster had clearly implied that whoever was in there might kick up a fuss, maybe start shouting or banging on the door. Barrett knew the foundation's activities went into some legal gray areas. But until now, he had not pondered just how questionable its methods might be.

What am I a part of? Am I like one of those men in uniform who just obeyed orders?

No matter how much effort Barrett made to stifle the disturbing thoughts, he could not be free of them. He had to know. Slowly the guard stood up to look at the heavy steel door of the cell. At just below his head height there was the viewing slit. It was about the size of a letter box.

I'm not supposed to look inside. Orders are orders.

"But what if they're bad orders?" he murmured, and reached up to open the slit.

The interior of the cell was dimly lit, but it was possible to make out its occupant. He saw a small figure wearing pajamas, apparently asleep, on a low bed. It was obviously a child. Small bare feet were visible, while long dark hair covered the face. As Barrett watched the child turn over, he saw a girl's face, her eyes were closed. He guessed she was about seven, but it was hard to tell. Now, when she had moved, he noticed that one of her ankles was bound to a steel chain.

"Oh God," he said, stepping back and slamming the slit

shut. "Oh God."

They're keeping a child prisoner, he thought. *Experimenting on a child.*

He felt a surge of anger, righteous indignation at a terrible injustice. No matter what the purpose, he could not let this stand. He thought of his girlfriend, of the children they were talking about having one day. Once more, images of past atrocities flooded his mind.

But how can I help her? I can't even open this door. If I could do that maybe I'd have a chance of getting her out of the building.

The phone rang, making him jump and look around guiltily. It rang twice more before he could focus enough to run over and answer it. It was Forster.

"Were you asleep, lad? What took you so long?"

"Sorry sir," he replied, trying not to mask his confusion. "Just – just taking a walk up and down the corridor, otherwise I get–"

"Never mind," interrupted Forster. "Is everything alright?"

"Yes sir," said Barrett. "All quiet."

"Okay then, listen carefully. In about half an hour I'm coming down to open that door so one of the scientists can access the room. She needs to do some tests. Don't ask why. It's been done before, and there have been no problems. Got it?"

"Yes, chief," said Barrett. "I'll be ready for you."

Chapter 2: Tricks of the Trade

"Okay!" said Zoffany brightly. "This last experiment is a bit way-out, but worth a try."

"No more white noise?" Denny asked. "No more blinkers?"

"No, this is much simpler, I promise," Zoffany replied, gesturing Denny to a low couch in the corner of the laboratory. "It's a form of hypnotic regression. Also, you can have a lie down after lunch."

Oh great, thought Denny. *Because I just love having my mind probed and poked.*

Denny's uncertainty must have showed in her face.

"You don't have to do it," Zoffany said. "I just thought it might help us understand just how much influence the Interlopers can exert over our minds."

Denny nodded, and climbed onto the couch.

"So this is like in the movies?" she asked. "I lie back and you dangle a shiny object in front of my eyes?"

Zoffany gave a full-throated laugh, and Denny felt herself trusting the woman more.

"No, that's a bit old-fashioned," the scientist assured her, as she closed the blinds, then sat by the couch. "All hypnosis really involves is relaxing someone to the point where their subconscious mind can be accessed. It's a lot like daydreaming."

"Okay," murmured Denny, trying to loosen up. "Relax me, doc."

"Think of your good place," suggested Zoffany. "Like a tropical beach. If that isn't too clichéd for you. Some people prefer mountains, or a forest, or–"

"Beach is just fine with me," Denny said, closing her eyes. "Kind of disappointed you won't be dangling a watch, though."

***

"Pleasant lunch?" asked Benson, as Gould entered the chairman's office.

"Very good," Gould replied. "She accepted the Machen

assignment."

"Hmm," said Benson. "You did stress the need to be discreet and not go charging in the way she did at Malpas?"

"I made that very clear," Gould replied, sitting down opposite his boss. "Of course, that might just make her more likely to take risks."

"Speaking of risks," Benson said, "here is a little experiment I thought you would like to see."

Benson operated a remote and the blinds closed, plunging the office into near darkness. At the same time, a large screen lit up, showing a monochrome video feed. Gould recognized it at once as security camera footage of the sub-basement level. In a corridor, a man in a dark uniform was sitting outside a large door.

"Is that – Cell 101?" Gould demanded. "Has something happened?"

"Movement," Benson said. "Our guest finally emerged from her coma, or whatever it was, earlier today."

Gould nodded thoughtfully as Benson flicked to another camera. Inside the cell, the Interloper was sitting up on the bed, staring at the door. Despite knowing that it was a monster that had killed several human beings Gould still felt his stomach lurch. The entity perfectly mimicked the appearance of a child. He had to struggle against his emotions not to see the creature as his long-lost sister.

"What's it doing?" he asked. "What is it staring at?"

"Doctor Zoffany and her team suspect that it is exerting some kind of psychic influence," replied Benson. "But we are not sure how powerful the effect might be. Hence, our decision to put a somewhat naive and impressionable young man on watch outside. He's a new recruit. If I'm right, the drama is about to begin. Ah, yes."

Benson switched views again. Now the security guard was rising from his chair as Forster and a female scientist walked up to him. There was a brief conversation, the guard nodded and took out a Taser, then Forster opened the door.

Things happened very quickly after that. The guard shoved the Taser into Forster's back. Forster jerked, puppet-like, then slumped against the wall. The white-coated woman began to retreat only for the guard to attack her, too. When the scientist was twitching on the floor, the guard bent to remove something from Forster's belt.

"Keys," explained Benson. "He's clearly thought it through. Or had it thought through for him."

"Oh God," said Gould. "He's going to let it out!"

"That does seem to be the plan," Benson said calmly, and switched back to the cell interior. The guard was going through Forster's keys one by one, eventually finding the one that unlocked the shackle on Lucy's ankle.

"You can't let that thing go free in this building!" shouted Gould, trying to control a rising sense of panic. "You know it's a killer!"

Benson gave his thin, humorless smile.

"Calm down, Edward," he said. "You're quite safe here."

***

"Don't hurt me, mister!" pleaded the little girl, seemingly unable to grasp what Barrett was saying.

"It's all right!" the guard insisted, unchaining her. "I'm going to get you out of here. You can go home!"

The girl let him scoop her up and carry her out of the cell. Forster and the scientist were still moaning and twitching from the Taser hits. Barrett walked quickly out of the cell and strode along the corridor.

"Are we going to see my mummy?" asked the girl, her head buried in his shoulder.

"Yes, that's right, poppet," Barrett replied, heading for the elevator. "We'll find your mummy and you'll be fine."

He swiped Forster's ID card on the reader by the elevator. The doors opened and he got inside, putting the girl down.

"What's your name?" he asked. "I'm Noel."

"I'm Lucy," said the girl, looking up at him with huge, unblinking eyes.

"Okay Lucy, we're going to get you out of here," he said firmly.

In the back of Barrett's mind, a small, sane voice was warning him to stop, but he brushed it aside.

I've got to save her. Get her out of here. No matter what the cost.

He took out his telescopic baton, formed a mental picture of the foyer and the quickest way out into the street. Once in public he could always call for help, for the police. The challenge was getting the girl past the guard at the main desk and the other guy at the door. Barrett visualized bursting from the elevator, taking out the first guard with one blow, getting the second before he could respond.

Tight margin, he thought. *But it can be done.*

"Get ready to run out of the big doorway after me, Lucy," he said. "Can you do that? Follow me?"

The girl nodded, stood up. There was a familiar chime as the elevator stopped moving. Barrett moved forward, braced himself, leaning forward with the baton at chest level. The doors slid open.

"Hello, Noel," said a familiar voice. "Taking a little break?"

Davenport, Forster's deputy, was standing just behind a group of four guards in full riot gear. For a moment, Barrett felt something urging him to attack regardless. It was an insanely violent impulse. Then common sense reasserted itself and he slumped, his baton falling to the floor of the elevator.

"That's very sensible," said Davenport, stepping forward.

Something brightly-colored hurtled past Barrett. In the time it took him to realize it was the pajama-clad little girl, she had already fastened herself onto one of the guards. The man yelled in pain and fear as the impact knocked him onto his back. The other guards flinched in obvious surprise, seeming to be moving in slow motion compared to Lucy. Davenport, reacting far more quickly, lunged at the tiny figure with a long, black rod. There was an electric spark as the cattle prod connected.

Lucy jerked, spun round, and detached herself from the guard. Barrett stared at the wounds to the man's face, saw that the little girl had somehow sprouted talons on her hands and bare feet. She seemed taller, now, spindlier, and her face had changed shape. Davenport jabbed at her with his cattle prod a second time, but before it could connect, she had knocked it aside. Snarling, she bounded over the injured guard, heading for the door. But when she reached it, the door was locked.

Barrett gaped as Lucy tore at the handles with her weird claws until two of Davenport's men threw a net over her. She began to tear at the net until Davenport shocked her a few more times, then she lay gasping, curled up like a wounded animal.

"What – what is she?" asked Barrett. "What's going on?"

As he spoke, he felt a cloud lifting from his mind. The influence that had gradually taken him in its grip during his shift was gone.

"Good question," said Davenport. He pointed to a corner of the ceiling. Barrett looked up and saw the security camera.

"Mister Benson's idea of entertainment," Davenport went on. "I think you gave him value for money."

***

Denny was in her good place, imaging a tropical shoreline and waves breaking on white sands. Zoffany's voice came from far away, out of the clear blue sky.

"Now move back in time," the scientist said. "Remember your colleagues at Malpas Abbey."

Denny's imagination conjured up the familiar team that had made a moderately success show about the paranormal. Brie, Matt, Marvin, all appeared, improbably dressed in beach attire – Bermuda shorts, Hawaiian shirts. But they said nothing to Denny, gave no hint of recognition. All of them were dead, slain by Interlopers. Except Frankie, who was missing, presumed alive but not in this world.

As she thought about Frankie's fate, the pleasant vista started to darken. The sea receded, the sky faded to pale gray, and the beach became a grim wilderness. It was the unearthly landscape of the Phantom Dimension.

"I don't want to be here," she muttered, starting to feel alarmed. "This is not my good place anymore."

"Okay, pull back," said Zoffany, soothingly. "Go back to the beach, the sun."

But Denny could not pull away from the grim, alien world. Instead she felt herself carried forward, over the reddish soil, towards the tunnel where she had gone in search of Frankie. She tried to resist, but an irresistible force drew her on. She was underground now, hurtling towards the chamber she remembered all too well. In the dark cavern, she again came face to face with the being that had posed as Lucy, Gould's long-lost sister.

"Hello again, Denny," said the creature, in its high, childish voice. "Thank you for coming to see me."

"No!" Denny shouted, writhing now. She could hear Zoffany's voice, far more distant now, trying to bring her out of the trance. But instead she was drawn closer to the diminutive entity, which reached up and grasped her face. She felt once more the crawling sensation in her mind, black tendrils groping through memories and feelings. She fought against the creeping incursion, lashed out with her mind against the invader.

This is not a memory, Denny thought. *This is happening now.*

"I can bring her back," whispered Lucy. "If you help me."

"... three, two, one!" said Zoffany.

Denny was back in the drab laboratory, the scientist anxious, leaning over her.

"You okay?" Zoffany asked. "I was a bit worried there."

Denny sat up, took the scientist by the arm.

"Lucy is still alive, isn't she?"

Zoffany looked shocked, then embarrassed.

"How – I mean, why do you say that?"

"Because I felt her," Denny replied. "She reached out to me. Made me an offer, in fact."

"You contacted her telepathically?" Zoffany asked, eyes widening. "You're sure?"

Denny nodded solemnly.

"And I'm also sure that you and Gould lied to me about her being dead," she said. "Is there anything else I should know?"

Zoffany looked around, then leaned closer.

"Look, this is strictly between you and me ..." she began.

***

"That was reckless in the extreme!" exclaimed Gould, knowing even as he spoke that Benson might well demote him for insubordination. The chairman had punished underlings who had made far milder criticisms of his methods.

"You're too personally invested in this whole project, Edward," Benson said, apparently unperturbed.

The chairman gestured at the screen, which showed the security team carrying Lucy back to her cell. Barrett was still looking baffled, while Forster and the scientist had recovered from their tasering.

"Now we know," Benson went on. "We had an inkling about the Interloper's mental abilities, but now we can be sure. Prolonged proximity lets them – or at least, some of them – unlock more than our fears and fantasies. They can shape our thoughts, channel our impulses. In this case, it was relatively easy."

"Easy?" Gould erupted. "Turning a professional soldier against his commanding officer–"

"Former soldier," Benson corrected. "And a naïve young man by any standard. He was set to guarding a cell, which implies a prisoner. From that it was relatively simple for the Lucy being to undermine his self-control, triggering what would appear to be distressingly moralistic impulses."

Gould snorted at that, but said nothing.

"Imagine," Benson went on, switching off the video feed, "imagine how effective such a being could be if we could somehow control it."

Gould stared at his boss for a couple of seconds before speaking.

"You can't be serious?" he finally asked in an unsteady voice. "Those things are killers!"

"Precisely!" Benson put in. "And if we can somehow get the upper hand, they could be killers in the service of the right side. Shape-changing, telepathic, able to sway weaker minds – the potential is immense."

There was another brief silence.

"But you don't approve, do you, Edward?" Benson went on. "This has always been more of a personal crusade. Your poor sister, trapped over there, still awaiting rescue? That's a wildly unlikely scenario."

"Not impossible," snapped Gould. "We know humans can survive for extended periods in the PD."

Benson shook his head.

"We have one example of that – not a happy instance. But if you want to cling to hope, Edward, you must do so. Just don't let it influence your decision-making. You may go now."

***

That night Doctor Russell Wakefield followed his usual routine. After making himself a ready meal he ate it in front of the TV. Then he caught up on some electronic 'paperwork' from his medical practice. By the time he had finished it was nearly ten pm. As was usual now, he began to feel nervous anticipation.

Will she come tonight? She doesn't come every night. I wish I knew for sure that she's coming. Did the fact that I examined Isobel Bavistock mean that she will come? I said the things she wanted me to say. Didn't mention any anomalies ...

Marie's visits were irregular, unpredictable. Whenever Wakefield asked if she would come back the next night she would answer 'Maybe! If you're a good boy.' Or something along those lines. He had once accused her of manipulating his emotions, keeping him off balance, playing him. She had laughed, and then asked if he wanted her to stop visiting him. He never made the mistake of accusing her of anything again. Every time he contemplated an end to their nights together, the same thought arose.

To lose her again would kill me.

He washed up the dishes, put away his laptop, and went upstairs to get ready for bed. After cleaning his teeth, Wakefield stood at the bedroom window looking out across the valley. Night had long since fallen, and creatures of the night were moving. He caught a glimpse of a pale shape moving, swooping over the meadow beyond his garden.

Owl. Night predator. Silent killer.

Wakefield tried not to think about the cruelty and violence that dominated the natural world. He had become a doctor to save lives, alleviate suffering, make people happy. And after he and Marie had gotten married, Wakefield had been happy, too. They had spent eight years together. And then a stranger, some maniac the police had still not caught, had killed Marie and left her mutilated body on the edge of Branksholme Woods.

She so enjoyed walking there. I didn't like it, she called me foolish. Went for a hike alone.

Wakefield shuddered at the memories of bleak years that had followed his bereavement. It had been a gray period. He had done what so many medics did and self-prescribed, rapidly taking things to excess. First, he had tried to find a way to sleep, then he had sought drugs to numb the pain of everyday existence. Eventually he had been unable to get through the day without pharmaceutical help. And then everything had changed; the impossible had happened.

"Hello, Russ," Marie had said, on the night she had come back.

She had knocked at his door just before midnight. When he had opened it, she had stepped inside, while he had retreated before her in stunned silence. Her whole manner had been so commonplace, as if she had just been away for a few days at a conference, or visiting relatives. When in fact she had been dead for three years.

"You're dead," he had said, feeling like an idiot as the words came out of his mouth. "I'm imagining this. You can't be real. Oh God."

Marie had followed him into the living the room, smiling, holding out her small, pale hands. Her feet, he saw, were bare and caked with dirt, as if she had walked over miles of open country. Her clothes seemed to be a mish-mash of rags – the sort of stuff people put into charity collection bags. But she was still beautiful, even more beautiful than he remembered, in fact. Her face, her body, the way she moved, her voice, all were perfect.

"You're a ghost," he had stammered, reeling back until he was pressed up against the living room wall. "Or I'm dreaming."

Marie had given a shake of her head and reached out, taken his hand, held it to her. The warmth of that touch changed his entire world. She was flesh and blood, not an illusion. She had come back from the dead. The only love he had ever known had been given back to him. She had led him upstairs and they had made love. And when he had awoken the next day, she had gone. But the muddy footprints on the floor were still there to prove she had walked back into his life. She had taken some of the clothes and shoes he had never been able to throw out. And there had been a note on the pad beside the phone.

Back Soon My Darling – M xxx

The childish, spidery handwriting was nothing like his wife's fine cursive. That had been his first inkling that it could not really be Marie. As her night visits continued, he grew more doubtful, but never dared ask outright. It was partly for fear of losing her, partly for fear of what her answer might be. Then, just a few weeks ago, she had asked him to do something for her, something questionable. And he had done it. He had lied about the children, about their heartbeats, blood pressure, and other things.

But if it isn't Marie, who could it be? She knows so much about me, what I like, what I feel ...

There was a click, the sound of the front door being opened, then closed. She had taken a spare key that first time. He felt his heart race as her footsteps moved along the hall, mounted the stairs. He held his breath for the few moments it took for her to reach the bedroom doorway. Then she was standing before him, impossibly alive once again.

"Marie," he began, moving toward her. "Oh, Marie."

She reached out and put a finger to his lips, began to undo his clothes with her other hand. Every move she made was the right one. In life, after years together, there were times when their lovemaking had seemed routine, stale. Now she pleasured him in every conceivable way, knowing exactly what to do, and when to do it. He allowed her to push him gently back onto the bed. Kisses, playful bites, caresses all did their work.

It can't really be Marie.

Wakefield's treacherous thought formed despite his sensual joy. At the same moment, she stopped moving, reared up, and looked down at him. Her face was blank, devoid of her usual playful half-smile.

"Does it matter?" she asked in a low voice.

"No," he said feebly. "No, not really."

Chapter 3: The Valley of Fear

Two days after her last session with Doctor Zoffany, Denny was on her way to Machen. This involved taking the train from London as far as the small city of Hereford, then on to the Welsh border by rental car. Before she left, she changed her appearance, shedding her on-air look in favor of shorter, darker hair and minimal make-up.

During the long train journey, she tried to focus on the task ahead, despite nagging doubts about the foundation's aims.

Focus, she told herself. *Gotta get a clear idea of what the situation is.*

Denny began by checking the history of the town, and found plenty of facts and figures. Machen's population was less than four hundred at the last census. It relied mainly upon agriculture and tourism. Pictures showed a few streets of attractive stone cottages nestled in a river valley. There was the usual village church, some more modern buildings such as a school and a medical clinic. There was also the Black Swan, which had been able to find her a room, it being October and well out of season.

Bored with general data she switched to more specific matters and typed in 'Machen War Memorial'. This yielded a number of claims on history sites, some contradicting one another. The one point everyone seemed to agree upon was that not a single man from Machen died in the First World War. This was, she realized as she read on, extraordinary. The war had been the most devastating in British history, and war memorials were set up in every city, town, and village after 1918.

Except for Machen, she thought. *Statistical fluke? Like a lottery win?*

One comment stood out.

'Check the church – there is a memorial inside to local men killed in the Second World War.'

She made a note to follow that up, though she could not see any obvious connection to the Interlopers. Then she moved on to the child abduction case. It was only briefly covered in the national and local press. This was because the search had only just gotten underway when the youngsters were found, safe and well.

When Gould's sister vanished, she thought, *there was a much longer delay before the Interloper replacement turned up.*

The three children were aged seven and eight, and had gone missing during a school trip to a place called Branksholme Woods. A picture of the woods made Denny pause, then do a quick internet search. Sure enough, some of the hits showed the area had an odd reputation. One entry in particular made her sit up. It was a paragraph from a nineteenth century travel guide to the West of England.

> *'Gypsies are said to avoid the woods because they fear that their children would be taken by unspecified beings that inhabited it. There seems no basis for this superstition, other than the notorious ignorance of the unlettered Romany.'*

"Prejudiced much, Mister Victorian Writer?" she murmured, searching for more data. "Aha!"

Here was another excerpt from a guide, this one pointing out historic sites. It claimed that, in the 1930s, archaeologists had found 'a pagan altar' in Branksholme Woods. Unfortunately, that was all the entry said. Denny searched in vain for more information on the altar, but was unable to find even a basic description.

"Great," she murmured. "Maybe it's still there, or maybe it's somebody's garden ornament by now."

She made another note.

At Hereford, she picked up her rental, which was a jeep. Denny reasoned that she might have to tackle some country roads. She had practiced with right-hand drive vehicles in the last few weeks, which proved to be a good idea. She had hoped that British roads outside London would be less confusing, but without GPS, she would have gotten lost almost immediately.

Denny arrived at her destination just before dusk. After she crested a gentle ridge, she pulled over to take in the view. Under clouds that threatened rain, the town seemed to huddle in its valley. Branksholme Woods was on the opposite side of the valley, and in the evening sunlight, it was bright with autumn colors.

Looks pretty pleasant now, she thought. *But so did Malpas Abbey.*

A sharp knock jolted her out of her reverie. A man was bent over, looking in through the passenger side window. He was about fifty, with a straggly beard and what looked like farmer's clothes. She toyed with the idea of simply driving off, but then decided not to alienate any of the locals. She lowered the jeep's window.

"Hello!" she said.

"You lost?" asked the man.

"Nope!" said Denny, doing her best to sound perky. "Just taking in the view. Is there a problem?"

The man peered suspiciously at her.

"You an American?" he asked.

"Yeah!" she replied. "Guilty as charged. I'm visiting your quaint little town, taking a little vacation."

"Right," said the stranger, as if vacations were vaguely disreputable. "Well, this is a bad place to stop, like. Some of them come around that corner way too fast. You might get yourself rear-ended."

Denny resisted the urge to make a risqué joke and thanked him for the advice instead.

"I'm Denny Purcell," she said, reaching over to extend her hand.

The stranger did not reciprocate.

"I daresay you are," he growled, and walked away.

Denny put the jeep in gear and drove down into Machen.

"Arrived safely," she said to herself. "Natives not necessarily friendly."

Denny found the Black Swan without incident, parking outside the pleasant, stone-built inn. Inside, a few early evening drinkers were clustered around the bar when she walked in. A pleasant-looking woman in her mid-thirties was tending bar, along with a sullen-looking teenage girl. Denny introduced herself.

"Mel Bavistock," said the woman, shaking hands. "Nice to meet you."

"Mutual," returned Denny. "This place is really lovely!"

"I'll come and help you with your luggage," Mel said. "Get you settled in."

After Denny had been shown to her room they chatted for a while. Denny repeated her cover story – an off-season tourist interested in history and old buildings. She then managed to work the conversation around to Mel's family. Her 'old man' had, Mel explained blithely, decided to 'bugger off to London' rather than stay with her when their daughter was born. Life was hard as a single mother but she wasn't complaining. Mel did not mention Isobel's disappearance and Denny decided to leave the topic alone.

After Mel went back downstairs, Denny unpacked, then stood looking out over the valley. It was a pleasant view, but the looming presence of Branksholme Woods made her slightly uneasy. She took out her laptop and added to her notes. She ended with, 'If I meet one of the children, will I know if they are human? I have to assume I will get some kind of vibe. But how far can I trust my instincts?'

Sighing, she closed the laptop, put on her jacket, and went downstairs.

"Is there anywhere I can get something to eat?" she asked Mel.

"Well," the landlady replied, "I can do you a nice pie and chips, or how about some pasta? And we've got apple crumble for dessert."

"Pasta sounds about right, and maybe I'll try that – is a crumble what we call a cobbler?"

They established that it probably was. As there would be a short wait for the food, Denny decided to take a quick walk and get her bearings. The autumn night air was already chilly as she left the Black Swan and stood for a moment, wondering which way to go.

Downhill and across the river leads to the woods, she

thought. *Uphill leads to the church.*

Denny set off uphill, but had only gotten a few yards when she heard light, fast footsteps coming up behind her. She turned, slightly alarmed, to see a diminutive figure in a huge, ancient overcoat. As the pursuer came closer, she was revealed, by the light of a streetlamp, to be an elderly woman. At the same time, Denny's nostrils wrinkled in distaste.

She sure smells of cat, she thought.

"I knew it!" the woman exclaimed, looking up at Denny. "It's you, isn't it? I saw you getting out of that car and I thought, it's her off the telly!"

Oh crap, Denny thought. *Busted.*

"I think you're confusing me with–" she began, but the woman cut her off.

"You're on that program, America's Wackiest Ghosts!"

"Actually, it's–" Denny retorted, annoyed as always when someone got the show's title wrong. Then she saw the woman's expression and realized she'd fallen into a trap.

"Caught you!" confirmed the old lady. "I may look a bit barmy but I never forget a face. That's one of our favorite shows, I think we've seen all of them."

"Okay," Denny said. "You got me. Guess it'll be all over town by this time tomorrow, right?"

Let's see of the old reverse psychology works.

"Of course not!" said the old lady indignantly. "You're working undercover, aren't you?"

Denny nodded.

"Well, you're in luck," the woman went on. "Mrs. Brenda Molesworth can keep a secret! And I've got your first clue for you!"

Despite her reservations about the woman's state of mind, Denny allowed herself to hope Brenda might have some useful local knowledge. She let the little woman drag her over the road to the open doorway of her cottage. Here the smell of cat urine was even more pungent.

"Erm, Brenda," Denny said, flinching as the odor hit the back of her throat, "can you just tell me what's bothering you?"

"They've all gone!" wailed Brenda. She gestured sadly into her hallway. "All my girls and boys. All gone!"

Denny hesitated, then realized what the woman meant. Despite the stink, she allowed Brenda to usher her into the gloomy hallway, then through into a chaotic living room. Evidence of feline occupation was all around – scratching posts, baskets, a variety of toys. But not a single cat was in sight. The smell was all that remained of Brenda's 'girls and boys'.

"When did they leave?" Denny asked.

Instead of replying, Brenda switched off the light, then went to the window and lifted a net curtain. The old woman jerked her head for Denny to come and look. Denny stooped to peer out at the same angle as Brenda, and found herself looking up at the Black Swan.

A small, pale face was visible at one of the second-floor windows.

"All my cats left me the day she came back from the woods," said Brenda. "That cursed child. Isobel."

***

Snide little bitch, Jack Larkin thought, watching the jeep winding its way into Machen. *Looking down her nose at me.*

After the American woman drove off, Larkin continued along the road until he reached the turn to his cottage. His home lay half-hidden among a clump of old ash trees. It suited his furtive lifestyle. Since he had inherited the place he had worked intermittently as a laborer, but it was common knowledge that he made most of his money from poaching. Depending on the season, people said, you could always go to Old Jack for a pheasant, a rabbit, or a nice juicy salmon.

Tonight, though, as he laid out his gear, Larkin had other, and far bigger, game in mind.

Larkin made himself a sandwich and ate it while the night came down over the Wye Valley. The radio said the rain should hold off until later. He packed a satchel with tools that might come in handy and then – after switching off the light – put on some military surplus night vision goggles. They showed him a monochrome world; ghostly, but detailed enough for him to get about the valley without a torch.

"All right," he said to himself. "A hunting we will go, Jack my lad."

The urge had come upon him unexpectedly, surprising him with its intensity. It had happened a few days' earlier. He had been out taking partridge from the edge of Branksholme Woods. Most locals shunned the woods at night, and a few were wary of it even in daylight. That was all the better from Larkin's point of view. He despised superstition but was happy to reap its benefits.

On that particular night, he had wrung the necks of half a dozen sleeping birds and stuffed them in his sack without seeing another human soul. It was a fair haul and he was thinking about making his way home when he saw her. She was coming up from the clinic, which was also the home of Doctor Wakefield. Larkin had dodged behind some bushes to watch the woman pass by and head into the woods.

Something about the way she moved disturbed him, fascinated him. Roused him. He had followed her, trying not to make too much noise as he crept into the trees. But despite his well-honed skills, he had lost her. One minute her pale shape had been moving a few yards ahead of him. The next, the image had blurred, vanished, leaving no trace of movement. Leaving him frustrated, and angry. As he tramped home with his haul of pheasant corpses, he had resolved to have the woman next time.

It had been many years since Larkin had tried anything with a woman. He had no interest in nonsense like 'relationships'. He knew what he needed, and he had only ever gotten it when the woman struggled, bit, fought. In his younger days, he had become adept at seeking vulnerable prey, targeting those who would not dare speak out, or would not be believed if they did.

Once he had been careless, though, and served a couple of years for assault. That had made him cautious, and over time, his urges had become less pressing. But the sight of the strange woman leaving the doctor's house had made him feel young again. So every night since, he had haunted the place where she had appeared, hoping to have his chance, and rediscover the old, sadistic joy.

Larkin closed his cottage door and set off down towards the river. He would bag a few more birds, then lie in wait near Branksholme Woods until the first light of dawn. It might be another pointless vigil. But for some unaccountable reason, Larkin felt that the American woman was a kind of omen, a sign that change was in the air.

I feel lucky tonight, he thought.

***

Denny arranged to meet Brenda the next day and went back to the Black Swan. When she crossed the road, she looked up at the second-floor window, but there was no sign of the child.

Best not read too much into this, she thought. *But it is weird that a whole bunch of cats would vanish overnight. If that's what happened.*

"Did you have a nice walk?" asked Mel Bavistock when Denny re-entered the bar.

"Yes, very bracing," Denny replied. "I met your neighbor from over the street – Brenda, the cat lady?"

The landlady frowned.

"Oh her! She's gone a bit strange over the years," Mel said. "Living alone with just those moggies for company – not surprising. This table all right for you? The food will be another five minutes."

"It's fine."

Denny let Mel lead her to an alcove by a real log fire and ordered a light beer. When Mel brought it over Denny asked if she knew any experts on local history.

"I'm really into old buildings, monuments – stuff like that," she added.

"Oh, not really my thing," Mel replied, wrinkling her brow in thought. "The vicar might know something, but he's not been here since a very long time. Then there's Doctor Wakefield, his family goes back a long way."

"The town doctor?" Denny asked. "So he's actually from here?"

"Oh yes," Mel said, setting down cutlery and a napkin by

186

the beer glass. "Old Machen family. Trained up in Edinburgh, but came back and took over the clinic."

Mel lowered her voice, leaned a little closer.

"Poor man's had a tragic life," she said. "His wife was murdered a few years back, shocking it was. And they never caught the man who had done it. We were all terrified – I didn't go out after dark for months."

Denny was genuinely surprised. From her research, she knew how rare serious violence was in these little English towns.

"That is terrible," she said. "What happened?"

"All anybody knows is that poor Marie was out walking out on the hills – she liked walking. Terrible state she was in, when they found her."

Mel looked around, lowered her voice even more.

"They had to use a closed coffin," she whispered. Then she straightened up and was back to her old jolly self again. "But let's not dwell, as my mum used to say, 'You're here to enjoy yourself.' And I reckon your supper's ready."

The homemade lasagna proved to be very tasty. As Denny ate, she checked messages, but nothing had come from Gould or anyone else at the Romola Foundation. She sent a simple *'I've arrived safe and sound'* text to Gould, then pondered what Zoffany had told her. She had been turning over in her mind the revelation about Lucy.

If they deceived me about that, what else are they holding back?

Her decision to accept a job with the foundation seemed questionable, to say the least. But the 'Malpas Massacre' had made her just notorious enough to block a return to regular TV work. Also, she wanted to try and rescue Frankie – she owed her friend that much.

No, she concluded for the umpteenth time, *even if there's mutual distrust, Romola is the best of a very limited range of options.*

Later, in her room, Denny had her usual struggle to sleep in a strange bed. In this case, it was a strange bed with a lumpy mattress, and the room was stuffy. The heating was set to maximum, and Denny could not figure out how to turn it down. She made a mental note to ask Mel in the morning and then opened the window before returning to bed.

Denny tossed and turned into the small hours and finally managed to fall into a fitful sleep. She was disturbed by fragmentary dreams of the living and the dead. One particularly convoluted sequence involving Frankie, Lucy, Gould, and the underground temple at Malpas Abbey. Matt, her former lover, appeared, trying and failing to hold in his entrails.

"Sorry babe!" he exclaimed, as if he had made a laughable, minor gaff. "Guess I really screwed the pooch on this one!"

With the twisted logic of dreams, Denny found herself venturing into the Phantom Dimension, but this time did not find Lucy. Instead, she encountered Frankie in the Interloper tunnels. Frankie was trapped in a network of white fibers that grew from the walls. Denny began to hack away the living network, only to feel a tap on her shoulder. She spun around to see Frankie standing behind her.

"I'm the real one," said the newcomer, smiling.

"No," shouted the prisoner. "I'm real, she's an Interloper!"

"You gotta choose one," said the second Frankie.

"There's a test," Denny said. "I know there's a real simple test."

The second Frankie smiled wearily.

"That's a pretty dumb idea. You were fooled last time. You'll get it wrong again."

Then the second Frankie began to change, human features fading away as teeth and talons emerged. Denny turned to free the first Frankie, the one that logic dictated must be her friend. But that one was changing, too, tearing itself free of its bonds with vicious claws. The false friends closed in on her.

The dream ended in a piercing scream. It was impossible to tell if it was human or animal, but to her half-awake mind, it suggested pain and terror in equal parts. Denny sat up, unsure of whether the sound had been in her head or outside. She got up and looked out across the valley. Beyond the streetlights of Machen, the land was dark. If the scream had been real, it was not repeated.

***

Larkin saw the woman making her way up the hill from the clinic and felt an old, powerful stirring. It was as exhilarating as poaching but promised far more satisfaction than mere profit. Through his night-vision goggles, he could clearly make out the woman's athletic stride, her long legs, and the confident demeanor.

I'll look forward to knocking that confidence out of you, darling. Hope you beg. Better not scream, though. Soon put a stop to that.

Larkin stayed in cover at the edge of the woods, watching as the doctor's 'fancy woman' strode past into the undergrowth. He waited until she was almost lost to view before setting off in pursuit. She was fairly quiet, not making the usual racket of a town-dweller at night. But he did not need to hear her to track her. She still showed up clearly, a light patch in the dark vista.

He had been in pursuit for a couple of minutes when she suddenly stopped. Larkin froze, wondering if she was aware of being followed. But if she was wary or afraid, her behavior made little sense. She seemed, so far as he could tell, to be taking off her coat. Larkin could not figure out why she would do such a thing, as the night was cloudless and distinctly chilly.

Unless she's getting ready for a bit more rumpy-pumpy, he thought.

He cursed under his breath. It had never occurred to him that the mystery woman might be going to the woods for another sexual assignation – that she might have another lover besides Wakefield. The idea made him angry because it introduced a complication. He would not risk encountering another man.

The whore, he thought. *Typical small-town trollop. Probably charges 'em for it.*

Larkin waited for the mystery man to appear, but there was no sign of anyone else. And instead of lying down, the woman set off again, walking deeper into the woods. Puzzled, he resumed his pursuit, but after a few seconds, she stopped again. This time, to his bafflement, she took off her shirt and hung it on a low branch. She removed her jeans, and slung them over a bush. Then she turned to look directly at Larkin, and waved.

"Hello, big boy!" she shouted. "Come and get me!"

Larkin's stomach lurched in confusion.

How can she see me? It's impossible in this gloom!

He felt an urge to turn and flee back to his cottage. As if sensing his indecision, she turned her back to him, wiggled her behind, then stuck her hand in the air, showing a middle finger.

"You scared, then?" she called over her shoulder. "What's the matter, old man? No more lead in your pencil?"

Anger welled up again, the fury blotting out all reason. Larkin could not bear a woman laughing at him, mocking him, making him feel weak. He began to crash through the underbrush, all pretense of stealth gone.

"I'll show you who's scared, you little slut," he growled.

She giggled, dodged behind a large tree trunk. Larkin charged on, almost falling over a root. When he rounded the tree, she was nowhere to be seen. Then he saw a pale shape a dozen yards away.

How did she move that fast?

Shrugging off the thought, Larkin resumed the chase. But by now he was feeling his age. His blood was pounding in his ears and his knees seemed liable to give out. Hatred and the deep-rooted need to hurt the woman gave way to physical distress, and he slowed down, then stopped, bent double and started wheezing.

Without turning to look back, the pale figure halted too. Then the woman turned and started to walk back towards him.

"Losing interest, Jack?" she shouted.

Something about her voice seemed strange to him. It seemed thicker, and deeper than before. A sense of unease came over him. This was not the way the drama was supposed to unfold.

No good if they're willing, he thought. *Got to be scared.*

She got closer, and he straightened up, made a fist, preparing to knock her down as soon as she came within reach. As she got closer, the night-vision goggles revealed more of her face, her body. Again, he sensed something wrong. Her limbs seemed thinner and longer than before. Her fingers had grown, and the nails were now several inches long. Her face was much less attractive, too. In fact, she looked hideous, her mouth protruding like a muzzle, her eyes tiny black beads inside deep sockets.

Without thinking, Larkin began to retreat. The woman dropped to all fours and bounded forward. Larkin gave a cry of alarm as she leaped and struck him square on the chest. He fell flat onto his back, lashing out with his fists. None of his blows seemed to have any effect on the monstrous being. Its inhuman face came closer and he saw that the tubular mouth was lined with needle-like teeth.

"What's up, Jack?" it breathed. "Changed your mind halfway through the game? I don't think so!"

"Get off me!" he yelled, trying to shove the nightmarish being away.

"Now you're hurting my feelings!" it replied. "Toying with a girl's affections!"

He felt vicious teeth sink into his flesh and then, with a sudden jerk of her head, she ripped away most of his nose. The pain was unbearable. He gave a gargling scream as blood flooded his mouth.

"Turnabout is fair play," growled the being.

"No!" he moaned. "Let me go!"

The creature laughed.

"Can't do that," it crooned. "You might go and tell tales, get me into trouble."

"I won't! I promise I won't!" he screamed.

The monster shook its head.

"Let's cut to the chase, Jack," it said. "We both know what it is you're really afraid of."

It plunged vicious talons between his legs. There was a ripping sound, an excruciating blast of pain shot through him, and he saw the monster hold up a near-shapeless clump of flesh.

Through the agony, Larkin felt himself grow suddenly cold. Blood loss had become critical. He knew that he was about to die. All his hatred, rage, and lust had long since evaporated, replaced by a basic, desperate desire to live. Then that, too, flickered out like a candle in the night.

Chapter 4: Creatures of Light and Darkness

The next morning, Denny got up and had breakfast at the Black Swan. Her order was taken by Phoebe, the grumpy teen who tended the bar in the evenings. In response to Denny's hearty 'Good morning!' Phoebe managed a grunt and a frown. An attempt to discuss the weather failed and Denny gave up on small talk.

She sent a message to Gould, phrasing it carefully. *'Couple of possible leads,'* she wrote. *'Will check out kids today if possible.'*

Mel emerged from the kitchen with Denny's scrambled eggs. They began to chat while Phoebe sat at another table playing with her phone. It was just after eight when Denny saw Isobel Bavistock clearly for the first time. The little girl, clad in a neat school uniform, emerged from behind the bar as Mel was refreshing Denny's coffee. Isobel had large blue eyes, a spray of freckles across her nose, and very fair hair in bunches.

"Hey, who's this?" Denny asked, making sure to beam at the child.

Isobel just looked blankly at the newcomer, then stared down at her shoes.

"Aw, guess she's shy," Denny said to Mel. "And real cute!"

"Didn't used to be so shy," Mel replied, with a faint smile. "Gone a bit quiet lately, though."

The woman bustled around the bar, putting on her daughter's coat, then scooping up a pink satchel with a unicorn logo.

"I'll just walk her along to school, now," she said to Denny. "Anything you need, just ask Phoebe."

Yeah, right, thought Denny, glancing at the sulky waitress. *No doubt about her being a real person. No Interloper could be that miserable.*

Denny watched as Mel took her daughter outside. She had noticed the small school as she drove into town. It was about fifty yards from the Black Swan. Denny's table was in the bow-fronted window, and as she looked out, children of Isobel's age started going by singly and in groups. None of them were accompanied by adults. Yet Mel Bavistock was clearly unwilling to let her daughter venture out alone for even a few minutes.

When the landlady returned, they chatted some more. Denny talked about the weather and her journey from London before casually working her own – purely imaginary – niece into the conversation.

"Yeah," she said, "my sis worries about her, says she doesn't really make friends, she's too quiet, kind of nervous all the time. I guess she has a point, but sometimes kids just go through quiet phases, don't they?"

Mel gave Denny an appraising look, then shrugged.

"Well, I suppose they're all little individuals," she said, picking up dirty plates. "And Isobel's not as chatty as she used to be. But that's not surprising. She had a bit of a fright a while back."

"Oh, that's too bad," said Denny, putting on her most sympathetic expression.

"It was nothing, really," Mel began, "but at the time we all got a bit worked up about it. I suppose what happened to poor Marie Wakefield was in our minds."

"What happened?" asked Denny. Then, seeing Mel hesitate, she added quickly, "No, I shouldn't ask. None of my beeswax."

The landlady took the plates out to the kitchen, then returned with fresh coffee and an extra cup.

"Phoebe," she said. "Washing up won't do itself, will it?"

The teen stomped out sullenly. When she was out of earshot, Mel sat down at Denny's table.

"You know," she said, "maybe talking to someone from outside Machen would help. There are some things about it all – I don't know. It just seems like …"

Denny was leaning forward, smiling encouragingly, but Mel was no longer looking at her. Instead, the woman was staring out of the window, mouth open. Twisting around, Denny was confronted by two small faces looking in. They were a boy and girl, both ginger-haired, also wearing the now-familiar school uniform. They were gazing straight at Mel, their green eyes unblinking.

"Who are they?" asked Denny.

"They're the Hawkes twins," said Mel hastily, standing up. "Isobel's friends. I'd better be getting on, if there's nothing else you want?"

"No, I'm fine," said Denny. "If you feel like talking later I–"

"I'm all right, really," Mel interrupted, turning away. "I'll be out back if you need me for anything."

Denny stared as the landlady rushed out of the room, then looked back out at the two children. But the twins had already gone. Denny finished her toast in silence, as the cup of coffee Mel had poured for herself grew cold.

***

Gould tried to concentrate on routine work but his thoughts kept returning to the prisoner in the sub-basement. It had been weeks since he had seen the Interloper in the flesh. The thought of encountering it again made his skin crawl. Yet, at the same time, he knew that it might hold the key to easing his own guilt. The guilt he felt at failing to save his little sister from the Interlopers decades earlier.

Eventually he gave in to temptation, closed the file he had been working on, and clicked on the security system icon. As a senior operative, he had access to the various closed-circuit cameras around the installation. However, he found that this did not extend to the one in the special confinement room numbered 101. The number irked him more than it should have.

Benson being pretentious again, he thought. *As if it's all just an intellectual game.*

Gould got up and walked along the corridor to the Security Watch Room, where he found a small team supervised by Forster. Among them was Jim Davison, one of the survivors of the 'Malpas Massacre'. A wall of screens showed various parts of the foundation's complex HQ. A single large screen in the middle of the array was currently showing the atrium.

"I was wondering when you'd show up," said Forster. "Now our guest is awake. Bring up the cell, Jim."

The large screen flickered, and Gould felt his chest tighten as the creature called, Lucy appeared. It was no longer clad in little girl's brightly-colored pajamas, but a white hospital smock. The creature lay on its side, knees drawn up. Shackles were attached to its ankles and wrists. A black metal collar was fastened around its neck and, like the shackles, chained to the cell wall.

"As you can see," Forster said, "it's reverted to its human form. A perfect facsimile of a child. According to Zoffany, you'd have to conduct a fairly detailed examination to determine that it wasn't human. Apparently, there are some inconsistencies in the heartbeat, things like that. Zoffany reckons a brain scan would show more radical differences, but of course that assumes we can get that thing into a scanner."

"If this footage gets out, we'd be in for it," added Davison. "Nobody would believe it's not a little girl. Human trafficking, child abuse, God knows what."

Gould nodded, not trusting himself to speak.

Why did I want to see that thing ... that monster?

"Because you wanted to see her face again," said the prisoner.

"What – what did it say?" Gould stuttered.

Forster and Davison exchanged a significant glance.

"That's the first peep we've had out of it since the escape attempt," the security chief explained. "It obviously knows you're watching."

"I can bring her back," said Lucy, looking straight at the security camera. "How about that, Edward? Would you like your sister back?"

Gould felt the room start to spin and clutched the back of Davison's chair.

"Maybe you shouldn't be here, Ted," said Forster quietly.

The rest of the team was pointedly not looking at Gould. He shook his head.

"I know all about its tricks," he pointed out. "And so do you. They're all deceivers by nature."

"That's not what he's thinking, guys," Lucy said. "But you knew that already, didn't you?"

"I don't suppose we can speak to that thing from here?" Gould asked.

"No, no need for that," Forster replied. "We just have directional mics in the cell."

"Okay," Gould said. "I'll let you get on."

Back in his office, he tried to resume his routine admin work. But the creature's words haunted him. He thought of his failure to save Lucy, the real Lucy, decades ago.

I was just a little boy, he said. *I could hardly fight those things.*

But he still condemned himself for losing her.

After an hour or so, he gave up on work and signed himself out. He needed fresh air in his lungs, oxygen in his brain. Walking in a nearby park, he watched a young woman supervising her small children as they fed the eager ducks some bread. The birds, Gould knew, should not be fed bread. There was even a warning sign right next to the family.

It's bad for the ducks, he thought. *But they crave it, nonetheless.*

He thought of the Interlopers. They clearly craved entry into the human world, a dimension radically different to their own. And it was definitely bad for them, the very laws of nature differing from those in the Phantom Dimension. The Interlopers encountered at Malpas, for all their ferocity, had literally fallen apart after a few hours in this reality. The laws of physics, as humans knew them, acted like some corrosive acid.

So why isn't the Lucy-monster decaying? Gould asked himself. *What is different about that particular one?*

The question had been posed many times before, most notably by Benson and Zoffany. The foundation's experts on biology had struggled to answer it. The tentative hypothesis was that Lucy represented some kind of new, improved model – a super-Interloper. It was an obvious notion, and might well be true. But now a different, if related, idea began to form in the back of Gould's mind. He pondered what it would take for a being to adjust to a different kind of physics. As he continued his slow walk around the duck pond, one possibility occurred to him.

Some kind of shield – but what kind of shield would protect a being against natural laws?

A little girl in fairy wings rushed by, brandishing a plastic wand topped with a tinsel star.

Magic, thought Gould. *Nice, simple answer that solves nothing.*

***

After breakfast, Denny changed into outdoor gear, including some new hiking boots, determined to explore Machen and the surrounding countryside. She had been careful to bring a waterproof coat with substantial pockets. Into these, she put her phone, along with the only weapon she had, which was a small can of cheap hairspray. Tasers and police-style pepper spray, she had been informed, were as illegal as guns for civilians.

What had been a fine morning had become overcast and blustery, with the threat of rain later. Her first destination was St David's Church at the end of the main street. Her route took her past the school. As she came abreast of the school gates, a bell rang and children flooded out into the yard. Despite the cold, damp weather, they began to play games and simply race around with childish energy.

Same in any country, she thought, smiling.

Then she noticed that three children were not moving, just standing in the corner of the yard. As she grew nearer, she saw that the three were Isobel Bavistock, and the Hawkes twins. They were looking straight at her with blank, unblinking expressions. She then became aware of something else. Although the schoolyard was full of little kids burning off surplus energy, none of the others came too close to the silent, unmoving trio.

Could be imagining it, she thought. Then she saw a young woman looking across the yard at her from the school's main doorway. A teacher had spotted a stranger paying attention to the kids. Denny resumed her walk to the church.

When she got there, the building itself seemed unremarkable. She had seen dozens like it on her drive from Hereford. She went inside to check out the internet commentator's claims about a war memorial. Inside she found some leaflets, but none mentioned military matters. She began to scrutinize the walls, searching for some kind of plaque.

Sure enough, she found one, listing casualties from World War Two. She snapped a picture with her phone, then decided to examine the rest of the interior for anything out of the ordinary. She soon concluded that St David's was a remarkably dull edifice and was about to leave when the vicar appeared. He introduced himself as the Reverend Samuel Arkwright.

"I'm Denny," she said carefully. "Over here getting a dose of good old English culture."

"Well, that's very heartening," said Arkwright, who was a plump thirty-something with a receding hairline. "An American visiting after the tourist season's over, braving the English weather. Perhaps our fame is spreading?"

"I guess so," she said. "One of the things that attracted me to Machen is folklore, myths and legends, all that quaint stuff you get in the Welsh borders. Do you have anything along those lines here?"

"Along those lines?" queried the priest, raising an eyebrow. "I doubt it, not really my area. Although—"

Arkwright paused and looked past Denny. She followed his gaze to a featureless, whitewashed wall.

"There was a mural painted there," the priest explained, indicating the wall. "Way back in the Seventies someone uncovered it during a refurbishment. They covered it up again almost at once. But it was quite something, by all accounts."

Denny peered at the wall. She thought she could just make out shapes, a few dark patterns beneath the faded white.

"I guess it was some kind of religious picture?" she asked, hoping the opposite was true.

"Opinions vary," Arkwright said. "But I know my predecessor was very keen for it to be covered. He painted over it himself, much to the chagrin of the archaeologists who wanted to study it. Quite a row at the time, I believe."

"Any photographs?" Denny asked.

The priest shrugged.

"I don't know. I've certainly not seen one."

Denny thanked him and left, pausing in the church porch to make a note.

Mural – Seventies. Find pic?

In the churchyard, she paused, scanning the townscape, seeing nothing especially interesting. Raising her eyes, she looked across the river at Branksholme Woods. The gray clouds cleared for a moment and a ray of sunshine reached down, bringing out the reds and golds of autumn leaves. The small woods looked far from menacing. But from her experience at Malpas Abbey, she knew that appearances were often deceiving.

Might as well get it over with, she thought. *At least I'll get some fresh air and exercise.*

Denny set off at a good pace, taking a few pictures along the way, and trying to convey the impression that she was just another tourist. Locals smiled and said 'Good morning!' as she passed, a novel experience for someone who had spent the last few weeks in London. She began to feel more optimistic about her assignment. Even if she went back to the Romola Foundation having drawn a blank, she had at least seen a beautiful, easygoing corner of England.

She had just set off up a winding path to the woods when she became aware of the sirens. Looking back at Machen, Denny saw flashing blue lights. A car and a van with police markings were winding their way through the narrow streets. She stood watching as the vehicles slowed to cross the hump-backed bridge, then stopped at the bottom of the track. Dark-uniformed figures climbed out and began to ascend the hillside.

Denny felt conflicted. Her instincts told her to get as close as possible to the scene of the incident – whatever it was. But she also knew it would be unwise to draw the attention of the police again in so short a time.

Mysterious deaths happen when I'm around, she thought. *Not a good look in the eyes of the law.*

She decided to play it by ear, standing just off the path as a group of police officers climbed the hill. One man in plain clothes glanced at Denny, but did not show any sign of recognition. Emboldened by this, she decided to continue her innocent tourist routine.

"Excuse me?" she said. "Are the woods closed off or

something?"

A young constable stopped.

"Sorry, Miss, but we're going to cordon off a large area, so no point in going up."

"Oh, right," she said, not having to feign disappointment. "Has there been an accident?"

"I can't comment on that, sorry," the policeman replied, and followed his colleagues up the hill.

Denny suppressed an impulse to follow them and set off back toward the town. A car marked with a caduceus symbol was now parked next to the police vehicles. A middle-aged man was just closing the door. The bag he was carrying jogged Denny's memory. She had seen similar bags before, at crime scenes in the US.

"Doctor Wakefield?" she asked, as soon as he was close enough to hear.

The man stopped, appeared surprised, and slightly annoyed.

"Yes?" he said. "And you are?"

"Sorry," Denny said. "It's just someone mentioned you to me as an authority on local folklore. I wonder–"

"This is hardly the time or the place," he said brusquely, and walked past her.

Fair point, she thought. *But now I know who you are.*

Denny walked back into town, passing a group of people walking the other way. She realized that they were on their way to form the obligatory crowd of rubberneckers standing behind a police cordon. Discreetly, she dawdled by the bridge, taking pictures of the river with her phone, and trying to glean some information.

"They say it's old Jack Larkin," observed one man.

"What's left of him," said an elderly woman, with relish. "Torn up, something awful, just like poor Mrs. Wakefield was."

The small crowd moved on, and Denny stood looking up at Branksholme Woods.

Could be a coincidence, she thought. *But how likely is that?*

She thought back to the horrific violence that had occurred at Malpas Abbey. That had been weeks before the disappearance of the local children, of course. Then a thought struck her. It was so obvious she swore under her breath, cursing herself for being so stupid. She knew from personal experience that the Interlopers, in their own parallel reality, experienced time differently from human beings. A few minutes there amounted to several hours in this world.

So, from the perspective of the Phantom Dimension, the children from Machen had vanished almost immediately after the events at Malpas.

***

The senior police officer raised a hand to stop Wakefield. The doctor stopped at the police cordon, which sealed off the eastern edge of Branksholme Woods.

"You don't have to do this, Russell," said the detective. "We can get another medical examiner to deal with it."

"That's ridiculous," responded Wakefield. "I'm right here, now. Why bother somebody in Hereford or Taunton?"

"It's a bit ..." the officer hesitated. "I think it might be a bit difficult for you, given what happened to ..."

Again, the detective hesitated, not meeting the doctor's eye. Then he took a breath. "Given what happened to Marie, I mean," he said quickly.

Oh God, Wakefield thought. *I know what it is. What the body will be like. The injuries. The mutilations.*

"We're both professionals," Wakefield said evenly. "If you can cope with it, so can I."

The officer looked levelly at the doctor for the first time, then nodded, and led him into the woods. Neither man said anything during the couple of minutes it took them to reach the scene. A photographer was taking pictures from various angles. It was a familiar sight to Wakefield. But the victim was startling, horrifying even.

"Couple of my blokes had to throw up," the detective said. "Glad I just had toast and coffee this morning."

"There's no doubt about the identity?" Wakefield asked, trying to sound professional.

"Jack Larkin," the officer confirmed. "His wallet was still

in his pocket. No sign of attempted robbery. In fact, he looks like he fell into some kind of agricultural machinery, but–"

"But that's not easy to do in the middle of a small forest," completed Wakefield.

The doctor knelt beside the body – or what was left of it. He took out a small mp3 recorder and started to make notes. It was an automatic process born of years of experience in forensics. He spoke the words – laceration, castration, viscera – while struggling with memories of Marie.

No, he thought. *The two Maries. The real one who died like this, and the false one who came to replace her.*

"I know it's tricky," the detective said carefully. "But could you give us a rough idea of the time of death?"

Wakefield recalled the time that the false Marie had left his bed. Then he calculated how long it would have taken her to climb the side of the valley, reach the woods. All the while, he was pretending to take temperatures, test degrees of rigor, and follow usual procedure.

I'm assuming she moved no faster than a real person could, of course. They say the dead travel fast. If only she was a ghost ...

"I'd say between four and five this morning," he said, standing up. "No later than five thirty."

The detective looked slightly surprised.

"You're not normally so sure after a first glance," he pointed out. "What's different about this one?"

Wakefield shrugged, started to pack away his forensic kit.

"Sometimes you can just tell."

Nobody had mentioned Marie. Wakefield stood up, paused, waited for the detective to say something about the two killings. Wakefield had not examined his wife's body. It was against official procedure. But he had called in a favor and seen the county medical examiner's final report.

Same killer, he thought. *Same slash wounds, punctures. Great strength. Doubt as to the sort of implement used. Nobody mentioned claws then. Probably won't now.*

He was about to go when a thought occurred to him.

"Will the woods be closed off?" he asked.

The detective looked puzzled, glanced around at the

brightly-colored markers, the taped cordon.

"No, I mean after today?" Wakefield persisted. Hearing himself he thought, *God I sound demented.*

"We haven't got the resources," the detective replied slowly. "You know that. We have to get it all done before dark."

"Then you'll pack up, right," Wakefield said, trying to sound casual, shaking the detective's hand. "Well, if there's anything – you know."

She will be free to come again, he thought, as he made his way out of the woods and into the weak morning sunlight. His heart surged at the thought of her, the feel of her body, her eyes looking into his, her moans, little gasps. He disgusted himself. A line of verse occurred to him. He could not recall if it was from a poem, or the Bible.

After such knowledge, what forgiveness?

Wakefield walked down to his car, making plans for the evening.

Chapter 5: Dead Man's Diary

After Wakefield's rebuff, Denny wandered back into the center of Machen. The town had woken up and the small main street was busy. She asked someone if they knew the way to the Copper Kettle, and was directed up a side street. The small teashop was already half-full of people she assumed were tourists. She took a seat, checked the menu, and ordered a pot of tea along with something called an Eccles cake, simply to discover what it might be.

While she waited for the tea to materialize, she took out her cell and looked up 'Church of St David, Machen, mural'. The search results startled her. Among the words associated with the mural were 'Satanic', 'un-Christian', 'bizarre', 'pagan'. She spent several minutes exploring history and folklore sites.

Eventually she found a picture of the mural, but it was a small, grainy black and white photo. Enlarging it merely lost almost all the detail. It seemed to show a vaguely-defined black mass to the left of the scene, and a group of people on the right. Something was going on in the middle of the picture. Oddly angular figures were crouching over something on the ground. It was easy to imagine them as Interlopers, but Denny was aware of the hazards of wishful thinking.

She decided to send the link to Gould along with the message: '*Any higher quality pics of this?*'

Her tea arrived. An Eccles cake turned out not to be a cake, but a flaky pastry shell containing currants in a kind of syrup. Denny was taking a picture of her half-eaten 'cake' when Brenda turned up. A few heads turned when the old lady came in, but when she reached Denny's table there was no distinctive wave of feline odor. Brenda had also dressed in new, reasonably well-matching clothes.

"Thought I'd dress up nicely," Brenda said, putting a large shopping bag on the floor as she sat down opposite Denny. "I don't socialize much – and don't pretend to be surprised by that, dear."

"Have the cats come back?" Denny asked, keen to change the subject.

Brenda shook her head sadly. She leaned forward and

lowered her voice, as if imparting a secret.

"I dread to think how they're faring on their own."

"Cats are pretty resourceful," Denny pointed out. She started to tell an anecdote about one of her mother's cats, which had grown fat by scrounging meals from neighbors.

"We thought he was missing," she concluded. "But all the time he was being pampered by half the families on the street!"

"You're a very kind girl, trying to reassure me and all," Brenda said. "But I'm not here to talk about my missing babies. There's a mystery about those children, and I want to help you solve it."

Great, thought Denny. *My Doctor Watson is the town's Mad Cat Lady.*

"I know what you're thinking dear," Brenda went on. "I'm not going to follow you around getting in the way. I just wanted to help point you in the right direction."

Denny braced herself for a rambling anecdote or a wild theory. But instead, the old lady reached down, to the bag by her seat.

"These were my great, grand-uncle's," explained Brenda, producing a battered cardboard box. "Lord of the manor, he was. Hard to believe, I know, looking at me now."

"Okay," said Denny warily. "Family heirlooms?"

"Valuable for your research," Brenda went on, nodding and smiling.

She opened the box to reveal an assortment of items. There was a smaller box, covered in faded red leather. Brenda took it out and opened it, showing the contents proudly to Denny. There were three medals, metal crosses with faded colored ribbons.

"These are from the First World War, I'm guessing?" Denny asked.

Brenda nodded.

"Major Reginald Pelham, Third Herefordshire Infantry," she explained. "His Campaign medal, and the Distinguished Service Order, and the George Cross."

"He must have been a brave soldier," Denny opined, gingerly examining the medals. She had no idea how significant the British decorations were. But they looked impressive. They reminded Denny of her grandfather's Vietnam medals. And, inevitably, of the old man's bitterness at the way he had been treated when he came home.

Brenda nodded, satisfied at Denny's response. She closed the little box and placed it in the bigger one.

"Oh, yes," she said. "He was courageous, nobody ever doubted that. Not sure if he was entirely wise, though."

She picked up a dog-eared book with a worn black cover. It looked to Denny like a small pocket diary, a view confirmed when Brenda handed it to her.

"This is his war diary?" she asked.

"Yes, I think it might help," Brenda said. "It tells a story that's hard to believe, but it makes sense. Someone like you, who's seen the paranormal at work, might find it more credible than regular historians."

There was something else in the box, an object that seemed out of place. Brenda saw Denny looking and picked up what looked like a crude pendant. A purple stone was suspended on a length of blackened hide.

"This is for you, too," said Brenda. "I've never felt comfortable with it in the house."

"What is it?" Denny asked, weighing the stone in her palm. It seemed oddly light, and she vaguely wondered if it might be hollow.

"A talisman," Brenda replied. "That's one word for it."

The woman reached over and put her hand on Denny's.

"Don't put it on!" she warned. "You can never trust any of their gifts."

Amen to that, Denny thought, *if we're talking about the same kind of folks.*

"What is it?" she asked.

"Read Pelham's diary," Brenda said quietly. "But not here in public. Let's just have our tea."

***

Gould was summoned back from the park by a message from his boss. He knew that Benson would be aware of the incident with Lucy. He expected to be reprimanded for interacting with the captive without permission. But he found that quite another matter was occupying the foundation's chief.

"Ms. Purcell's report intrigued me," said Benson, gesturing Gould to take a seat. "Much more successful than I had expected. You were right to recommend her."

Forster was already in the chairman's office. The security chief and Gould exchanged brief nods.

"It seemed fairly routine to me," Gould responded. "She arrived, she checked the place out, she observed the children."

Benson gestured at the large screen on the wall. The blinds of the office were already closing. The screen came to life, showing a single image. Forster gave a low whistle.

"Quite," observed Benson, drily.

"But this is ..." Gould began, still trying to process what he was seeing.

The picture was a color photograph of a wall painting. Gould recognized the mural that Denny had linked to in her email of that morning. But this picture was much more detailed. The dark mass on the left was now clearly a crude likeness of a forest – evidently Branksholme Woods. On the right were a crowd of medieval folk. A priest and a woman in a hooded robe stood slightly apart from the group. They were holding what seemed to be jeweled pendants. In the middle of the scene, three oddly-proportioned figures stood over a swaddled infant lying on the ground.

"The earliest known representation of the Interlopers, I believe," Benson remarked. "Proof that they were present in Machen about six or seven hundred years ago. And that this Covenant referred to was of very long standing."

"Children," said Gould.

"Is this child a sacrifice?" asked Forster. "Maybe a protection racket?"

Benson shook his head.

"Note the items given to the priest and that woman, who I assume was the local witch. Two different traditions working together in rather special circumstances."

Forster leaned forward, squinting at the screen.

"Are those jewels or something? Precious stones?"

Benson turned off the screen, leaned back in his chair.

"That is what I want to find out. And that means providing Ms. Purcell with some backup. No–" Benson held up a hand as Gould began to speak. "I think you're a little too close to the issue. Forster, send Davison down. Have him pose as a tourist, make it clear to her that he has the final say on any radical steps she might contemplate."

"Understood," said Forster. "He'll be on his way in a couple of hours. Should he take any special gear?"

Benson waved an elegant hand.

"I think we can leave it up to him," he replied. "Thank you."

Forster got up and left in silence, carefully not looking at Gould as he passed the latter's chair. After the office door closed, Benson remained silent as seconds passed, gazing at his hands folded before him on the desktop.

"I know this is designed to throw me off balance," Gould said, eventually. "It's a very obvious ploy."

"But knowing it is a ploy does not stop it from working," murmured Benson, finally looking at his subordinate. "Which is my point with regards to our guest downstairs. If it were to plant certain ideas in your mind, you would be suspicious. But if they were attractive enough you might still act upon them."

Gould bridled at the imputation.

"You think that monster could influence my mind?" he said. "After all I've seen, everything I've been through?"

Benson gazed at Gould, his eyes half-closed, his mouth twisted up in his familiar humorless smile.

"It could influence anyone's mind," he said. "Think of Barrett, that hapless raw recruit. It took Lucy less than an hour to radically subvert his sense of duty, not to mention his basic commonsense."

"I'm not some young lad just out of the army," retorted Gould.

"True," said Benson. "You are a veteran field operative and a remarkable theorist. But it knows you. Has been close to you."

Gould stood up, feeling slightly absurd, knowing that

storming out of the office would merely make his situation worse.

"What's this leading up to, Benson?" he snapped. "Am I on gardening leave from now on, or what?"

Benson shook his head.

"Check your emails," he said. "I have an interesting case for you to look into. It's up in the Lake District, not far from Carlisle. People have been seeing strange creatures in the hills. Could be significant."

"Let me guess – you're sending me a few hundred miles out of the way to look at some internet rumors," stated Gould, flatly. "Is Siberia fully booked?"

Benson sighed, folded his hands on the desk in front of him, looked down at his interwoven fingers.

"You can choose not to go," he said. "But that would be unfortunate for your prospects here."

**

Denny decided to read the war diary back in her room at the Black Swan. She returned to the inn to find Phoebe, the grumpy teen, serving a handful of pre-lunchtime drinkers. Mel was nowhere in sight. Eyes followed Denny as she passed through the bar and mounted the stairs to her room. She made a point of smiling at the stone-faced British boozers. Then she waved and gave a cheerful 'Hi!' She knew it confused them.

Pelham's handwriting was not very good, and varied in quality – dependent, Denny thought, *on the kind of pressure he was under.* Early entries dealt with basic training in 1914-15, and she found herself skimming these. Eventually, though, Pelham was sent to the front line in Belgium, where he joined the British Expeditionary Force.

Denny soon learned that trench warfare consisted mostly of long periods of boredom and occasional flare-ups of vicious fighting. The diary began to seem repetitive again after Pelham got used to the routine. He hated the food, he had lice, there were rats in the trenches. Occasional bright spots included periods of rest behind the lines. Skimming some more she almost missed the first reference to something unusual.

April 4th 1916

My unease about the Covenant has never quite gone away. All through basic training, I wore the talisman delivered by Ma Wakefield. Many times, I took it off, looked at it, and thought about discarding it. But I could never bring myself to get rid of the thing.

I still cannot quite believe what happened on that night. No one mentioned it again – not one of the men from the town who joined the army when I did. I think we all pushed the memory to the backs of our minds. But then things started happening that were not easy to explain. I began to hear mutterings about so-called Jonahs in the regiment – men it was unlucky to be around. Invariably the 'Jonah', if identified, would be a man from Machen.

Soldiers are superstitious folk, of course. It is easy to discount rumors of this sort. But yesterday something happened that I cannot easily dismiss. It was just after dawn and we were making the best of a cold breakfast in the forward trench when the sound of artillery broke out on our flank. The Germans were bombarding a position to the south.

We immediately took cover as best we could, knowing that the enemy might well extend his barrage to us. Sure enough, small stuff – mostly light field guns – opened up on us just after eight. Then something landed in the trench a couple of yards away. It splashed down into a couple of inches of filthy water, an anticlimactic sound. But I could see that it was a heavy mortar round, and that it would probably kill everyone in my unit if it went off.

Without thinking, I hurled myself into the puddle, covering the bomb with my body. I closed my eyes, feeling sure that I was about to meet my Maker. I remember thinking that I wanted to die instantly, blown cleanly to atoms, rather than feel my guts blown out. A second passed, then another, and I was still alive, still conscious. The sound of the artillery bombardment continued. I heard my company sergeant swear profusely.

I opened my eyes, then gradually got to my hands and knees. Underneath me, the mortar bomb looked unremarkable, a dull-colored cylinder with a few letters and numbers stenciled on the end. I stood up carefully and retreated around a corner of the trench, where the rest of my men were huddled.

"It's a bleedin' dud," the sergeant exclaimed.

"Jesus Christ, what a lucky bastard," muttered another man.

"Well done, sir," said a third.

Today, I learned that the colonel, having heard about what I did, has recommended me for some kind of medal. Perhaps I deserve one. But even if I receive it, I don't think I will feel especially proud. Because what happened after I got up and walked away led to more rumors, sidelong glances, doubts.

The sergeant delegated two young privates to go and clear the 'dud' from the trench. It's always a ticklish business, handling faulty ordnance, but I was looking on and I saw them do nothing wrong. No, it was clear enough what happened. The first man was just about to crouch down next to the bomb when it went off. He was killed instantly. His comrade was behind him, partially screened from the blast. He lived long enough to be taken back to the field hospital. From what I saw, he lost his eyes, much of his face. I am ashamed to think it, but it might be more merciful if gangrene sets in and he dies rather than live like that.

After the wounded man had been evacuated, the men started talking about what might have caused the explosion. Some were naturally inclined to set it down to sheer bad luck. A faulty fuse,

*something nobody could take
account of. But others looked
furtively at me and passed
comments when I was out of
earshot. I asked the sergeant what
was being said, and he seemed
uncomfortable.*

*"Just a lot of daft talk, sir," he
insisted. "Nothing to worry about."*

*I wish I could believe that. But
I think the damage is done, now. I
am a 'Jonah' from Machen, too. I
fear that the trust that forged
between me and the men under my
command over so many months
has begun to unravel.*

What the hell is the Covenant? she wondered. The word
was vaguely familiar.
She looked it up and found that it did not, as she had
suspected, have anything to do with the paranormal. Or at
least, not directly. It was an old-time term for a binding
agreement. But the reference to 'Ma Wakefield' made her
wonder about witchcraft. She varied her search terms and
found one image of the Devil making a 'Solemn League and
Covenant' with a witch. Denny made a note of this and went
back to Pelham's diary.

April 9th 1916

*First thing this morning the cry
went up.*

"Gas! It's gas, boys!"

*A cloud of oily, greenish-
yellow vapor drifted in from No
Man's Land. It had been released
from the German front line
trenches and carried our way by
the prevailing wind. Despite the*

alert being sounded promptly,
some of the men were slow to put
on their gas capes and respirators.
One, a seventeen-year-old called
Priestley, started panicking. It
turned out that his respirator was
faulty and gas had leaked in
through the filter. A corporal did
the sensible thing, ran along the
trench – despite a hail of enemy
fire – to the forward supply depot
to get a spare. Priestley had lost
his reason by this point. He tore off
his mask, and in his terror, began
inhaling great lungfuls of poison.

I took off my respirator and
put it on Priestley. Part of me
knew this was madness, that the
gas would kill me or at least leave
me blind, or crippled. As soon as I
removed the mask, the sting of
chlorine made me start to retch.
Yet another part of my mind was
telling me to test the talisman, to
see how far I could push this
supposed good fortune that the
Covenant brings. Perhaps a part
of me also wanted to show the men
that I was like them, an ordinary
mortal.

In a matter of moments, I had
collapsed and was heaving,
bringing up the morning's
porridge and eggs. My eyes
streamed, it felt as if my throat
was on fire. I must have lost
consciousness for a moment,
because the next thing I knew,
spring sunshine was falling across

the trench. The attack was over, all trace of the gas vanished like morning mist. Faces looked down at me.

"He's all right," said one, and the man offered me a hand to get up.

I thanked him, of course. But the tone of his voice, the expression on his face, spoke volumes. He and the others were full of doubt and suspicion. How could their captain have survived unscathed without a gas mask? I ask myself the same question as I write this. I have a sore throat. My eyes are slightly reddened. But my breathing is unimpaired

Could the enemy have blundered in some way? Was the gas less effective than normal? No. After all that I have seen since coming to the front, I have no doubts concerning the efficiency of German industry. The explanation for my good fortune, I am sure, lies back in Machen, or more precisely in Branksholme Woods.

Now, when I close my eyes at night and try to sleep, I see those creatures taking the child. My life, the lives of all my fellow townsmen, for one innocent.

It was a bad bargain.

June 8th, 1917

So many months during which nothing strange occurred –I had almost persuaded myself that the so-called Covenant was indeed nonsense. But after the events of last night, I can never deceive myself again.

Three of us were on guard in a forward trench. Myself, Sergeant Paterson, and Private Welch were, as usual, rationing out our supply of cigarettes. As the officer, it always behooves me to share my 'cigs', as they call them. It was just after midnight when I felt the usual craving, took out my cigarette case, and offered it round. The usual muttered thanks was followed by the flare of a match – the sergeant lit his own cigarette, then offered to light mine.

I had just inhaled the first blessed lungful of tobacco when I saw that Paterson had not nipped out the match, but was lighting Welch's cigarette too. Welch, a new recruit fresh from training, could have had no idea what Paterson was doing wrong. How such an experience NCO could have made the error I do not know. It's a fundamental rule – lighting the first cigarette alerts Jerry to your position. Second cigarette, time to take aim. Lighting the third cigarette means the sniper is squeezing the trigger.

I think I shouted something, an incoherent warning, but it was too late. A tremendous blow struck me on the left side of my chest, just above the heart. I fell backwards, certain that I was mortally wounded. But instead, I simply lay in the dried mud, feeling a throbbing ache spread across my upper torso. It was Paterson who fell, forwards across me. I felt a gush of hot liquid soaking my uniform. He had been hit squarely in the throat. The burning match fell from his hand, guttered, went on.

Welch was frozen in shock, so I had to heave the sergeant's body off myself. I assumed that two shots had been fired, and that one had somehow grazed me, while the second had killed Paterson. Then I remembered my cigarette case in my jacket's breast pocket. I took it out, and while I could not see it, I could feel the dent the sniper's bullet had made. It had ricocheted off and killed Paterson.

The talisman had done its job again.

November 11th 1918

Well, it's over. The rumors were true – an Armistice has been signed with the Germans, and the Kaiser has gone into exile. It was my task to convey the news to the men this afternoon. They managed a faint cheer, but I could see that they were exhausted. Perhaps, also, they were skeptical,

unwilling to believe any good
news after enduring so many
years of suffering.
No word yet of when we will
be going home. There is talk of an
occupation army for Germany, of
peace talks that will last for
months. So, I cannot take it off.
Though all reason dictates that
this trivial pendant cannot shape
my fate, I will not remove it until I
am sure that I will return home.

Denny turned a few more pages, but Pelham did not mention the talisman again. Instead, he wrote about the gradual demobilization of the British army, of precious letters from home. Then, on December 24th, he wrote,

Christmas Eve, my fourth in
the king's uniform. I am so far
from home in a foreign land. The
talisman feels heavy around my
neck, now. Since the fighting is
over, I feel I should take it off.
What can happen to me now? I
will take it off. I must take it off.

The last sentence was underlined, the pencil pressing so hard that it had gone through the thin paper.

Denny felt a sense of trepidation as she turned more pages. At first, it seemed that Pelham would make it home to his family. But then she found a reference to 'some kind of outbreak'. More remarks about 'influenza' spreading among the soldiers of all nations. Then Pelham simply stopped writing, in the middle of an entry.

It took her a few moments to find the correct historical data. In 1918 the so-called Spanish Flu had killed more people than all those who had died in the Great War. She looked up Sir Reginald Pelham and confirmed that he was one of the victims. His wife and young children had also died in the epidemic, 'extinguishing the ancestral line', as the internet history site put it.

Denny put the diary back in the box and picked up the pendant again. She thought of the story, 'The Monkey's Paw.' So many cautionary tales contained the idea that wishes granted merely led to disaster. And yet Pelham did not strike her as a foolish, gullible man falling prey to superstition. She flipped back and forth through the diary, trying to find out more about the mysterious 'Covenant', but gave up after a few minutes. She would have to read the entire book to make sure.

Perhaps more importantly, though, was the reference to Ma Wakefield. She tried to determine if this woman might be an ancestor of Doctor Wakefield, but this time the internet let her down. British records of births, marriages, and deaths were hard to figure out. What's more, some old paper files had been lost – to fires, floods, wartime air raids.

Denny's phone chimed. She checked it to find an email from Gould. Opening it, she gasped at the color photo of the church mural. Clearly, there had been a long-standing tradition in Machen, the mysterious 'Covenant' going back into medieval times. She remembered Gould's theory that once the Interlopers had existed in something like harmony with primitive humans. Things the false Lucy had said during its attempt to kill Denny supported this idea, that an old agreement had broken down.

She thought of the list of World War Two dead in the church. Evidently, no paranormal protection had been offered to Machen's menfolk in 1939.

Why would that be?

"Because nobody knew how to ask for it, dumb-ass," she said aloud.

The more Denny thought about it, the more sense it made.

After 1918, the world had been in chaos, what with revolutions, technological change, the Wall Street Crash and its aftermath. Denny was no expert, but she recalled enough history to know that small farming communities in the US had suffered badly between the wars. A little Googling showed that a similar crisis had hit British farming. A town like Machen would have been badly disrupted.

If anyone was still alive who remembered the old ways when another war came, they were obviously in no position to revive them. The war and the flu epidemic, plus general social upheaval, had ended the sinister tradition. The Covenant had simply been forgotten, lost with so many other, more innocent folk customs.

And now they're back, she thought. *Replacing children, killing adults. No mention of any Covenant. No communication. But why?*

***

After Gould left, Benson turned on the monitor again. Lucy was apparently asleep, curled up on its small, Spartan bed. But a few moments after Benson began watching, the creature opened its eyes and looked up at the camera. Benson grew tense, leaned forward. He imagined his mind reaching down into the sub-basement, tendrils of thought penetrating Room 101.

Can you hear me?

Lucy nodded, face serious.

What do you really want?

Lucy smiled at that.

"Everything," she said. "We want your world."

Benson frowned, focused his thoughts again.

Why?

"Because ours is nearly finished, you silly man."

What is happening to your world?

"Collapsing, dying, failing."

But how can you survive in this world? It is too alien, too hazardous.

The false child's smile faded. She turned away from the camera, stared at the cell door. Then she curled up again, facing the wall.

Benson sent the question again, repeating the demand for information for several minutes. Then he gave up and simply watched the creature, wondering if it really had gone to sleep.

"If you won't tell us," he said finally, "we'll just have to find out for ourselves."

Turning off the security feed, he brought up the latest report from Denny Purcell. Then he brought up the color photograph of the Covenant mural from the church in Machen. A few mouse clicks allowed him to enlarge the central section of the image. It was clear what the priest and wise woman had obtained in return for the newborn.

"Charms or amulets," he murmured quietly. "Worn externally, of course. By human beings. But what about inhuman beings?"

Benson brought up in the internal video link to Doctor Zoffany's office. He explained what was required. Zoffany protested, Benson insisted, and mentioned what Lucy had said.

"If one views this as a war for survival," he said patiently, "extreme measures are more than justified. Prepare the subject for X-ray. If I were a betting man, I would put the object we're looking for somewhere in the upper torso."

"If it's in the head ..." Zoffany began.

"Then we will need a very discreet and quite unscrupulous brain surgeon," Benson put in. "Let me worry about that kind of detail."

Chapter 6: Beauty, Beast

After finishing Sir Reginald Pelham's diary, Denny took pictures of the most interesting pages and emailed them to Gould. Then she put the journal back in Brenda's battered cardboard box and took out the mysterious pendant, holding it up in the sunlight by the leather cord. The rough-hewn, purplish stone gleamed faintly, but did not convey any sense of mystical power.

Maybe I'm not on the right wavelength, she thought. *But if it is a protective talisman, perhaps being too flashy would be a disadvantage? More likely to be stolen.*

As she stared at the stone, she tried to imagine how such a protective charm would work. It was too simple to say 'magic' and move on. Besides, blithely accepting any kind of magical powers offended her journalist's desire to dig deeper, get at hidden truths. Denny cast her mind back to Malpas Abbey, and the way electronic devices had malfunctioned in the so-called temple.

Gould's Geiger counter, she remembered. *That didn't work at all.*

Gould had spoken of the laws of physics being distorted or suppressed near the portal to the Phantom Dimension. *Maybe the pendant worked in the same way?* Denny vaguely recalled a TED talk on quantum theory. It had been complex and she had fallen asleep towards the end. But the central point of the expert had been simple enough.

Probability, she thought. *The world works by probability, with all sorts of complex variables influencing every event.*

"So," she said to the pendant as it spun slowly in the light, "are you a legit good luck generator?"

Denny put the cord around her throat, then tucked the pendant down the front of her shirt. She had not even thought about the action, but once it was done, she felt a slight dizziness. She remembered the first time she had gone on a roller coaster as a child – the feeling that her stomach had suddenly become weightless.

"Now all I need to do is buy a lottery ticket," she said, and had to suppress half-hysterical laughter.

Another message arrived, and this time it was from Benson, not Gould. Denny had still not met the mysterious chairman, but here he was, pointing her at a supposed lead. It was a news story from several years earlier. She raised her eyebrows as she scrolled down the front page. The headline was clear enough.

LOCAL DOCTOR'S WIFE SLAIN

The picture of the victim looked like a passport photo, but it could not disguise her beauty. Denny found herself reading between the lines of the report. Even hardened police officers had been 'shocked by the ferocity of the attack', which had occurred 'just after sunset in the vicinity of Branksholme Woods'. When she put the report together with what Mel had told her, it suggested an Interloper had killed Marie Wakefield.

Why her, though? And why kill anyone after so many years of inactivity?

Then Denny gasped, struck herself dramatically on the forehead with a fist. She had assumed that the Interlopers had simply stopped appearing after 1914. But how did she know? More digging was required.

She acknowledged the message, then pondered her next move. Wakefield now seemed central to her mission – an expert on local folklore, a widower whose spouse was possibly an Interloper victim, and now the medical examiner in a similar case. But how to approach him?

Honesty is the best policy, she thought. *Up to a point.*

Denny looked up the number of the local National Health Service clinic. Doctor Wakefield was listed as the only GP. She dialed the number and got a receptionist, who at first was unwilling to convey a message to her boss.

"Tell him it's about the murder of Mrs. Wakefield," Denny said. "I guess you've got my number on your screen there. I'm staying at the Black Swan for the next few days."

It was nearly lunchtime, and Denny went downstairs into the bar to check if they served midday meals. Surly, Phoebe rolled her eyes and informed Denny in a monotone that they did not.

"Could you recommend any local restaurants?" Denny asked.

"There's a chip shop down the road," Phoebe replied, with zero enthusiasm.

"Thanks, Pheebs!" said Denny, enjoying the look of irritation that flitted across the teenager's face.

From now on, you are Pheebs, she thought. *Maximum annoyance.*

Fish and chips sounded good, so despite Phoebe's recommendation, Denny decided to give the place a try. As she left the Black Swan, she almost ran into Mel Bavistock, who was laden with packages and looking harassed. She accepted Denny's offer to help with food and other provisions.

"Normally we get stuff delivered," Mel explained. "But I've had to make an emergency run as the firm's van broke down. Car's full of unhealthy stuff the punters like."

"Can't be easy running a business and looking after a child," said Denny as they carried packets of snacks through the bar. "No time for yourself."

"No," Mel agreed, bustling around the small kitchen.

"If you need any help, like a babysitter for Isobel, I'm right along the hall," Denny added.

"Oh, she's very self-reliant," said Mel, not meeting Denny's eye. "But thanks for the offer."

"Okay," Denny said quietly, putting her burden down. "Guess I'll be going now."

Mel looked up, then and smiled wearily.

"Sorry I've been a bit short with you, it's just ..."

The woman gestured around her at piled of unwashed crockery, pint
glasses, empty beer bottles.

"Right!" Denny said. "Gets on top of you. Like I said, if I can help make it a bit easier, just ask."

"I will!"

Mel smiled again, and Denny left her busily trying to bring order to the chaos in the kitchen.

***

Russell Wakefield went through the morning's patients on autopilot. Like most rural doctors, he had too many patients, but few general practitioners wanted to move to a place like Machen. As the only MD in town, Wakefield was the man most in touch with members of the community. He knew far more about Machen folk, he often reflected, than the vicar. The church on Sunday was half-empty. The clinic's waiting room was almost always full.

As he examined an elderly farmer's ingrown toenail, Wakefield tried to suppress memories of Larkin's body, what was left of it. He tried even harder not to think of what Marie – the real Marie – must have looked like when she was found in virtually the same spot. His thoughts slowly crystallized around one central idea.

They targeted me from the start, he thought. *They killed her all those years ago because they knew they would need me one day.*

As he referred the farmer for day surgery at the county hospital, Wakefield ticked off facts in his orderly mind. He was the one man who could suppress anomalous data about Isobel Bavistock and the Hawkes twins. He had contacts in the police, and would know how much, or how little, attention the authorities were paying to events in Machen. And he could read the pulse of the community, sense if unease and suspicion were growing among locals.

So far, there's precious little sign of it, he thought as he sent the farmer away with forms and contact details. *Now there's been a killing, people have something new to talk about.*

Wakefield sat up, blinking, at the thought. He realized that he had missed an obvious point. Killing Larkin had not been a random act of violence, any more than Marie's murder. A killing fed the very human desire for gossip, the more sinister and grisly the better. It easily trumped the temporary disappearance of three children who had come back safe and well.

Officially, at least, those kids are safe and well at home. Thanks to me.

The doctor struggled with conflicting emotions, turbulent

ideas. He had always thought himself a good man, not someone who would willingly overlook evil. Not a collaborator, but one who resists. But he knew that the police, no matter what his status, would never believe that his dead wife had returned to seduce him into joining some kind of weird conspiracy.

Wakefield reached for the intercom.

"Janice? I'm going to have to finish early today, reschedule all appointments after three please."

"Yes, Doctor," replied the receptionist. "And I've sent you a message about a personal call earlier today."

"Thanks."

Wakefield frowned at his PC screen. An American reporter had called, saying something about Marie's death.

Bloody vultures, he thought. *That didn't take long.*

Then he realized that the reporter was calling from Machen. There was no way someone could have got here so quickly from London, the only likely base for a US correspondent. So the woman calling herself Denny Purcell had already been in town when Larkin was killed. Given how few tourists came to Machen out of season, it was hard to see her arrival as a coincidence.

Purcell, he thought. *Like the composer. But why do I feel I've heard it somewhere else lately?*

He put off calling in the next patient to Google the name. The phrase 'Malpas Massacre' appeared repeatedly as he scrolled down links. Opening what he considered a reliable news site, he reminded himself of the details.

Three people dead. One missing. Horrific injuries. Police baffled. Case still open.

Now it was clear.

She knows. She's seen them.

The intercom buzzed, and Wakefield knew that Janice must be fending off impatient locals. He closed the web browser, making a mental note to find out more later. Then he got up and took some items from the locked drugs cupboard, and put them into his bag. He took a deep breath, reached for the intercom.

"Send the next one in, Janice," he said. "I'm ready now."

***

Denny sat on a bench opposite the church and ate her fish and chips.

Watching the world go by, she thought. *Or at least, Machen's tiny fraction of it.*

Her phone chimed and she licked her fingers clean before checking her emails. This one was from Forster, the head of security at the Romola Foundation. Denny frowned at the contents. Jim Davison was a nice guy, and at Malpas he had shown himself to be courageous. But she resented the imputation that she needed some kind of minder.

No point in objecting, though. They'll just ignore it.

Denny saw no reason to alter her plans. She wanted to talk to Doctor Wakefield about his wife, last night's murder, and the returned children. And she needed to explore Branksholme Woods, to see if there was an obvious gateway to the Phantom Dimension. All this in addition to getting close to Isobel, or the other children, to see if they showed any overt signs of being Interlopers.

I'm almost sure they are, she thought. *But almost ain't good enough.*

A family walked past, a mother and father with two small children. The kids were complaining about not having sweets or ice cream, not wanting to go for a walk in the country. The mother was promising treats in the near future in return for co-operation now.

Could an Interloper fake being a child well enough to be a pain in the ass? A whiner, a nuisance? Or even a kid who's scared of the dark?

Denny then thought about what she would do if she were sure that Isobel Bavistock and the Hawkes twins were Interlopers. Would Benson order her to kill them? Or stand back while Jim killed them? It seemed insane to even contemplate it. But such creatures could hardly be allowed to roam freely among humans.

What if they're just the first of many?

The thought had been preying on her mind since she had

first seen the twins. If the Interlopers could replace three children, why not thirty? Or three hundred? This in turn raised questions about how many portals to the Phantom Dimension there were around the world.

What might be happening in other countries? Back in the US?

Denny had a sudden, surreal vision of children all around the world being slowly replaced by millions of Interlopers. She knew this was unreasonable, but it was hard to dismiss the horrific idea.

More likely Machen is just an experiment, she told herself. *A test to see how long they can get away with it. Or am I making the mistake of attributing human ideas to them?*

She felt frustrated by the sheer lack of data on what was going on. She got up and went over to a trashcan to throw away what was left of her lunch. A small dog scampered up to her, sniffing, attracted by the food smell. Its owner tried to haul her pet back on its long leash, apologizing to Denny, who made a fuss of the floppy-eared animal as it licked salt and vinegar off her hands.

Just following instinct, she thought. *Smart, but not too rational.*

She was still unsure where the balance between instinct and intellect lay with the Interlopers. It was another mystery she was yet to unravel.

***

After he had finished with his last patient, Wakefield checked the contents of his bag again. Then he thanked Janice and sent her home early. Like many rural doctors, he lived in a house that incorporated his clinic. And he did not want anyone around as he made preparations for the evening.

She might not come, he told himself.

Images of the killing flashed into his mind. He tried to blot them out. He stared out of the window at the autumn sun, which was sinking towards the hills. It was hard to believe so much evil, so much violence, could occur here. One of the reasons he had moved back to his hometown was its sleepiness, its sheer dullness.

Marie found it a bit too dull.

Wakefield pushed the unwelcome thought away and turned his back on the reddening October sky. He went into the kitchen and laid out various items, most of them innocent enough. Anyone glancing at the scene might think the doctor was about to attempt a little DIY.

If she comes, will I be able to do it?

He thought of the strength of the being that had killed Larkin. The man had been old, yes, but also active and strongly-built. It had been very clear that there was not a great deal of fat on Larkin's body. But his attacker had overpowered him.

So I've got to level the playing field, Wakefield thought, double-checking that he had everything ready. When he was sure he had everything he needed to carry out his plan, he put all the items out of sight around the bedroom. One final preparation involved placing a photograph in plain sight. Then he made himself a microwave meal and ate it while watching the television news.

It was almost dark when he finished eating. He realized as he washed up his plate and cutlery that he had no idea what the news had told him.

She won't come. She will come. She might come.

Wakefield turned on lights all around the house, trying to banish shadows altogether, not quite succeeding. He had often felt lonely since Marie's death, but now — for the first time, he felt vulnerable. Not a man in possession of his home, but a potential victim. He turned on his stereo, raised the volume on Brahms' German Requiem. The powerful chords filled the house, but did not make him feel any more secure. He turned off the music.

I can't do this alone, he thought. *I'll screw it up. I'll fail.*

Wakefield paced up and down in his living room for what seemed like an eternity. He considered calling the police but dismissed the notion, as he had done innumerable times before.

Well, officer, at first I thought my wife's ghost had returned for energetic sex on a regular basis, but in fact it's some kind of demon that's taken her form.

On impulse, he checked his messages again and called Denny Purcell, but ended the call before she answered. He was about to call again when there was a soft click from the hallway. The front door was being opened with a key. Then the hall light was switched off.

***

Denny had spent her afternoon in Hereford, which was the closest place where Jim could find a place to stay at short notice. He had tentatively suggested that he could pose as her British boyfriend and stay at the Black Swan. Denny had vetoed the plan despite Jim's assurance that there would be 'no funny business'.

"Funny or serious," she had said, "I sleep alone. We'll just have to find you somewhere closer. There are holiday cottages for rent in Machen, try one of those."

After comparing notes on the investigation, Denny had driven back. She was parking the jeep outside the pub when her phone rang briefly. Frowning, she finished parking and then checked. The number was unfamiliar. She hit the call back. It rang a few times then went to Wakefield's voicemail. Rather than leave a message, she decided to go straight to the clinic.

As she backed the jeep out into the road, she glanced up again at the front of the Black Swan. Isobel was looking down at her. The small, pale face was impassive, apparently devoid of emotion. Denny shuddered, focused on the road ahead.

I'll be seeing you later, she thought. *Whoever or whatever you are.*

She arrived at Wakefield's home to see that there were no lights on downstairs. An upper window, presumably a bedroom, was lit, but as she got out of the jeep, Denny could see no one inside. Then she caught a glimpse of movement in the window. It was impossible to tell in that split second if the figure had been a man or a woman. Curtains were drawn, and then the light behind them went out.

Or even human, she reminded herself.

She went up to the door and was reaching for the doorbell when she hesitated. She tried the door handle. It was open.

***

Wakefield tried to blot all thoughts from his mind when she appeared at the door of the living room. She paused to look at him, smiling quizzically.

"Hello, Russ," said the false Marie. "You seem a little agitated. And why are all the lights on?"

She reached out a pale, slender hand and flipped the switch. In semi-darkness, now, she walked over to him, put her hands on his shoulders, and drew her to him. Her clothes were cold from the chilly night air. He knew the body beneath them would be warm.

"So tense," she said, massaging his shoulders. "Long day at work, darling? I know how to relax you."

She reached down and took his hand, tried to lead him out of the room. He resisted, and she stopped, eyebrows raised.

"Don't tell me you're not in the mood, darling?"

Her expression was still amused, half-mocking. She let go his hand and took off her coat, threw it onto the sofa.

"I ... I want to know something," he said, dismayed to hear his voice falter. Marie lifted his hand and laid it on her breast.

"You know all you need to," she whispered. "Don't spoil this, Russ. I came back. Changed a little, perhaps, but still me. Still the woman you love."

Wakefield's attempt to suppress all his confused, disturbing thoughts failed. Images of the corpse in the woods flooded his mind's eye, jumbled together with memories of Marie.

"Try not to think about it," she said, pressing herself against him.

Her eyes were level with his, just a few inches away. Wakefield felt a wave of acceptance wash over him, dark thoughts fading as he began to anticipate another bout of lovemaking. Again, she took his hand and lead him out of the room and up the stairs. This time he did not try to resist. As they climbed the stairs, she began to undress him, and herself, teasing and caressing him all the while.

"You need this," she murmured. "You need me. And all I need is your love. Be faithful to me, Russ."

They entered the bedroom, and she moved quickly to draw the curtains and turn off the light. Wakefield turned on a small lamp on the bedside table. It was a familiar routine. But this time something was slightly different. Beside the lamp, stood a framed photograph of Marie Wakefield. He had put it in a drawer after her death, unable to face the reminder of his loss. Now it reminded him of just how far he had betrayed her.

"Oh, Russ," she said. "We can't have that. You're just upsetting yourself."

She strode around the bed and turned the picture face down. As she did so, her back was to him. Wakefield reached under the pillow for the syringe, which he had filled earlier. Marie was straightening up, turning, when he stuck the needle into the back of her neck and pushed the plunger. She gave a piercing screech and moved with terrifying speed, spinning around and lashing out. The needle broke off in her body, but he had already injected her with a massive dose of morphine.

Wakefield jumped back, but she was way too fast for him. She caught the side of his head with an open-handed blow that sent him reeling across the room. He crashed into the dressing table, then fell to the floor. He looked up to see the false Marie standing over him, a dark shape with the dim light behind her. She seemed to be changing shape as he watched, losing her familiar soft curves, becoming thin, wiry.

"You idiot," she growled, her voice become deeper, the words more crudely formed.

There was enough in that syringe to kill anyone, he thought desperately.

"Any human being," she said, reaching over her shoulder and pulling the needle out, throwing it aside. "Not enough–"

She paused, swaying, seemed to stagger, then drew upright again. Wakefield tried to shuffle away from her, felt around for a weapon, but there was nothing. She stepped forward, crouched over him, her hands pinning him down. He felt sharp talons cutting into his flesh. When she spoke now the words came from a mouth that was elongating into a kind of muzzle.

"I didn't kill her," the creature said, its words now heavily slurred. "I became what you wanted. That should have been enough."

"Let me go!" he cried, trying to shove the monstrous being away, but failing.

"I'll just have one last kiss," it grunted.

The funnel-like mouth-parts descended toward his face. Wakefield twisted his head aside, closed his eyes, and continued to yell for help. Then his frantic struggles seemed to prevail, all of a sudden. There was a hissing noise, followed by another screech from the monster.

"Get up!" said a new voice. "I think I blinded it."

Wakefield looked up to see a second shape holding out some kind of canister and directing a spray into the face of the creature. It lashed out with claw-like hands, but seemed much slower and clumsier than before. The newcomer dodged and there was more hissing. A strong scent was discernible, now. The creature fell back onto the bed, flailing and grunting. Gradually its movements died down, but it continued to twitch and heave spasmodically. It was certainly not dead.

The morphine's working, he thought. *Just not so well as I'd hoped.*

"Come on, doc!" the woman said, reaching down to help him to his feet. "We need to tie this thing up. Got anything to–"

The woman stopped when Wakefield reached under the bed and pulled out a box containing four rolls of duct tape, plus a length of nylon washing line, and a large plastic garbage bag.

"Let's get its feet secured first," he said. "I take it you're Denny Purcell? Pleased to meet you. Thanks for the assist, as they say."

Chapter 7: Sex and Violence

Denny stared down at what looked like a half-naked woman tied up on the bed. The Interloper had returned to the form of Marie Wakefield shortly after they had secured it. The hairspray and morphine both had no obvious lasting effects. The creature was not struggling against its bonds, but simply staring up at its captors.

"There's this guy I know," Denny said to the doctor. "He might be able to – to deal with it."

As she spoke she thought, *I sound like a gangster offering to have someone 'disappear'.* But Wakefield merely nodded.

"I never really thought that far ahead," he said. "I've been improvising since this morning. Since I realized that this ...this *thing* must have killed Marie."

Denny looked at Wakefield closely for the first time. She saw a man in his mid-forties, slightly paunchy, with a face that was handsome in a careworn way. He seemed wired, still on edge despite having subdued the creature.

Is he telling me the whole truth? Denny wondered.

"Were you planning to kill it?" she asked quietly.

"Of course he was!" said Marie. "He always wanted to kill me. The original me, that is. The first version was a bit of a slut, you see. On the night Marie Number One died, she wasn't just out for a walk. She was ready for a roll in the–"

"Shut up!" Wakefield shouted, stepping towards the bed, fist raised.

Denny caught the doctor's arm, pulled him back.

"Don't let them manipulate you," she warned. "The more emotional you get, the easier it is for them. Fear, desire, greed – you name it, a powerful emotion is a handle they can grab hold of. Self-control can block them. Focus."

Wakefield shook off Denny's hand, but stepped back, and went to the window. He ran his fingers through his untidy, graying hair, looking out into the night. The doctor squared his shoulders, seemed to reach a decision.

"This friend of yours," he said. "Will he kill it?"

Denny explained that she had no idea what Jim might do, but she felt the need for backup. She sent Jim a message that simply read,

CAUGHT A LIVE ONE, MEET YOU AT BLACK SWAN. HURRY!

"Thing is," she went on, "often, they simply die after exposure to our world."

Seeing Wakefield's puzzlement, she tried to explain that most Interlopers could not survive for long outside the Phantom Dimension. The doctor stared at her, then at the false Marie.

"It's true, darling," said the Interloper. "I'm like Cinderella. Sort of. If I don't get home before dawn, I fall to pieces. Quite literally. Will you enjoy watching that?"

"Shut up, you murderer," Wakefield growled. "I'm not your puppet anymore."

"Let's talk downstairs," said Denny quickly. "That thing is tied up pretty good."

In the living room, Wakefield poured himself a large Scotch. Denny turned down the offer of a drink. They talked, she explained what had happened to her at Malpas Abbey to gain his confidence. She explained that the foundation she worked for called the creatures 'Interlopers', and was building up research on them. But, after a brief hesitation, she decided not to mention that she had ventured into the Phantom Dimension and returned.

Not strictly relevant, she told herself, *besides, he might think I'm a random crazy person. I'm asking him to take a lot on trust.*

After Denny had finished explaining why she was in Machen, she gently probed him over how he had become a tool of the Interlopers. His explanation was both convincing and disturbing.

"So all they wanted you to do was verify to the police and parents that the children were normal?" she asked, after he had finished.

Wakefield grunted in assent, not meeting her gaze.

"And were they?" she asked quietly.

Wakefield shook his head, took a last gulp of his Scotch.

"No, they were anomalous in all sorts of ways. Low blood pressure, intermittent pulse, and peculiar eyes. The pupils seemed hypersensitive to light. But you'd have to know what you're looking for – they certainly pass for human. And I told myself that perhaps they were, that they had simply been changed in some way."

"But you think they were replaced?" she asked.

Wakefield shrugged, looking guilty and miserable.

"Everything in my medical training tells me that's nonsense," he said, in a pleading voice. "If somebody came to me and said their child had been replaced by some kind of – some kind of alien, I'd recommend they be detained under the Mental Health Act. But on the other hand, after what I've seen in this town. In this house ..."

He looked up, and Denny thought of what they had left trussed up on the doctor's marital bed.

Poor guy's been in a mess for a good while, she thought. *They played him.*

"One more question," she said. "The obvious one."

Wakefield looked at her.

"Oh, that. Believe me, I've thought about it. A lot. But I still don't know what they want with human children," he said. "I asked her once, she flat out wouldn't tell me. I didn't dare push it."

Didn't want to lose your Marie-shaped sex doll, thought Denny, then felt guilty for feeling so superior. *What would I do if a fake Frankie turned up? Kill it, just like that?*

"I can't be sure, of course," Wakefield went on. "But I've always been interested in folk tales, and there's a Scottish ballad called 'Tam Lin' that might–"

He broke off as Denny's phone rang. Jim was on his way from Hereford with what he referred to as a 'containment and disposal kit'. He would arrive in Machen in about twenty minutes. Denny did not ask what it included. What she had seen of Interloper deaths had not been pretty. She explained the situation, including the fact that a large dose of morphine had had some effect, but not for long.

"In about half an hour, I have to go and meet my ..." she hesitated to say 'superior'. "My colleague from the foundation. Will you be okay? I need to show him how to get here from the town center. Then we'll deal with ... with the Interloper."

Wakefield poured himself another Scotch and took a gulp.

"I'll be fine," he said. "We locked her in. What harm can she – I mean *it*, of course, what harm can it do?"

"Nothing physical," Denny said. "But remember, it can read your mind and influence it."

"I know," Wakefield said, suddenly sounding weary after his earlier tension. "It always knew what I wanted, how to stop me thinking, asking obvious questions."

"Come and make me a cup of coffee," Denny said. "And tell me about this legend you mentioned."

***

Mel Bavistock noticed Denny's jeep pull into the car park, then reverse out again a minute or so later. She was mildly curious as to where her guest might be going on a weekday evening. But there was a queue of customers waiting to be served at the bar, and Mel had to focus on keeping her business afloat.

A few minutes later, during a lull, Mel asked Phoebe to take charge.

"I'm just going to tuck Isobel in," she said to the surly teen.

"Don't be all night about it," grumbled Phoebe.

"I won't," Mel replied. "And don't you lounge about like a great pudding girl, when there's people waiting to be served!"

Leaving Phoebe seething with silent resentment, Mel climbed the stairs to the second floor. She passed the guest room to the door at the end of the corridor, which opened into the apartment she shared with Isobel. As she let herself in, she hoped to hear the sound of the television. The sound of a normal kid wasting their time. If it were on, Mel could gently rebuke her daughter for watching it when she should be brushing her teeth, getting ready for bed. But the living room was silent, the TV screen a dark mirror. Since she had come back from Branksholme Woods, Isobel had lost interest in what had been her favorite shows. And she had gone to bed on time, without protest, every night.

Like a good little girl, Mel thought, as she crossed to the bedroom door. *So why does it seem so wrong?*

The bedroom door was a few inches ajar. Mel paused, listened, but heard nothing other than the faint sound of the jukebox from downstairs. She pushed the door a little wider and sidled in. Faint moonlight, through open curtains, showed a small shape beneath the bed sheets.

Mel tiptoed over to the bedside, her eyes adjusting to the gloom. She could make out Isobel's head on the pillow. The child was facing upward, eyes closed. Mel leaned closer, listening for her daughter's breathing. She could not quite hear it, could not feel the gentle wash of the girl's breath.

Isobel stirred, then mumbled something. Mel thought she heard the phrase 'I'm like Cinderella', and smiled. Isobel had loved the picture-book and the film. Now she never touched her books, never asked to watch the DVDs, never asked to dress in a princess outfit.

Perhaps it's just the trauma, Mel told herself. *Like the way she's gotten so fussy about what she eats. Kids aren't tiny adults, after all.*

Isobel stirred again, turning her head so that her face was illuminated by a shaft of moonlight. For a moment, Mel forgot her anxieties about her daughter. She leaned closer still, and a strand of her hair fell onto the sleeping child's face.

Two dark eyes opened, stared up into hers.

"Mummy," said Isobel. "What's wrong?"

"Nothing, love, go back to sleep," Mel said, kissing the girl on the forehead, then standing upright.

"You used to read me stories," Isobel said. "Read me one now."

"I haven't got the time, love," Mel said, truthfully. "I have to get back downstairs. Shush now, and go to sleep."

She was almost at the bedroom door when Isobel's voice came again.

"Do you still love me, mummy?"

Mel stopped but did not turn around.

"Of course I love you, poppet."

I don't love her enough, though. I'm not a good mother. I'm holding something back.

Mel tried to suppress the accusing thoughts as she pulled

the door almost shut behind her. But the voice in her head, now all too familiar, followed her back downstairs to the bar. Even as she worked the beer pumps, collected glasses, bantered with the regulars, the small, persistent voice continued to condemn her. It had always been there, a niggling presence. But since Isobel and the Hawkes twins had vanished and come back the voice had grown louder, more insistent. It was wearing away at her character, she knew, robbing her of judgment and self-respect. But she could not quiet it.

I don't do enough for her. She's so shy and sensitive. Needs protecting. I nearly lost her once. That was my fault. Poor excuse for a mother. Not good enough.

***

Wakefield stood in his darkened living room, looking out at the taillights of Denny's jeep as it wound its way along the lane into town.

Just a few minutes more, the doctor thought. *Then I can be rid of that foul thing forever.*

He finished his third Scotch of the evening and went to get another, then slammed the glass down by the bottle.

What a cliché. The boozy doctor with the disastrous marriage.

Despite his best effort to suppress them, memories of Marie swarmed in his mind. Moments he had shared with his wife vied with images of the imposter, the two blurring in a sensuous mix of desire and betrayal.

Never see her again.

The thought would not be silenced.

Never touch her again. Never feel that ecstasy, that release from all your cares.

Wakefield reached for the Scotch again, poured himself a good measure. He was just raising the glass to his lips when he heard a dull impact from upstairs. He listened intently but the sound was not repeated. It had sounded like something falling to the floor in the bedroom. He imagined the false Marie writhing, biting, clawing herself loose from the tape on her wrists and ankles.

Wakefield took a gulp of Scotch, put the glass down, and went into the kitchen to get a knife.

***

Denny dipped the jeep's headlights, and saw the signal returned by the unmarked, white van outside the Black Swan. She pulled up alongside Jim and rolled down the window.

"Ready to roll, big fella?"

Jim gave a thumbs up, then jerked his head to indicate the contents of the van.

"I've got an airtight bag and some preservative chemicals, so if it dies we still might recover an intact body."

"Great!" she said. "You know there's a third party, Wakefield?"

"Yeah," Jim said. "Will he be a problem?"

"I'm not sure," she admitted. "I couldn't order the guy around in his own house, but the quicker we get back up there the better. He seemed pretty shaken up."

"Let's get moving, then. Monsters to destroy and all that jazz."

As she U-turned the jeep, Denny looked up at the pub. Isobel was standing at her window, looking down. An uncomfortable thought struck Denny. She had taken it for granted that Interlopers had psychic abilities. Yet she realized that, until now, she had been thinking of them as sci-fi aliens, creatures that would naturally communicate in their own strange tongue.

But what if they can communicate telepathically with one another? That would make sense. And if one of them is held captive so near to the gateway, they would all know and maybe do something.

Denny drove fast out of town, back towards Wakefield's home. In the rear-view mirror, she saw the headlights of Jim's van start to fall behind as he tackled the unfamiliar country lane by night.

***

"We never did experiment with bondage," said the false Marie. "Never too late to start!"

She was lying on the floor by the bed. When Wakefield had entered the bedroom she had been contorted, bent to an inhuman degree. Her face had been elongated, sharp teeth trying to reach the tape that secured her arms behind her back. Now she was immobile, staring up at him. Her face quickly returned to the perfect likeness of his dead wife.

"You're sure you never want to see me again, Russ?" Marie demanded, pouting in a way that he remembered all too well.

Her 'poor little me' look, he thought. *Twist me round her little finger. Or claw, in this case.*

Instead of speaking, he took a few paces into the room and held up the knife.

"Ooh, sado-masochism, now, is it?" she asked. "Well, you'd better get on with it. Those killjoys from Romola will be back soon."

"I'll kill you, you monster!" he shouted, but did not move closer.

You can't do it, said an insistent inner voice. *You need her too much, want her too much. Imagine losing her. Imagine a life without her. Forever.*

"Who's the real monster?" Marie asked. "I did everything you wanted. All the things she never would do. For you, at least. She did them for other men, though, didn't she?"

"Shut up!" he shouted. "Just shut up or I'll ..."

Now he did take a step closer, holding the knife out in front of him with both hands. Part of him wanted to drive it into the beautiful, smiling face. But he also felt the urge to cast the weapon aside and enjoy one last, frantic session of lovemaking.

That's insane, he thought, even as his arms lost their strength and the knife sagged until it was pointing at the floor. *I'm going crazy.*

"If you cut me loose, I'll make it worth your while, darling," Marie purred. "Remember, if you let me go there's no proof I ever existed. Forget that silly American's lies. I'm the reality. I'm what you always wanted. What you can still have."

"No!" he said "You're a monster. I don't – I won't!"

This time the wave of desire was almost overwhelming, as if every cell in his brain had been caressed by phantom fingers. The body of the imposter became more voluptuous as she writhed slowly towards him, her skin seeming to glow in the dim light. He dropped the knife, reeled back, reached for the dressing table to stop himself from falling. A tide of raw lust was beginning to overwhelm him.

There was a crash from downstairs as the front door was slammed open against the wall.

"Oh, thank God," Wakefield breathed.

"Oh," pouted Marie, "is it the White Hats, come to spoil our fun?"

He staggered out of the bedroom onto the landing to look down into the hallway, already forming the words to welcome back Denny. But the figure that loped into view was not Denny – was not human at all. It scurried quickly to the foot of the stairs and began to run up towards Wakefield, peering at him with tiny, dark eyes in deep sockets. Claws scraped on the banister rail as it reached the landing and paused, half-crouching, preparing to spring.

Wakefield threw himself back into the bedroom, slammed the door, flattened himself against it. There was a small bolt on the inside, and he drew it.

"That won't keep him out," Marie said. "But if you let me go, you won't be harmed. I promise. We still need you, Russ."

That's true, he thought. *We could go back to how it was before.*

Then he thought again of the corpse he had examined that morning, its viscera scattered, face and limbs hideously mutilated. Wakefield stooped, picked up the knife, and retreated as the new Interloper charged the door. The door bounced on its hinges, and there was a distinct crack of wood giving way.

"Tick tock, Russ," said Marie, staring at him. "Deal's still on the table. Or the bed, if you like."

***

Denny left the engine running and jumped out of the jeep, not waiting for Jim as she raced to the open front door. Feeling slightly ridiculous, she held her small spray can in front of her as she moved more cautiously into the hallway. There was a commotion upstairs, a man shouting, and a high-pitched screech that might have been an animal. Denny looked around, saw Jim running after her carrying what looked like a nightstick.

"They're in the bedroom!" she shouted, and rushed up the staircase.

She found the bedroom door hanging crazily at an angle, and saw rapid movement inside the dim-lit room.

"Doctor?" she shouted, pausing in the doorway.

She heard a muffled cry that might have been *'Help!'* Rushing into the room, Denny skidded, almost fell. The deep-pile carpet was slick with some kind of liquid. At the same time, she became aware of a stench, one she had first encountered at Malpas. It was the smell of an injured Interloper. She saw two figures struggling in a corner of the room and rushed toward them, only to trip and fall. She landed on something soft and yielding; a warm body that moved.

Denny realized that it was the false Marie just as the creature's distorted face loomed up in the gloom. The entity's circle of vicious, sharp teeth lunged toward her. Denny screamed in panic fright. But the hideous muzzle did not fasten onto her face. Instead, the Interloper seemed to pause, as if unsure of its target. Then the creature gave a high-pitched whine and shied away.

Denny scrambled to her feet and leapt away from the monster, then turned to the two figures still locked in their struggle. She could see now that Wakefield was lying underneath a second Interloper, stabbing frantically at the creature with a large knife. As Denny watched, the Interloper collapsed onto the doctor, who continued to drive the blade into its back. Black blood spurted from numerous wounds, and Denny realized she had slipped on this noxious fluid.

"What's happening?" Jim shouted from the doorway. At the same moment, a bright beam of light shot into the room, blinding Denny for a moment. When she recovered her sight, Wakefield was heaving the inert body of the Interloper off him.

"Very impressive," said Jim. He put his flashlight on the dressing table and stepped around the false Marie. "Seems you didn't need any help, doc. Not everybody could take on one of those things."

Wakefield was kneeling beside the remains of the second creature.

"I think I got a bit carried away," he said, dropping the blackened knife.

"Understatement of the year," murmured Denny.

"Been building up for a while," said Wakefield, standing up. He looked over at the fake Marie. "I couldn't kill you, even now, but I found a way to relieve the tension."

The surviving Interloper, now returned to fully human form, gave no sign of hearing the doctor. Instead, it was staring up at Denny. Its expression was blank, with no hint of faked human emotions.

What's your problem? Denny wondered.

Taking a step closer to the creature, she squatted just out of reach. Marie continued to gaze blankly at her.

"It knows you all right," Jim observed. "Don't get too close. I'll get the stuff from the van."

"Stuff?" asked Wakefield, looking confused.

"Quite a mess there, needs cleaning up," Jim said, gesturing at the remains in the corner. Denny glanced over, quickly looked away. It was already clear that the Interloper's body was breaking down, flesh melting into dark, fetid liquid.

"I'll bag it and tag it," Jim explained, as he turned to leave. "And then I'll put her ladyship into a nice secure box."

Again, the reference to Marie prompted no reaction from the Interloper, which continued to scrutinize Denny. Denny realized that the creature was not looking at her face but somewhere just above her breasts.

Of course, she thought, as she remembered the one material piece of evidence she had found since arriving in Machen. Denny reached down and took out the crude stone pendant. In the radiance of Jim's flashlight, its purple color seemed brighter, almost lurid. Denny took the pendant from around her neck and dangled it in front of Marie, who gazed at it in apparent fascination.

"What's that?" asked Wakefield, leaning forward to look more closely.

"Not sure," Denny replied. "But it was given to a human by the Interlopers. It's some kind of talisman. It seems to recognize it."

Marie suddenly emitted a sharp growling noise, a low and utterly inhuman sound. The Interloper arched its back and then wriggled swiftly away, stopping only when it collided with the bedside table.

"She doesn't like it," Wakefield said wonderingly. "I've never seen her react like that. Never seen fear at all."

"And you're calling her 'she' again," Denny noted. *Old habits …*

"What is it, Marie?" she asked, shuffling forward and holding the pendant closer. "Don't like it? Why? It brings good luck to people, right? What's not to like?"

Because they're not people? So maybe, instead of good luck …

On a sudden impulse, Denny swung the pendant towards Marie.

"Here," she said. "Catch!"

When she let it go, the pendant, trailing its dark lanyard, traced a short arc toward Marie's face. Moving with uncanny speed the Interloper flung up its arms to bat the talisman away. The purple stone was flung over the bed, into the room's far corner, where it landed amid the remains of the decaying Interloper. There was a sharp hissing sound. Looking over at the mess of bones and rotting tissue, Denny saw that decomposition had accelerated. A cloud of oily vapor was rising from what was now a crumbling skeleton.

"Bloody Hell!" exclaimed Wakefield. "What is that thing?"

"One of your ancestors got it for a guy called Pelham," Denny said. "It's supposed to be a good luck charm."

"Not for those buggers, obviously," grunted Jim. "Seems to burn them like phosphorous."

"One of my ancestors?" Wakefield asked.

Seeing his puzzlement, Denny asked if he had heard of a

wise woman called 'Ma Wakefield'. He shook his head.

"Okay," she said, "there's a diary back in my room you should check out."

The doctor nodded, then looked over at Jim, who was now busy in the corner of the bedroom.

"You might want to consider getting a new carpet, doc," observed Jim. "I can't see your regular cleaner tackling this."

He was shoving what remained of the dead Interloper into a transparent plastic bag. Denny went over and retrieved the talisman from the bubbling mess, then wiped decaying organic matter off the stone with a paper tissue. She replaced the stone around her neck, then turned to Marie again.

"Why does it harm your kind?" she asked.

Marie snarled at Denny. She was clearly not willing to co-operate and was no longer even faking the human form convincingly. Her face was too angular, the mouth protruding, eyes sunken.

"How are you going to take her away?" Wakefield asked Jim, who was leaving with the remains of the dead Interloper.

"Best thing is to wait for it to perish naturally," said Jim over his shoulder, with an emphasis on the 'it'. "Then I can bag it and tag it."

Wakefield looked shocked, but said nothing. Instead, he sat on the bed and put his face into his hands.

I thought we were the good guys, Denny thought, looking at the cowering creature. She got Jim's flashlight and shone it onto the false Marie, which raised its ragged claws to shield its eyes. Now Denny could see that the Interloper was showing signs of decay, once smooth skin becoming rough and uneven.

"You'll be gone, soon," she said. "Wouldn't you rather go home?"

Wakefield began to protest, but Denny held up her hand for silence.

"Show me the gateway," she said. "Show me the portal to your world, and I'll let you live."

The creature lowered its claws. There was still something of the woman it had mimicked in the face that spoke.

"If you let me go, I will show you."

"Why do you want to know where this gateway is?" asked

Wakefield.

Denny reached down and picked up the doctor's gore-clotted knife. She thought of the legend the doctor had told her.

"So, I can go through it," she said. "Maybe save some kids. Maybe save a friend of mine."

Chapter 8: Creature of the Night

"You must be going barmy!" exclaimed Jim. "You can't just let that thing go."

He had returned from the van with a body bag and a bottle of preservative chemicals. He had found Denny sawing through the tape around the Interloper's ankles with Wakefield's carving knife.

"It'll show us the gateway in Branksholme Woods," she explained. "That will save us a lot of pointless thrashing around."

Jim began to protest, but Denny interrupted, raising her voice.

"Firstly," she said, "we should find the gateway on general principles, right? Then if Benson wants Forster and his guys to encase it in concrete, like they did at Malpas, then they'll know where to go."

Jim gave a reluctant nod as Denny stood up.

"Second," she went on, "I don't feel comfortable letting a living, thinking being just die because we tied it up. It's one thing to kill in self-defense, but this feels too much like murder. Murder by neglect, maybe, but still ..."

The Interloper, wrists still bound, pushed itself upright against the wall. As it stepped forward, Denny noted that it had left a dark trail. She assumed it was now shedding decaying tissue.

It's already falling apart, she thought. *We need to move fast.*

"Get downstairs and into the back of the van," she told it, cuttings its hands free so she didn't have to help it up "We'll drive you to the woods."

Jim looked as if he might protest, but then sighed and stood aside as the creature loped out of the room and down the stairs.

"How do you know it won't try to kill you?" asked Wakefield.

"One, it couldn't kill me because I wore the talisman," said Denny. "Two, it's in bad shape and getting weaker by the second. It might not even make it. When these things drop to pieces, it's really fast."

Denny rode in the back of the van, feet away from the creature, again holding the talisman in her hand. In the front, Wakefield guided Jim up to Branksholme Woods. The journey took a few minutes, but by the time they pulled up near the tree line, the stench from the dying Interloper was almost unbearable.

Denny threw open the doors of the van and jumped out. As the creature struggled to climb out, she unthinkingly reached up to take one of its arms. As soon as she felt the pulpy flesh, she realized what she had done, but forced herself to help it to the ground. The entity gave no indication that it was even aware of her help. Once its feet touched the ground, it began to limp urgently into the trees.

Normally, those things are so fast we can't follow them, Denny thought as she followed. *This one's barely managing a brisk walk.*

She wondered, not for the first time, what desperation would prompt any intelligent being to enter a world where the very laws of nature were toxic to it. The doctor's account of the old folk ballad had given her a vague clue as to what the Interlopers' motives might be. If she was even vaguely right, they needed to move fast.

At Malpas, I went into the Phantom Dimension and survived, she thought. *I can do it again.*

Denny knew that she had been allowed to escape so she could bring the false Lucy with her. It had been a staged rescue. Lucy had almost convinced the foundation's team that she was indeed a little girl, Gould's younger sister, abducted decades earlier. Mere chance had derailed the Interloper's plan that time.

What if I'm fooled again? Denny wondered. *But if I do nothing, I'll damn sure be saving nobody.*

They arrived at a clearing. In the gloom, it was impossible to see anything that might be a gateway. For a few seconds, Denny wondered if the fake Marie had simply led them on a wild goose chase.

It might be under orders not to let the enemy know where the gateway is, she thought. *Like a soldier on a suicide mission.*

Then Jim crashed into the clearing and swung the beam of his flashlight around, illuminating tree stumps and fallen boughs amid wild ferns and nettles. The Interloper was now on all fours, crawling through the underbrush.

"There it is!" cried Jim, focusing the light on the area just ahead of the creature.

In the artificial light, Denny could just make out a rippling sphere of disturbed air, like a globular heat-haze. It was fixed in place about three feet above the ground. Wakefield appeared at her shoulder, gasped in astonishment.

"That's some kind of portal to another dimension?" he asked.

The Interloper was under the shimmering sphere, now. It tried to stand, failed, tried again, collapsed.

"Crap," said Denny, racing forward. She tried to lift the creature but it was too heavy.

"Some help, guys?"

After brief hesitation, Wakefield and Jim joined her, and between them they half-threw the Interloper into the sphere. The globe of strange energy pulsed, darkened, then emitted a faint reddish glow. For a moment, Denny thought she could see through it to the nightmarish landscape of the Phantom Dimension. She had a fleeting vision of ruins stretching across a bright red plain under a pale, colorless sky. Then the gateway was transparent again.

"I'll let you file the report on this one," said Jim.

"I'll make sure you get plenty of credit for your contribution," Denny said, smiling wryly. She took out her phone. "Okay, let's get this location pinned."

"You're not just going to dive straight through, then?" asked Jim.

"Watch that tone, mister, or I might just do that," Denny warned, only half-joking.

Jim looked suitably abashed.

Remembering when she went through and he stayed behind, recalling her first foray into the Phantom Dimension.

"I'll try and prepare a bit better this time," she said, in a softer tone. "And I'll need your help."

Denny finished noting the location on her phone's mapping app and they set off back to the vehicle. Denny had to stifle several yawns, then gave up.

"We could all do with some sleep," Jim commented. "Big day tomorrow, apparently."

"You really think that pendant will protect you?" asked Wakefield.

"Your ancestor, the wise woman, gave them to the soldiers who served in the First World War," Denny said.

She gave them a potted version of Pelham's diary and her theory that the talisman's powers somehow involved the clash of different sets of 'natural laws'.

"That's one for the eggheads," Jim commented sourly. "Sounds like Gould's quantum double-talk. Gives me a headache."

Wakefield's response was more thoughtful.

"So they traded something powerful and dangerous for human infants," he mused. "And this went on for centuries?"

"Yeah," Denny said, "but remember, time flows much faster here. So to them it might have been a short-term arrangement."

"Yes!" Wakefield said, now sounding intrigued. "Different physics, different time flow, and strange materials with variable properties."

Jim groaned.

"Oh God, my brain hurts! And I've got to drive all the way back to bloody Hereford."

"You could stay at my place," Wakefield said, surprising the others. "After all, we don't know whether those creatures will come back."

"Okay," Jim said. "Save time tomorrow, I suppose. Yeah, why not?"

This could be the beginning of a fine bro-mance, thought Denny, trying not to smile.

***

"I doubt they will try again tonight," said Jim, from his position slumped on Wakefield's couch. "Great booze, by the

252

way. Better not have too much, though. Stay alert and all that."

"Yeah," said the doctor.

He was gazing out onto the moonlit valley again.

Poor bastard, Jim thought. *If I'd been through what he's suffered, I'd have lost it well before now.*

"So, what was this about a legend Denny was talking about?" he asked

He asked mainly to distract Wakefield from brooding. Jim had heard many folk stories and fairy tales that might – at a pinch – be linked to the Interlopers.

This one is probably just the usual old guff, he thought.

Wakefield turned from the window, leaned against the sill.

"Oh, you mean Tam Lin? It's a fairy tale from the Scottish border region. Tam Lin is a handsome young man, and the Queen of the Fairies sees him and decides to make him her plaything."

"Lucky lad," said Jim with a wry grin.

"At first, yes," agreed Wakefield. "The Queen has her minions kidnap him and bring him back to her realm. Tam enjoys himself, and doesn't seem too bothered at being her love-slave. But then comes the kicker. Every seven years the Fairy Queen must pay a tithe to Hell. A sacrifice, in other words. And Tam Lin, a mere human, is it. That's when Tam resolves to escape, with the help of his girlfriend, Janet, who's actually the hero of the story. There's a lot more, involving shape shifting ..."

Jim leaned forward.

"So, changing form is something this legend ties to so-called fairies?"

"Oh yes," the doctor nodded. "Plus, the power to sway people's minds."

Jim sat back, and took another sip of the doctor's single malt whiskey.

"It does sound credible," he said, slowly. "I've never heard of this. Maybe the foundation should spend more time on folktales and a bit less on weird science."

Wakefield laughed.

"One can do both, given sufficient funds," he pointed out. "Okay, I'll get you a spare duvet. Oh, and should we prop furniture against all the doors, do you think?"

"Mmm," said Jim, distractedly.

So you think the Interlopers are taking humans, the best specimens they can find, as offerings to something else? Kids preferably, younger adults if none are available?

Jim thought about what Davenport, one of Forster's clean-up team, had told him about graffiti at Malpas Abbey. One message that had apparently appeared after the carnage was over kept popping back into his mind.

THERE ARE WORSE THINGS THAN US

***

After bidding goodbye to her companions, Denny returned to the Black Swan, feeling burned out by everything she had just experienced. The ever-helpful Mel had given Denny her own key, but the pub was still open. From the cluster of people at the door she guessed it was what the Brits called 'chucking out time', when people in cities vacated pubs and either went home or went 'clubbing'. Machen, Denny assumed, only offered home as an option for its revelers.

Denny pushed through the crowd, ignoring a few ribald remarks, and entered the bar room. Mel was being cheerful but persistent in her attempts to get the last few drinkers to finish up and leave. Phoebe was slouching back and forth, collecting glasses and bottles.

"Hi Mel! Hi Pheebs!"

Denny got a satisfactory scowl from the teen and a cheerful 'Hello' from Mel. She offered to help with closing up, but Mel insisted that she get to bed.

"You look dead on your feet," the landlady added. "Overdone the walking? Often get that with big city types."

"Yeah, that must be it," Denny said. "Overdid it on the first day!"

The exchange did not quite feel right. Mel's tone was a little too bright, as if she was putting on a show of normality. Something was clearly weighing on her mind. As she climbed the stairs, Denny wondered how much she should or could reveal to Mel. If the woman's own daughter had been replaced with an Interloper, it seemed only right to tell her. But if Denny was wrong, it could prove disastrous.

Maybe the kids were just – changed in some way? Hypnotized, something like that?

If Isobel and the Hawkes twins were real human children, it would simplify things. Denny would have one less reason to venture into the Phantom Dimension.

One less reason to look for Frankie, she thought. *That's what this is about. The fact that she was taken and I just can't help feeling it should have been me.*

Denny had got into the habit of analyzing her own motives since arriving in England. It was not a pleasant pastime. Sighing, she took out her laptop and typed up a report, and emailed it to the foundation. She made a point of including the Tam Lin legend. She hesitated to go into details about the talisman, but then added a concise paragraph.

> 'The object appears to have a powerful negative effect upon Interlopers, and they are keenly aware of how dangerous it is.'

No doubt Jim will have his own say on tonight's events, she thought.

She was too tired to wonder if Jim would soft-pedal in his report, or condemn her for recklessness in letting the fake Marie go. She brushed her teeth, flung herself into bed, and shut her eyes. At first, sleep would not come. She simply became frustrated as well as tired. She told herself this was because of the noise from the street, where a few late drunks were still shouting what might have been compliments or abuse.

Assuming they can tell the difference, she thought. *Brits sure like their beer but so many of 'em can't take it.*

The shouting died down eventually, but, still, sleep did not come. Rolling over onto her side, Denny felt a dull irritation and realized it was the pendant. She sat up and took it off, placing it on the bedside table, then lay down again. Sleep finally came, but it was not peaceful. Almost at once, Denny found herself dreaming of another world. A world in a state of disintegration, a world falling ever more rapidly into chaos.

***

Mel Bavistock mounted the stairs again. Dog-tired, she moved slowly, feeling every second of her thirty-eight years in her bones and muscles. Thirty-eight was not old, she knew that. It just felt ancient at the end of the day.

Used to be a time I ran up here, she thought. *Never do that again. Knackered every night now.*

She paused outside the guest bedroom, and listened. There was no sound of radio or TV. Mel wondered if she should share some of her concerns about Isobel with Denny, who seemed a sympathetic listener. In a small town, it was hard to talk to someone about your problems without being the subject of gossip. Unkind remarks had already been made about the fact that she had let her eight-year-old daughter go astray in Branksholme Woods.

I was just preoccupied for a few minutes, she thought, as she walked towards the door of her apartment. *Now all the old biddies think they can call me a bad mother.*

She was inclined to slump onto the couch and watch late-night TV with the sound low. But she forced herself to go into Isobel's room again to check on the child. As she drew close to the small bed, the nagging inner voice resumed its harsh monologue.

Bad mother – neglect – selfish – don't love her enough ...

"I do love you, more than anything!" she whispered, sitting carefully on the edge of the mattress. "I'd do anything for you."

Isobel stirred slightly but did not open her eyes. Again, Mel tried to feel the love she told herself was there, intense and real. But something prevented her, choking off the emotion. It were as if a cold, hard stone was lodged somewhere in her throat. She could not quell the inner voice. But when she got up and left the bedroom the voice dwindled, became manageable. It was always there, but seeing Isobel seemed to make it worse, scrambling Mel's thoughts and feelings.

Maybe I should ask Doctor Wakefield, she thought. *He might give me something. Pills.*

A few minutes later, she was under her duvet trying to get to sleep. The noise outside had quickly died down. Now only the occasional car broke the silence, and threw sweeping rays of light across the ceiling. Mel felt weariness submerge her anxieties. Then, on the brink of sleep, she heard the sound of a door being opened nearby.

***

"Been a while," said Frankie, who in Denny's dream had her camera perched on her shoulder as usual. "Okay, let's get this shot lined up."

Denny was in the nightmare world of the Phantom Dimension. Around her were ruins, long-eroded remains of what might have been a city. The Interlopers, she knew, now dwelt underground in crude tunnels. In the sky and on the distant horizon were huge, strange entities.

"Frankie?" she said. "What's going on?"

"Got a show to make!" replied her friend. "Tick-tock, we're on a schedule here."

Denny felt chastened, even though she knew she was dreaming, despite the absurdity of the situation. She was standing in an unearthly wilderness under a sky filled with black stars. A bitter wind blew across the rolling red plain. And she was expected to present a show about the paranormal.

"The paranormal," she said, following the familiar script. "Ghosts, poltergeists, spirits, doppelgangers, demons – do they exist? We aim to find out. Do supernatural beings haunt the earth? Do monsters lurk in the shadows? Welcome to another episode of ... of ..."

Denny hesitated, forgetting her lines, despite having spoken them dozens of times.

"Sorry, sorry – can we go again?"

Frankie lowered the camera, shook her head.

"Sorry, that was the last take."

As Denny began to protest, a shadow fell across them. Frankie dropped her camera and ran, shouting for Denny to follow. Instead, Denny felt herself compelled to turn, and look up. A towering form, vast as a skyscraper, was moving ponderously toward her. Though, at least a hundred yards away, it blocked out half the sky. It tore up the reddish turf, producing a cloud of dust that swept into Denny's face. Shielding her eyes with her hand, she could just make out a huge column of dark, glistening flesh, writhing tentacles thicker than tree trunks. Now came a sound so deep she felt it rather than heard it.

Denny fell backwards, and found herself in her bed at the Black Swan. The pale, yellowish glow of a street lamp filtered through a crack in the curtains. Denny heaved a sigh of relief, sat up to check the time on her phone. Then she realized she was not alone. The bedroom door was open, and a small figure stood at the foot of her bed.

"Isobel? Is that you?"

Without replying, the girl walked around until she was standing between Denny and the faint light. The small intruder seemed oddly larger, more imposing.

"I couldn't sleep," said Isobel. "I had a bad dream."

"Well," said Denny, still fuddled by her own nightmare, "maybe your mommy can–"

But before she could say anything more, Isobel had climbed onto the bed and was trying to wriggle under the covers.

"I don't think this is right," Denny exclaimed, but Isobel had already grabbed her around the neck. She could not bring herself to push the little intruder away.

Is she too strong for a real kid? God, I don't know, Denny realized. The small body pressed close to her.

"Tell me a story," said Isobel. "Then I'll go to sleep."

Denny was about to protest, but then a thought occurred to her.

"Okay," she said. "A long, long time ago, there was a young – a young prince called Tam Lin. One day when he was out riding his horse, the Queen of the Fairies saw him, and decided that she wanted him to come live with her. So, she had her warriors follow Tam Lin and ..."

As she continued her improvised version of the folk tale she felt Isobel grow tenser, until eventually the high-pitched voice demanded, "Stop! I don't like this story. I don't want to know how it ends."

Denny reached over and turned on the bedside light. She looked into the tiny, pale face a few inches from hers.

If she's an Interloper, she thought, *she could kill me right now.*

"Well, how about I tell you all about this amazing adventure I had when I went through a magic gateway into another world?"

As she spoke, Denny was reaching past Isobel toward the talisman, which she had laid beside her phone. Isobel grew very still as Denny lifted the stone by its strip of hide. She dangled the pendant above the small head.

"And," Denny went on, "I found this amazing, scary world, full of monsters?"

"I don't like monsters!" whispered Isobel urgently.

"Aw," Denny said, "don't be scared! Monsters can't get you if you have a magic charm like this one. Would you like me to–"

"If you kill me," Isobel hissed in voice suddenly devoid of any childishness, "you know it will destroy the mother!"

Denny froze. Small hands that now felt colder, scalier than before, detached themselves from her arms and neck. The Interloper wriggled away with startling speed, sliding off the bed onto the floor, careful to avoid contact with the hanging pendant. The creature stood up, still far too close for comfort, its form starting to flow in the dim light. Denny wound the lanyard around her hand so that the stone was sticking out from her clenched fist.

If I have to go down, she thought, *I'll go down swinging.*

"What's going on?" asked Mel from the doorway.

A moment later, the light clicked on, dazzling Denny. She blinked, squinted, and by the time she could see clearly again, Isobel had run across the room and wrapped her arms around Mel's waist. The creature whimpered, a perfect facsimile of childish distress. Denny hastily shoved the pendant under her pillow.

"I'm scared mummy!" Isobel sniffled.

"Sorry, Mel, that's my fault," said Denny, climbing out of bed. "I think she was walking in her sleep. I know you're not supposed to wake a sleepwalker, I just got shocked when I saw her standing there."

"Right," said Mel, uncertainly, looking from Denny to Isobel and back. "Okay, Izzy, let's get you back to bed."

Denny made a point of accompanying Mel and the creature into the family apartment. She watched Isobel carefully. The creature avoided her gaze, its eyes downcast. Now that she knew for sure, Denny wondered how she could have ever been uncertain about the girl.

How could a mother not know? Denny wondered. Then she answered herself. *Then again, what mother would believe such a crazy notion?*

Denny lingered in the living room, listening while Mel put her 'daughter' to bed. She felt a pang of remorse. Sooner or later, she would have to tell the woman the truth. It made sense to do it sooner, given the risk all Interlopers posed. But she had no idea how Mel would react.

She could call the cops, Denny thought. *Accuse me of being a threat to her kid. And by any reasonable standard, she'd be right. I'd be no use to anybody in jail. They could cancel my visa, throw me out of the country.*

Denny was still struggling with the dilemma when Mel emerged, running fingers through her tangled hair. Mel gave Denny a weary smile, gestured at the sofa.

"Sorry she woke you up," said the landlady, in a low voice. "Let me make you a cup of hot chocolate? I was going to have one."

"Chocolate's great!" Denny replied, also lowering her voice.

Mustn't wake up the little girl next door, she thought ruefully. *God this is hard.*

As they sat and sipped their chocolate, they engaged in desultory chatter. Denny carefully avoided being too specific about her job, talking about 'media work' and 'TV production'. Mel was interested, but seemed preoccupied.

Not hard to guess what's on her mind, Denny thought.

A sudden storm broke over the valley. Rain lashed the window, and Denny gave an involuntary shiver.

"British weather," Mel remarked. "Not ideal if you want to see the sights."

"No," Denny agreed. "But kind of nice to be indoors. Like in a story by Dickens or one of those guys."

Mel gave a murmur of assent, glancing back at Isobel's bedroom door.

"You worry about her a lot, I guess," Denny said softly. "I remember my mom getting totally frazzled over me and my brothers."

"Poor woman, one's enough for me," Mel said, with a wan smile. Her tone was not as light as her words.

"I've seen quite a lot of people who've been through stressful experiences," Denny began, carefully. "Adults, kids. Sometimes they undergo what seems like a total personality change, you know?"

Mel looked at her, expressionless, her fingers wrapped around the steaming mug of chocolate.

"I remember one case," Denny went on, "where a mother thought her child had been replaced by someone else. That it wasn't her daughter anymore, you know?"

Mel nodded.

"Doctor Wakefield told me it's trauma and stress," she said, her voice quivering slightly. "He said if I just act like nothing's changed, things will go back to normal."

"I met Doctor Wakefield earlier today," said Denny.

"Oh, really?" Mel looked surprised. "Why was that?"

Denny took a breath, about to launch into a full disclosure of everything; Interlopers, Wakefield, the gateway in the woods. But then she choked back her words.

If I tell her, Isobel will know. That might be a death sentence.

She also thought of Lucy's outburst as the Interloper had tried to kill her. About how much the Interlopers hated human beings for ruining their world, somehow. Denny took a gulp of hot chocolate, then put the mug down on a low table.

"Oh, I just asked him something about local folklore,

family history," she said, standing up. "Nice guy. Guess I'd better get some shuteye, now."

Chapter 9: Worse Things than Us

The October dawn was just breaking when Mel crashed into Denny's room.

"What did you do to her?"

Denny struggled up onto her elbows, eyelids still gummed with sleep. Mel stood over her, eyes red, disheveled.

"Do what?" Denny asked, beginning to suspect what had happened.

"It's Isobel," Mel said, and for a moment, Denny was afraid that the woman was going to attack her. But then Mel started pacing back and forth, firing off disjointed sentences as Denny got out of bed. Panicking openly now, Mel took Denny's hand and dragged her into the apartment.

"Tried to get her up – her face, her skin, it's wrong – she can hardly talk – but she said it was you!"

"Mel," Denny said, going up to the woman and putting her hands on her shoulders. "What is it that I have done?"

Instead of answering, Mel gestured to where Isobel was lying on her bed, gazing up at the ceiling. The Interloper was clearly in distress, jerking and quivering. Denny went closer, moving cautiously, and understood what Mel had meant. The small, heart-shaped face was haggard, colorless, and pebbly in texture. And there was a slight whiff of a smell Denny knew well – the stench of Interloper decay.

Crap, she thought. *It must have been too close to the talisman for too long.*

"When did this begin?" she asked, feeling sure she already knew.

"I don't know!" wailed Mel. "But we have to get her to the doctor, and I haven't got a car, and–"

"Come on," Denny said. "You get her ready while I put some clothes on."

A couple of minutes later, Mel was carrying Isobel downstairs behind Denny. The being Mel thought of as a child was wrapped in a tartan blanket. The day was overcast and a steady rain was falling as they rushed over to the rented jeep.

"Oh God, what's happening?" Mel cried as Denny opened the rear door.

Isobel's face was being worn away by the rain. Streaks of viscous, brownish liquid were running down the decaying cheeks.

"We need to get her back to the woods," Denny said. "Wakefield can't help her."

Mel looked at her, eyes huge with astonishment and panic. "What? Are you mad?"

"Just get in, I'll explain on the way," Denny went on. "You've got to trust me. That's not Isobel."

"What?" Mel repeated. "What are you talking about?"

This time, however, Denny heard doubt in the woman's voice.

"Trust your instincts, your judgment," Denny persisted, as she reversed hastily into the main street. Her driving was sub-par, she knew, but fortunately, it was well before Machen's rush hour.

"Isobel and the other two kids were abducted, and replaced," she went on, slewing the jeep around and heading for the bridge. "Isobel's a changeling, a kind of supernatural creature. Or an alien, whatever term you prefer."

Don't get lost in the details, Denny warned herself. *Stick to the point.*

"Isobel is still alive in – in another world," she said, trying to sound totally certain. "I know where the gateway to that world is and I think I can go through and get the kids."

Mel, glimpsed in the rear-view mirror, was staring open-mouthed. But then her expression changed. Denny saw her look down, scrutinizing the diminutive figure, the decaying head resting on her lap.

No mother should have to face this, Denny thought.

"I know it sounds crazy, but do you believe me?" she persisted.

Mel said nothing as the jeep raced over the hump-backed stone bridge, leaving the road briefly before landing with a sickening jolt. The impact produced a grunt from the fake Isobel. It was a deep, animalistic sound, nothing like a child moaning in distress.

"Oh my God."

Denny could just make out Mel's words over the engine,

the rain, and the steady beat of the windscreen wipers.

She's coming around, I guess.

"But – how can this be true?" Mel demanded. "Wouldn't we know if these things existed, kidnapped people?"

"Some people *do* know, let's leave it at that," Denny retorted. "Will you help me get her to the gateway?"

Mel nodded, and a thought struck Denny. She held her phone out behind her.

"There's a number, Jim, call him for me now," she ordered. "I'll need his help."

"Doing what?" Mel asked as she took the phone. "Is it – dangerous?"

"Very, but only for me," Denny replied.

"You've done this before, been through this – this gateway thing?"

Denny made an involuntary clutch at the pendant that she had put on under her shirt.

"Yeah, but I'm holding a better hand than last time. Now make that call!"

***

Wakefield was having breakfast and a somewhat awkward conversation with Jim when the call came. Jim put Denny on speaker and they listened as she explained the situation – with occasional cursing at a tricky bend in the road.

"I'll be right there," Jim said, dropping his fork. "If you want to come, Russ–"

"No problem," Wakefield replied. "I half-expected there'd be a crisis with the children. I'll get my medical kit."

They took the van, with Wakefield navigating, and soon parked beside the jeep. There was no sign of Denny, Mel, or the Interloper. But the back door of the jeep was open. Jim looked inside, recoiled.

"What is it?" Wakefield asked.

Then the stench hit him. Even in the weak light of the autumn dawn, he could see dark stains on the upholstery.

"They fall apart quickly," Jim explained, opening the doors of the van. "Rot away in front of your eyes."

"But getting it back into this Phantom Dimension, that will save it?"

Jim shrugged, then took a double-barreled shotgun out of the van.

"Not an expert, mate – but why else would it want to go home? Here, can you carry this?"

Jim handed Wakefield what looked at first like a leash and harness for a seeing-eye dog. Then he realized that it was far more substantial, a bespoke restraint made of steel and Kevlar.

"You're going to try and control it, once you're on the other side?" Wakefield asked.

"That's the plan – hastily improvised," said Jim, taking out a small backpack. "The harness is child-sized so we could try and capture one safely. But now, well ..."

He slammed the van doors, turned towards Branksholme Woods.

"I half-expected she'd try to cross over again. This time I'm not letting her go in alone."

***

"Bloody Hell," Jim said. "It's a city. They're actually civilized. Sort of."

It was true. They had fallen from the gateway onto a kind of raised platform made of pale, rough-hewn stone. Around them stretched hundreds of square buildings, each about the size of a bungalow but with flat roofs. They had doorways and windows, all just gaps in the walls. No glass or wood was evident. Here and there much larger structures towered above the smaller structures. Everything seemed to be made of the same pale stone.

Above them a pale, sunless sky radiated an unpleasant, harsh light. Jim winced, put on a set of wraparound shades. He stared up at vast, drifting entities Denny called the Black Stars. As far as she could tell, all of the huge predators were floating too high to endanger them. And there was no sign of life anywhere on the ground.

"So where is everybody?" Denny asked the Interloper.

Instead of answering, Isobel jumped to its feet and

scampered to the edge of the platform. Jim hauled on an improvised leash, jerking the creature onto its back. Denny winced at seeing a being that still looked like a sick child being treated so brutally. The creature was still wearing pastel-colored pajamas. Seeing Denny's expression, Jim shook his head.

"No room for sentiment," he said. "You taught me that last time."

"True," Denny conceded. "Okay, second and last time of asking Izzy ..."

She reached down and lifted up the talisman.

"You want me to step a little closer? You know I'd do it. We're doing this, with or without you."

The fake Isobel had apparently stopped dying. Its face was ravaged by scars and swellings, but no longer weeping rancid brown pus. It had reverted to its true form, with sharp talons, a tapering muzzle, and deep-set, piggy eyes. When it spoke, Denny struggled to make out the words, formed as they were by a circular mouth rimmed with needle-sharp teeth.

"Keep away! I will lead you there. Children are safe."

Yeah, that's the deal, Denny thought. *But how likely are you and your people to keep to it?*

As they set off after the creature, she realized that she had suddenly begun to see the Interlopers as people. They were monstrous and deformed by human standards, perhaps. But she could not deny that they were a race of intelligent beings with their own history, culture, and presumably ethics of a kind.

We must look hideous to them, she thought. *Yet they risk everything to venture into our world.*

"Better late than never," it hissed over its shoulder. "We have no choice but to try and live among you. No matter how vile you are."

Jim looked from the creature to Denny, raised an eyebrow.

"Izzy's reading my mind," she explained. Then, raising her voice, "So why not cut to the chase and just tell us why you're doing all this?"

Isobel's only reply was a grunt. It continued to lope along

ahead of them, moving faster now. It was apparently gaining strength, or confidence. They were jogging briskly along what passed for a street, a dusty track-way between two rows of square buildings.

Now they were closer and her eyes had adjusted to the weird light, Denny could make out more detail. The Interlopers' architecture was not quite so crude and stark as she had thought at first. There were traces of elaborate carvings on stone lintels and around the unglazed windows. But many of the buildings showed signs of damage, with large cracks running from ground to roof in some cases.

"Are we in an earthquake zone or something?" Denny asked.

Again, Isobel said nothing.

"Black ops," Jim suggested. "Top secret."

"Hell, yeah," Denny agreed. "Or maybe it doesn't know."

"Yeah," Jim went on. "Probably just a dumb grunt obeying orders."

Isobel stopped, turned to look at the humans.

"Reverse psychology!" it croaked painfully, then turned to lope onward. "Not play your games."

"Sod off, bloody mind reader," mumbled Jim.

Denny peered ahead through the ski goggles she had brought from London, part of some general gear she had only half-expected to use. Slung across her back was a crossbow – legal in England, just like Jim's shotgun. Before they came through the gateway, Jim had politely asked if she knew how to use the medieval weapon. She had explained that she had made a short documentary about medieval weapons for her journalism course and had 'kind of picked it up'.

That was a few years back, though.

She glanced up, and saw that one of the Black Stars had descended so that she could now clearly make out the huge, single eye in the center of the five-pointed body. Tendrils, still thread-like at this distance, were unwinding from the vast arms.

"We'd better get under cover soon," said Jim.

Isobel snorted, perhaps out of amusement. It was no longer possible to read any human emotions into the creature's responses.

But it can still read us, Denny reminded herself.

"Can we go into one of these – these houses?" she asked.

Without replying Isobel swerved through a doorway. They followed and found themselves inside a featureless room. At first, Denny thought it was empty, then saw eyes gleaming in the murk. Denny removed her shades and saw that, in the corner, a group of Interlopers was huddled. Jim raised his gun, but the creatures showed no sign of even noticing them, let along attacking.

"What's wrong with them?" Jim whispered urgently.

"Scared." Isobel reached up slowly and pushed the gun barrel up toward the ceiling. Its voice was now barely comprehensible. "All people scared."

"Of what?" Denny demanded, but again the Interloper ignored her, squatting down in the middle of the room.

Jim flattened himself against the wall and worked his way along to a window. He took a quick glance outside, jerked back.

"That thing is rising again," he said. "Give it a minute."

Jim stopped, frowned. A vibration ran through the floor, a distant rumbling that grew, then dwindled. It reminded Denny of a London Underground train passing beneath her. The Interlopers in the corner reacted by emitting high-pitched screeches and cowering even closer together. They covered their heads with their claws.

When scary things get scared ...

They did not talk for another minute or so. Denny tried to calculate exactly how much time had already passed in the outside world, could not focus, gave up, and guessed at several hours. Jim looked out again.

"It's gone, I think."

They set off again, leaving the terrified Interlopers behind, weaving their way through a labyrinth of dark alleyways. Eventually they emerged into the open, or very nearly did. Ahead of them was a long, low heap of rubble, beyond which was the kind of bleak, reddish plain Denny had seen before. On the horizon, a huge, dark object loomed. It reminded her vaguely of Mount Fuji in shape, only stretched upwards. The mountain, if that's what it was, seemed to be shrouded in mist around its base.

"City walls, yes?" Jim asked Izzy, gesturing at the rubble, which seemed to stretch all the way around the settlement. "Not very effective, it seems."

"There," it said, raising a claw. "There! Sacrifices out there."

"They're just pegged out in the open?" Jim asked, staring incredulous into the hazy distance.

"Remember, to the kids it's just been a few hours, not weeks," Denny reminded him. "They won't be starving yet. Maybe dehydrated, though."

"Sacrifices to what?" Jim demanded, jerking on Isobel's leash again. "What else is out there? Come on, terrify us!"

Isobel looked up into the man's face.

"Eats souls. Younger is better."

"Thanks," said Jim, trying to sound sarcastic. "That's a big help."

He looked up at the Black Stars, then back at Denny. So far as she could see, none of the drifting creatures were descending. But out on the red plain they would be very obvious targets.

"We've got to go," she said.

"Thought so," he grinned. "Let's get some more exercise."

Isobel balked at leaving the city. Instead the creature pulled at its leash, screeched and snarled. No threats, not even a shotgun pointed at its face could persuade it to move.

"We should kill it now," Jim said.

"It knows we won't," Denny sighed. "Let it go."

As she said the words, she noticed that the creature was in *Frozen*-themed pajamas.

Isobel fled back into the nearest alley without another sound.

"A bit of taunting would have been nice," Jim grumbled, as they clambered over the low line of shattered stone.

"Yeah," Denny said. "Nothing says 'You Are Now up Shit Creek' like your native guide fleeing in panic."

***

"What do we do if they don't come back?" asked Mel Bavistock. "They've been gone for ages! Oh God, what do we do?"

She looks to me for guidance, Wakefield thought.

"Time flows much more slowly there," he explained, struggling with the concept himself. "According to Jim, a year there is like a decade here – something like that."

"A year?" Mel's eyes were huge with shock, now.

Brilliant, he thought. *I couldn't have used minutes and hours?*

"But Jim said that Denny has been into this – this other dimension," he went on. "And she came out again after a few hours. So we can wait here, maybe take turns."

Mel collapsed, all the stress of the morning finally taking its toll. She fell clumsily into the undergrowth, crying in fear and frustration. Wakefield helped her up and led her to a fallen tree-trunk. It was a chill morning, and he put his jacket around her shoulders.

"I'm so sorry," he said, taking a tissue from his pocket. "Sorry for my part in this."

"I don't care!" she exclaimed, then blew her nose. "I don't care what you've done, I just want my daughter back!"

What are the chances? Wakefield wondered. *Slim, is what my fear says.*

"I don't know much about these people," he admitted. "But they know more than we do. We have to trust them. I do."

As he said the words, he realized he did not really mean them. He simply knew so little about Denny and Jim that he was clutching at hope, not thinking things through. He looked over at the shimmering, translucent gateway into the Phantom Dimension. It seemed slightly smaller than before. He almost commented on this, then thought better of it.

"Should we call the police?" sniffled Mel.

The suggestion was so bizarre, so unexpected that Wakefield almost laughed. He tried to imagine the detectives, whom he routinely worked with, solemnly taking down his testimony. The questions they would ask, before having him detained under the Mental Health Act.

Poor old Russ, he could imagine them saying in the canteen. *Pressure finally got to him. And the booze, of course.*

"Probably best not to involve them at this stage," he said carefully.

He got up and fetched his bag.

"I always carry a flask of coffee," he said. "Want some?"

***

The three small figures were covered in a web of pale strands that flexed and pulsed. It was a living cage, like the one Denny had cut away from the fake Lucy. This time there was no doubt that the captives were human, though. Even from here, she could hear a wailing, the weak cries of children seeing the first hope of rescue. They began to run, but then the reddish dirt darkened with a vast shadow. Jim spun around, aimed upward, and fired his shotgun. A black, whip-like object lashed Denny across the face. She looked up, saw most of the sky blocked out. The Black Star was within reach, but Jim had apparently stung it. The vast creature gave a spasm, retracted the wounded tendril, but others began to reach down. Denny ducked, knowing it was irrational given the exposed position.

But there's no way those kids have been out here for weeks unless ...

Isobel had told the truth. The Black Star's tentacles flailed, withdrew, reacting far more violently than they had when simply shot. The creature's body rippled, then it began to rise, gradually gaining speed. Denny could just make out bulges along the arms, wondered if they were organic sacs containing hydrogen or some other gas. Shrugging, she turned to the prisoners. Jim was already striding forward, taking out a large hunting knife.

"Don't worry, kids, we'll soon–"

The force that had repelled the Black Star from the children struck Jim. He recoiled, dropping the knife, and fell to his knees. Denny rushed forward, got her hands under his shoulders, and dragged him away from the white web. She heard despairing cries from the children, felt a pang of shame, rage at their situation.

"Like a kick in the balls, only in the brain," Jim gasped. "Jesus Christ, that hurts worse than stepping on Legos in the dark."

Denny had to laugh despite herself. She held up the talisman.

"Okay," she told him, "let's see if this trinket always works to counteract their magic, science, whatever."

She scurried forward, picked up Jim's knife, then took two hesitant steps. She was just a few inches past the point where Jim had collapsed when she felt a stabbing pain between her eyes. It grew quickly as she advanced, building into a migraine that clouded her vision with pulses of green radiance.

Denny was crawling by the time she reached the web-work. She felt more than saw the living bonds, and could just make out the children's cries. She began to cut away the bonds of the nearest small figure as the pain pushed her to the brink of blackout.

They must be protected from this pain, she thought. *Or this web-creature only radiates outward ...*

It was almost impossible to think, but she kept working. The white web gave more quickly than she had expected, and as the strands parted, she felt a slight but real diminution in the pain. She wanted to slash violently at the strands, but the danger to the children kept her sawing with the hunting knife. She became aware that a sticky liquid was running down her arm.

Yeah, bleed out you bastard!

"I want my mummy!"

The voice was Isobel's – the real one – audible above the wailing of the Hawkes twins.

"We'll get you home," Denny managed to croak. "Don't be scared."

The word 'scared' was drowned out by a noise so deep she felt more than heard it. If they had been on earth, it would have suggested some vast machine, perhaps a warship entering harbor. Denny could not believe such technology existed in this world. It must be a living thing.

The earthquake, in the city. Cracking the walls. The cry of a living thing.

"Denny! Hurry up!" called Jim.

For the first time, she heard outright panic in his voice.

He can see what's coming, she realized.

The stabbing pain was just bearable now, so she could stagger to her feet and pull the real Isobel free from the white web. The creature was dying, or at least retreating, the strands untangling themselves and withdrawing into the reddish soil. The Hawkes twins were suddenly free and ran to Denny, grabbing her around the legs. Jim appeared, scooping up a bawling twin under each arm, and ran back the way they had come. Denny had glimpsed his face. She clutched Isobel and followed, not daring to look back.

It's the living mountain from my nightmare, she thought. *The sacrifice was going to keep it away from the city.*

The blast of sound came again, much louder now, almost deafening her. After her ears stopped ringing, she heard something else, a roaring like a waterfall, or an avalanche. It was the noise of a colossus on the move. In pursuit. Denny risked a glance over her shoulder.

The roughly conical shape that had loomed on the horizon was now much closer. It was still shrouded in haze around its base, but Denny realized that was because it was moving. The sides of the colossal entity consisted of glistening grayish-white tissue dotted with roundish shapes. She could not make out much detail. She did not particularly want to.

Nothing that big can move too fast, she told herself. *Like a man trying to catch a fly.*

Then she thought of a man trying to step on an ant, and forced herself to run faster.

They reached the outskirts of the city and began to weave their way among the low-rise houses. By now, some inhabitants had come out of hiding, but were milling in confusion or fleeing from the approaching menace. Once an Interloper blocked their way, its arms raised in what might have been menace or simply surprise. With her free hand, Denny raised the talisman and ran straight at it, forcing the creature to hurl itself aside.

Again, the deep roar of the colossal creature ran through the earth under their feet, sending up spurts of dust. There was a crash, and the side of a house fell into the alleyway ahead of them. Looking back as they scrambled over the shattered stone, Denny saw the mountainous being, just visible through a rising cloud of dust and debris. It was hard to judge, but the monster seemed to be well inside the ruined city walls. And it was now getting visibly larger by the second. She could now make out what the round bulges on its sides were. Not growths. Grotesque human faces, dozens of yards across.

We're not going to make it, she thought. *We're gonna get stepped on.*

Jim stumbled on rubble, dropped one of the Hawkes twins, and struggled to pick the terrified child up again. The rumbling roar from the colossus was almost unbearably loud, now. But even as she covered her ears, Denny realized that it was not just an animal sound. There was a hint of something she had never expected to hear. A series of distinct syllables, just perceptible amid the immense blast of sonic energy.

Denny turned to Jim, reached up to pull his face down, kissed him. He reeled back, comically surprised.

"You get them home," she said. "I've got an appointment with an old friend."

"What the—"

She held up a finger to Jim's lips, raised the talisman with her other hand, then got down and talked to Isobel.

"Can you run fast?" she asked.

Isobel nodded. Denny could see the girl was trying to be brave, but almost ready to cry.

"Then run!" she said.

"That stone won't protect you!" Jim shouted. "That's crazy!"

"Get going," she shot back, and began running back towards the moving mountain. "I'll see you later, maybe!"

***

The gateway darkened for a moment, then a child fell through and started crying. Mel rushed forward, recognized Michael Hawkes, and hesitated. She bent down and picked up the boy, just in time to be hit in the small of the back by Trudy

Hawkes. By this time, Wakefield was helping, in a haphazard way. Jim arrived with Isobel in his arms, and was followed by a blast of heat.

"Isobel!"

Wakefield noted that Mel, to her credit, did not simply drop the Hawkes boy, but instead tried to gather up all the children. Jim handed Isobel over, and there were several minutes of talking, crying, confusion. But it was clear from Jim's expression, as much as his words that he did not expect Denny to be coming back.

Explanations were attempted, then abandoned. But one problem presented itself.

"What about the fake twins?" Wakefield asked.

"I can call in a special unit," said Jim, trying to brush red dust off his jacket. "We can – well, take them discreetly, with your help."

"You mean call them in for some kind of check-up?" Wakefield asked, looking at Michael and Trudy. "I suppose that makes sense. The parents trust me."

The twins were scruffy and pale, but like Isobel, they seemed unharmed. Seeing Wakefield's expression, Jim patted him gently on the arm.

"Believe me, Denny would think this was a fair exchange," he murmured.

Wakefield nodded. They conferred some more, slightly apart from Mel and the children, so as not to be overheard. Then they agreed to go back to the clinic to make sure the children were okay, and find them something to eat.

"I'm sorry, Mummy," Isobel kept saying, as they found their way out of the woods. "I promise I won't wander off again."

It was mid-morning, now, over four hours since the expedition had departed through the gateway. As they approached the edge of the trees, Wakefield saw flashing lights, and his heart sank. His receptionist would, of course, have found the clinic and his home empty, and given recent events, would have called the police. Either she or the police would have found the fetid residue in the bedroom. Denny's jeep and Jim's van would be visible from the town.

QED, he thought. *No bluffing our way out of this one.*

When they emerged, two uniformed officers rushed over to them, followed by paramedics. There were blankets and hot drinks for the children. There was talk of statements being taken, and Jim was looked upon with some suspicion despite the children insisting loudly that he 'and the nice lady' had saved them. A detective whom Wakefield had worked with on and off for years beckoned him aside.

"Okay," he said, "I can cut you a good bit of slack here, since all the kids are accounted for. But anything you want to say – anything at all to help when I have to report to my boss – much appreciated, eh?"

For a moment, the officer's words did not sink in.

"All the children?" the doctor asked.

The detective looked quizzically at him.

"Yeah, the Bavistock kid and the Hawkes twins. Are we on the same page?"

The fake twins are gone, Wakefield thought, looking out over the valley. *But they didn't go back through the gateway.*

"Come on, Russ," the detective pleaded. "Look at the bloody press, they're here already. Christ, it's the BBC. Come and sit in the car."

"Okay," Wakefield began. "These kids have been through the wringer, and I think that killing yesterday must have triggered – some kind of subconscious urge to return to the scene of their own trauma. It does happen in these cases. I can cite research ..."

By the time he had finished improvising, Wakefield had almost convinced himself.

***

As she grew nearer, the huge voice sounded again, deafening her with its plea. The words rang through the ground, the air, her flesh, and bone.

DENNY. HELP ME.

She realized how stupid continuing to run towards the thing was. She glanced back to see that Jim and the children had gone. She could see Interlopers scrambling over wrecked buildings in panic, but no sign of the humans.

Before the advancing wave of dust overwhelmed her, she looked up, straining to see again the vast, distorted face that had not at first registered – so unlikely that this was its location. The face that promised some kind of closure. The oversized face on the side of a living mountain that apparently ate souls.

"Not looking your best, Frankie," she said, glimpsing her friend's features for a moment. "But I guess we've both been through a lot."

Denny clutched the talisman and closed her eyes, half-expecting to be simply crushed. But the words spoken in the immense voice gave her hope, of a kind. The Eater of Souls was studded with images of the humans it had absorbed. Most of the vast faces on the surface of the entity were those of children, but a few were adults. Frankie's was one of the best-defined.

Because she's not been fully consumed, Denny told herself. *I must believe that. Something of her survives in there. I must believe that, I must!*

Chapter 10: Victims and Survivors

"But," protested Zoffany, "I think we've established that the resilient Interlopers almost certainly aren't equipped with one of these – talisman devices. Davison's testimony states quite clearly–"

Benson casually waved his chief scientist to silence.

"The fact remains that Lucy, and the children of Machen, were able to survive in our world for far longer than they should have been able to. We need to know *why*. Analysis of tissue and blood samples has failed to find anything new. Whatever it is could well be inside."

Zoffany began to object to this line of reasoning, but was again discreetly ordered to shut up.

"Dissection is the sensible option," Benson went on. "The bad news is, after making a few discreet overtures, we have been unable to find a reputable surgeon willing to undertake the task."

The chairman paused, looked down at his desk, brushed an imaginary speck of dust off the mahogany surface.

Bastard, Zoffany thought. *Frigging mind games, like a Bond villain.*

"And the good news?" she could not help asking.

"You get a bonus after you cut it open."

Four hours later, preparations were complete.

"So, you've all read the briefing?"

Harriet Zoffany stared at each member of the security team in turn. A couple of guards failed to meet her eye.

"I'll recap for the benefit of anyone who is unclear on the details," she said. "What we're dealing with is *not* a child. It is not a little girl. It is an alien entity that has killed at least one person and injured several more. Understand?"

There were nods, grunts of affirmation.

"Some of you," she went on, "may be wondering why we are doing this in the middle of the night. Mister Benson decreed it, so that there would be fewer non-essential personnel around. Minimizes the risk to innocent bystanders, should we screw up."

After they had donned their respirators, Zoffany led the

team from the elevators to the corridor where Room 101 lay. Outside the cell door, Forster was already waiting. He was supervising a technician who had sealed the edges of the door and then pumped in nitrogen gas. The heavier-than-air gas was now at just under adult head height, totally immersing the prisoner. Zoffany had staked her reputation on this subduing the creature without proving fatal.

"Okay?" she asked the security chief.

Forster nodded and the technician removed the pipe from a hole drilled in the observation window. Looking inside the cell, Zoffany saw Lucy lying motionless on the bed. The scientist felt her heart rate increase as she wondered if she had in fact killed Lucy. Then the small, pajama-clad figure stirred. A leg flexed, pulling weakly at the chain that shackled it to the wall.

"It's still alive," she said, stepping back from the viewing slit. "Assume it will be alert and able to attack. Restrain arms and legs before undoing the shackles."

And may God forgive me for this, she thought. *There's more than one inhuman being involved in this.*

***

Denny struggled blindly in darkness, panicking as she felt her lungs fill with a vaguely acrid fluid. Every breath she tried to take drew the luke-warm fluid deeper inside her. Eventually she blacked out, certain that she was dying, only to wake again. She was adrift in what seemed total blackness. Her limbs were not exactly tied up, but the gelatinous substance around her made movement difficult. Her eyes were open, but coated with an unpleasant greasy film.

If I keep struggling, I'll exhaust myself, she reasoned. *And I'm not dying, clearly. Not yet, anyway.*

Instead of fighting the gelatinous stuff, she tried to focus on what had gotten her here. She remembered looking up at Frankie's face, impossibly huge as it bulged from the surface of the monster. Then she had been swept up by a kind of pseudopod that had gradually absorbed her.

It carried me inside, into the belly of the beast.

'Denny? That you?'

Frankie's voice sounded in her head, apparently coming from all directions and none. It was faint, but very audible above the sound of Denny's pulse hammering in her ears.

"Frankie?" she tried to say, only to gag on the dense fluid. *Which must,* she reasoned, *be feeding me oxygen. Because I'm not inhaling air.*

'Don't fight anything with your body, Denny! Fight with your mind! Form words with your mind!'

Denny struggled to speak silently, imagining the sound words would make.

'This any good?'

The reply came instantly.

'That'll do! Okay, I've got good news and bad news. Want the bad first?'

'Okay,' Denny signaled.

'We're being eaten. Real slow, the way big beasts do it … but eaten nonetheless.'

Denny felt panic rising again, although she had always known this was the most likely scenario.

'And the good news?' she asked.

There was a pause, and Denny was about to ask again when Frankie replied.

'We're going to redefine the concept of bringing something down from the inside.'

Denny tried to laugh, forgetting there was no air in her lungs. She became aware that she was not, in fact, in total darkness. There was a faint, greenish glow in the distance, a blob of light linked to her by a few filaments of dimmer radiance. She blinked, then closed her eyes, but the pattern did not vanish.

'Frankie? I'm seeing some kind of network with – I guess my mind's eye?'

'That's me!' Frankie responded. 'Keep looking, kind of. See the rest of us.'

Sure enough, dozens and then hundreds of luminous strands materialized around Denny, a huge network extending far into the distance. They were, she realized, like veins of precious mineral inside the living mountain.

'Psychic links,' Frankie explained. 'But most of the humans are scared kids, hard to get much sense of out of them. The Interlopers in here just don't give a damn. Fatalistic. Still, you're here now. Really appreciate you following me through!'

In her own mind, she's only been here maybe a few hours, at most, Denny reminded herself. *No point in going into that.*

'How does this work?' Denny asked. 'Can I talk to anyone?'

'Yeah,' Frankie replied. 'But the further away they are, the harder it gets. It's almost impossible to mind-share with Interlopers outside the creature. And, like I said–'

'Interlopers?' Denny interrupted. 'Tell me more about that.'

Before Frankie could reply, Denny felt a wave of movement pass through the dense fluid around her. It was a slow-moving spasm within the vast organism. At first, Denny assumed it was just part of the colossal creature's normal behavior. But then the wave came again, and she felt it shift her body with a definite jolt.

'What was that?' Denny asked.

'It's what we were hoping for,' Frankie replied. 'Can you feel the stone getting warmer?'

Denny focused her attention on the talisman. Was the stone transmitting heat to her body? It was hard to tell in the luke-warm surroundings of jelly-like tissue.

'Not sure,' she admitted. 'I might be imagining – Whoa!'

The third wave was violent, a seismic shock that must have embraced a large part of the mountainous Soul Eater.

'That's what we were all banking on,' Frankie said. 'The talisman is the one thing it can't digest. That's why all of us in here – the ones who can still think, at least – wanted you to come.'

Before Denny could frame a reply, the Soul Eater began to heave and shudder in a continuous outburst of discomfort. Now the heat coming from the talisman was unmistakable. The stone was affecting the vast predator at least as violently as it had harmed the Interlopers.

'What happens now?' Denny managed to ask as more

ferocious convulsions hurled her back and forth inside the glutinous darkness.

'With luck, it throws up,' Frankie replied.

Oh great, Denny thought. *I get to be a pavement pizza.*

The buffeting from the throes of the monster was so violent now that it was hard for Denny to think. She had no idea which way up she was, and the mucilaginous tissue was now uncomfortably hot. And getting hotter.

Broiled alive, she thought. *What a way to go.*

But now the darkness around her was giving way to a faint glow.

I must be nearer the skin of the beast.

'I can see—' she began to signal, but before she could finish, one final, tremendous spasm flung her up toward the light.

***

Lucy wailed like a terrified seven-year-old as the guards pinned her down and fastened the restraints. Zoffany hoped that the others weren't feeling as conflicted by the situation as she was. Her mind knew that they were dealing with a dangerous, inhuman creature. Her emotions – no doubt boosted by Lucy's psychic powers – screamed that a child was in distress.

Fortunately, Forster had picked his team well, and the creature was soon laid on a gurney and wheeled briskly through the under-level corridors. A gag reduced the screams and sobs, but Lucy continued her convincing act all the way to the door of the medical research unit. When the team took her inside, however, the creature fell silent. Lucy stared around her with huge, dark eyes.

Zoffany glanced up at the camera in the corner of the room. Benson was expecting success from his chief researcher, not doubt and hesitation. Lucy's gurney was wheeled under a modified X-ray machine and the creature's head placed in a special clamp. Zoffany had expected the captive to struggle, but it remained still. The security team withdrew to the doorway, knowing what was coming.

This might be easier than I thought, she thought as she retreated behind a lead screen. *But we still don't know what effect the radiation will have on it.*

"Right," she said to a technician. "Fire it up."

There was a deep hum, a click. The machine was re-positioned by a remote control and another image taken. The procedure was repeated until Lucy's body had been scanned from all angles.

"Now, we'll see," Zoffany murmured. "The moment of truth."

She stepped out from behind the screen, beckoning Forster's team back in. The last position of the X-ray unit had placed it between Zoffany and the gurney. As she stepped around the bulky machine, she saw that Lucy had managed to tear one arm free and was slashing at its restraints with razor-sharp talons. After a brief struggle, Forster's men subdued Lucy with a steel net and cattle prods. The creature lay curled on the tiled floor while Zoffany reported to Benson that the first phase of the plan was complete.

"There was no kind of talisman in that body," Zoffany declared. "No magic amulet to change the laws of nature."

"I can see that," the chairman replied. "I can also see that the internal organs are fascinating and that the subject is proving awkward. I've received some information from one of our field operatives that might be of use to you."

As Benson explained, Zoffany started to shake her head.

"A huge overdose of morphine?"

"Apparently it does subdue them, if only for a few moments," Benson said simply. "That country doctor seems to have performed a very worthwhile experiment."

Zoffany looked at Lucy, still writhing in the steel net, surrounded by guards. It would be impossible to do anything with the creature unless it could be immobilized in some way. The last time it had been rendered inactive had been with a massive blow to the cranium. Compared with that, a drug overdose was at least more scientific.

"Very well," she said. "I'll try it."

"Don't kill it," Benson cautioned. "Unless it is unavoidable."

After Lucy was knocked out, Zoffany prepared for exploratory surgery. She carefully drew a dotted line down the sternum and called for a scalpel.

I'm going to be the first person to explore the internal organs of a non-human intelligence, she thought. *But the Nobel committee won't be getting a nomination.*

The scientist began to cut into the pale, colorless flesh. Dark fluid leaked out, ran in rivulets down the creature's ribcage into a gutter.

"I will first expose the heart and lungs, or more precisely the Interloper organs analogous to those," she said, glancing up at the camera. "It seems reasonable to assume that functionality–"

Lucy opened her eyes and lifted her head, looking straight at Zoffany, and her features returned to those of a defenseless child. Zoffany was so startled that she froze. One of Forster's guards took a jab at the creature with his electric prod.

"No," Zoffany warned. "Just put in a morphine IV, should have done that earlier."

One of her lab assistants clumsily inserted the needle into the creature's neck. Lucy did not flinch, but simply looked down at the incision on its chest. Then it looked up at Zoffany again and spoke in a breathy, little-girl voice.

"Denny says hi," it said, as its head fell back onto the operating table. "And she'll be back soon."

Zoffany hesitated, then started cutting again.

***

"Say Aaah for me," said Wakefield.

"Aaaaaah!" replied Isobel, loudly.

Wakefield shared a smile with Mel Bavistock.

"I think she's made a remarkable – let's call it a recovery," he concluded.

Mel nodded. Wakefield had noticed that she never let her daughter get more than a couple of feet away from her.

Can't blame her, he thought. *She's been through hell. And so has her little girl.*

"Are you sleeping all right?" he asked Isobel.

The girl nodded.

"I thought I would have nightmares about that bad place, but I didn't," she said.

"And you know it's best not to talk about it if you want to keep the nightmares away?" Wakefield said in his best 'kindly uncle' voice.

Isobel nodded, looked up at her mother.

"I promised I wouldn't say anything. And so did Trudy and Michael."

"That's right, dear," Mel replied, absent-mindedly tidying her daughter's hair. "Least said, soonest mended."

Three days had passed since the return of Isobel and the Hawkes twins. As before, Wakefield supported the official line that the traumatized children had returned to Branksholme Woods in some vaguely-defined 'cathartic gesture'. The media feeding frenzy had soon abated when it became apparent that nobody else had been brutally slain. Jim Davison had prevailed on Mel not to reveal Denny's disappearance.

"Well, that's about it for now," Wakefield said, standing up and getting a lollipop from a jar on his desk. "Here, don't tell the dentist I gave it you."

After the Bavistocks had gone, the doctor finished the day's online admin. After his receptionist had left, he stood for a moment in the empty waiting room. Then he went into his house, changing into old walking clothes, and set off up the hill toward Branksholme Woods.

Jim was getting ready to leave when Wakefield entered the clearing. The gateway, Wakefield saw, was still present. At twilight, the shimmering globe was just perceptible under the trees.

"Nothing going on?" asked Wakefield, already knowing the answer.

"Just a few hikers passing by – didn't see me," replied Jim, shouldering his backpack. "I'll be back to relieve you at midnight. Looks like rain, so—"

Wakefield ran past the other man, heading for the shotgun that leaned against a stump. A figure was forming in the gateway. By the time Wakefield had picked up the gun, a clearly-defined human form had appeared.

Or at least, it looks human, Wakefield thought.

The figure fell onto the leaf-mold with a thud and gasp. It was not Denny, Wakefield could see that. The newcomer was feminine but far too small, the hair too short. What's more, the person was caked in a layer of yellowish gunk that looked something like congealed bacon fat. She got up and crawled out from under the gateway, then collapsed.

Exhaustion, thought Wakefield, but then remembered some medical cases he had seen. *Or someone who hasn't been able to walk for a good while.*

"Who are you?" snapped Jim, stepping forward and holding out a cattle prod.

"Jim?"

The voice was weak, rasping, but the name was clear.

"Frankie?" Jim said, lowering the prod. "Oh my God."

The gateway darkened again and another figure fell through. This one, the doctor recognized. Denny, too, was covered in the hardening mucous. Jim took a step back, glanced at the puzzled Wakefield.

"We can't be sure it's really them, not without tests," he said.

"Feel free to test us all," Denny said, struggling upright, and then moving swiftly out from under the gateway. "But you'd better be ready to put in some overtime."

"What–" began Jim, but before he could ask what Denny meant, the sphere darkened, and a third mucous-encrusted figure fell onto the forest floor. Denny dashed forward and picked up what Wakefield saw was a small boy. The child's eyes were huge with fear.

"See, Jimmy, I told you it was okay," Denny said soothingly. She looked up at Wakefield, grinned. "We came through first to show them it was safe."

The boy made a gagging sound and a lump of hardened mucous came out of his mouth.

"Here," Denny went on, handing the boy to Jim. "This is Jimmy, your namesake! Maybe you could help clean the gunk off of them, guys?"

Wakefield nodded, baffled, and started to tear the encrusted organic matter from Frankie. The diminutive woman smiled ruefully, raised herself up on an elbow.

"Thanks," she said. "Proper introductions later, I guess. There were about a dozen of us in there, not quite sure. Some of them ..."

A frown passed over Frankie's face.

"Some had been almost totally absorbed, but their brains and nervous systems were still active. We didn't realize until we escaped. We had to leave them behind."

This is lunacy, thought Wakefield. *But I've seen so much madness already. Why not another dose?*

A fourth person fell through the gateway, this one a full-grown man. He lay inert, and Wakefield left Frankie to check on the man's pulse. As he reached down, he saw that the man's clothes seemed oddly archaic. The outfit reminded him of pictures he'd seen of his grandfather in working clothes. But this man was painfully thin, like a famine victim.

A time traveler, he thought. *Decades spent away in that evil place.*

"Yeah, he's been in there a good while," said Denny, seeing Wakefield's expression. "Probably the oldest survivor. See if you can help him, doc?"

They dragged the man to one side just before another small figure appeared out of thin air and landed with a pathetic squeak. Frankie was helping out now, moving slowly but with determination. As Wakefield examined the man, he found that almost all of his fat and muscle had been eaten away. Fortunately, his skin, while thin and badly abraded by his ordeal, was still mostly intact.

"I think we can save him, but we need to get them all back to the clinic," he said. "And after that, to an intensive care unit."

"We have good facilities at the foundation," Jim said quickly. "Otherwise, there'll be too many questions. I'll call it in."

"What happened to these people?" asked Wakefield.

"We were offered to the Soul Eater," said Frankie matter-of-factly.

"Soul Eater?" asked Jim. "What's that?"

"Let's just say it's big, dumb, and is getting over a terrible bellyache," Denny said. "But did the children get home all right?"

It took Wakefield a moment to realize that freeing Isobel and the Hawkes twins had happened only minutes earlier from Denny's perspective. Jim explained the situation. Denny frowned at one revelation.

"So the Interlopers posing as the twins are still on the loose?"

"They could be waiting for a chance to go back through the gateway," Jim pointed out. "Since we're going to have to leave it unguarded they could get home today."

"Yeah," Denny said, not sounding convinced. "I guess they could. I suppose they wouldn't want to stick around now that we know what they look like."

**

"It doesn't look like much," said Gould, turning over the dull purplish stone in his hand. "Hard to believe it can slay monsters."

"I know," Denny replied. "But believe me, it gets the job done. Any idea how it does it, by the way?"

Gould put the talisman back into a clear plastic container labeled 'Artifact #1' and closed the lid. He stared at the box for a few moments.

"The best theory we have at the moment," he said finally, "is that it somehow draws power from a singularity. A point where normal laws of space and time break down."

Denny frowned.

"Sorry, but isn't that like saying 'it's magic'?"

Gould shrugged.

"I suppose so," he admitted. "It certainly defies conventional analysis. There's talk of putting it inside a particle accelerator, bombarding it with protons, neutrons, helium nuclei – see if we can boost its energy."

"Or make it go boom. Cool," she said.

He isn't going to say it, she thought. *Up to me.*

"I'm sorry we didn't find your sister," Denny said, in a gentler voice. "We wanted to, believe me – but Lucy definitely wasn't there."

Gould nodded, not meeting her eyes.

"At least now you've got some protection," she pointed out. "We know there are other Soul Eaters, right? She was offered to another one, that's the logical explanation."

Gould looked up at that, frowning.

"That information was supposed to be classified."

"Tough," Denny said, "because when I was in there I got a lot of info about the whole setup. All of the survivors were linked in to this kind of organic internet, I guess you'd call it. Fragments of Interloper history, why their world is screwed up. Not everything, but a lot."

"And you'll tell us what you learned?" Gould asked, tentatively. "Full disclosure?"

Denny gave a thin smile.

"Not much point in me holding anything back when you have all those other guys in the basement, right?"

Gould reddened slightly.

"The survivors are being given the best treatment money can buy–" he began.

"Sure," Denny put in, holding up her hands in mock surrender. "I'm sure they are, but most of them are kids, and you guys are not their legal guardians."

Gould looked as if he would object to that, but then fell silent again.

Score another point for the trained journalist, she thought.

"Right," said Denny. "And all this tells me the Foundation – it's not what you claimed originally, is it? It's a hell of a lot bigger than some quaint old English charity looking into spooky happenings. I mean, maybe that's what it was, a long time ago when that Romola guy set it up. But now it's a front for something bigger."

Gould nodded, looking uncomfortable.

"I mean," Denny pressed on, leaning forward and jabbing a finger at the table between them, "there is no way you could do all this stuff without somebody in the British government turning a blind eye. Or maybe even *helping*? And if your government is aware of the Interlopers, at some level, I guess mine must be too, right? There's not much you guys don't share with the US. So if I go home tomorrow, I'll just get grabbed at the airport, end up at some secret base in Nevada, maybe?"

Gould glanced up at the camera that peered down at them from above the door. Denny looked up into the blank lens, gave a small wave.

"Hi Mister Benson!" she called in a mock-cheerful voice. "Can I have my paycheck now? With lots of overtime?"

Gould covered his mouth with a clenched fist, and gave a fake-sounding cough.

"Your first salary payment should be cleared by the end of the week, yes," he said. "Do I take it you want to leave the foundation?"

Denny kept looking up at the camera.

"No," she said, finally, turning back to Gould. "It's not like I can just walk into another job, not with such a weird, blood-stained resume. And before you ask, yeah, Frankie's in the same boat. So if Benson is agreeable, she'd like to join the team."

"That's a good idea," Gould said quickly, then he raised his voice a little and spoke in more measured tones. "Better to have someone with her knowledge inside the organization than outside as a ... I think the term is 'loose cannon'."

Yeah, thought Denny, *Benson wants to keep us close. Well, that could work both ways.*

"Okay," she said, pushing back her chair. "If there's nothing else, I've got an appointment with an old friend and a pizza."

***

"We shouldn't be down here," said Ben. "It's dangerous. Dad said so. And anyway, we're not supposed to leave the farm at all. Not without permission."

Zoe looked up at him with her implacable, dark eyes. Ben had always found his sister a nuisance. But in the last couple of days, she had become something else. He tried to shy away from the thought, but it kept returning.

She's scary, now. Not just annoying.

"Don't be such a baby," said Zoe, pulling at Ben's arm. The boy bridled at the insult, was about to retort that he was older by a whole fourteen months. He then looked into Zoe's dark, expressionless eyes and let her lead him on.

Maybe it's not the quarry, he thought. *There's plenty of other places down this lane. There's birds' nests, and the badgers up in the copse, and the gun platform from the war.*

But Zoe led her brother past all off the other attractions that fringed their farm, and kept going until they reached the fence with its faded signs reading DANGER and KEEP OUT. Zoe wriggled through a gap in the fence that was almost hidden by weeds, then stood waiting for Ben.

"I don't want to," he protested feebly. "Someone might see."

The thought of being caught by grown-ups, normally a worry, suddenly seemed a last vestige of hope.

"Don't you want to see yourself?" Zoe asked, tilting her head to one side. "Don't you want to see your twin?"

"I don't believe you!" he exclaimed. "I've got no twin! And if I did, why would he be living in a dirty old quarry that's full of water?"

"Scaredy cat," said Zoe. "Scaredy, scaredy, scaredy cat."

Then she turned and began to walk through the wild high grass. After a few moments, only the top of her head was visible. Ben heard a small, despairing noise come from his throat as he squeezed through the gap and started to go after her. It was easy to follow Zoe thanks to the straight pathway she made through the grass.

She wasn't this brave before, he thought. *It's like she's a different girl.*

When he caught up with Zoe, she was kneeling on the edge of the flooded quarry, looking down into the gray water.

"What is it?" he demanded. "Your magic twin a mermaid, then?"

Zoe looked up, and again Ben felt a chill of genuine fear. The wind rustled through the grass, and he looked around, again hoping for an adult to shout, wave his arms, order them home. But they were alone. He looked back down at his sister.

"Look, this is daft. I'm going home and if you don't come with me, I'll tell on you."

Zoe looked up, smiling now, then looked out over the water and pointed. Ben, annoyed and puzzled, could not make out what she was indicating. Then the surface of the murky water parted and something rose. It was red and white and had a face, or what was left of one. The face was that of Zoe, the eyes and mouth open.

"We didn't weight it down properly," Zoe said, standing up and turning to face him. "We won't make that mistake with you."

Ben gave a strangled cry of panic and staggered back. The grass rustled around him, and he froze. The rustling continued, and Ben noticed despite his panic that there was no wind. Zoe stepped forward, raising her hands. Her nails were no longer tiny pink ovals, but growing rapidly to become black talons. Her face, likewise, was changing, no longer the familiar pink oval of a little girl.

Ben spun around and started to stumble through the grass, His mind was spinning in fear-induced confusion, but all his instincts drove him toward home, the safety and sanity of his mother and father. They would save him. They had to. Behind him he heard a crashing as the creature sped along the narrow trail. He ran faster, reached the fence, scrambled through, every moment expecting to feel claws raking down his back.

Ahead of him, on the dirt road, was a figure, hard to make out as Ben was weeping in terror. He began to wave his arms above his head as he ran.

"Help!" he gasped. "Help me please!"

The figure did not move, and Ben hesitated, came to a halt. He realized, as his vision cleared, that the stranger was too small for an adult. Behind him he heard wire creak, glanced over his shoulder, and saw a creature in Zoe's clothes loping toward him. Ben spun around, mouth open to cry for help again, but froze. The words failed to form in his throat.

He was looking into his own face.

* * *

Nightmare Revelation

Nightmare Series Book 3

Nightmare Revelation

Prologue: Underground, London

"Don't go down there!" Cristina jumped back in alarm, almost colliding with two young women emerging from the entrance of Hobs Lane station. The man who had shouted at her was shabby-looking, his hair long and disheveled, his face half-covered by an unkempt beard.

"Don't go down there! It's not safe!" he shouted, voice breaking with emotion.

"Another bloody nutcase," muttered one of the girls. "Ought to round them up."

Her friend shushed her. They walked on. But Cristina could not go away from the entrance to the Tube station. Her work lay inside.

"Please, sir, let me pass," she said firmly, keeping her voice level, trying to soften her accent. Sometimes people reacted badly if you sounded foreign but she had never managed a convincing English accent, even in small phrases. "Please. Sir. I must get to work now."

It was ten after midnight, but in the streets of central London, there was never total darkness. In the glow of streetlamps and passing headlights, Cristina could see that the man was not merely poorly dressed. He was obviously homeless, his feet wrapped up in newspapers that concealed any shoes he might be wearing.

The man frowned at her, then seemed to get an idea.

"You're from Poland, right?" Cristina sighed, started to protest, then thought it might antagonize the man, who could well be mentally ill.

Always, they assume I'm Polish, she thought. *But if I say Romanian, they call me a bloody gypsy. If I'm lucky.*

When she said nothing, the man stepped forward, looming over Cristina. He was close enough now for her to smell his bad breath, and the scent of sweat and urine from his clothes. Even in the cold February night, the odor carried. Cristina wrinkled her nose and took another step back.

"You lot from Eastern Europe," the strange man went on, "you know there are monsters, like vampires, werewolves? Your church teaches you to shun the doings of evil spirits!"

I'm a qualified science teacher working as a bloody cleaner in this big, dirty city to make money to help my sick child, she thought, anger rising. *Who are you to make assumptions about me, smelly Englishman!*

But instead of speaking her thoughts, she nodded mutely, still keen on not angering him.

"Well, then," the vagrant continued. "You should know there are things like that in this city, now. Demons! Monsters! Unholy creatures from the Pits of Hell!"

The man waved his arms, and Cristina saw his knuckles were scarred. She glanced past the stranger, calculated that she could duck past him, run for the station entrance, and call security.

"I've seen them on the tracks, under bridges, in the old, abandoned sidings!"

The man was ranting now, arms flailing ever more wildly. She could see the whites of his eyes, looked away, but then saw the gap-toothed mouth with its ropes of saliva, gobbets of spittle flying towards her as he went on and on.

"What's this about?" Cristina looked over her shoulder to see a young police officer. She had been raised to fear and mistrust the police in her homeland, but in England, she had not found officers corrupt or brutal. She started to speak but the homeless man started scolding the officer.

"The government knows about it! How could they not know? Those things are using the tunnels–"

"All right, pal, that's enough."

The officer waved the man back, and it worked. Suddenly Cristina's personal space was free. She realized that she had been holding her breath. But the tense situation seemed to have been defused as suddenly as it had started. The gangly homeless man started to shuffle away along the street, muttering to himself. The police officer looked down at Cristina, smiled. She felt her face flush and hoped he could not see it in the poor light.

"He's harmless, miss," he said. "Take care. There's plenty around who aren't."

She stood watching for a moment as the policeman walked off after the vagrant, taking his time, showing that he was confident, in control of his territory.

A good-looking young man. Kind eyes. Nice rear, too.

She shook her head to dispel pointless thoughts and hurried into the station, then made her way around the ranks of ticket machines to the small storage room. There, she changed into her overalls, collected her mop, and filled her wheeled-bucket with warm, soapy water. She almost forgot to tie up her long, dark hair, and tuck it under a soiled canvas cap. Despite rushing, she was still a good ten minutes late when she reached the platforms via the service lift.

The last Tube train had gone nearly twenty minutes ago, and security had finished their final sweep. There was nobody else around. The silence was profound, the escalators and air conditioners had been switched off automatically. She glanced up at the closed-circuit TV camera, and wondered – as she always did – if anyone was actually watching over her. From what she knew of security guards, the answer was almost certainly 'No.' Cristina began mopping the platform, sweeping smaller items of garbage off onto the track. As she worked, she felt an all-too-familiar weariness begin to weigh down her limbs. She was trying to hold down four cleaning jobs, all with different contractors. She had gotten up at four that morning, grabbed a sandwich at lunchtime, another at six.

Dead on my feet, she thought. *That's what the English say, dead on your feet.*

"Crissi." Cristina stopped, leaning on the mop, head tilted. She had been dog-tired many times before, and nodded off on a bus or in a cafeteria. But she did not think it was possible to dream when you were actually working.

"Help me, Crissi."

The words were spoken in Romanian. They echoed down the empty platform. The voice was familiar.

Impossible. Cristina began to mop vigorously at the worn tiles, carelessly slopping gray water over her trainers. The voice was familiar, but the person the voice belonged to was long dead. She reasoned the voice was a symptom of her terrible fatigue. She would finish up quickly.

Yes, I will do what they call a 'half-arsed job', she told herself. *And if I lose this gig, there are plenty of others.*

Always plenty to clean in a big, dirty city.

"Help me, Crissi."

The voice repeated the phrase, over and over, and it sounded so plaintive that she had to stifle a sob. She flung the mop down, the crash of the plastic shaft on the tiles drowning out the voice. It paused, as if startled by the racket, then resumed its plea, its tone even more urgent.

"Shut up," she said, quietly at first, but then getting louder as she felt herself growing angrier. "Shut up, Constantin!"

As soon as she said the name, the voice stopped. *As if Constantin is a magic word,* she thought.

She had not seen Constantin since he had left their provincial home and gone to the capital to be, in his words, a businessman. A few months later, his emails and phone calls had stopped. When Cristina had gone to try and find him, everyone had claimed ignorance. The police had not cared. There were too many missing persons. Eventually, an old police sergeant had told her that Constantin had been involved in drugs and was probably dead, buried in the foundations of an office building or flyover.

But maybe he came to London instead, she thought. *To flee from his enemies, creditors, gangsters.*

"Crissi, I need your help."

This time the voice was weak, hesitant. She looked up towards the platform at the gaping tunnel mouth, a vast round O of blackness. It was the only place that Constantin could be. She walked up the platform, slowly at first but then gathering pace as hope took possession of her weary mind. She stopped by the tunnel entrance, leaned out cautiously over the track.

"Constantin? Is that you?" she hissed.

In the darkness, she could just make out a pale shape. She was a little shortsighted, and the figure could have been anyone.

"It's me, Crissi. It's your brother." Cristina felt her heart miss a beat, then start hammering wildly.

"I can't see you properly. Can you come closer?"

"No! I can't let them see me."

Tiredness left her struggling with her thoughts until she worked out what he meant.

"You mean the cameras?"

"Yes," said the voice from the darkness. "But you can come to me. They turned off the power, Crissi, it's safe." Cristina looked down at the track. The third rail gleamed dully silver.

"What are you doing in there, Constantin?"

"Hiding, of course! Easy to hide in London. Lots of places underground. You know that."

She was puzzled for a moment, but then it was as if a doorway had opened and let a host of new ideas into her head. She saw the familiar London she walked through every day, but now the concrete and tarmac beneath her feet was transparent. Underneath ran cables, conduits, water mains, and the myriad tunnels of the Underground network. And there were older tunnels, plus medieval cellars, wartime shelters, secret government bunkers, hundreds of hidden places once useful, now forgotten. And all beneath the vast, bustling city.

Of course there are lots of places to hide, she thought. *That must be what that homeless man saw. People like Constantin, the smarter outcasts and fugitives, seeking warmth and safety under the earth.*

"Okay," she said, sitting down on the edge of the platform. "Wait there. I'll come to you."

Once her feet struck the dirty ground between the rails she knew she could not turn back. She began to step carefully along the tracks, squinting into the gloom. In the uncertain light that spilled from the platform, she could just make out a pale figure crouched low against the curving tunnel wall.

"Constantin? Oh my God, are you naked? What has happened to your clothes?"

Overcome by emotion, she rushed forward, almost tripping on the rails, desperate to embrace her brother again. But as she drew nearer, she saw that the body before her did not look very much like that of a young man. In fact, its small stature and soft curves were more feminine than anything else, as was the mass of dark hair hanging down the crouching figure's back. She hesitated, her hands falling to her side. The desperate belief that she had found her long-lost sibling evaporated.

"I ... I don't understand. Where is my brother?"

Without replying, the pale shape sprang up, moving with extraordinary speed. Cristina screamed, reeled backwards, and tripped on a rail. She fell painfully, onto hard metal, and gasped as the wind was knocked out of her. The pale creature that had mimicked Constantin leaped forward, landed on her chest. Its long, sinewy fingers fastened around her throat.

Dark hair brushed her face as Cristina fought for life, all weariness forgotten in the struggle. She tried to pry the gripping hands loose, but in vain. Desperately, she clawed at the half-hidden face, but her arms were not quite long enough. She only succeeded in sweeping aside the thick veil of hair.

No, no, it cannot have my face.

"Oh, but it does."

They were the last words Cristina heard.

***

"Hello there, darling," said the security guard. "Knocking off early, are we? Bit naughty!"

The young woman with long, dark hair said nothing, simply continued to walk toward the exit. The guard walked after her, keeping a few yards behind so he could take a long look at her figure.

Weird, the guard thought. *She's normally one of the chatty ones. What's her name again? Maria? Most of them are called Maria. Damn, now if I call her Maria, she'll be peeved.*

He picked up his pace to overtake the woman, noting that she was still wearing her overalls. And one of her shoelaces had come unfastened. He pointed this out to her and she stopped, bent down, and started to fasten the lace again. Her hands, he noticed, moved clumsily, as if she were suffering from severe cold. Yet it was not particularly chilly indoors.

"In a hurry, are we?" he said.

Again, there was no response. Instead, the woman stood up and walked to the exit where a large sliding door sealed Hobs Lane off from the rest of the city. The guard hurried forward again, taking out his key card.

"Here you go, love," he said, swiping the card, then tapping in a code on a keypad. An electric motor whined and the door began to lift slowly, revealing the sidewalk. The guard looked down at the woman, who was staring blankly ahead.

"Long day, I bet?" he offered. "Mine's just starting, of course."

"Yes," she said, without looking at him. "Long day. I go home now."

The guard felt suddenly resentful of her attitude. He had been kind to this woman in the past, offering her cups of tea, overlooking her occasional tardiness. And now she was treating him in such an offhand manner.

Stuck-up bitch, he thought. *What's she got to feel so superior about?*

"Well, don't do anything I wouldn't do," he grunted. "So that leaves you free to do just about—"

His hand was almost on the woman's right butt cheek when her hand shot around behind her and grabbed his wrist. The small, delicate-looking head spun, dark hair flying.

"Hey," he protested, "it was just a bit of fun."

The woman stepped forward, her small, cool hand still gripping his wrist like a vice. Now he could see her face more clearly, her eyes were great, dark pools with no apparent boundary between pupil and iris.

Did she have those eyes before? Of course she did. I just didn't notice, is all.

He began to struggle against her grip, brought his other hand up in a threatening gesture, only to have her seize that one too. The guard felt a sudden terror, an awareness that he was alone with this apparent madwoman.

"So alone," she murmured, and a small, oddly dark tongue flicked across her lips. "So frightened."

Then, as quickly as it had begun, the weird confrontation ended. The woman freed his arms and ducked under the still-rising door. He cursed after her, feeling brave again. The door rose up a couple of feet higher and revealed an empty street. He closed the main door and went back to check on the cleaners' store room.

"Bloody hell!" he exclaimed. "She didn't even put her

damn bucket away."

He set off back to his desk to fill out a report.

Chapter 1: Over-ground

Denny was floating in a warm, tropical ocean. The blue of the sea was so beautiful that she smiled at it, sure that she was in paradise. Other people around her were mostly drifting but a few swimming languidly, kicking themselves along with oversize fins. One swimmer moved a little closer, giving her a thumbs up. She looked through the plastic snorkel-mask to see that it was Frankie.

Hey, she mouthed. *Thought I'd lost you.*

Frankie mouthed back, *I know,* then gestured upward, at the shimmering ceiling of the ocean surface. Denny returned her friend's thumbs up, and kicked out. But her feet did not propel her forward. Instead, she felt her feet pinioned, trapped in some unyielding substance. She looked down. A dark, mountainous object was rising beneath them. She could make out a vast, corrugated mass of roiling protoplasm. Dotted here and there, on its surface bulged, huge, distorted faces. Each face was a bulbous expanse of cartoon-like despair. Denny knew these to be the faces of its victims, the beings whose essence the vast entity needed to survive and grow.

Soul Eater. It found us again.

Denny kicked more frantically, but instead of freeing her ankles the action seemed to draw her deeper into the colossal body. She sank to her knees into the semi-transparent tissue. She looked over at Frankie, but her friend was also caught. One by one, all of the swimmers in the warm sea were snared, sucked into the nightmare monster.

Nightmare! That's what this is. Not real at all. Just a bad dream.

The knowledge did not free her. The awareness that she was dreaming only seemed to make her sink faster into the glutinous tissue. Soon the sticky outer layer engulfed her head and she was inside the Soul Eater. Around her, through the semi-transparent flesh of the creature, she saw other bodies in attitudes of panic and despair.

A gigantic quivering wave in the protoplasm that held her spun her body around, and she was now facing downward. Small glowing patches grew larger, until she could make out roughly human outlines. Denny didn't want to look, but couldn't close her eyes. The shapes were the earlier human sacrifices the Interlopers made to this hideous quasi-deity. The beings of the Phantom Dimension, almost driven to extinction, had found that offering humans to the greedy colossus bought them more time until the creature grew restless again.

These victims had been consumed skin and muscle first, then organs and skeleton, leaving only the brain and nervous system. The Soul Eater needed their minds, hijacking them to keep its own vast, alien organism functioning. Their brains, Denny knew, could live for years within the living mountain.

Another ripple in the protoplasm spun her and doubled her up, and now Denny was looking down at her own body. Or rather, at where it used to be. Fragments of bone and flesh were falling away. Nerves trailed through the dark tissue, tracing the shape of a body now dissolved, consumed. She could not escape the Soul Eater. What little remained of her would be trapped here, serving the inhuman purposes of a colossal beast.

"No!"

Denny sat up in darkness, reached out to feel her arms, legs, then her face. As sleep receded, she recognized the bedroom of her small rental apartment in central London. The time by the clock radio was 3:35 am. She sighed. She was due at the Romola Foundation for more tests and questions at nine, sharp. This was the second time in one night where she had been awoken by a dream of the Phantom Dimension. The first one had been a lot worse.

Maybe the third will be cute and cuddly. Hell, I need to pee anyways.

On the way back to bed, she made a quick diversion across the living room to look out of the window. Despite the freezing winter night, London was busy. Groups of people, mostly young, were apparently staggering home from nightclubs. The famous black taxis plied a busy trade. As she looked down at the street, a young woman in a short, sequined dress fell out of a cab, and on hands and knees puked in the gutter.

"In my day, we waited until we got home, young lady," Denny murmured.

Raising her eyes, she could just make out the St. Paul's on the other side of the river, the dome of the cathedral floodlit. Denny recalled a famous picture of the beautiful building in wartime, St. Paul's surrounded by fires, indomitable in the face of human evil.

Hope wasn't misplaced then. Good did triumph. Imperfectly, but still it triumphed.

After she got back into bed, another image came to Denny, this one a hybrid of history and nightmare. Behind St. Paul's loomed a Soul Eater, a moving mountain easily larger than the cathedral. Though she tried to dispel the vision, her tired mind returned to it every time she closed her eyes.

The flowing mass surrounded the ancient building, smashing down its walls like a mudslide wrecking a fragile log cabin. The dome cracked, fell into the foul mass, and the living tide of darkness flowed on, its body studded with thousands of faces. Vast, caricatures of human faces, each one frozen in a scream of fear and torment.

Denny sat up, groped for the remote, and turned on the TV. Channel hopping past news, sports, and the porn that her employers had apparently decided she might need. There were plenty of dramas about serial killers, mostly men stalking women in dark apartment buildings.

Eventually Denny found an old movie station that was halfway through showing an old black and white British film she had never heard of, 'The Day the Earth Caught Fire'. She was about to flick past it when she realized that it was about journalists. Becoming interested, she found that it was the first disaster movie she had seen with reporters like herself as heroes, as opposed to shallow idiots who ask scientists dumb questions and cause mass panic.

Denny stayed with it. A character gave a helpful recap, explaining that nuclear testing had knocked the Earth off its axis. The resulting change in temperature was destroying civilizations. The superpowers were now planning to detonate H-bombs at both Poles in the hope of correcting the problem before everyone got baked in a literal sense. And an old-school newspaper editor decided that he needed to prepare two front pages. The camera zoomed in on headlines.

EARTH SAVED. EARTH DOOMED.
At last, she thought. *A bit of harmless escapism.*

***

Sallie Murray took a deep breath and carried the breakfast tray into the dining room. Outside the windows of the farmhouse, large, fluffy snowflakes were falling onto the frozen mud of the yard. It was a bleak time of year, a time when Sallie struggled with the recurring depression she insisted on calling 'the winter blues'. She forced a smile as she placed steaming bowls of porridge in front of her children, Zoe and Ben, and her husband Jon.

"Snowing again," she said, sitting down. "Looks like it might lie, Jon."

Her husband grunted, dug into his porridge.

"Still, no chance school will be closed over a little sprinkling like that," she went on, turning to Ben. "Is there, darling?"

The boy looked at her for a moment, then down at his breakfast. His sister looked out at the snow, then turned to Sallie.

"No, mummy," Zoe said. "Everything will be fine."

Not for the first time, a chill went through Sallie at her daughter's words, followed by a pang of intense guilt.

Why do I feel like this? How can I suddenly stop loving my own children? What kind of god-awful mother am I?

The weird revulsion she felt for Ben and Zoe had crept up in her over the last few weeks. It was hard for Sallie to pin down any event that had triggered the change. In fact, lately, the children had been better behaved than ever before. And they had done their homework and chores on time, without being nagged. They seemed indifferent to the television, watching it if she put it on, going to bed as soon as she told them to.

The only real problem, so far as she could tell, was a deterioration in their handwriting. They were both producing straggly, printed letters that did not much resemble their earlier, better efforts.

Hardly cause for alarm, she told herself for the hundredth time. *Kids today spend so much time on tablets and laptops that handwriting is like some weird, old-fashioned skill.*

Her train of thought was interrupted by her phone. A neighbor was inquiring about their dog, a wayward collie that kept escaping to the Murray farm. Zoe and Ben always made a huge fuss over the dog, ignoring instructions not to feed it tidbits.

"No, Jackie, I'm sorry," Sallie said, "we haven't seen Fenton. Have we, kids?"

She waited for the children to respond, but they continued to scoop up spoonfuls of porridge.

"Answer your mother," growled Jon.

"No, we haven't seen the dog," Ben said, without looking up.

"Sorry, Jackie, the kids say he's not been round, but we'll keep an eye out for him. Yes, I know, it is pretty bad, but I'm sure he'll have more sense than to stay out in weather like this. Gotta go, bye!"

After breakfast, Sallie gave out lunches to the husband and kids, and saw them off at the door. Jon went first, unsmiling, delivering his usual peck on the cheek, only grunting as she asked when he might be back. The children's kisses felt just as perfunctory. She stood musing unhappily as she watched them set off across the farmyard towards the main road.

"Just a minute!" she shouted, giving way to a sudden impulse. "I'll get my coat and see you to the bus-stop."

It's just a harmless little experiment, she thought, as she rushed back inside to grab her coat. *Not a mad thing to do. Not mad at all.*

Ben and Zoe were waiting at the farm gate, showing no sign of impatience or annoyance. As soon as she caught up with them, they recommenced their walk, Ben on one side of Sallie, Zoe on the other. The snow was falling more swiftly now, the flakes so dense that she could barely make out the early morning traffic passing a quarter mile ahead.

Please, please be normal, she thought. *Please react the way I know my kids would react to their mother seeing them off in front of their schoolmates.*

The children stopped abruptly, each one turning to look up at her.

"Mummy, please don't come with us to the bus-stop," Zoe pleaded. "We're not babies."

"Yeah, mum, it'll be dead embarrassing in front of the other guys," Ben added. "Not cool."

Sallie laughed, trying to sound casual.

"Of course, silly me," she said, taking a pace back. "I just worry about you when ... when the weather's bad, you know."

"We know how you feel," said Zoe, matter-of-factly. "But there's nothing to worry about."

"Nothing to worry about, mother," said Ben. "Nothing at all."

Then, without another word, the children turned and walked on. Zoe's tiny figure vanished into the blizzard first, then Ben's. Sallie stood looking after them, only vaguely aware of the icy flakes settling on her face, starting to clot her hair with moisture. Only the sudden scream of a siren out of the storm brought her back to awareness of her surroundings. Red and blue lights flashed briefly in the swirling whiteness, then vanished.

Sallie turned, and set off back to the farmhouse at a run. Suddenly she felt the full force of the cold, its chill cutting through her coat and jogging pants, reaching up through her old runners to numb her feet. The farmhouse loomed into view, and she began to anticipate the warm glow from the old kitchen range.

Then she heard the whimpering. It was barely audible through the blustering wind and the sound of her shoes on the frozen track. The noise seemed to be coming from the old pig-pens to her left. Sallie paused, beating herself with her arms to generate some warmth, then walked over to the fence. The plaintive sound was a little louder now. Sallie climbed through the fence and picked her way through the deepening snow, to the derelict pens.

At first, she thought it was a heap of discarded clothing, an asymmetric splash of red and black on the pervasive whiteness. Then it moved, and Sallie put a hand to her mouth to stifle a scream. She knelt in the bloody snow, wanting to reach out and somehow repair the poor creature. But too much of the ravaged body had been ripped away, scattered. Fenton, the silly dog who kept running away from home because he loved kids, died the moment she looked into his eyes.

***

Trains were running on the Thames line, but they were not stopping at Hobs Lane.

"She caused problems for one of the fluffers," said Davenport as he led the way onto the platform.

Jim Davison looked at the security man, raised an eyebrow in amusement.

"Is that the title of your sex tape?" he asked, with feigned innocence.

Davenport replied with a single-fingered gesture, then pointed towards the mouth of the tunnel at the end of the platform.

"Fluffers," he said, "as you should know, mate, are machines that clean all the fluff from the rails. Used to be done by hand. Bloody awful job. Now every underground rail system has clever little robots that do a sweep in the early hours."

"They have to clean the tracks daily?" Davison asked. "Why? Rat droppings?"

Davenport gestured at the tunnel.

"People are a lot dirtier than rats. Hundreds of miles of tunnels, millions of people moving every day. That's a lot of skin cells, hair, general detritus best not thought about."

Jim thought about it, regardless. He felt a chill at the thought of so much random organic matter being shot along the Tube's tunnels, by the pressurized waves of speeding trains.

"So," he said to Davenport, "these machines scrub the crud from the tracks?"

The other man nodded.

"And when they encounter some organic matter that's too big to move ..."

Rather than complete the sentence, the security man strode forward towards the yellow and black tape that marked the police cordon. That morning, Davenport and Jim had been issued with Home Office passes for the first time. Forster, the head of security, had put it succinctly.

"Shit has hit the fan, and we've been drafted. Official security contractors to the department. Homeland security sub-division."

Jim, who had served with Special Forces, said nothing. He knew from bitter experience how messy chains of command and territorial struggles could get. He thanked a young, female police officer who lifted the tape so they could duck under it. Then a senior officer was explaining just what was waiting to be bagged up at the end of the platform.

"Young woman, maybe mid-twenties to early thirties," said the detective. "Badly smashed up, not much left of her face. However, the preliminary examination suggests that she wasn't hit by a train. The medical examiner thinks she was strangled first, then the body was stripped, and only then was it mutilated. Face destroyed, and fingerprints removed simply by snipping off the fingertips."

Davenport nodded, looking slightly bored.

Just another day at the office, thought Jim. *When we treat this stuff as routine maybe we're already halfway to hell.*

"Any idea what kind of weapon was used?" Davenport asked.

"Our guy's not sure," said the officer, with a slight emphasis on the 'our'.

Resents sharing information with us, Jim thought. *But he's not sure how unhelpful he could safely be. Good.*

"Well, how about a bladed weapon, like a machete?" Jim suggested.

"See for yourself," replied the officer. "Looks like a disturbed individual with a knife to me. No ID, naturally, but we're running DNA. That will take a few days. Of course, if she's not on the Home Office system ..."

They all knew what that meant. A Jane Doe in a city of nine million legitimate residents, maybe a million more tourists and other travelers, plus uncounted illegal migrants. London was a global hub where unusual and often inexplicable deaths occurred frequently. The police inspector half-turned, indicated the body lying half-concealed by a canvas screen. The Romola Foundation team stepped forward, but Jim stopped short of squatting next to the corpse as Davenport did.

I've seen wounds like these before, he thought. *Malpas Abbey. Only then they were inflicted on living bodies. Why change the MO now?*

"Yeah, we've seen enough, thanks."

Davenport stood up, and Jim saw his face was pale, and heard his breathing, fast and shallow. The other man began to speak, then a Tube train approached with a rumble like thunder, blasted through the narrow confines of the platform. The wave of hot air with the tang of electric ozone made Jim blink, rub his eyes. When he opened them, the body was being manhandled into an opaque plastic bag.

What a bloody awful way for any life to end, Jim thought. *Regardless of who or what is responsible.*

"Might not be them at all," Davenport muttered as they ducked under the cordon. "There are so many sick bastards in this town. Human monsters."

"Let's hope so," Jim concurred.

Maybe not this time, he thought. *But the Interlopers must figure it out at some point. The swarming, anonymous life of a modern city makes it their kind of place.*

***

In a white room, Denny sat in a chair that reminded her of visits to the orthodontist. Her head was strapped into position, electrodes on her skull. In front of her face, a series of pictures appeared on a screen. She had been told that in a room along the corridor one of the survivors of the Phantom Dimension was in a similar position. The difference was that the 'target' person's screen was showing a kind of psychedelic pattern designed to relax their mind and make it receptive. The idea was to determine if some kind of telepathic link existed between those who had been captives of the Soul Eater.

The images that changed at intervals of ten seconds were usually mundane, but sometimes baffling. Close-ups of nondescript machine parts or pictures of bizarre modern art would appear after a series that went dog, tree, child, automobile. Denny did as she was told, trying to mentally transmit the picture into the ether. But despite her best efforts to co-operate, the Soul Eater is what kept appearing in her mind. The creature of a nightmare that she knew was all too real, albeit in another world.

Eventually, Denny grew tired and was about to ask for a break. She looked up at the closed-circuit TV camera that stared unblinkingly down at her from a corner of the room, and gave a weary smile. But before she could speak, the door opened and the foundation's lead scientist hurried in.

"You're doing well," said Doctor Zoffany. "But I think that's enough for one morning."

Zoffany began unstrapping Denny's head and removing the delicate monitoring gear, all the while keeping up a stream of inane, comforting chatter. The chief scientist had an almost maternal manner that Denny had sometimes found irritating, but not today. Days earlier, Zoffany had noticed the dark patches under Denny's eyes, and suggested some kind of medication.

The in-house medical team could prescribe mild sedatives, Zoffany pointed out. Denny had turned the offer down, having seen too many people in her profession use prescription meds as a crutch. She was starting to regret that refusal now.

"I wonder if—" she began, but was interrupted when a white-coated technician entered.

"How is he?" Zoffany asked.

The newcomer looked pointedly at Denny, then back at her superior.

"Let's not keep secrets from our own operatives," said Zoffany, pointedly.

The technician reddened slightly.

"Sorry, Doctor," she said. "It's just that the subject has had … well, a bit of a melt-down. We've put him under sedation."

"What was the problem?" Denny demanded, feeling sure she knew the answer already.

"Apparently," the technician said slowly, looking from Denny to her boss, "the only images he got were of that – thing. The Class Two creature in the PD. Nothing else."

"Crap."

Denny felt a pang of guilt as Zoffany dismissed her underling with a request for a full report by noon.

"Not your fault," the scientist went on, reaching out to give Denny a brief hug. "I think we've proven that whatever psychic capacity was developed in you is linked to that entity."

Denny nodded, and bit her lip. Then a thought struck her.

"She said Class Two – what does that mean?"

Zoffany gave a wan smile, picked up an old-style clipboard and started to tick boxes.

"You may have noticed that science is about classifying things, whether we understand them or not. Interlopers are Class One beings – we know they're intelligent, though we've never given one an IQ test. The Soul Eaters, and those other beings, the Black Stars, are Class Two – intelligence of animal level, at the very least. Perhaps as smart as whales or dolphins, or as dumb as sea urchins."

Denny made a noncommittal noise.

"The Black Stars just seemed on the lookout for prey on the ground below them," she pointed out. "I got the feeling they were dumb. Vicious, but dumb."

Zoffany looked up from her clipboard for a moment, her pen poised.

"A Martian landing at a random point on Earth might get exactly the same idea about us humans. Depends on who you run into first."

"Especially if your imaginary Martian looked, smelled, and tasted exactly like an enchilada," Denny added. "Which would seem to be our problem with the Soul Eaters."

Zoffany gave a short bark of laughter as she finished filling in her form.

"Doc," Denny went on. "I wanted to ask something. I'm still having nightmares about being engulfed, swallowed, or whatever, and I wondered ..."

Denny hesitated.

Maybe popping pills isn't so smart, she thought, as a new

concern struck her. *Meds can impair your concentration when you're awake.*

"Yes, you're right," Zoffany said, looking Denny in the eye. "In my opinion, there is still a link between you survivors and the creature. That's why these nightmares keep recurring. In a sense, you're still inside it. Part of you did not escape, if you'll excuse the imagery."

Denny stared at the researcher, open-mouthed.

Holy crap. On some level, I knew this all along, but it took a near-stranger to make it clear.

Zoffany looked puzzled at Denny's reaction.

"Sorry," she said. "Isn't that what you were going to ask?"

***

Sallie Murray called her neighbor to report the death of Fenton. She tried to avoid saying too much, merely that she had discovered the body. When Jackie came to recover her pet, Sallie showed her the corpse, which was now almost covered in snow. This was followed by an hour of confusion, tears, anger, as they both tried to come to terms with the loss.

"But what could have done this?" Jackie kept asking. "It couldn't have been a fox, could it?"

Sallie produced a steady supply of tea and sympathy, and suggested badgers. Or perhaps a pack of wild dogs. Jackie called the police, and the RSPCA. Sallie deterred her from also contacting the local newspaper.

No need to make more fuss than necessary, she told herself. *I have nothing to hide, nothing at all.*

After the uniformed men and women had come and gone, after the still-tearful Jackie had gone home, Sallie felt guilty, furtive. She tried desperately to recall when she had last seen Zoe and Ben play with Fenton. It had not happened for at least a week, perhaps longer.

And then she reflected on the fact that the dog had known – as dogs often do – when the children got home from school. She remembered the way Fenton had bounded up to them as they walked along the track from the road. She tried to visualize that happening yesterday, just after dark. Sallie pictured the amiable creature running up to her children. But then the vision darkened, and she could not imagine what could have happened next.

What led to a disemboweled corpse of a good-natured family pet?

From sheer habit, she put on some coffee, went to the fridge to get the milk. On the door of the fridge was a selection of drawings by Zoe. One was a family group, with all four members labeled. The writing was childish, but controlled, not the lopsided scrawl Zoe was producing lately.

Forgetting the coffee, and trying to put Fenton out of her mind, Sallie got her laptop and tried to make sense of a single, puzzling fact.

'How does handwriting work?' she typed. It seemed a stupid question, but, in her stressed-out state, she could not think of a better way to phrase it. A list of links appeared. She scrolled down, up again, unsure how to assess the merits of the data on offer.

I don't want to become just another nutcase looking at crazy websites, she thought. *But I'm on the verge of becoming just that.*

She learned a lot in the next couple of hours. Handwriting was a far more complex skill than she had realized. It was not something you can simply learn the way you'd learn a fact, like when a battle happened or who was the king on a particular date. No, it was to do with muscle memory, like the skills of a top gymnast, or a musician. It was, in a way, as singular a feature as a fingerprint. And of course, over time a normal child's handwriting became more disciplined, distinctive, grown-up. All the experts agreed on that.

And my kids' handwriting suddenly changed to the point where it's barely recognizable. As if, she thought, *they were trying to disguise their writing by making it really bad. Or they had somehow lost the knack. But why both Zoe and Ben? What could undermine that skill in both of them at the same time? Makes no sense. No, it's as if they're not really my children at all...*

Her runaway thoughts hit a solid brick wall of incredulity. But no matter how she tried to suppress the nightmarish thought, it returned. She started another Google search, this time finding it less of a struggle to choose the right phrase. Soon, a host of links sprang up. Half an hour later, she had a name for what might be a form of madness possessing her.

'Capgras Syndrome, also known as Impostor Syndrome. The belief that someone we know well, often a family member, has been replaced by a stranger who looks and sounds just like them. Sufferers can become angry, even violent, if it is put to them that they are deluded.'

"I'm a very deluded woman," she said aloud to the empty kitchen. "A normal person doesn't suddenly stop loving her own kids. It's me that's gone wrong, not them. I'm mentally ill."

She looked over at her reflection in the window, a startled-looking face reflected against the backdrop of whirling snowflakes.

Chapter 2: Impostor Syndrome

"Sorry I'm late," said Frankie, a little out of breath. "There was some kind of accident on the Underground. Schedule's all messed up. Much British complaining."

"Oh," said Denny, feeling a tinge of apprehension. "Not another bomb scare?"

She glanced around the restaurant. Nobody seemed to be particularly tense or excited, and most were looking at their phones.

"Nah," Frankie said, sitting down in the seat opposite her friend. "I think somebody fell under a train. Or jumped. They found a body, anyways."

"Oh God, how awful," Denny said casually, handing over her menu. "No hurry, it's not like they're busy."

I'm getting kind of blasé about mangled corpses, Denny thought. *Not a great character trait, but there it is.*

They were grabbing an early lunch in a small, relatively cheap eatery in central London, not far off the tourist trail. But it was a dismal winter morning and only a handful of tables were occupied. Piped pop music made it unlikely that they would be overheard. But Denny still lowered her voice and leaned forward when she wanted to discuss work. They had decided to meet at a series of random public locations to minimize the risk of being bugged by the Romola Foundation. As a result, they had discovered some nice pubs and coffee shops, but also had some lousy meals.

"So, you been cleared by the foundation?"

Frankie nodded without looking up from the big, laminated menu.

"According to Ted Gould and his minions, I'm a hundred per cent human. Who knew? I should ask him for a certificate. There's a few people back home who really need to see it."

"Gould's not so bad," laughed Denny. "He's just a bit uptight and pretentious, maybe. But he's been through a lot."

"I know," Frankie replied. "Must have been hell to hear so many abductees had returned, then be told none of them is his sister."

"Hey," Denny said. "Let's not dwell on the bleak stuff. This is old pals having lunch. You ready to order?"

Frankie nodded.

"I think I'll have a salad. I used to love spaghetti and meatballs, but now ..."

Denny shuddered, thinking of the mountainous, tentacled monstrosity that had come close to absorbing them.

"We're a long way from the Phantom Dimension now," she pointed out.

"Are we?" Frankie asked, looking up now. "I thought it was right next to us, wherever we are."

The simple remark made Denny freeze, staring at the other woman.

"God," she said. "It never really struck me before. I mean, I was kind of thinking of it as another planet, you know? Like, somewhere on the other side of a Stargate or something. Only without, well, all the pyramids and stuff."

"Not according to Ted Gould," Frankie pointed out. "He was very keen to explain his theories. No matter how much I yawned and looked at my watch."

Denny had to laugh. Frankie was back to her old, irreverent self.

"So what did Gould say about the Phantom Dimension?"

Frankie shrugged.

"A lot of scientific terms I didn't understand. Einstein got a mention, and that Hawking guy. He tried to illustrate something by folding up a piece of paper. Oh, and apparently we're supposed to believe in a multiverse now – lots of universes lying alongside one another. Or stacked on top of one another. In a higher dimension."

Denny frowned. Like most people, she had watched a few science documentaries, but often the effect of cosmic speculation was to make her feel small and stupid.

"So, this multiverse," she said, "Gould thinks there could be more Phantom Dimensions? Sheesh."

Frankie made a helpless gesture.

"Too much of a bad thing, I reckon. But he thinks all of them have a common origin. The Big Bang spawned lots of universes, maybe an infinite number."

Denny struggled with the idea of multiple universes, tried

to grasp at a familiar notion.

"So, there's like one universe where Hitler won the war? Is that it?"

"That's just what I said!" Frankie exclaimed. "He looked at me like I'd just belched in his face and said it was a 'trivial example'. Because he means parallel universes with different natural laws and stuff, not just different history."

Denny gave up trying to grasp Gould's ideas second-hand.

"But what's that got to do with Interlopers walking around right next to us?"

They paused as a waitress appeared, and gave their orders. As soon as the waitress left, they resumed their discussion.

"So Interlopers could be walking among us, right now," Denny said, "only we can't see them and they can't see us?"

Frankie nodded.

"That's how I guess it works. We could be inside a Soul Eater and not know it."

"Don't!" said Denny, a little too loudly.

She glanced round, but the bland pop music had apparently covered her outburst.

"Hey," Frankie said, quietly. "Let's count our blessings. Some guys weren't so lucky."

Denny tried not to visualize the remains of the Soul Eater's victims, most of their bodies, being disgorged onto the alien desert. Little remained of them but their brains and spinal cords.

"Gould thinks the Soul Eater actually needs brains, preferably human, to function," Frankie went on. "That's why it leaves the gray matter until last."

Denny nodded, not trusting herself to speak. She wished she had not ordered a mushroom risotto. But they only had a limited amount of time until they had to report to the foundation. They needed to get their stories straight.

"Frankie," she said. "We've held out on them over – the reason. The motive. Whatever we call it. We're still okay with keeping it to ourselves?"

Frankie shrugged.

"Knowledge is power," she said. "That bastard Benson can't be trusted. I heard about what he did to the Lucy

Interloper. Sure, it was a killer, but it had its reasons."

And now that thing is in pieces in a freezer, Denny thought. *She's right. There's nothing ethical about Benson and the rest of them take their orders from him.*

"Will the other survivors blab, though?" she asked.

"I think they're too badly traumatized," Frankie replied. "Remember, I was in touch with them for a while longer than you. Most of them were too terrified to think straight, thinking they'd been dragged into Hell or something like it. Maybe they did pick up some information, but it'll just be bits and pieces."

"So we play dumb," Denny declared. "We were sucked inside that thing, we escaped from it thanks to the talisman."

The waitress returned with their orders, smiling as she placed the plates down, seeming to want to linger and chat on a slow lunchtime. The girl wore a crucifix, and Denny wondered if all such symbols could trace their origin to the strange stones of the Phantom Dimension. When the waitress left, she suggested this to Frankie.

"Gould would love that," Frankie grinned. "Him and his theories. Has he had any luck with the talisman?"

"Not that I know of," Denny replied. "I think they're scared to monkey with it too much in case they break it."

"Oh, they'll break it sooner or later," Frankie declared. "Ka-blooey! It's what they do. Over-confident white guys in expensive suits giving orders to nerds in white coats. Between 'em they'll break pretty much anything."

***

"X-Ray, ultraviolet, infrared, microwaves," said Harriet Zoffany. "And yet we have bugger all to show for it."

"Frustrating," said Ted Gould. "But it obviously supports the singularity theory. It's impervious to scientific analysis as we understand the term. Therefore, it represents science we don't understand."

"Which is to say," said Zoffany, turning over in bed to face him, "that it supports the existence of magic. Which I am not going to put in my report to Benson."

Gould brushed a strand of hair from the scientist's

forehead, raised himself up on one elbow.

"Mentioning Benson in bed," he pointed out. "That's a paddlin'."

"Like to see you try and spank my arse, old man," Zoffany retorted, with feigned pugnacity.

"So we're agreed, it's a paddlin'?" he laughed, and they wrestled for a while. But the precursor to a second round of lovemaking was never followed through. A sudden shouting and hammering on the adjoining wall froze them in mid-tumble. Raised voices were those of a man and a woman, at first. Then they were joined by another man, one with a hoarse, menacing voice. The first man went quiet, while the woman continued to complain.

"Dispute over a business arrangement, I'm guessing," Gould said quietly. "Something tells me they won't be going to court over the contract."

"God, these cheap hotels," Zoffany moaned, stretching. "Well, no time for encores this morning, anyway. I need to risk that shower and get to my team meeting."

"Fair enough," Gould said, unhappily. "At least we know Benson won't be watching us in glorious Technicolor. Unless he's bugged every grotty knocking shop in the capital."

"Don't joke about it," she replied, sliding out of bed. "I wouldn't put anything past that man."

Thanks to Benson, she thought, *we meet in the grubbiest, most sordid places. We can't be sure of privacy in our own homes, let alone our offices or labs. And when people ask what I do, I say, 'Oh, I work for this quirky little charity that looks into the paranormal'.*

As she was getting dressed, they resumed their discussion of the talisman.

"No way could we get it into any particle accelerator without legitimate paperwork, funding, the whole shebang," Zoffany pointed out as she reapplied her lipstick in front of the room's brown-specked mirror.

Gould grunted in agreement as he pulled on his pants.

"Civilian facilities aren't secure, anyway," Zoffany went on. "And the military would simply take over. And we can hardly send it out of the country."

"Don't open that can of worms," Gould warned. "Benson gets very touchy if you mention NATO or the Pentagon."

"Classic control freak." Zoffany finished her make-up, took a step back, tried to fix her hair. "Oh, screw it, I'm supposed to be a mad scientist, so I'll have Einstein hair."

Gould stepped up behind her, tried to put his hands around her waist. Zoffany grabbed his hands and raised them to her breasts.

"I wish," she said, "we could reach some kind of permanent arrangement? Preferably before you get permanent brewer's droop and these puppies reach my navel?"

Gould gave a slight laugh.

"This can't go on forever," he said. "It's obvious the situation is unstable, in both worlds. There's going to be some kind of showdown."

Zoffany turned around, and held out Gould at arm's length.

"Showdown? Not the word I wanted to hear. Like crisis, invasion, apocalypse."

Gould shook his head firmly.

"It's their disaster, not ours," he said. "The Interlopers are desperate, trying to find a way to escape the end of their world. That doesn't mean they should take over our world. Or wreck it."

No, she thought. *But it doesn't mean they can't.*

***

Was anything worthwhile ever decided at a goddamn team meeting?

After heaving a huge sigh, Denny looked around the conference table, saw only faces illuminated by the screens of phones. Zoffany glanced sideways at Gould. The latter's phone chimed, and a second later, Gould's face reddened slightly.

Oh, get a room guys, Denny thought, trying not to smirk.

She self-consciously began to turn off her own phone, then saw an email alert. It was from her mother. She hesitated, then switched off her cell.

Sorry, mom. Still can't really explain where I've been,

who I'm with, or what the hell I'm doing. Mainly because I only understand half of it myself.

"Benson always late for meetings?" asked Frankie, to the room in general. "Some kind of mind game?"

"No," Gould said, looking startled. "He's normally early."

"He still has another thirty seconds," added Forster, the head of security, looking up at the wall clock. "So strictly speaking–"

The door opened, cutting off Forster's remark, and a man entered. Denny took in an expensive suit, jowly features, watery eyes, and thinning white hair. The man had a confident manner but didn't look as if he had even *walked* past a gym in years. She concluded that Benson was a typical corporate type. She felt slightly disappointed as well as relieved. She had been expecting a Bond movie villain, and instead Benson was just another old, white guy with a silk tie.

Then a young woman walked in, also suited and businesslike. She was tall, voluptuous, and walking a little too close behind the elderly man. Denny read the body language as they walked behind Gould and Forster, concluded they were having an office affair.

That doesn't sound like Benson's style at all, she thought. *I was wrong. Is this a coup or something?*

Confirmation came in a flurry of movement among the British. Gould half-stood, Forster frowned in puzzlement, while Zoffany looked surprised.

They know this guy, but they've never actually met him 'til now, Denny thought. *Come to think of it, I've seen that face somewhere.*

Then a second man entered, and Denny took in a sharp breath. The newcomer was tall, at least six-four, and thin. Not only his chest and hips, but even his shoulders seemed narrow for his height. His head seemed abnormally large by contrast. He walked with a smooth, long stride that suggested strength under tight control. The man's age was hard to judge from his smooth features, deep-sunk eyes and hairless cranium. Denny guessed he was over fifty, less than seventy.

Yep, this is him all right. Creepy as hell.

Benson looked straight at her, and she fought the desire to

look away. Instead she blinked, cursed herself. But by now the chairman of the foundation was moving on. He stood at the head of the table, gestured to the two strangers, who took seats to one side.

"Ladies and gentlemen," said Benson. "As you can see we have a distinguished guest. Those of you who know Sir Lionel will need no introduction, but for the benefit of our American friends ..."

Denny found herself listening to the sound of Benson more than the words. The chairman's voice was startlingly deep, as if coming from some cavern under the earth. It was hard to believe it emanated from that narrow chest. Though almost expressionless, the voice was also oddly hypnotic. So intrigued was Denny that she almost missed the introduction of Sir Lionel Bartram. Benson did not mention the pretty, young woman, or give any indication that he acknowledged her existence.

"Sir Lionel, as I'm sure some of you know, is Minister of State for Internal Security at the Home Office," Benson explained, then proceeded to make introductions. Denny and Frankie were 'Ms. Purcell' and 'Ms. Dupont', and now classed as Special Field Operatives. Denny resisted the urge to ask if that meant she would get a raise. She also wanted to ask the name of Bartram's PA, whose job seemed to consist of smiling prettily at the old man now and again.

After Benson had finished, Bartram rose somewhat wheezily to his feet and began to talk. He had an upper-class British accent but sounded to Denny like a politician from anywhere, and one that had enjoyed too much fine dining at the taxpayers' expense. After a few words of praise for the foundation and its 'brave paranormal investigators', Bartram talked in vague terms about the 'threat posed by non-human entities to our way of life'. Denny had to struggle not to zone out. She had heard so many similar waffling speeches as a young reporter, even the topic of shape-shifting monsters from another dimension could not make it interesting.

Wonder how much this guy really knows? Denny thought. *Benson does not look the over-sharing type.*

After Bartram had finished, Benson said nothing. Gould

looked around the table, and then cleared his throat.

"I'm very glad the government is taking the Interloper threat more seriously, Sir Lionel," he said. "But does this mean we will have more resources to tackle it?"

The minister leaned forward, but before he could say anything, Benson raised a long-fingered hand.

"I think," he said, "that this is far too early to discuss funding and equipment issues, Mister Gould. The minister is simply here to get to know us, get a feel for our work."

Benson stood up, and again Denny was surprised by the way the man did not seem to be built to the same scale as the room. Benson was like a normal, if deeply unappealing man, viewed in the distorting surface of a fun-house mirror.

An Interloper would do a better job of looking human, she thought.

"Forster," said Benson. "Perhaps you could begin the tour by showing Sir Lionel our security arrangements?"

As Forster ushered the minister and the unnamed woman out of the room, Benson started to fire questions at Gould and Zoffany. It became apparent that research on the talisman had stalled.

"However, the survivors rescued from the Phantom Dimension," Zoffany said, "have given us some useful data on the large organisms known as Soul Eaters."

"Anything that can kill them?" Benson said, looking at his chief scientist from under drooping eyelids.

"Not as yet," Zoffany admitted. "But realistically, given the size of the gateways we know of, these behemoths could hardly enter our world."

The scientist looked over at Gould, evidently for support, but he did not meet her eye. Instead, he appeared fascinated by a point on the wall somewhere above his lover's head.

Oh crap, thought Denny. *What have I been missing?*

"Insufficient progress," drawled Benson, dragging out each syllable. He walked over to the window, ran the tips of cadaverous fingers absentmindedly along the sill. "We need more data, preferably from captive Interlopers. If necessary, Gould, you and Forster's people must go into the PD and get them. Deploy adequate force. Professionals. Do not rely on amateur heroics in the future."

Benson paused, looked at Denny for a moment, then turned his unblinking gaze back on Gould. Gould did not protest, merely looked miserably uncomfortable.

"Well," said Benson, after a brief pause. "As we have had our introductions, I think it is time we all returned to our respective posts."

He started to walk out of the room, then paused at the door, rubbing his fingertips with his thumb. Then he left. Denny heard quiet sighs of relief from the others, then realized she had joined them.

"Okay," said Gould. "Back to what passes for work, I suppose."

***

Denny and Frankie spent the hour after the meeting briefing some of Forster's men on the Phantom Dimension. The questions they were asked ranged from dumb to not-so-dumb. But it was clear that the ex-military types recruited by the foundation had a fixed mindset as to what they were going to be dealing with. Denny sensed Frankie's frustration with the cocksure attitude of the security operatives as her friend's responses grew more sarcastic. But in the end, it was Denny that snapped.

"Look!" she heard herself shouting. "You're going up against shape-shifting creatures that are smart, fast, and can disembowel you before you can aim your fancy guns. And if the Interlopers don't get you, there are Black Stars that can swoop down and grab you from above. And that's before the Soul Eater scoops you up in its nice, big tentacles and swallows you like a really fat guy swallows a chocolate-coated peanut."

There was a moment's silence. Then someone at the back snickered.

"Fine, be assholes, go and do the macho thing," Denny sighed, then turned to Davenport. "I think we're done here."

The friends did not speak as they made their way to the canteen and got what passed for coffee, plus some glazed donuts. After they had sat for a while, Frankie broke the silence.

"You think we blew our Christmas bonus?"

After she'd finished laughing, Denny leaned back, gestured with her half-eaten donut.

"I don't know if it's because we're women or American or both, but those guys—"

As often happened, having someone else to trash talk brought them together. They were laughing loudly when Gould appeared and asked if he could join them.

"Sure," Frankie said. "How are things in your multiple worlds?"

That set the women laughing again. Gould gave a slightly strained smile.

"I see the implications of quantum theory continue to fascinate the layperson," he said. "Well, as it happens, we may have made a breakthrough."

"Some kind of anti-Interloper death ray?" Denny suggested.

Gould shook his head.

"Not my field. No, we sub-contracted some theoretical work to a few people at Cambridge, and they came up with a remarkable algorithm that could be used in conjunction with a civilian satellite to detect anomalous microwave emissions—"

Gould continued to explain, but Denny could tell from Frankie's expression;

He thinks he's dumbing it down for us, she thought. His faith is touching in a way.

"Can we cut to the chase, professor?" Frankie interrupted. "What's this in aid of?"

"The gateways," Gould said patiently. "We might be able to spot them from space when they open. We tested the system on the two examples we know and it seemed to work."

"Seemed?" Frankie responded. "That's a fine old ass-covering word, Ted!"

Denny nudged her friend.

"Let's just say," Gould went on, "that we've been getting anomalous readings."

"I just love anomalous readings," Frankie said, in a mock-seductive voice.

327

Gould sighed.

"Would you like to come and actually see the system in operation? Consider it an informal briefing."

Now why would you want to do that? Denny wondered. *You haven't been an over-sharer before now.*

She did not say anything, though, simply followed Gould and Frankie through a maze of corridors to a large room filled with screens and nerdy personnel. Denny noticed that one of the young men was playing a video game when they came in, but quickly minimized the window when he saw Gould.

Some things never change, no matter who you work for.

"Okay," Gould said to the gamer. "You seem to have a spare moment; would you mind firing up Gatescan?"

The young man reddened as he followed the order. Denny and Frankie stood behind the tech guy's chair as a basic map of the Earth appeared. A dotted green line was the path of a satellite, Gould explained.

"Now zero in on any region at random, give us the latest sweep."

Denny expected to see England appear, but instead the young man clicked on a region of northern Asia. There were no national boundaries marked, so Denny guessed it was Mongolia, or maybe Siberia. The view zoomed in some more. A scale in the corner of the screen went from hundreds to tens of kilometers. Three sharp points of orange light appeared on the screen.

"Nothing to get excited about," Gould explained. "Those will be short-wave radar installations. Very distinctive signal. We're looking for something a bit different, a fluctuating signal that's blurred at the edges."

"I'll speed it up," said the tech guy, clicking on a slider bar.

The orange lights remained steady, then one flickered out.

"It's running data gathered on the satellite's last pass," Gould explained. "That was probably military radar being tested, so – What the hell is that?"

A diffused cloud, reddish-brown in color, had appeared on the edge of the screen for a split second, then vanished.

"Was that a gateway?" Frankie asked.

Gould did not answer, but reached over the young man's

shoulder to rewind the video, then pause it. The ocher blue was, Denny saw, nearly ten kilometers across. She did a quick calculation, came up with over six miles.

"No way," she said.

"No," said Gould, in an expressionless voice. "As I said, it's experimental. We're still working the bugs out of the system."

***

Harriet Zoffany swiped her ID card through the reader, then keyed in an eight-digit code. The door unlocked itself with a click, and she entered the Maximum-Security Area. The entire sub-basement was off-limits to all but foundation employees with top clearance.

But there's always a higher level of clearance, she reflected. *Always more secrecy, more paranoia.*

A small, naked body lay on a slab. It was open from throat to groin, flaps of skin folded back and pinned, rib-cage split open. A casual observer might not have noticed anomalies, but to Zoffany, the peculiarities of the creature's internal structure were always striking, and still somewhat baffling.

But then, she thought, *a casual observer would more likely be freaking out over the fact that we have apparently dissected a child.*

Zoffany leaned close, nostrils wrinkling. She never quite got used to the smell of disinfectant, despite working with it most days. But it helped mask the other smell, of Interloper slowly decaying. It was a stench that had filled her nostrils when she had cut Lucy up to try and find some reason for the creature's ability to survive in the human world.

God, what have I become?

The creature's eyelids flickered, opened, focused on the scientist. Zoffany jumped back, collided with a tray of instruments, sending scalpels and spreaders clattering to the tiled floor. No matter how often it happened, the reaction always spooked her.

I'm the most inept executioner in history, she thought. *If time taken is a factor.*

The dissection would have killed any earthly creature.

Lucy had become inert, but tests showed that the alien tissues were still alive. The best theory Zoffany had was that Interlopers went into a state of hibernation when they experienced major trauma. In this case, she suspected, the body was too far gone to survive but was taking a long time to die. Zoffany was under strict orders not to kill it.

Benson had been keen to discover some equivalent of the talisman, a special object that created a protective field around the creature. But all Zoffany had found was bone, cartilage, organs, blood vessels. Not human, but getting there. She suspected that she knew what made Lucy and the other so-called 'endurers' different from the rest of their kind. But she had not yet told Benson. Actual data was proving elusive. And Zoffany was not sure she wanted to admit the truth, even to herself.

"Too ... long."

The words were croaked out of the cracked, black lips. The voice was still recognizable as that of a child, a perfect imitation.

"Too ... long ... dying."

Zoffany swallowed, tried to keep her voice steady.

"You could tell me," she said. "Tell me what we want to know, then I'll kill you. I have acid, hydrogen peroxide, cyanide. Something will work."

The face that looked very much like a tormented child's, smiled up at her.

"So ... generous. Humans. Killers ... all."

Zoffany composed herself and picked up the surgical instruments.

"If you change your mind, I'll be back to check on you tomorrow, same time."

She was already opening the door when she heard the croaky voice repeating what had become a kind of mantra for the dying monster. Zoffany did not hurry, but was glad that the door slammed behind her before she heard the end of the familiar sentence.

"There ... are ... worse ... things ... than ... us."

Chapter 3: Fake News

Timandra Clay looked out over the grassy expanse of Wimbledon Common. The great tract of open land was whitening rapidly just as twilight darkened the city. Behind her, the TV weather forecast informed her that the snow that had hit the western parts of the island had now reached London.

"Brilliant," she murmured, and shivered in anticipation of her run. "Should have done it this morning. No help for it now, though."

Lionel had gone back to his constituency for a meeting after their morning visit to the Romola Foundation. This had left Timandra on her own in the flat that Lionel paid for out of his expenses, in some convoluted way. She had asked him, once, when they were in bed together, if she were part of some kind of tax dodge. He had laughed, but not answered. Then he had left to attend a meeting of the standing committee on internet pornography.

One day, she thought, as she pulled on her running spikes, *he'll leave his wife and marry me.*

It was Timandra's unspoken mantra, repeated so often that some days she almost believed it. On this bleak afternoon, though, with the light failing, it had little force. She hit the street, jogged across the road, and focused on her run. Soon she was pounding along one of the footpaths, waving to other runners, saying 'Hi' to neighbors walking their dogs. Soon she was warm enough to almost forget the blizzard that was blowing in her face out of the darkness.

A dog started barking frantically, and Timandra felt a twinge of fear. She had once been chased and bitten by an untrained Rottweiler some idiot had let off the leash. But then she saw that this dog, a black bull terrier, was straining at the leash. Something near the path had set it off.

Rabbits, maybe, she thought, as she passed the cursing owner. *Or more likely rats.*

She checked her fitness tracker and saw she was still several thousand paces short of her daily target. She contemplated going further, but then decided to go home and defrost a pizza instead. Retracing her steps, she passed the dog-walker again. The terrier was still pulling at its leash, trying to drag its diminutive owner off into the storm.

Timandra slowed, stared at the whirling flakes. *Is someone out there?* If so, they were moving fast. For a moment, she thought it was a runner, then it dawned on her that the figure she had glimpsed was not moving like a runner. It had been bounding like an animal, crouching low then leaping forward a few yards only to stop again. She thought of hyenas in wildlife documentaries, creatures with oddly short hind legs, long forelimbs.

A very strange predatory lope, she thought. *But it must be one of these weird, fashionable dog breeds. They're everywhere.*

She waited to hear the animal's owner shouting for it. No human voice came. One of the lamps that lined the footpath flickered, and she picked up her pace. She started to look around to see if any other people were ahead of her, walkers or runners she would pass on the way home. She could see nobody.

Because it's frigging February and blowing a bloody blizzard. You could have done this before work. Prize idiot.

Timandra reached the edge of the vast, open space without incident, though. The road was now busy with rush hour traffic and she waited impatiently to cross, glancing around, trying to look casual. A couple of times she thought she glimpsed the crouching, bounding creature. It was very pale, pale all over in fact.

A hairless hyena. The latest must-have pet for London's obscenely wealthy cosmopolitan elite.

The thought made her laugh out loud, dispelling her apprehension. The front door of her apartment building was visible, and now a gap in the traffic let her run over. A few seconds later, she was inside the hall. She took off her sneakers and carried them up the stairs. Three minutes later, she was turning on the shower, then hurling her cold, wet clothes into the laundry basket.

Timandra wrapped an old robe around herself, glanced out of the window. *One thousand acres of open land and I can't see any of it, only a vague blur that marked the rough position of streetlights.*

The buzzer of her intercom sounded. The old lady who lived on the ground floor was always forgetting her keys. Timandra padded over to the doorway on bare feet, pushed the button.

"Hello?"

"Sorry to be a bother, dearie. I've locked myself out again."

The voice from the speaker was tinny, distorted, but something about it made Timandra wonder if it really was Mrs. Bradford. She hesitated, finger over the door button, until the urgent little voice sounded again.

"Please hurry, dearie," it said. "I've got a casserole in the oven."

Doesn't she always? They'll probably bury her with one.

Timandra smiled, pushed the button, heard the distant sound of the front door banging back against the lobby wall.

"You in all right?" she shouted into the grille. It was a ritual they went through. The old lady would reply with profuse thanks and promise to bring a 'nice bowl of casserole' up later 'for my young friend'. But this time there was no response.

Oh well, maybe she was in a hurry, she thought, feeling slightly annoyed.

Despite the apartment's central heating, she was starting to feel chilly, so she ran into the bathroom and tested the water. It was a little too hot, so she adjusted the mix. Before she could step under the jet of steaming water, her own door buzzer sounded.

Who the hell is this?

As she retraced her steps across the small living room she could just make out Mrs. Bradford's plaintive voice.

"Hello dear? I've got something nice and warm for you to eat after your run."

Smiling resignedly, Timandra undid the chain and unlatched the door. It was only as she began to turn the handle that something occurred to her.

How did she know I'd been out for a run? I normally go in the mornings. And if she wasn't at home when I went and came back ...

She was still opening the door, an automatic reflex, when she saw that what was crouching in the hallway was nothing like an elderly lady. Timandra Clay's last coherent thought, as the creature hurled itself at the six-inch gap she had unwittingly offered it, was that it did indeed looked a little like a white, hairless hyena.

Except that it had her face.

***

Theresa Bradford was not quite quick enough to catch the person who was let in. She started hobbling to the door as soon as the buzzer sounded but by the time she reached the spy-hole, the incomer was already halfway up the stairs. Theresa just caught a vanishing glimpse of a shadow on the wall. Then the hallway light, which was on a timer, went out.

"Oh, well," she said to her cat. "I don't suppose it was her fancy man. He's not so light on his feet, is he Percy? Surprised he hasn't croaked from heart failure, the sounds we hear. Shocking, isn't it?"

Percy was sitting on the sofa on the far side of the room, staring across at his human. Normally, all Theresa had to do was go near the door for the cat to start winding himself around her ankles, meowing to be let out. The worse the weather, the more Percy wanted to experience it, before demanding to be let in again about thirty seconds later. But this time he showed no intention of leaving his comfortable seat.

"Not feeling well?" asked Theresa, going over to scratch the old tom between his ears. But before she could touch him, Percy spat at her, back arched and tail fluffed up. Then, as the old lady flinched in surprise, the cat leaped down and ran into the kitchen.

"You're not getting any more Whiskas!" Theresa said crossly, as she followed the animal. "Not with that attitude, young man."

Suddenly she halted, cocked an ear. There had been a noise, faint but unmistakable, from the flat upstairs. It was a feminine voice, crying out, suddenly stifled. It was followed by the sound of something falling, what might have been a struggle. Then there was silence for a few moments. Theresa began to become concerned. *What if an intruder had attacked Miss Clay?*

Then she heaved a sigh of relief. The phone rang, and it was answered immediately. Theresa heard the sound of Miss Clay's voice. Though she could not make out the words, the tone was familiar, and unmistakable. It was what the old lady thought of, with a thrill of disapproval, as a 'sexy voice' – low and teasing.

"Shocking behavior!" she hissed.

Percy was squeezing himself into a space behind the refrigerator, a hiding place he always took to when strangers were about. But this time there was no plumber or electrician to be scared of.

Silly creature, she thought. *Going dotty in his old age, no doubt.*

She inspected her latest casserole. It was done, a steaming concoction of beef and vegetables. Not for the first time, Theresa decided to go up with a bowl for the young lady. It would give her the chance to look inside the flat, if only for a moment, and see if she could catch a glimpse of that dirty old man. Or some of the strange toys that were sometimes lying around the place.

"You sure you don't want out, Percy?" she shouted as she opened her front door.

The cat did not respond. Muttering about ingratitude, Theresa climbed the stairs to the first floor, put the bowl down outside Miss Clay's apartment, and then rapped gently on the door. After a few moments' silence, the door handle began to turn.

***

The padded envelope was waiting for Denny when she returned to the apartment. She picked it up, gave it a gentle shake. It had been dinned into her at the foundation that she should take 'reasonable precautions', and that included not opening strange parcels. She had asked Forster if he thought the Interlopers were going to send letter bombs via Royal Mail. He had not found the idea amusing.

"No," he had said. "I think they might send something far worse. Something that pops out and fastens itself on your face, for instance."

Denny shuddered at the thought and studied the envelope. The address was handwritten, the writing unfamiliar. She turned it over and saw no return address. However, it was post-marked 'Hereford'. Denny relaxed. There was one person in that part of England who knew where she lived. Someone she could trust.

Sure enough when she tore open the package, it contained a note on letterhead, from the clinic of Doctor Russell Wakefield in Machen. As she scanned the message, she recalled that Wakefield was a folklore expert with, presumably, a lot of local contacts.

'Dear Denny,

Checked out local museums for Great War memorabilia. Someone found this for me. Had been stashed away with other trinkets, no obvious historical merit. Don't want to keep it here in case it draws wrong kind of attention. You could give it to RF if you like.

Best, RW.'

Denny felt her heart speed up as she reached inside the package again and found a smaller envelope, plain brown and sealed shut, that had been shoved right down at the far end. It was a lumpy object a little smaller than her thumb. She tore open the inner envelope and a purple stone fell into her hand. A quarter-inch hole had been bored through it near one end so that it could be hung around its user's neck. But there was no cord in the envelope.

"Yeah," she said softly. "I could give it the foundation. If I liked."

Denny thought back to her conversation with Frankie, and Gould's theory of a 'multiverse'. She imagined Interlopers and Soul Eaters moving invisibly through the city in the parallel Phantom Dimension. And she remembered the rage of the Interloper posing as Lucy Gould, Ted's missing sister. The creature had somehow blamed human beings for the decay and collapse of their world. Somehow, these wild ideas had fit together, but she despaired of how to go about it.

In the meantime, I could do with something to shift the odds in my favor.

She put the talisman under the small desk lamp, but like the first one, it showed no peculiar features. It was like a crudely-worked bit of colored quartz. Denny thought about going out and buying a piece of string or maybe a shoelace to turn it into a pendant. Then it occurred to her that the security scanner at the foundation might well be triggered by the stone.

I have no idea what this thing might do to that kind of tech, she thought.

Denny went over the routine she had gone through that morning when entering the organization's headquarters. Then she got her keys from her jacket. The key ring would not fit through the hole in the stone. She took out the small sewing kit she always carried, got a length of black thread, and fastened the talisman to her key ring.

Hide it in plain sight. The security guys don't know anything about the talisman. Or are they talismen? Whatever. Just so long as none of the senior guys are there when I log in. That's a risk I'll have to take.

Denny got up to replace the keys in her jacket. Then she changed her mind and shoved them into her jeans pocket instead.

Closer to the flesh the better, she thought. *So at least my butt will be protected from dark forces.*

Denny almost sent Wakefield a message thanking him. She just stopped herself from thumbing the icon on her phone, and then deleted the message, cursing her naivety. She had no reason to believe that her bosses were bugging her, of course.

But I'd be a damn fool to assume they weren't.

***

"So," said Jon, without looking at her. "What sort of day have you had?"

Sallie stared at her husband, wondering what to say. For ten minutes after returning home he had grumbled about feed prices, European farming regulations, the inability of 'this damn country' to grit roads when it snowed. The usual mundane talk of a tenant farmer.

How can I tell him what I think, or feel, or fear? He'd think I was mad. Stress. The 'winter blues'. A reasonable explanation.

"Sal?" Jon said, looking up from the local paper to frown at her. "You all right? Why so quiet?"

"It's nothing," she said. "It's just ... Fenton's dead."

She proceeded to tell Jon about discovering the body, emphasizing how upset Jackie was about her pet, skipping the parts involving the police and RSPCA. She did not want him to think she had 'brought trouble', as he would say. Uniformed officials on the farm unnerved him, and she never inquired too closely why.

"But what could have killed a dog that size?" Jon said, the paper forgotten. He got up and started pacing, then stopped at the window to look out at the encroaching twilight. Snow was still falling, though less heavily than before.

"The kids," he said. "Will they be back soon?"

"Yes," she replied, glancing at the kitchen clock. "The bus ..."

Jon was not listening. Instead he was unlocking the gun cupboard, taking out his twelve-gauge, shaking cartridges out of a box onto the table.

"Jon," she protested. "I don't think there's any real danger—"

Again, she stopped, and not just because her husband was continuing to disregard her words. Sallie had a sudden moment of insight.

No way could any animal hurt those kids, she thought.

They can look after themselves.

Jon paused in loading the shotgun, stared at his wife.

"What is it?" he asked. "Is there something else? Did you see something, an animal?"

Sallie shook her head.

"It's not that," she said. "It's just – at first, I had this crazy idea."

Sallie buried her face in her hands, felt great heaving sobs shaking her.

Jon unloaded the gun, and put it on the table. For the first time in months, he gave her his undivided attention. He leaned against the kitchen table, reached down and took her in his arms. His hands were big, clumsy, and rough with working in all weathers. As he held her close, she started babbling all her wild thoughts into the front of his jacket. She jumbled together her puzzlement over Ben and Zoe's handwriting, their changed behavior, and the horror she had felt as she knelt by the dog's corpse.

Eventually, she ran out of words. She sniffled, heard the sound of the central heating boiler firing up. Jon stroked her hair, murmured something she could not make out. Sallie lifted her head, looked up at him.

"Oh God," he said, staring at her. "I thought I was just imagining it all."

Sallie laughed, aware that she sounded almost hysterical with relief. But before she could say anything, there was a familiar sound. It was a series of rhythmic thuds, as small feet kicked snow off their shoes against the back doorstep.

The children were home from school.

***

Denny was about to turn off the TV and go to bed when she received a text message. She frowned at the screen. She did not recognize the sender and thought about deleting it at once. Her thumb hovered over the screen, then felt an impulse to gamble. She touched Open.

What the hell? If it's a virus, I could get a new phone on expenses. Probably.

339

The message contained a link, nothing more. Again, she gambled, and nothing disastrous seemed to occur. Instead, she found herself on a popular video streaming site she had used many times in her previous job.

The video on offer was Russian, judging by the Cyrillic writing in the title and the accents of the people involved. The clip was poor quality and looked like it was taken by a phone. The viewpoint was the rear seat in the cockpit of a small aircraft. The pilot and co-pilot were visible, then the camera swung around to aim out the side window. The plane was flying over a forest covered in snow, and Denny thought of Siberia. But her knowledge of Russian geography was patchy, so she could not be sure. People were talking loudly over the drone of the engine, perhaps enjoying a joyride.

The chatter got louder, more excited, and there was much pointing. At first, it was hard to make out what was causing the excitement. Then Denny realized that what she had taken for a dark cloud was hard-edged and symmetrical. The plane turned in a wide arc as the chatter got even louder. There was alarm now amid the excitement. The airborne object was closer as the aircraft spiraled in. Denny did not need a translation, she had seen similar situations before. Some passengers were urging the pilot to turn away, but he was dismissive.

The camera wobbled, the view veering wildly, until it settled again and focused on the mystery shape. Denny took in a sharp breath. Now the aircraft was circling at a higher altitude than the object. Its shape was apparent despite it being so dark in hue that light seemed to fall into it. A central hub, roughly cylindrical, from which radiated five tapering arms. It was several hundred feet across, though size was hard to estimate against the backdrop of the forest far below.

A Black Star.

The plane continued to circle, then the video cut to a more distant shot. Denny sighed with relief. They were at least moving away from the creature. The video ended, like most amateur footage, abruptly and with no kind of credits. She scrolled down the comments. A minority were in English. The first one she could read described the clip as,

'TOTALLY FAKE RUSSIAN BS LOUSY FX CRAP'. The next few were no more thoughtful. Most seemed to think the video was a viral marketing campaign for a forthcoming alien invasion movie. There was a consensus that, as spaceships went, the Black Star was 'lame'.

Denny tried to search for other sightings of what might be entities from the Phantom Dimension. After struggling with mainstream media, she soon found herself surfing conspiracy sites and ended up reading semi-literate prose for a good two hours. She read about sea serpents, Mothmen, Sasquatch, and a range of other creatures that she would once have dismissed as hoaxes, or symptoms of drug abuse. Now she was not so sure.

You see crazy and do crazy, how can you not believe crazy?

Denny tagged a few accounts that might be valid. There were many tales and theories concerning CHUDS – Cannibalistic Humanoid Underground Dwellers, said to lurk in the sewers of New York.

"Where else? But they could be Interlopers."

Denny went back to the original video. She was almost sure that Gould had found it, and sent it to her. But whoever it was, they clearly did not trust her enough to communicate openly. Or maybe they, too, assumed the foundation had hacked Denny's phone?

God, I need some sleep. Monster-free sleep.

She was brushing her teeth when a thought occurred to her. She picked up her phone and opened the video link again. This time she paused the clip and then zoomed in on the Black Star. The result was a blurred mess, but she could see what seemed to be fragments of dark debris falling into the forest below.

Is it dying?

She moved forward, frame by frame, trying to find a clear image. Eventually she got one. It was obvious that flaps of ragged flesh were hanging from one of the Black Star's immense arms. Then she found another definite sign that the creature was decaying. One of the dangling tentacles fell off the underside of the drifting colossus, and fell spinning into the trees below.

They're as vulnerable to earthly conditions as the standard-issue Interlopers.

She felt an odd sense of regret at the thought of the huge, floating predator suddenly cast into an alien world. Denny had no reason to believe that the Black Stars were anything other than predatory animals. Despite the horror she had felt when the creatures had tried to capture her, she also felt pity.

An animal mind, feeling its body disintegrating, failing to understand why it's dying. A casualty of a crisis it could never grasp.

She ended the video and went to bed. Before she settled down, she put a notebook and pen on the bedside table. She had decided that if her dreams continued unabated, she might as well try to write down what she remembered.

If I wake in the night, she thought, as she turned the light off. *And if I remember anything at all.*

***

Theresa Bradford found it difficult to get to sleep. Age and the discomfort of arthritis were partly to blame. But she was also worried about young Miss Clay. She lay awake listening until well after midnight, alert for the slightest noise from upstairs. But she heard nothing.

Well, the poor girl might have had an early night, she thought. *Even young people go to bed early sometimes.*

Theresa could not quite convince herself that the answer was that simple. When she had taken her casserole up to her neighbor, she had been startled at the appearance of the girl. She thought back to the encounter, tried to remember what Miss Clay had said. There was nothing odd about the words, she decided, but the tone of voice had been strange.

And her face. What was wrong with her face?

"Oh, bugger it, I can't sleep like this!" she muttered, and heaved herself ponderously out from under the duvet. Percy, who was curled up in his favorite spot at the bottom of the bed, gave a grumpy meow. Then the cat, sensing the possibility of the fridge being opened, jumped down and ran ahead of her into the kitchen.

"You'll be lucky," she told the animal as she filled the kettle.

While she was waiting for the kettle to boil, Theresa stared out of her small kitchen window into the night. Wimbledon Common was dotted with lights. The snow had stopped falling and the night was clear, giving the vast expanse a magical appearance. But Theresa did not find it enjoyable, and turned on the kitchen light. She could now just see her reflection in the dark mirror of the window glass.

God, you look awful. And so old.

Then the idea that had been worrying at the back of her mind for hours surfaced. She knew why there had been something wrong with Timandra Clay's face. It was so simple that she laughed out loud. The girl's face had looked completely natural. For the first time, she had seen her neighbor without lipstick, powder, eyeliner, mascara.

"She wasn't wearing any make-up, Percy! That was all. She'd probably just been into the shower. These girls today, they wear far too much on their faces. Good that she's looking more natural, isn't it? Yes."

Theresa was so relieved to have solved the mystery that she celebrated with a chocolate digestive biscuit, and even gave Percy an extra helping of Kittybits. She went back to bed to sip her tea, and drowsiness began to overcome her. She placed the teacup on the bedside table and curled up again, feeling content. She had almost drifted off to sleep when another thought struck her.

Did she have time to take a shower? Hadn't she just come in, and then taken a phone call?

But by then, tiredness had claimed the old lady, and the questions faded into a dreamless slumber.

***

Ted Gould sent the video link, from his second phone, to Denny and Harriet Zoffany. Neither responded, but he assumed both would guess he was responsible. It had not taken him long to find the evidence of the incursion. He hoped that the research staff had not followed his example, but they were a smart bunch. If any of them had found the video and followed procedure, they would tell him.

And I'll have to tell Benson that the boundary is starting to collapse. Far sooner than we had expected.

When footage taken by Denny in the Phantom Dimension had been analyzed the previous autumn, it had caused alarm. Vast entities had been heading toward the Malpas Abbey gateway. But it was assumed that, even if the beings could somehow enlarge the portal between dimensions, the human world would have years to prepare. The time flow in the PD was so much slower, it made sense to believe in a comfortable margin.

What they had not taken into account was that Class One entities might be about to penetrate our world in other places. Nobody knew what the Russians, Chinese, or a dozen other nations were doing about the issue. Gould had a strong conviction that they were doing nothing.

The more authoritarian the state, the more it can ignore pressing problems.

"Maybe we deserve what's coming," he said aloud.

The bleak statement broke the silence in his apartment. Part of him hoped that he was being bugged, that Benson heard him in his despair. Despite years of doing the chairman's bidding, Gould still did not understand his boss. He disliked and mistrusted Benson, but could not grasp what made him tick. All he could be sure of was that Benson had the backing of the government and the foundation's trustees.

Gould frowned, took out his 'secret' phone again. He searched for the Romola Foundation, something he did from time to time to see just how well-cloaked his employer was. Sure enough, the foundation was still listed by the government's charity regulator as a 'body devoted to research into the paranormal and related issues'. Gould grimaced as a quote from the visionary poet Blake occurred to him.

"A truth that's told with bad intent," he murmured, "beats all the lies you can invent. Pity you're not still around, mate. You might be just the kind of lunatic we need at this hour."

The Charity Commission website gave a few other

snippets of information. It was notable that other charities offered pictures of their bosses, workers, major donors. The Romola Foundation only listed Benson and the trustees. No pictures. Gould tried to remember if he had ever met one of the trustees, as they were required by law to hold regular meetings and supervise Benson's activities. But try as he might, he could not recall anything about them. The list of commonplace British names told him nothing. A web search found no further data on any of them.

They're probably just a bunch of upper-class nonentities, Gould concluded, *claiming expenses, signing off on the accounts, and just letting Benson do his thing.*

He flung the phone down on the sofa, then poured himself a whiskey as a nightcap. As the pungent spirit hit the back of his throat, he felt a warm glow. It did nothing to improve his mood at first, but after finishing a full glass of Scotch at least his unhappiness had blurred around the edges.

***

Jon and Sallie Murray got the children to bed without difficulty. After that, they said little to one another; she busied herself with household tasks, while he worked on his laptop in the kitchen. They would normally have settled down to watch TV around nine before getting to bed early. But on this particular night, neither made a move towards the living room sofa.

We're avoiding each other, she thought. *We don't want to talk about it while they're in the house.*

Sallie went into the kitchen, filled the kettle.

"Want some tea?" she asked, without looking at her husband.

"Yeah, I'll have a cup," Jon replied.

After she had made the tea, she set the cups down on the table between them and took a seat opposite Jon. Then she reached out and placed her hand over his, clutching it as he tried to pull away. His face was illuminated in the glow of the laptop screen. He still did not look at her.

"We've got to talk about it," she whispered urgently. "We

can't just let it slide. Not now. Not after the dog."

"Do you seriously think," he said softly, still not looking up from the screen, "that those kids – our kids – could do something like that?"

"Somebody did it," she insisted. "I don't believe it was a wild animal. And neither do you."

"Remember when Zoe saved that ladybird from the stream?" Jon said. "She insisted on it having a bed made from a matchbox and some cotton wool. So it could get better after nearly drowning. Ben made fun of her, sure, but as soon as she cried, he stopped."

"I know–" Sallie began.

"That was last summer," Jon said. Now he did raise his eyes to hers. "I was so proud of them. I got that glow when I talked about them. So proud. How can they have changed so much since then?"

"I don't know how it's happened," Sallie admitted. "But I found out some things ..."

She told Ben about her research, her suspicions, her doubts. After the first minute or so, he shook his head, seemed about to object. But as she pressed on, his face became pale, confused, even more unhappy than before. When she had finished he said nothing for a few moments, then closed the laptop.

"There's been some talk going 'round," he whispered, leaning forward. "About something weird that happened with kids over the other side of the county. Place on the border, called Machen."

"Where did you hear this?" she asked.

"Old Bert down at the garage," he admitted. "I know he's a bit daft and drinks too much cheap cider, but he does have family out that way."

Sallie said, "So what did he tell you?"

"Kids disappeared in the woods, then came back ... but changed," he explained. "Not acting right. All withdrawn and quiet, like. And there were killings. Story gets a bit garbled about that, you know what Bert's like. But I heard–"

Jon's eyes widened as he stopped talking, then leaned back. Sallie knew before she turned around what he had seen.

In the doorway behind her Zoe stood, staring at her parents. Zoe was dressed in Disney princess pajamas, dangling a cuddly panda from one tiny hand. Yet looking at the small figure, Sallie felt a definite chill of dread.

"I can't sleep, daddy," said Zoe. "I'm frightened."

"Oh," Jon said, standing up. It was his established role to comfort Zoe, despite Sallie's half-serious opposition to the 'Daddy's girl' approach. This time, though, she sensed Jon's reluctance as he made his way around the table to kneel, with open arms, before Zoe. The child ran forward into her father's embrace.

It looks so right, Sallie thought. *Anyone else looking at this would see it as normal. Touching, even. But really, it's like actors in a play.*

Zoe had buried her face in Jon's shoulder, but now she looked up sharply. Sallie flinched, tried not to show how disturbed she was. Zoe's face was expressionless as she murmured something into Jon's ear.

"Oh, is that so?" he replied, his voice hearty. "Well, I'll come and check."

Jon lifted Zoe and stood up. He looked back at Sallie, and she saw all too clearly that he was afraid, and fighting his fear.

"What is it?" Sallie asked.

"Oh, don't worry, love," said Jon, trying to sound nonchalant. "She says there are monsters in her room. Just some silly old monsters. I'll take care of it."

Sallie sat, wringing her hands, as her husband carried their small daughter upstairs. She thought of the torn and bloodied carcass of the dog, and listened intently as low voices carried down the stairs.

What can I do? Sallie asked herself. She looked at her phone lying on the table. *Can I call the police and tell them our children might be planning to kill us? What evidence do I have, really?*

She went through the mental list of oddities, changes, impressions. If she spoke them aloud to a police officer, she would sound like a lunatic. And yet she and Jon both shared the same fear, a dread of their own offspring.

And now they've separated us.

The new thought stunned her with its simplicity. The children were far smaller and weaker than their parents, but together they could tackle one. And Jon, by far the stronger of the two, had just been lured upstairs.

Into the dark.

Sallie rose and walked slowly to the foot of the stairs. She could hear nothing, now, except the familiar grumbling noise from the boiler. Then came what might have been a cry, quickly stifled. The voice was not that of a child. There was a startling thud as something struck the bedroom floor.

Sallie retreated, shaking her head in desperate denial, until she collided with the kitchen table. A shadow appeared on the staircase, a shadow cast by something low, crouching, moving on all fours. She reached behind her, groping for the phone.

"Jon?" she said faintly, as if his name could somehow conjure him up.

It can't be Jon. Oh God!

A small shape came into view, and turned its head towards her. It had a muzzle, not a face, but the hair hanging in pigtails to either side of the monstrous visage was as familiar as the Disney princess pajamas.

Sallie screamed, knocked the phone onto the floor, and got down to scrabble for it. Then she changed her mind, went to slam the kitchen door first. The creature that had been Zoe was already bounding on all fours across the hall. Sallie slammed the door in the creature's face, and pressed her back against it. A snarling noise, utterly inhuman, came from the other side of the door. A series of fierce blows pounded on the oak panels, but they held firm.

There was no lock, but a chair could be jammed under the knob. She stretched out an arm for the nearest chair but could not quite reach it. She slid down until she was on her backside and tried to hook the chair with her foot. She succeeded only in kicking it sideways. She tried again, and this time dragged it closer. Grasping the knob with one hand, she pulled herself upright and grabbed the chair, jamming it into position.

As if sensing what she had done, the pounding increased. Sallie got down and crawled under the table to reach her phone. But before she could reach it, the back door swung open. Locking up was part of the nightly ritual she and Jon went through just before going to bed. Ben had simply gone around the house from front to back.

With nowhere to retreat, Sallie tried to overturn the table to make an improvised shield as the pale entity bounded into the kitchen. It easily leaped over the table and landed on the cringing woman, talons flashing with dizzying speed. Sallie felt suddenly cold and numb, all fear departing with her life blood.

Chapter 4: City of Illusions

At Hobs Lane station, a different security guard was on the night shift. Just after midnight he waved the pretty, young cleaner through, and smiled, trying to make conversation about the weather.

"Cold enough for you?" he asked, cheerfully.

The woman looked up at him, then her mouth twitched up in a tight smile that vanished again almost instantly.

"It's cold enough for me, yes."

The guard was about to launch into a comparative discussion of wintry conditions in England as opposed to Eastern Europe. But before he could begin, the woman had moved on, not exactly running but walking swiftly. The guard was left ambling back to his small office, feeling slightly resentful.

Still, he thought, *it's that work ethic that brings them over here in the first place.*

The guard settled into his chair with a sigh and flicked through the security monitors. They showed, unsurprisingly, that both platforms were empty. He waited for the cleaner to appear.

There she is, he thought. *With her bucket on wheels.*

The woman began to mop the tiles, and the guard soon got bored. He took out his phone and started checking the football news. He felt moved to comment on a piece about his team, Arsenal. This quickly involved him in a fierce online dispute with a supporter of Manchester United, a not-uncommon situation. As the mutual mud-slinging escalated, he was half-aware of the tiny figure of the cleaner moving along the platform.

"Oh, sod off," he sighed eventually, and got up to get his Thermos flask of coffee.

It was only then that he noticed the cleaner had vanished.

"Where did you get to, then, darling?"

The guard flicked between different views, scrutinizing both platforms and the various tunnels and escalators. Then he got up and went outside his tiny office, into the atrium. She wasn't there, either. The guard knew that a body had been found on the tracks near Hobs Lane that morning. There was talk of the woman being a murder victim. In his mind's eye, he imagined a killer stalking the Underground tunnels in the small hours, preying on cleaners.

Don't be stupid. No way somebody could walk that far through the network and not be seen.

He realized he did not even remember the woman's name. He found the cleaning roster under a heap of free newspapers and fast-food wrappers.

"Daniela Wysko – Viskovich – bugger."

He gave up on the cleaner's surname and rushed to the lift. When he emerged onto the platform, he saw the cleaning gear lying, as if abandoned, near the tunnel mouth. His heart began to pound with genuine fear. The idea of a psychopath lurking in the vast labyrinth of tunnels under London was suddenly credible.

"Daniela?" he said tentatively, then realized he could not be heard more than a few yards away. He raised his voice, shouted her name again. The echo answered him. The tunnel mouth suddenly seemed huge, menacing. He wished that budget cuts had not left a bare minimum of staff at stations.

A sound came out of the darkness. It might have been a call for help. It had a plaintive quality, weak, feminine. The security guard had failed to get into the army or the police. He had always wanted, deep down, to be hailed as a hero, to see his name in the paper. In fact, he could see it now.

HERO GUARD SAVES WOMAN

No way are you going in there, he told himself firmly. *Go back up and call the cops.*

Before he could turn away, though, a flood of images cascaded through his mind. He saw himself not only rescuing Daniela, but her immense gratitude leading to steamy fun and more. She would become the hot, adoring young wife he had always deserved. He saw himself transformed from just another fat, middle-aged guy to a celebrity. He would appear on TV to be modest and witty. He would found a charity, travel the world promoting good causes, and never have to work again.

You're being an idiot, said a small voice, which he ignored as he climbed ponderously down onto the track. But as he walked into the darkness, he was smiling, despite the pounding of his heart. A phrase he had always liked occurred to him.

"A date with destiny," he murmured. "Oh yes."

He took out his flashlight and shone it into the tunnel, the beam glancing off the steel rails and damp, gleaming walls. He could just make out a vague figure, small and still, about a hundred yards ahead.

"Daniela?" he shouted again.

Instead of coming towards him she stepped back, disappeared.

"Don't be afraid, Daniela," he said in a wheedling voice. "I'll protect you."

Protect her from what?

He tried to ignore the small voice of skepticism, but here in the dark it was hard not to be nervous. The visions of his future as a lovable hero-next-door were still intense, but fear was fighting back against optimism. He resolved to go back and call the police if she continued to head further into the tunnel.

Then the flashlight's beam found her. She was crouched down, dark hair falling over her face. He reached out to touch her on the shoulder.

"Daniela?"

She turned her head, and he saw her pretty, pale face smiling up at him. She stood and reached out, taking his hand, playfully pulling them closer together. It was his fantasy made real, the attractive woman suddenly finding him desirable.

Why is she doing this in a tunnel?

Again, he quelled the small, troubling voice as Daniela started to unbutton his jacket. She worked quickly with long, clever fingers, and in seconds she had stripped him of his jacket and shirt. She bent down and started working on his pants. They fell around his ankles.

"Oh God," he breathed.

The flashlight beam wobbled, played over the tunnel wall. It picked out a leg, a hand, a glimpse of a face. The small figure was pale, dressed in a cleaner's overall. It looked a lot like

Daniela but before he could focus on her, the stranger dodged to one side, heading behind him.

"Hey!" he exclaimed. "You brought a friend?"

No, the skeptical voice warned, *she came alone.*

He turned the flashlight down again and saw Daniela. She looked up at him with what might have been a grin. It was hard to tell, as what should have been a face was a now elongated muzzle. The eyes were small, dark, deep-sunken. But it was the mouth that made him gasp in terror, held up a hand to ward off the sight. The mouth was lined with dozens of needle-sharp teeth. The creature hissed at him.

"Christ!"

He reeled back only for sinuous fingers to wrap themselves around his throat from behind. A moment later slender legs wrapped themselves around his waist. The weight of his assailant sent him staggering, and he fell to his knees. One kneecap connected with a rail and the pain blinded him for a moment. His flashlight skittered away, stopped, cast a useless patch of light on the wall.

"Help!" he screamed, clawing at the talons gripping his throat.

The first creature, the false Daniela that was not killing him, did not respond. It was too busy gathering up his discarded uniform.

I only wanted to be a hero.

Bittersweet, it was his last thought.

***

Denny awoke after a night of disturbed sleep, with only the vaguest memories of her dreams. Her face in the bathroom mirror reminded her of a former college friend who had dropped out thanks to a serious meth problem. She had interviewed the girl as an assignment.

"I didn't even get the fun a drug habit can bring," she grumbled, stepping into the shower.

A few minutes later, she felt refreshed, and took her first sip of coffee. As she was waiting for her breakfast oatmeal to be microwaved, she checked her phone. Frankie had sent her a video of a Wiener dog dressed in a fire truck costume chasing an angry cat around an apartment.

Some things never change, Denny thought, smiling.

She moved on to news feeds. Inevitably her browsing around the Russian video had produced a rich crop of craziness. Some algorithm had decided she was interested in not only Bigfoot sightings and sea serpents, but also conspiracy theories about lizard people from outer space. One 'revelation' claimed the Queen was just such an alien. Denny chuckled, then swiped on to the next item.

CALI FISH KILL BAFFLES SCIENTISTS

She frowned at a picture of people on a beach picking their way among mounds of silvery corpses. Skimming the story, which came from a mainstream source, she could see that it was mysterious but not obviously related to the paranormal.

Fish kills? Hardly my cup of tea.

She scrolled down, stopped, stared. There was another image, this time of the sea taken from the air. The caption read 'A Coastguard aircraft was in the area when the strange incident occurred'. Hundreds of dead fish drifted on the blue ocean. Flocks of gulls were circling, though none seemed to have alighted to feast on the corpses. The angle was shallow, the plane had clearly been some distance from the focal point of the mass death. However, Denny felt sure that there was an unusual symmetry to the drifting carrion.

The pattern was blurred, but still quite discernible. It was roughly star-shaped. Denny imagined a Black Star dying slowly, drifting down to the surface and poisoning marine life as it sank, slowly dissolving, into the depths.

"Strike two," Denny thought. "One over the Pacific, one in Russia."

She was dressed and ready to go when she remembered the notepad beside her bed. She glanced over, saw that it had apparently been moved. When she checked, she found a few scrawled words slanting down the page. They were hard to decipher, but she thought she recognized 'chamber', 'cocoa', and what might have been 'queer'.

"Great," she muttered, tearing off the page and shoving in her jeans' pocket. "Now I'm setting myself puzzles."

***

Sir Lionel Bartram sat in the back seat of his ministerial Daimler and checked his watch. Timandra was late. This was not unusual. He had not hired her for her punctuality. But Bartram still felt mild resentment that his personal assistant should take his tolerance so much for granted.

After all, he thought, *the girl's getting more out of this than I am.*

He checked his phone. She had not replied to his last message. Or any of the previous three. Bartram leaned over, looked up at the apartment building through the limousine's bullet-proof glass.

What on earth is keeping the little fool? Has she overslept?

Bartram suddenly thought of Timandra sprawled luxuriously in bed, next to her a young, handsome, virile man. The unwelcome thought was followed by a far worse one. Like most career politicians, Bartram was a risk taker, like a compulsive gambler. He knew it, but could never control his urges enough to be wholly safe. Timandra was just the latest of a string of young mistresses. None of her predecessors had gone to the press.

But in these days of Twitter and online shaming, she doesn't need to.

"Would you like me to go and ring the doorbell, sir?" asked his bodyguard, turning around in the front passenger seat.

Bartram thought he detected a slight hint of mockery in the police officer's voice. The man might well have sensed Bartram's discomfort. As a minister with a security brief, he could hardly travel without armed protection. But between the bodyguard, the chauffeur, and various civil servants he was left with little time to enjoy Timandra's company.

"No," he said brusquely, "I'll do it, I need to stretch my legs."

He distinctly heard the officer sigh and felt a mild rush of pleasure at forcing the man to get out into the freezing cold.

Bartram picked his way carefully over the icy pavement and jabbed at the door buzzer. After a moment, there was a click.

"Is that you, Tiger Pants?"

Without meaning to, Bartram looked around to see if his bodyguard had overheard. The man coughed, covered his mouth with a fist.

I'll get him replaced, Bartram thought, then turned to put his mouth close to the grille of the intercom.

"You're running late, I have a meeting with the Home Secretary at ten. I need to prepare–"

"Come on up, darling."

There was a buzz, a louder click, and the door opened.

"I haven't got time–" Bartram began.

He hesitated. His mind was suddenly flooded with amorous thoughts. He saw Timandra in the special outfit he loved so much. He remembered many previous moments of delight. Again, his gambler's instincts rose up, the thought of opportunistic shagging all the more tempting because it was so reckless.

"I'll be down in a few minutes," he called over his shoulder as he pushed the door open. "You wait in the car."

The old busybody who lived on the ground floor was just opening her front door as he tried to sprint up the stairs. He gave her a curt nod, secretly wishing she would expire from heart failure. She was one of many loose ends in his affair with Timandra.

Far too many loose ends. I will get caught at this rate. But oh God, it's worth it.

***

"So, this is weird," said Davenport. "Check it out."

Jim Davison watched the poor-quality video of a woman mopping an Underground platform. He could not make out the sign from this angle, but assumed it was Hobs Lane. They were in Davenport's office, a small cubbyhole that seemed little used, as befitted a top field agent.

"Weird, as in somebody actually working hard for a living?" Jim remarked after half a minute. "I suppose you could sell this as some kind of art installation. Good feminist angle."

"Keep watching. Our contact at the Scotland Yard passed this along first thing. Surprised they got the footage this quickly, given all the cutbacks."

Davenport jabbed a finger at the tunnel mouth. Then Jim saw it, the way the cleaner stopped, seemed to listen. Although the angle was poor, he could just make out that she was speaking. Then she walked along to the end of the platform, and after seemingly pausing to listen, climbed down onto the tracks.

"Bloody hell!" Jim half-expected to see her killed instantly by the voltage, then remembered that the current would have been turned off.

"Malpas Abbey, yes?" Davenport said. "Underground gateway? This could be another one. And you know how those creatures can lure people in. Make you see people you love, or want to bonk! And put ideas in your head."

"Yeah, all that's true," Jim conceded. "But in Machen, the gateway was at the top of a hill in a forest. And remember Gould's account of his sister being taken. That was pretty much at sea level. So, you're reading a hell of a lot into the behavior of a woman who might just be, I dunno, mentally ill? Or a part-time rat collector?"

"Keep watching, mate," Davenport said, looking pleased with himself. "It gets better."

The cleaner went into the tunnel, vanishing into the darkness. Davenport wound forward just over six minutes. A figure appeared in the tunnel, gradually became clearer. Even in the poor-quality footage, the person was clearly wearing the cleaner's overall, jeans, and sneakers.

"Hard to tell if it's exactly the same face," Davenport remarked. "But what a neat trick if they are coming through down there."

Jim leaned back in his chair, and his head connected with a filing cabinet. He swore, partly at the pain, partly at the problem.

"How the hell could we investigate the Tube network without drawing too much attention? We can't close the

Thames Line, or even part of it. At least half a million people must be using it every day."

Davenport nodded at the screen.

"Do it at night. Nobody about except security and cleaners. We tell them it's counter-terrorism, make it very clear that they're to tell no one. Then some of them will blab to their mates, partners, whatever, and that's our cover established."

"Rather you than me," Jim replied. "Not keen on enclosed spaces, myself."

Davenport gave a knowing smile.

"Oh come on!" Jim protested. "I did Malpas Abbey, then that mayhem in Machen. Isn't there some other idiot who'll stick his nose into monster territory?"

"You're looking at him," replied Davenport. "Hey, it's probably nothing. But we're keeping it to ourselves for now, right? Just in case. And who better to probe this particular mystery than someone with time in the field?"

Jim conceded, with bad grace, and the two began planning their investigation. As before, Jim found himself growing enthusiastic about the assignment once the practical issues had to be tackled. He brought up a map of the London Underground system on his laptop and pointed to the Thames Line.

"Okay," he said, "first thing is tunnels tend to go in two directions. So we've got Hobs Lane, suspect area, right. But at the other end of that tunnel is Wyndham Road. That's nearer to the heart of the city. And if they kept going the other way, they'd get to Wimbledon Common – it's not that far for things that move as fast as Interlopers."

Davenport made a skeptical sound.

"Yeah, but nothing's been reported at Wyndham Road," he observed.

"Because nothing's happened?" Jim riposted. "Or because the Interlopers have done a far better job at covering their tracks? Like Gould always says, absence of evidence is not evidence of absence."

"Quite the little Poirot, aren't we?" Davenport said, but Jim could tell his colleague was impressed. "So we need to check security staff at both stations."

They agreed to start at Hobs Lane and work their way along to Wyndham Road that night. In the meantime, checks were to be carried out on the night security force and the cleaners. Forster, Davenport explained, had squared it with Benson as a special operation that nobody else need know about.

"What about backup?" Jim asked. "Two guys is one less than sensible."

"Not many people available," said Davenport. "Most of them are down in Herefordshire, preparing for another venture into the Machen gateway. But we'll still have a couple of guys positioned outside each station. They'll come in if we call them via the emergency radio system."

"Are we gonna be armed?" Jim asked. "And please don't let it be Tasers or gas."

His colleague reached down behind his small desk and Jim heard the sound of a locker being opened. Davenport took out a semi-automatic pistol, checked the ammunition clip, put it down on the desk, muzzle pointed away from both men.

"Short range weapons with stopping power," Davenport said. "I know you'd prefer a shotgun, pump action?"

Jim murmured his assent, looking at the gleaming Beretta. Numerous movies about a zombie apocalypse came to mind.

Shoot 'em in the head, he thought. *That's the only way to be sure.*

"Check with you later," Davenport said, rising to offer his hand and signaling the meeting was over.

"Right, I'll check out some body armor as well as the twelve-gauge," Jim said, and after a brief handshake, he set off back to the training section. As he made his way through the labyrinthine corridors of the Victorian building, he passed some familiar faces, nodded, shared a joke with one.

Any one, he knew, might in theory be an Interloper. They still did not have an infallible way to tell them apart without taking a blood or tissue sample, followed by a test lasting an hour. It was impossible to test everyone every day.

If they're in London, in force ...

The thought would not complete itself. Jim was rather glad of that.

***

After climbing two flights, Bartram was wheezing a little. As soon as he arrived outside the second-floor flat the door swung open, and there she stood in all her glory. He was wheezing a little from his exertion, but the sight of her perked him up. In her Perspex stripper heels, Timandra was nearly a head taller than Bartram. She glanced past him, raised an eyebrow.

"He's waiting downstairs," Bartram explained. "We don't have long, but I couldn't resist you my – ow!"

She reached out for his tie and pulled him into the apartment, slamming the door with her near-naked butt. Her hands were busy with his clothes, her full lips seemingly fastened onto his mouth by suction. Bartram felt a twinge of alarm. She had never been so assertive before. More often she had been coy, a shy creature he could mold to his needs. There was no trace of that girl now.

"I say!" he spluttered, more in surprise than protest.

She stopped kissing him and held his head in her hands, looking down into his eyes.

"Don't you like this? Isn't it what you always wanted?"

"Oh yes," Bartram sighed, realizing that this confident, passionate lover was indeed what he had always fantasized about. It would have been unmanly to admit to her that he wanted her to take control, dominate him, make him her slave. His entire political career had been based on traditional values, especially concerning 'a woman's place'. But now it was happening, being dominated was more pleasurable than anything he could have imagined.

Timandra practically hurled Bartram onto the bed and straddled him.

"You're sure they won't come prying, knocking on the door?" she demanded, her voice much huskier than normal.

"No, they wouldn't dare!" he replied.

"We have plenty of time?" she insisted.

"Plenty, Oh God yes!"

There was a mirror on the ceiling above the bed. It had come with the apartment, which he had taken over from another member of his party when their mistress had moved on. While Bartram did not particularly enjoy seeing his short, flabby body exposed, there was something wonderful about watching Timandra writhing on top of him.

If anything, she looked more beautiful and sensuous than ever. Lately, Bartram had noticed his young mistress becoming slimmer, more 'buff' as the young folk called it. He had not said anything but found the obsession with fitness unappealing if it sacrificed curves for muscle. But there was no trace of that now. Her hourglass figure reminded him of the fantasy women of his boyhood, when his first sexual awakening had led him to his father's stockpile of well-thumbed magazines.

Bartram peered more closely at Timandra's face, and was reminded of a girl in one of those long-defunct publications. The shape of her lips, the expression in her eyes, all echoed the soft-porn starlet. The resemblance was striking, yet he had never noticed it before.

Funny how the subconscious plays tricks, he thought. *But that explains why she turns me on, of course. Fantasy of youth and all that.*

By now, Timandra had managed to remove all of his outer garments while continuing to kiss and caress him. He noted with approval that she had suddenly become far more skillful in the arts of seduction. She flung his socks into the corner of the room and then sat up, looking down at her sprawled paramour. Again, Bartram could see himself clearly in the ceiling mirror. He could not pretend to himself that he looked like a stud, lying there in baggy Y-fronts and vest.

A beached whale, he thought sadly, and the intense passion of the moment began to fade. *It doesn't help that it smells a bit in here.*

The odd odor was hard to define, but might be down to a backed-up drain. He wrinkled his nose.

"What's the matter, Tiger Pants?" breathed the girl, smiling down at him enigmatically.

361

"Oh, nothing, Sugar Buns," he replied, trying to get back into the moment.

Timandra ran her hands through her hair. Hair that somehow looked less abundant than it had seemed a few moments before. Even more oddly, the girl's figure was no longer a voluptuous hourglass. It was as if her flesh had somehow flowed down her torso, shrinking her breasts and enlarging her belly.

How could I have missed that tummy bulge? Bartram thought. *Not to mention those rather thick thighs.*

"Not quite beach body ready, eh?" she said, voice silky, and oddly menacing.

"Oh, no–" he began.

Before he could say something complimentary, Timandra laughed and to Bartram's displeasure, slapped his considerable stomach with both hands. It did not seem playful, and it hurt. Before he could protest, she punched him, hard, in the gut so that he wheezed and brought up some of his breakfast. Then her hands were around his throat, squeezing with extraordinary strength.

As he struggled to tear her hands free, he saw her face change. She developed jowls, her eyes grew smaller, her nose turned red – what his wife called 'a boozer's conk'. The hairline had receded, now, so that only a few wisps of hair remained around the fringes of a bald scalp.

It's me, my God it's me!

With a tremendous effort, born mostly of blind panic, Bartram managed to heave the freakish assailant off him. His near-double fell sideways onto the carpet while he rolled off the opposite side. This put him further from the front door, but just a few feet from the bathroom.

I can lock myself in, wait for help – yes, that's what I'll do!

He staggered to the door, tore it open, hurled himself inside and slammed the door behind him. A moment later, a heavy weight struck the door and nearly knocked him down. Again, adrenaline came to his aid, allowing him to keep the door shut just long enough to turn the latch. Another blow almost jolted the door out of its frame. Bartram realized, with a sinking feeling, that waiting for help was not an option. And his phone was in his jacket, which was lying on the floor by the bed.

"Come on out, Tiger Pants," cooed the monstrous being. It now sounded deeper, more masculine, but still had a trace of Timandra's girlish voice.

Bartram whined in terror and confusion. He realized that if he smashed the bathroom window, he could shout for help. Simply breaking it might be enough. He tried to recall the layout of the flat, whether his security man would be likely to hear the shattering of glass. But his mind was not up to the task, so he simply started looking for something heavy enough to do the job.

"Don't you want your Sugar Buns anymore?"

The mocking plea was followed by a crash and a splintering sound. Bartram could not see anything on the shelves that might break a window. Then he thought of the shower head, which he recalled was metal. He yanked open the door of the shower cubicle, and the real Timandra fell out. She would have fallen face down, except that her head had been twisted around so that she was looking at him over her shoulder.

Bartram fell on his backside and screamed just as the door gave way. His doppelganger entered, still clad in a purple velvet basque and fishnets. The face that looked blankly down at him was his entirely, but the hands that reached for him were the black-taloned claws of a waking nightmare.

***

"How much longer do we give the old perv?" demanded the government driver.

Rather than bicker, the bodyguard just grunted and got out of the limousine. But he had not even reached the door of the block when it opened and Bartram came out.

"Ready to go, sir?" asked the bodyguard.

"Yes," said Bartram, tersely, walking past the Scotland Yard officer.

The bodyguard glanced over at the driver, who was

keeping a straight face, then hurried forward to open the car door. Bartram got in without another word and sat, staring ahead, while the officer hurried around to get in on the other side.

"Young lady not coming, sir?" asked the driver.

"No," Bartram replied instantly. "She's not feeling very well."

No, thought the bodyguard as he fastened his safety belt, *I wouldn't either if I had to shag an old blimp like you.*

There was a pause while the driver waited for the minister to buckle up. When Bartram showed no sign of fastening his seatbelt, the bodyguard gave a small sigh, reached over and did it for him. The driver caught the bodyguard's eye, raised a quizzical eyebrow, then eased the Daimler into the rush hour traffic.

"Sorry to hear that, sir," the bodyguard said. "Lot of bugs going 'round, this time of year."

This attempt at conversation achieved nothing. Bartram continued to stare ahead as if in a trance. The bodyguard found his gaze drawn to the old man's face, though he knew he should have been keeping alert for potential threats. There was something not quite right. Then he saw it. The minister was wearing eyeliner and lipstick. There was not much of it, and it had been clumsily applied. But the make-up was definitely there.

Bartram suddenly turned to look at the bodyguard, who gave a wan smile and turned his attention to the traffic. Out of the corner of his eye, the officer saw the minister take out a hankie, lick it, and start dabbing at eyes and mouth.

No wonder the bloody country's in a mess, he thought. *Still, this could all make a choice chapter for my memoirs, if I ever get to write 'em.*

Chapter 5: Revelations

Gould and Zoffany met in a cheap diner for breakfast. They were surrounded by shift workers. Gould felt incongruous among cleaners, truckers, nurses, taxi drivers, and other bleary-eyed folk looking forward to a well-earned day in bed. His well-cut suit was as out of place as his newly-shaved chin. He felt relief when Zoffany arrived, especially as she looked even less like a regular in her business-like pants suit.

But at least none of Benson's little friends are likely to be here, he thought.

Gould smiled and half-rose when Zoffany walked over to his table, but she barely managed to nod, eyes downcast. At first he thought it was because of the venue, then he realized that she looked drawn, tired. Unlike him, she had not slept well, if at all. He leaned toward her to kiss her cheek, indifferent to the crowded room. But she gave a small shake of the head and sat down at once.

"Not feeling too good?" Gould asked.

She shook her head, began playing with the handle of her bag. She still did not look at him. A waitress came up, dumped a laden plate in front of Gould, and asked Zoffany what she wanted. She ordered coffee. When the girl had gone, Gould asked, "What's wrong?"

Zoffany took a deep breath and started to talk. She rattled off a string of technical terms, some of which were familiar to him. He had heard her talk this way before, and recognized it as a defensive reaction. It might be explained by her being in a strange place, but that seemed unlikely.

She's had more disconcerting experiences than the menu in this place, he thought. *Is she going to break up with me? The whole workplace affair thing might be too much for her.*

Gould reached out and touched Zoffany lightly on the back of one hand. She jerked back, then looked up at him for the first time.

"Sorry," he said. "Look, if this is about us—"

"Oh God no!" she said loudly, so that heads turned at nearby tables.

"No," she insisted in a lower voice, "not that. That's not what I want. But if you–"

"Why would I?" he interrupted. "You're the best thing that's ever happened to me."

Cheesy, he told himself. *She'd be entitled to dump you after that.*

Zoffany reached out and took Gould's hand. He felt her quivering with emotion.

"It's about the tests on the – the false Lucy," she explained. "I got a batch of results back this morning, and I need to tell you before the meeting."

Gould felt himself grow rigid at the mention of the creature that had imitated his sister.

"Dissection found nothing, as I understand it," he said, keeping his voice low. So far as he could tell, nobody was paying attention to them now.

"Yes, we were looking for something like the talisman," Zoffany replied. "An implanted shield of some kind. A field generator, if you like, that would keep them alive in our reality. But it was more fundamental than that."

Gould nodded.

"A talisman seems to shift probabilities in the wearer's favor," he said. "Not good enough if we're talking about general metabolic collapse."

"Yes, which is why X-rays and ultrasound scans found nothing either," the scientist went on, looking even more uncomfortable. "It needed something at the cellular level. Which is why I had tissue samples sent to Zurich for analysis."

Gould felt her fingers tighten on his.

"There are human cells distributed throughout the Interloper Lucy's body," she said. "It's a more advanced form of life support, a symbiosis if you like. More advanced than the external symbiont used to keep George Blaisdell alive for all those years in the Phantom Dimension. He was some kind of test subject, I assume, to see if the two forms of life could be made compatible for extended periods."

Gould nodded, wondering why this breakthrough should make Zoffany so nervous. She had not relaxed her grip.

It's a triumph, he thought. *Benson will be delighted.*

"So," he said slowly, "if we were to damage the human cells in some way, the Interloper would decay as usual?"

"Mmm." Zoffany responded brusquely. "But that's not – there's something else. I had the human DNA analyzed, tested it against examples we have on record. To see if it had been taken from any of the people who escaped at Machen."

"And there's a match?" he asked.

She nodded. Gould was startled, then his mind began to come up with possibilities.

"So it was Frankie Dupont's? She was over there for a while–"

He stopped, looking at Zoffany's tormented expression.

"It was a close match to your DNA," she whispered. "Not identical, but close enough for a sibling."

Lucy.

"So she could still be alive, Ted," Zoffany insisted, both her hands now clasping his. "I had to let you know before Benson and the rest. We're not talking about huge numbers of cells, here, no more than a nurse might take for a blood sample and …"

To Gould, the room seemed to become silent, as a great rushing sound began to overwhelm him. He saw Zoffany's lips moving, then looked down at the table. It occurred to him that his coffee was getting cold, the fried eggs on his plate congealing.

"Thanks," he said. "I know how hard this was for you."

Suddenly the room was back to normal. There was the chatter of weary customers, the clink of cutlery, and the tinny pop music from Capital FM. And there was Zoffany, reaching out to him again, trying to explain something else.

"The Lucy Interloper," she said, glancing around and leaning closer. "I told you that we dissected it. What I didn't say is that dissection *didn't* kill it."

***

Denny checked in at the front desk, smiling at the guard on duty, who was evidently in a grumpy mood. She vaguely recognized the young woman, but perhaps she did not recall

Denny.

"Please put all your metal objects in the tray," the guard said. "That includes phones, keys, belt buckles. And step through the archway."

Denny took out her keys, and put the phone and her key ring into the plastic tray. She forced herself not to look at the guard as the woman waved her through the security barrier. As expected, there was no alarm. Denny turned, walked around the desk, and reached for her possessions. She made a point of taking the phone first.

The more precious item to a person with nothing to hide, she thought. *Keeping it realistic.*

She did not bother smiling at the guard as she scooped up the keys, turned away, started to tuck the talisman into her pocket again.

"Hey!"

The guard had to be talking to Denny. She was earlier than usual, and there was nobody else in the foyer. She turned, looked at the stocky, short-haired young woman, but did not go back to the desk. Instead, Denny raised a quizzical eyebrow.

"You've seen them, right?" asked the guard.

It took Denny a moment to realize what the woman was talking about.

"Interlopers? Sure," she replied, keeping her voice level.

The guard glanced up at the closed-circuit TV camera.

"How hard are they to kill?"

"They're pretty tough," Denny said, taking a couple of steps nearer the desk. "Harder than a human being, I would think. But I've seen it done."

She's just worried, she thought. *She didn't sign up for this.*

"In that briefing you said they're really fast," the guard continued. "And they can look like anybody. So if I get separated from my team—"

The woman stopped, looked past Denny as the elevator dinged. Glancing around, Denny saw two young women emerging from the lift. Again, she recognized them. They were cleaners she had sometimes encountered when she got in early.

"I'd better get going," she told the guard.

"Lots to do, eh?"

"Yeah, right."

The young woman dismissed Denny and focused on the approaching cleaners. Relieved at getting the talisman through the checkpoint, Denny did another smile-and-nod, and again got blanked. But then, as one of the women passed a few inches away from Denny, the cleaner looked sharply at her, and seemed to trip and almost fall. Her companion grabbed her arm and helped her keep her balance.

Must work them like slaves, Denny thought, as she got into the elevator. *Maybe she's sick and doesn't dare take time off to see a doctor.*

***

Jackie Marshall insisted on driving her son Josh to school that morning. After the killing of Fenton, she would not let him go anywhere alone. Josh had made a token protest at being treated 'like a baby', but had given in quickly. He, too, had been shocked by their dog's sudden, violent death.

"What was it, Mum?" he asked yet again.

He's looking for some kind of certainty, she thought. *A sense of someone in control, that grown-ups know what's going on and will fix it.*

"I don't know," she replied honestly. "If I did, I'd tell you. A wild animal, maybe."

"The last wolf in England was killed in the days of Shakespeare," he said. "Miss Dalby told us that."

"Well, Miss Dalby is right, about native wolves," Jackie said patiently. "But some misguided people have brought dangerous animals into this country from abroad. They think you can keep wolves, or lions, or tigers as pets."

"That's against the law," said Josh matter-of-factly. "The police should stop them."

"They do when they know about it," she said. "But the police rely on good people to help them, so you should always–"

"Look!" Josh shouted, pointing off to one side.

"Don't do that when Mummy's driving!" said Jackie.

But the boy was insistent. Jackie slowed, peered out of the window across the snowbound landscape. In the first light of morning, it was hard to make anything out. But for a second, she thought she saw two shapes that might have been dogs running into a plantation of pine trees.

"Wild animals," said Josh, looking at her round-eyed. "But not wolves."

Jackie could not be sure how much or how little she had seen. She decided to say nothing more and Josh seemed content to drop the subject. In fact, he looked so unhappy that she decided to drop him off quickly so as not to attract too much attention from the other kids.

"Remember, you wait here for me," she told him as he got out. "You don't go on the bus, don't talk to any strangers. If I'm late I'll call the school."

"Yes, mum," said the boy wearily as he climbed out of the battered Range Rover.

Jackie was about to add a few more warnings when she bit her tongue.

Don't want to show him up in front of his friends, she thought. *He's a sensible kid.*

Jackie was just pulling away from the school gates when a teacher she recognized appeared, waving her to stop. She rolled down the window, feeling her heart lurch. Josh's reports had been good. But there could have been other problems.

"Sorry to bother you," the teacher said, "but you live near the Murrays, I believe?"

"Yes," she replied, feeling only slight relief that this was not about her or Josh. "Is there a problem?"

"I'm not sure," the teacher admitted. "But the children weren't on the school bus this morning, which is odd. I did try to call Mrs. Murray to check but nobody answered. And recently both children have been very subdued ..."

The teacher trailed off.

Zoe and Ben have been a lot less outgoing than usual, Jackie thought. *And Sallie's been depressed.*

"I could call in on the way home," Jackie said. "It's not far out of my way. If they get a lift in from their dad there's no harm done."

"That would be great," the teacher said with relief.

The Murray farmhouse was dark as Jackie steered the Range Rover up the track, bumping over frozen, rutted earth. She would have expected to see a light in the kitchen, at the very least. When she pulled into the farmyard, she got another surprise. Jon Murray's car was still parked near the back door.

Maybe some kind of crisis, Jackie thought. *Accident, perhaps.*

Jackie tried to imagine the kind of problem that would make it impossible for anyone in the family to answer the phone. She thought again of poor Fenton's corpse, torn flesh and bloodied fur. Jackie felt a sudden impulse to leave, but instead she got out and went to the kitchen window. It was hard to see inside; the winter morning light was feeble. But she could make out the table, overturned at one side of the room. And from behind it, some legs in jogging pants protruded.

Oh God, Sallie.

Jackie ran to the back door, found it ajar, and went inside. Something sticky underfoot made her look down. The floor was black with a sea of congealing blood. The next coherent thought she had was when she had locked herself in her car and called 999.

***

"I would like to begin with classification," Zoffany said. "More specifically, the need for redefining what we've been calling 'modified' or 'enduring Interlopers.' The ones that seem to have indefinite lifespans in our dimension."

Denny glanced around the meeting room as Zoffany introduced the term 'Class Three' entities. Apart from Denny and Frankie, Gould and Benson were present. Forster was absent, however, and in opening the meeting, Benson had said nothing about this.

Probably some bureaucratic bullshit, she thought. *But maybe not.*

Zoffany was saying, "...those Interlopers modified at the

microbiological level to exist indefinitely in our world. Class Twos invariably died if they did not retreat to the Phantom Dimension."

"What do you mean by microbiological?" put in Denny. She sensed that Zoffany was skating quickly over some detailed stuff.

Zoffany looked at Gould, then said, "I mean Interlopers who have effectively been hybridized with human DNA."

"Holy crap!" breathed Frankie.

Denny was looking at Gould, who was flipping through a set of written notes. The Englishman was trying to look casual, unaffected by Zoffany's contribution. But Denny could see he was upset, hands quivering, face almost bloodless.

"Do we know what else, if anything, distinguishes the two types of enemy?" asked Benson.

Denny glanced up sharply from her phone. It was the first time she had heard the chairman use the word. It gave a military feel to the situation. The Interlopers did act as enemies of the humans they encountered, she knew. But the foundation was technically about research, not conflict.

Things are shifting, she thought. *Like layers of an onion being peeled away. How soon before we see what the foundation's really about?*

Zoffany shook her head.

"So far as I can tell they have the same capabilities, it's just the Type Threes are – for lack of a better term – armored against the corrosive effects of our reality."

"What's doing all this?"

Benson's pitch-black eyes focused on her.

"Please expand upon your interjection, Miss Purcell."

"We've seen Interlopers, old and new style," Denny went on. "They're not scientists, they're killing machines. But what's conducting experiments on people, conjuring up all these hybrid cells and symbionts and stuff?"

"That is a good question," Zoffany said. "It's related to another good question. The matter of Interloper reproduction."

"Where do little monsters come from?" said Frankie. "I did notice that those things, in their natural form, ain't got no junk on show."

"Junk?" said Benson in his sepulchral voice.

Despite the tension in the room, or perhaps because of it, Denny laughed.

"Sorry," she said. "My friend means they have no visible sex organs except when they, you know, create them for their fake human bodies. And when we were in the Soul Eater we got no sense that there are Interloper children, just different sizes. They grow, but they never mature."

"Quite." Zoffany said. "The lack of any obvious genitalia has been occupying my team for some time. A significant clue as to why they are apparently sexless is in the fact that they all seem virtually identical at the genetic level."

"You are saying that they are clones, Doctor?" asked Benson, his voice betraying genuine interest for the first time.

"So far as we can tell," the scientist replied. "While they imitate people, their basic biology is very different. They could be said to have a kind of telepathic hive mind, though normally I would shun such terms."

"So they're like worker ants!" exclaimed Frankie. "Which implies there must be some kind of queen who is reproducing–"

"Queen!" shouted Denny, reaching into her jeans pocket and pulling out the notepaper. "That's what it says!"

Four pairs of eyes watched as she tried to decipher her hasty night-time jottings.

"That's what I dreamed of, or part of it," she babbled, "I wrote 'queen', and 'chamber', and it's 'cocoon', not 'cocoa'. I can remember some of it now, in flashes. There's a queen, in some kind of egg chamber that produces both types."

Benson nodded, the only person showing no sign of surprise. Then he turned to Frankie.

"You have not experienced similar dreams, I take it, Miss Dupont?"

Frankie looked guiltily over at Denny, then shook her head.

"No, I took some stuff to help me sleep. After the first few times I just couldn't face the nightmares."

"Can't blame you," Denny said reassuringly. "I nearly went

there."

Everyone but Benson started talking at once until the chairman held up a languid hand.

"Thank you, everyone, for your contributions," he said. "The location of a queen, or similar entity, will be added to our list of priorities. With luck, our field operatives will be able to obtain some solid data in the immediate future."

Denny had a sudden epiphany and leaned forward over the conference table.

"Where's Forster?" she asked.

"Mister Forster," replied Benson carefully, "is leading a major tactical operation. In Herefordshire."

"You mean he's going to lead a team through the Machen gateway?" Denny stated bluntly. "Which is insane. There are Soul Eaters near that gateway, not to mention Black Stars and the Interlopers themselves!"

Again, Benson waved a hand dismissively.

"Mister Forster is perfectly able to lead an effective combat force in hostile terrain," he said. "Before he entered our employ he had a remarkable career in the private security industry."

It took Denny a moment to realize what he meant.

"He was a friggin' mercenary," Frankie grated. "I knew it. He has that vibe."

"We are fighting a kind of war," Benson went on, at the same time staring Frankie down. "An enemy whose numbers we do not know and whose capabilities are rapidly evolving is attacking our country. Our world, in fact."

"And you think shooting 'em up a little will make things better?" demanded Denny. "Why didn't you allocate people like me and Frankie to this mission? Forster's never even been into the PD."

"The advice that you gave his personnel will be invaluable," Benson said.

"How come we're not involved in this?" Frankie asked. "You had us giving some half-assed TED talks about the Phantom Dimension, but you don't trust us to go back? Is that it?"

Benson's expression did not change, but Denny was

convinced that Frankie was right.

"You think we can't be trusted," she insisted. "Because we're linked to the PD in some way. Our jobs here are a way of keeping us close, under observation."

"It was felt," Benson said, "that if you were apprised of any details concerning major operations, you might unwittingly alert the enemy."

Gould laughed, a mirthless sound. Everyone turned to look at him.

"I take it you have a different perspective on this?" Benson asked.

"A living Interloper is in this building," said Gould. "Or at least under it. And that Interloper has had regular contact with someone who has the highest security clearance. Isn't that so, Harriet?"

Denny saw that Zoffany, who was sitting next to Gould, looked more than surprised. She was horrified.

***

Doctor Russell Wakefield broke for an early lunch. He left his consulting room and walked through into the main body of his combined home and clinic. He made himself some coffee and put a ready meal in the microwave, gazing out over the valley while waiting for the oven. Another wave of bad weather had swept in over the Welsh border, and now a fresh snow was being added to last night's layer.

The kitchen window overlooked the town of Machen. Things had been quiet since the chaotic, bloody events of last autumn. Wakefield had almost started to think of it as the quaint, quiet town of the tourist brochures. But he knew that if he walked into the next room and looked out a different window, he would see Branksholme Woods. As far as he knew, the clump of trees still concealed a gateway to a close approximation of Hell.

The microwave pinged and he took out a piping hot mess of pasta, meat, and sauce. He kept resolving to learn how to cook something more complex than an egg, but somehow never got around to it. He was emptying the plastic tray onto a plate when the first of the vehicles appeared, crossing the bridge over the Wye. At first, he thought it was a small convoy of winter hill-walkers, who sometimes braved the valley in February. But as the three SUVs grew closer, he became suspicious.

The vehicles passed close enough for him to make out that they were full of young men and women in dark clothing. There were no markings on the SUVS, but the way they plowed up the snowy lane toward the hilltop was business-like. Wakefield saw one of the passengers looking back at him. The face looked vaguely familiar, but that was not an unusual sensation for a country doctor.

Shrugging off his doubts, Wakefield sat down to eat his lunch and tried to focus on the long list of patients he would be with that afternoon. But before he went back to his clinic, he went upstairs and took a look at the ridge above his home. The SUVs were parked close by the woods and tents were being set up near the treeline. About a dozen people were being given instructions by a man who was presumably in charge.

No way they're tourists, he thought. *Probably Romola Foundation. They could have let me know. Don't trust me, perhaps.*

Wakefield thought back to the way an Interloper had seduced and manipulated him for months. He had worked out that he was being used by the creature that impersonated his dead wife, yet he had not had the backbone to break free until the very last moment.

So maybe they've got a point.

Wakefield checked his watch. He had a couple of minutes before the next patient. He glanced out of the window and saw what might have been two lean dogs, roughly the size of greyhounds but with far paler coats, moving swiftly across the skyline. Before he could focus on them, they had vanished into a dip in the earth.

People should keep their dogs under control, he thought. *There are plenty of farmers who shoot first and ask questions later. And then some poor kid has lost their pet.*

Chapter 6: Closer Encounters

Fiona Lansing, Her Majesty's Secretary of State for Home Affairs, took a deep breath, turned to face the door, and tried to remember how to smile. She had had a few stressful days and the last thing she needed was to meet a grabby, old lush like Sir Lionel Bartram.

The man's a bloody dinosaur, she thought. *And God, if he brings that tarty little girlfriend of his I may hurl.*

A gofer opened the door and Sir Lionel walked in. He responded to the Home Secretary's smile with one of his own, and held out a hand. When she took it, he gave a firm, if slightly perfunctory shake. She also noticed that he did not look her up and down, as he had on every previous meeting. What's more, his eyes seemed clear and focused.

Is he on an AA course or something?

"Good to see you again, Fiona," he said, looking at her face rather than her chest. "Shall we get started?"

"Your assistant is not with you?" Lansing asked, looking past him.

"Oh, no, Timandra's got a spot of flu, I'm afraid," said Bartram, airily. "But I think I can manage without her."

The Home Secretary exchanged a glance with a senior adviser, who had been waiting discreetly by her desk. Normally she wanted an ally in the room when she was with Bartram. He sometimes said bizarre, offensive things that were worth noting for future use. But today she felt a witness might not be needed.

"I think we can make this an informal chat," she said.

"Quite so!" Bartram said as the adviser left, closing the door silently behind him.

They sat down on opposite sides of the ornate Regency fireplace and Lansing tried to make some small talk. As usual, jockeying for position within the government concerned her more than running the country. Lansing and Bartram were in rival camps within the party, but today he seemed willing to agree with her on every issue. He seemed to have also lost his old condescending manner, and if anything, seemed keen on becoming her ally.

"You must be reading my mind, Lionel!" she exclaimed at one point.

"Great minds think alike, Fiona," he responded.

If this is a personality transplant, she thought, *maybe we can get the rest of the cabinet done.*

"All right," Lansing said. "Let's get this over with. I have to make a statement on this terrible business in the West Country."

Bartram raised an eyebrow, expressing polite curiosity.

"A couple have been killed by some sort of maniac," she went on. "Their kids are missing. Nightmare for us, of course. I'll have to say something vaguely reassuring, but of course it's the local plods who are trying to deal with it. Surely you've seen the news?"

"Ah yes," Bartram said, nodding. "Terrible business. But I'm sure you'll manage to combine efficiency with compassion."

The comment was so close to what she wanted to hear that Lansing looked sharply at her subordinate. His expression was bland, innocent. She decided to move on to informal briefing.

"About the Romola Foundation," she said. "I understand you've actually looked it over?"

Bartram nodded, gave a self-deprecating laugh.

"Yes, indeed, and quite an experience it was. I don't claim to be an expert on the paranormal of course ..."

He gave another laugh, and she smiled politely.

"But I can't help thinking we have granted a little too much latitude to what is essentially a crackpot outfit."

"Crackpot?" she said, alarmed. "The prime minister was quite explicit about our support for Romola. She seems to think that these hostile beings – what do you call them?"

"Interlopers," said Bartram. "That's what they call these hypothetical creatures. Not very imaginative, in my opinion. But it speaks volumes about the amateurishness of the entire set-up."

Lansing frowned, glanced up at the row of paintings above the fire. Every single one showed a long-dead, male politician gazing down on her with what seemed like thin-lipped disapproval. She looked back to Bartram, who was sitting with folded hands, looking every inch the reasonable man.

Has he lost weight? Lansing thought.

"I was saying," Bartram went on, "they claim that these creatures from another dimension – preposterous idea in itself – are killing people right and left. But if you look at the evidence, it's pretty flimsy. There's good reason to believe that the Malpas affair was in fact a serial killing by these two rather shady Americans. They were present at Machen, too."

"But ..." Lansing tried to challenge him, but Bartram had a slick answer to every point she raised. Brick by brick he demolished her belief in the Interloper threat, pointing out that state funding for the Romola Foundation had produced zero material in return.

"All we have, really," he concluded, "is a heap of corpses, some fishy found footage, and a lot of tall tales. All wrapped up in pseudo-scientific jargon, of course. But still. You see my viewpoint, Home Secretary?"

"I can," she replied. "And I can also see the basis for a nice spending cut in this whole area. But how can we persuade the prime minister?"

"Well," said Bartram, interlacing his long, pale fingers. "According to my information they are planning a major operation that is supposed to recover crucial data – solid evidence of this alien incursion."

"Aha," the Home Secretary said, feeling herself on safer ground. "And if this very costly operation fails ..."

"My thoughts exactly, Fiona."

Lansing smiled, satisfied that a real solution to an annoying situation was on the horizon.

"You know, I never feel comfortable with all this stuff," she said. "It's like old Nigel at defense with UFOs. Not the way to conduct grown-up politics. Now ..."

She stood up and went over to her desk, pressed the intercom.

"I think we're ready for some tea, Jeremy. And could you rustle up some fruitcake?"

***

"I think you're reading far too much into this unfortunate situation," said Benson. "It was logical to keep our only enemy operative alive, and the sub-basement is our one secure location."

Denny was still trying to process the revelation that the Lucy-creature was technically, alive. Frankie was looking similarly stunned. Zoffany, meanwhile, was engaged in damage control.

"We don't know that Lucy is able to pick up anything," she insisted, "still less that it's able to transmit data to its kind."

"You can't prove a negative," Gould said bleakly. "No way to determine it's not sending details of all our activities back to ... whatever is in charge. The Interloper Queen, perhaps."

"Well, this big incursion will be a pretty definitive experiment," Denny pointed out, loudly. She jabbed a finger at Benson. "You must have known there was a risk. What the hell is this? Why do you keep putting people in harm's way?"

There was a shocked silence. Zoffany stared open-mouthed at Denny. The others looked away from both Denny and the chairman. Gould broke the silence.

"I don't think it's reasonable to accuse Mister Benson of deliberately–"

Denny exploded with anger at that.

"Come on Ted, you must have suspected it!" she said, slamming a palm down onto the table. "We were sent to make a dumb TV show about a haunted house. We barely escaped being massacred. Do you think Benson was hoping we'd just come out with some spooky footage?"

"With the benefit of hindsight ..." Gould said, but his voice lacked conviction.

"And in Machen I was sent alone, despite a long history of Interloper activity in the area," Denny went on. "My backup consisted of Jim, basically. Oh, and in Machen, a captured Interloper called for reinforcements and got them. So, you can screw this–"

Denny stopped. Benson had pushed back his chair and was standing up. Denny lost her train of thought; so improbably tall was the chairman.

"You can't be sure of that," said Benson, showing no other

sign of being perturbed. "It may be that, like us, they simply react when one of their operatives does not report in. As for the Lucy-creature, if Doctor Zoffany thinks we should kill it immediately as a security risk, I will of course sign off on the procedure. However, I think we have achieved all we can today. This meeting has over-run. Good afternoon."

A chorus of protest followed Benson to the door of the conference room, but he did not look back. They sat in silence, then Frankie spoke.

"Well, shit!"

***

"Right, listen up," said Forster, scanning the semi-circle of dark-clad operatives. "I've commanded some motley outfits in my time, and done some very questionable things. But–"

The security chief paused for effect. The nine armed men and women were paying attention. It was a cold afternoon, even for February in the English countryside, and a few flakes of snow were falling. Clouds of breath came from chapped lips. Down the hill in the valley, cars passing through Machen had their lights on, and moved slowly. The sky was a bleak gray ceiling of unbroken cloud.

This lot will soon be wishing they were back in the cold, where we're going, he thought.

"This is the first time I've led reconnaissance in force into another dimension," Forster said, with a wry smile. "A parallel universe, an alternate reality. Call it what you like, it's not like our world. Laws of physics as we know them don't quite apply. Now, you've all been briefed."

Forster paused again, focused on the youngest member of his team.

"You! How fast does time flow in the Phantom Dimension?"

"About ten times slower than in the real world, sir!" returned the young man.

"Correct, so I hope you've made it clear to your loved ones that you won't be home for dinner."

That got a slight ripple of laughter.

"But cut out this stuff about 'the real world'," Forster went on. "We're not going into dreamland. Nightmare-land, maybe – but everything you're going to see is real. First mission objective is to determine nature of threat. Second, try to obtain what's termed talisman material. Third, if we see one of those Soul Eater things, run like hell."

That got a louder laugh. They had all seen grainy footage of the mountainous entities and been thoroughly briefed on how fast they moved. It was clear that no weapons short of a nuke could touch the colossal predators.

Forster turned to his deputy, Clarke, who was working on what looked like a home-made mine detector.

"Is that thing working?" he snapped.

Clarke, a top-notch radio operator, shrugged.

"So far as I can tell, chief. It worked back at HQ when we tried it on that pendant. So it should be calibrated."

Forster grunted.

Looking for magic pebbles in what might as well be Hell, he thought. *Somewhere my career took a wrong turn.*

"Okay," he said, picking up his own shotgun. "Let's move out."

They set off into Branksholme Woods, moving in a single file. Forster noticed they were bunching up.

"Spread out," he said. "Not too much, but you might end up tripping over each other if any of those beasties are lurking in the trees."

"Or shooting each other," muttered Clarke, still fiddling with the detector.

"Ever the optimist, eh?" joked Forster, bringing up the rear.

The security chief paused at the edge of the small forest and took a last look around. He saw lights from the Wakefield clinic, thought of locals getting bunions treated, sprains looked at, and smiled.

My last sight of my world, maybe, he thought. *Well, there are worse places.*

A lithe shape moved swiftly against the stone wall that bounded the doctor's garden. It was pale, vaguely canine in shape. As the first vanished around a corner, a second creature appeared. Forster, who had seen some wild parts of the earth, frowned. But the animals were far away, and he had a team to lead. He turned and sent troops after his squad, into the darkness under the trees.

***

"No way," said Davenport, looking from Denny to Gould and back.

"But you've got to call it off!" Gould insisted. "They could be walking straight into a trap!"

Davenport shrugged helplessly. They were in the cafeteria, where Davenport was lunching with Jim Davison. Denny and Gould had decided, after much debate, to simply ignore Benson and try to prevent the Machen expedition from leaving.

"They'll be moving out, or in, right now," Jim pointed out. "So even if we could call them—"

"Radio silence," Davenport cut in. "It's compulsory. They only use short-wave communications within the team."

"They've got no back-up?" Denny asked, incredulously. "Isn't that military tactics 101, or something?"

Davenport clammed up at that, and got up to return his tray. Jim looked uncomfortable as the other man left. Denny sat down opposite and took Jim's hand.

"What is it?" she demanded. "Come on, you owe me."

"We're a bit over-stretched because of the Tube situation," Jim said unhappily.

"What Tube situation?" asked Gould. "First I've heard of this."

Davenport, returning, tried to keep Jim quiet, but failed. The Hobs Lane situation was quickly outlined.

"They could be in London?" Gould gasped. "And in contact with the Lucy-creature?"

"And Benson chose this moment to send the security team a couple of hundred miles away," Denny observed. "And send the remainder to do a sweep along a nice, dark tunnel. In the middle of the night."

The three men looked at her. Davenport was the first to

break the silence.

"Oh, that's bloody ridiculous!" he scoffed. "Benson's a weird bastard, but why would he sabotage his own organization?"

Denny looked around the table. Unlike Davenport, Gould and Jim both seemed confused, doubtful.

"Look," she said, "before I did some dumb show about ghosts I was a reporter on local news shows, then a bigger network. Believe me, I saw a lot of bosses screw things up at close quarters. It's usually because they won't listen to good advice. But with Benson, it's different. Something about that guy is off, so is his whole approach."

"What do you mean?" asked Jim.

"Malpas Abbey," she said. "Opening up the chamber that contained the gateway. That building had been abandoned for years. It was like Benson wanted to trigger an Interloper attack."

"But doing the show at Malpas was my idea!" protested Gould.

"Was it?" Denny asked, staring intently at him. "How did you first get to hear about my show?"

"I was allocated the task of–" Gould stopped. "Benson told me to check all media for possible evidence of Interlopers. He suggested I start with the US, because there'd be an abundance of data."

"Wow." Jim looked from Gould to Denny. "But that's not absolute proof."

"No," she admitted. "But then you came up with the idea of filming a British episode of the show at Malpas, is that right?"

"Yes," replied Gould, sounding more confident. Then a shadow passed over his face. "Except that, about a month before, Benson informed me the foundation had bought the whole Malpas estate."

"God, he really did set it up," Jim said, aghast. "He put a bunch of people there hoping there'd be mayhem, and there was."

"I think the term," Denny said, "is 'a target-rich environment'."

"Yeah," Davenport retorted. "But what about Machen? Who could have known how that one would pan out?"

"Maybe the idea was to get Denny killed," Gould said slowly. "Zoffany knew one operative was going to Machen, where the Interlopers had been active for a while. They just didn't reckon on her getting the talisman."

"Let's not waste time dotting the 'I's and crossing the 'T's," Denny insisted. "Just get in touch with Forster and tell him to stop!"

***

The incursion began smoothly. The team was all through the gateway and standing in the open space described in Denny's report. Behind them, the gateway was a pulsing black globe, offering an escape route. When Forster arrived, Clarke was already pointing the detector out over the Interloper city, or what was left of it. Many of the square, stone-built buildings were in ruins. As Forster's eyes adjusted to the weird glow from the sunless sky, he saw that in fact a swathe had been cut through the city. Forster swept the entire horizon with binoculars but saw no sign of a moving mountain.

Soul Eater, he thought. *Been and gone.*

"Over that way, boss," Clarke gestured. "Strong signal."

The techie, Forster noted, was pointing toward an intact area of the city. A mile or more of labyrinthine alleyways might lie between them and whatever was tripping the detector. Forster weighed the odds. What had been dubbed 'talismanic material' was a priority, but so was getting back alive with useful data.

Nothing ventured, nothing gained, he thought.

"Okay, people, spread out," Forster ordered. "Stick to the plan."

They made their way into what remained of the city. This time the commander took up a position in the center of the column. It was just as the last man in the unit was entering the alleyway that the first Interloper appeared. A pale figure, its head bowed, rushed across the path of the column. The leading guard fired reflexively. His shot missed, blasting a chunk out of the corner of a building.

"Cool it!" shouted Forster. "They can sense fear and panic. Keep a cool head and they can't–"

There was a crash, and a building collapsed into the alley, throwing up a choking cloud of dust. More shots were taken at an Interloper bounding away. The creature moved too fast, and dodged too well. The rearmost guard had been caught in the tumbling rubble. When she was pulled out, she was limping badly. Forster felt a sense of Deja vu, that an all-too-familiar situation was unfolding under the alien sky.

Classic tactic, he thought. *Using improvised weapons on a more technically advanced foe.*

"If that's the best they can do," he said loudly to Clarke, "there's nothing to worry about. All we have to do is get out of this rat-run ASAP."

He did not add that, with an injured comrade, they would take a lot longer now. He could see from the expressions of the experienced men that they did not need to be told.

And they've probably worked out, he thought, *that the enemy was expecting us.*

"Okay, move out!"

***

"No reply," said Gould, slamming down the headset. "They must have gone through."

The operations room was almost empty. The six 'quasi-rebels', as Gould had carefully dubbed them, arrived to find just one technician scrolling through a Reddit thread on serial killers. The man had quickly vacated his seat when senior staff appeared. He did not ask any awkward questions.

"Don't they have some guy back at base camp, or whatever they call it?" Frankie asked. "Isn't that the usual soldier-thing?"

"No point if you're going into the Phantom Dimension," Jim observed. "Remember, even if radio signals did pass through the gateway there's the time difference. If Forster could call for help it would be in slow-mo."

"Quite," Davenport said. "Which is why Forster decided to

put all his eggs in one basket, so to speak. It's an all-or-nothing attack."

"And they could be through there for months," Denny added. "Or years, even. Assuming they took sufficient rations."

"So what do we do in the next, say, couple of hours?" Frankie asked. "Find ourselves a large jigsaw?"

Denny glanced round at the technician, who was gawping at them from a few yards away.

"We might as well admit it," she said. "We've all had it up to here with Benson's BS. We don't trust him. And he's sent his private army away, so it's not as if the guy can shut us down, now, can he?"

The technician's mouth fell open a little more.

"Maybe you should take a nice long break?" Gould suggested. "Then you can say you didn't hear anything remotely untoward. Plausible deniability, they call it."

After the young man had left, they held a council-of-war. Denny and Frankie both thought simply telling the media everything they knew was the best option. Gould and Zoffany, having invested so much of their lives in the foundation's work, were less keen.

"People will think you've gone crazy," Zoffany pointed out. "And after all the deaths, all the mystery, they would have good cause."

"Also," said Gould, "encouraging reporters to blunder into this situation might simply get them killed."

Denny, pacing the length of the operations room, wagged a finger at them. She felt suddenly free after weeks of being stifled by the secretive, corporate culture of the foundation.

"You're missing the point, this is modern journalism 101," she said, "The idea is to make a stink and embarrass the powers that be to move on something they don't want to. Just mention that old fart, Sir Lionel Whatsit, and see what happens. God, why didn't I just take the risk before?"

Frankie, who was sitting on a desk swinging her legs like a bad kid in detention, put up her hand.

"Ooh, I know this one," she said. "We didn't want to get sent to Area 51 and be put in a cell next to all those aliens."

"Way things are going now that might be the safest place,"

Denny retorted. "No, I'm sick of being shoved around and put in harm's way. I'm going to take risks on my own terms from now on. Get yourself a camera, Ms. Dupont. Let's start making a guerrilla documentary about this dump. Instant journalism, straight onto the net by tonight."

Grinning, Frankie jumped down and left. Denny took out her phone, held it up to get all the Brits in shot.

"While she gets her gear, it's time for your close up, guys. Let's do some quick interviews, get us warmed up. Jim, how about you introduce yourself first?"

Jim did not look enthusiastic.

"Okay," Denny went on, holding out her phone at arm's length. "Hey there! My name's Denny Purcell. I used to present a TV show called 'America's Weirdest Hauntings.' Last year you may remember the series came to a sudden end amid, well, a lot of confusion, not to mention some very violent deaths. So, I'd like, for the first time, to tell you what really happened at Malpas Abbey. It all began when ..."

***

Jackie Marshall was one of the volunteers who agreed to go and search for Ben and Zoe. Over a hundred locals turned up to sweep the countryside around the Murrays' farm. The official police line was that an intruder had butchered the parents during the night. The children were believed to have been abducted by the same person, who was assumed to be mentally unstable. It was not stated explicitly, but Jackie and the other locals were sure the police did not expect to find Ben and Zoe alive.

Jackie was not so sure. She could not articulate her concerns, but as she joined the line of searchers, she wondered what they would find. A few traces of blood had been found outside the farmhouse, but the night's snow had erased any footprints. She kept thinking of the dead dog. She tried to imagine a homicidal maniac living rough in February, going unnoticed, and failed. But when she tried to formulate her own theory of what had happened, she hit a brick wall of fearful incomprehension.

The searchers, strung out in a long line across the rolling landscape, moved slowly. Jackie was at the center of the line, and soon the search reached a major obstacle. The old quarry lay right in the middle of the designated area. As she drew nearer to the fence, Jackie saw a group of police officers clustered around a gate. By the time she got within earshot, one was using bolt-cutters on the rusted lock. Soon the searchers were inside, and fanning out around the banks of the flooded quarry. As they worked their way through waist-high weeds, they were told to bunch up. Lines of sight were limited.

"Ideal place to dump a body," said a man she vaguely recognized as they emerged from the vegetation onto a cracked concrete path.

Jackie did not reply. She was looking out over the water and thinking of her own child. She tried not to imagine a pale, torn body spinning slowly in the icy gray waters. She stopped when she reached the edge of the pond, wondering which way to go around. Then she saw a low, dark object just breaking the surface.

It's nothing, she told herself. *Just some old junk. A mattress somebody dumped.*

But she could not stop looking, found herself pointing, heard a voice shout hoarsely, and realized it was her own. From behind her, as if by magic, two police officers in waders appeared, wielding boat hooks. There was more pointing and shouting. Jackie heard a roaring noise in her ears, staggered. A female officer took her arm and led her to a battered wooden bench; relic of a failed attempt to make the quarry a pleasant place.

"Put your head between your knees," advised the policewoman.

Jackie did as she was asked, closing her eyes. She heard splashing, a discussion she could not quite make out. Then she heard a clear warning to someone 'not to film the scene'. She opened her eyes and sat up, taking a lungful of the freezing air. The men in waders were standing near the shore. Other officers were looking down at what their colleagues had brought in. The half-submerged object was turned over, and a small arm flailed into the air, splashed down.

"Best not to look," said the policewoman, hand on Jackie's arm.

"That much decay in just a few hours?" said one of the policemen. "No way. Dead for days, maybe weeks ..."

An argument began, conducted in low voices. Jackie asked if she could go home. She was told that she could. She did not look back as she followed her faint trail through the wild grasses. She was on the road before she began to think.

Dead for days. Dead for days.

She thought of Josh at school, still unaware of what had happened to his friends. She could not understand what had happened to Sallie, Jon, Zoe, and Ben. All she could be sure of was that a violent, destructive force was loose.

So this is what it feels like ... to live in fear.

***

The edge of the Interloper city was in sight when what looked like children appeared. Naked and cowering, two little girls with dust-matted hair ran out of a side-passage and clung to a startled Clarke. The technician tried to shove them away but Forster could see the man was unwilling to risk injuring what may have been real kids.

"Tasers!" Forster shouted. "Knock 'em down!"

The children began to wail.

"Help us! We want to go home!"

Half the squad seemed to be scrabbling for Tasers, with the rest looking on, confused. Forster heard a mournful sound behind him and turned to see another thin figure approaching. This one appeared to be a young woman, clutching a few scraps of dirty clothes around herself. Forster had seen plenty of refugees, and thought he had long ago perfected the art of ignoring them. But this one's face reminded him of someone. He felt old memories stirring, and with them, confusion.

Mission! Focus, man! Overwhelming odds, it is not a human being.

He raised his shotgun, made a stabbing motion with it.

"Get back!"

The woman held out stick-thin arms. The face that looked

pleadingly into his was, he could not help noticing, very lovely. It reminded him of an altarpiece of the Virgin Mary in his school chapel. Every Sunday for five years he had stared at the unearthly visage, come to associate it with all that was good and pure.

Cheap tricks!

Forster fired into the beautiful face. It staggered back. There was a spray of blood, showing black in the strange light. The figure fell. There was a startled yell behind him, and Forster turned to see one of the small Interlopers had clambered up Clarke and was biting his face. Other thin, pale figures appeared. The heavy boom of shotguns and the crackle of Tasers were interspersed with screams, curses, scuffling. Clouds of red dust rose to obscure what had become a vicious close-in fight.

"Regroup!" Forster bellowed, as something struck him hard between the shoulder blades. He managed to beat off his assailant with the butt of his gun, then ran into the middle of the fray, hitting out left and right. The Interlopers were fast, but in the enclosed space, the sheer number of people striking at them offset their advantage.

"Withdraw to the gateway!" Forster shouted, shooting point-blank into the face of what had, a moment before, looked like a scared child. For every attacker that went down, at least one guard was also disabled or killed.

"Drop the wounded, save yourselves!"

Forster followed his own advice and made it back to the gateway. Half-blinded by dust, he at first thought the portal had closed. But as he got nearer, he saw that the sphere of darkness was still hovering. He glanced back and saw a dark-clad figure pounced upon by two pale, naked Interlopers.

Down to me, he thought. *Sole survivor. Not for the first time.*

Forster ran onto the stone platform and hurled himself into the dark globe. The weird, directionless light of the Phantom Dimension vanished, along with its dry, thin air. He found himself falling onto a patch of snow, rolled, and hit a fallen tree trunk. A shower of snow fell over him as the tree juddered. He panted, his breath visible as spurts of white vapor filled the crisp winter air.

Forster struggled upright, brushed snow off his jacket, and went to pick up the shotgun that had fallen a few feet away. As he moved over the snowy ground, he noticed the trail of boot-prints that led into the clearing.

Only one set of tracks going out, he thought. *What a bloody fiasco.*

Out of the corner of his eye, he saw the air shimmer and grow dark. The gateway was still open. He snatched up the shotgun, pumped another shell into the chamber, and waited. A crouching shape tumbled through, small and pale. Forster fired just as the Interloper was emerging from the sphere of troubled air. The creature gave a shriek and fell to the forest ground.

Forster took off his pack and opened it, took out a grenade – souvenir of a more orthodox job. He tore out the pin with his teeth and flung the small, gray ovoid into the gateway. There was a reddish flash and a sound like a distant rumble of thunder. He calculated that, if it had fully emerged on the other side, it would at least buy him some time.

With luck, it killed most of 'em. But whatever's happening in their world, I need to get moving in this one.

Forster got up and started to dodge between the trees, moving quickly but not running. He reloaded the shotgun as he went, using up the last of his cartridges. Every sound he made seemed way too loud. He kept glancing back, expecting any attack to come from the gateway. It was only when a small deluge of snow fell just ahead of him that he thought to glance up, and saw a small figure crouching in the leafless, black branches above. Forster began to raise the gun as the Interloper dropped down upon him. He fired but missed, cursing at the fast-moving target.

It would have to be a small one.

Chapter 7: Revelation, Two

After Frankie returned with a camera, Denny suggested that she and Zoffany go get the best evidence to support their case. Close-ups of an actual Interloper.

"You mean filming Lucy?" asked Gould.

"Yep," Denny confirmed. "That's a case where a picture is worth a thousand words."

"Yes, but most of those words will be along the lines of 'fake'," Gould protested. "It will be like that alien autopsy film."

"Except that we know the Interlopers exist," Denny pointed out. "And by the same logic there must be a whole lot of people around the world who know it, too. England is hardly unique. Interlopers must be known to some governments, quite a few scientists, maybe reporters. My guess is they're all waiting for someone else to make the first move – claim to know about real monsters, and get called crazy. At first."

She paused, smiling at the group.

"Well, I'm nominating us as the Crazy Committee. How about it?"

"Sounds reasonable, in the circumstances," said Jim, ruefully.

"You're not coming?" asked Frankie, brandishing her camera.

Denny shook her head.

"I saw enough of that particular – person when it tried to kill me," she said. "So don't get too close."

After Frankie and Zoffany had set off for the sub-basement, Gould asked, "What's the real reason for you not wanting to go downstairs?"

Denny glanced around the three men. She felt she could trust Gould and Jim up to a point, but Davenport was a relative stranger.

"Those things have a range, when it comes to mind-reading," she said carefully. "I think it's a few yards, at most. There's something I don't want it to know. And yes, I am keeping it to myself for now."

Gould shrugged, sat down at a PC and tried to get more satellite data. At first, it seemed as if the system was malfunctioning. The screen showed what looked like orange smog across much of the earth's surface. Then it occurred to Jim to ask if it had been swamped with data.

"The idea is to find gateways," Gould said, trying to get a clear image. "There'd have to be millions of them to overload the software."

"What if instead of pin-point gateways there were lots of broad regions?" Jim asked. "Would that foul it up?"

"We can't be sure of that," said Davenport.

"You sound kind of unsure yourself," Denny said, filming the screen. "Maybe you could describe what this equipment is supposed to do, Ted? Keep it short."

"Look," Davenport said, getting up. "I know you mean well, but this goes against my training, and my gut tells me it will end in tears. If you don't mind, I think I'll just take some unpaid leave."

After he left, Denny looked at what remained of the Crazy Committee, then took out her keys. Gould leaned forward, peering at the dull, purplish stone as she dangled it in front of them. Jim gave a low whistle.

"I guess I can trust you guys," she said. "If we can find the other talisman, maybe we can do that old-school military thing – take the fight to the enemy? By which I mean, get some actual footage of the Phantom Dimension, and release it to the world tomorrow."

"How?" Jim asked. "They know we're planning to scout along the tunnel, and that's the only gateway we know of."

Denny put her key ring away, leaned back against a desk, and folded her arms.

"Yeah, but the gateway can't actually be on the line, can it? I mean, trains would be going through into another dimension. People would notice. Questions in parliament, right?"

"How does that help us–?" Gould began, then paused. "Oh. Oh, I see your point. But if you're wrong ..."

"You want us to go into the tunnel between trains?" Jim asked.

Denny pointed at the map of the Tube. Between Hobs Lane and Wyndham Road was a disused side tunnel. It was, they had agreed, the likeliest place for a gateway. It was closer to Hobs Lane, and Denny had estimated that it would only take them ten minutes to get there.

"But," Jim protested, "the rails will be live. And there are only a few inches between the train and the tunnel wall. So if we get it wrong—"

"We get turned into hamburger," Denny said simply. "And then we get grilled."

***

After the last of his patients had left, Russell Wakefield went to look out at Branksholme Woods. The group of SUVs was still parked in a rough triangle, a few yards from the edge of the forest. There was no sign of movement. Wakefield shrugged, reasoning that it was none of his business. He thought he saw movement under the trees, something pale darting between trees.

"Play the hero, get yourself killed," he muttered.

He went into the lounge, poured himself a Scotch, and then turned on the TV. A local news bulletin was just ending. The presenter was talking about missing children, and a 'scene of carnage'.

Frowning, Wakefield picked up his phone and checked the news feed. It did not take him long to find the story. 'Farm killings – police appeal to the public for information.' He scrolled down and found that the crime scene was about twenty miles away. 'Concern is mounting', he read, 'for two young children who are missing'.

He thought of the Hawkes twins, who had returned from the Phantom Dimension, and their Interloper doubles, who had vanished. Then he put on his coat and decided to go and check. At the last moment, he paused and went back for his medical bag, and made a few preparations. Then, bag in one hand and phone in the other, he set off up the snowbound slope.

As he neared the unmarked vehicles, he caught sight of

movement at the edge of the woods. Some snow fell from a heavy-laden branch with a hiss. Wakefield raised his phone and filmed for a few moments, focusing on the area. Then he played back the footage. There was no sign of any living creature. He looked up again, and listened. All he heard was the squeak of compact snow as he shifted his weight slightly.

No birds, he thought. *There are never any birds when it happens.*

Then there was a dull booming sound that echoed along the ridge. Wakefield had lived in the country long enough to recognize a shotgun being fired. He half-ran up to the nearest vehicle, tried the door. It was locked. Out of the corner of his eye, he caught a glimpse of movement, a pale shape that darted out of sight as soon as he turned to stare. He flattened himself against the side of the SUV and speed-dialed 999.

"Police, yes. Emergency. I think there's been an accident involving a number of people ..."

He spent what seemed an eternity arguing with the emergency operator and then a bored desk sergeant. Fortunately, Wakefield, in his role as a former medical examiner, still had some influence. That, and the location he gave, seemed to galvanize the officer into a response.

"A unit will be with you shortly," said the tinny voice. "Do not attempt to tackle criminals yourself."

"Oh, I won't," he murmured, ending the call.

Wish I hadn't sent that bloody talisman to Denny Purcell, he thought ruefully.

He put the cell away and took out a hypodermic loaded with morphine. It had worked before, albeit for a short time. As he slipped the protective plastic cover from the tip of the needle, he heard a fast, rhythmic crunching. It was coming from somewhere on the other side of the SUV. He did not move, but held his breath, hearing the small footprints grow closer. Then they stopped.

A shock ran through him as something leaped onto the roof of the SUV. He crouched, rolled forward into the snow, and felt claws rip the back of his coat. The Interloper paused for a split-second, its long, razor-toothed muzzle agape. Then it leaped down, arms spread. He brought up the needle, but the creature easily knocked it aside.

"No more tricks," it hissed. "Bad doctor."

It brought its funnel shaped mouth down toward his eyes. The creature was smaller than he had feared, for all its speed and strength. Wakefield heaved it off him with the frantic strength of abject terror. But as soon as it landed in the snow, the monster sprang back to attack again.

He flung a handful of snow in the creature's face and felt a twinge of satisfaction as it gagged. The Interloper was bounding toward him again, colorless talons reaching for his face. He kicked at it, but it dodged so that his foot barely struck its shoulder, and resumed its attack.

I'm dead, he thought, but continued to kick and fling snow.

A dark figure appeared at the edge of the woods. As soon as Wakefield saw the man, the creature paused and spun round. The newcomer was already raising a gun as the Interloper leaped sideways towards the cover of the vehicles. The shot missed the dodging creature, and Wakefield felt the wind of it pass his head. Then the stranger fell to his knees, and Wakefield realized he was watching someone on the edge of exhaustion, or worse.

Wakefield felt around in the snow. He found the needle when it jabbed his thumb. Swearing, he picked it up and staggered to his feet, started to run towards his savior. As he got closer, he saw that the man was wearing a black, unmarked uniform. Great tears were visible on the left sleeve, and now Wakefield could see that the cloth was stiff with dried blood. A nametag read FORSTER. The name was vaguely familiar.

Did Denny mention a Forster? Or was it that Jim bloke?

Wakefield shoved the trivial thought aside and knelt beside Forster, whose eyes were half-closed. The doctor checked for major damage as best he could and found no evidence of severed blood vessels. For a moment, he considered giving the stranger a shot of morphine but then decided against it.

"Come on," he said, lifting Forster with one arm while picking up the shotgun with the other, "let's get you inside."

The man tried to speak, and a gout of blood spurted out of

his mouth.

Crap, thought Wakefield. *Internal injuries. He might not have very long.*

"Other–" coughed Forster, blood dribbling over his torn tunic. "Other one."

It took the doctor a long moment to work it out. By the time he did, he could hear twigs breaking behind them as a small, fast-moving creature bounded towards the edge of Branksholme Woods. At the same time, the first Interloper appeared from between two SUVS. It was also running on all fours.

"Wait," croaked Forster.

This time Wakefield got it. The closer the creatures were the less easily they could dodge. He raised the gun, pointed it one-handed at the first attacker. It instantly scampered sideways, reminding him of a spider with too few limbs. The sound of the second creature grew louder then stopped.

"Two hands," Forster said, again spitting blood. At the same time, he shoved Wakefield away and fell, face first, into the snow. Wakefield gripped the shotgun with both hands, nested the stock in his shoulder, crouched and turned on one heel. The first Interloper was just visible behind a vehicle. Wakefield glanced round and saw a second, smaller monster dodging behind a tree.

"Can't move!" he said despairingly. "You'll bleed to death! Forster!"

"Leave me!" the other man gasped. The snow by his mouth turned pink.

"I'm a bloody doctor!" Wakefield shouted, angry now as well as scared.

But he saw the logic of Forster's argument. He got up and started a crouching run towards his home, scouting the SUVs. It was impossible to keep an eye on both Interlopers, impossible to protect both himself and Forster.

Any trick I try, they'll know about it, he thought. *Always one step ahead. Unless –*

Wakefield thought of Forster, probably a professional soldier, always cool and collected in battle.

Thoughts clear and focused, always well-defined.

Wakefield tried to visualize an attack on the first Interloper. He conjured up a clear image of him throwing himself flat and firing the shotgun under the SUV, hitting the entity in the legs, crippling it. Almost before the scenario had played out in his mind, the Interloper darted out from behind its cover and Wakefield shot it. The creature leaped into the air, blood spurting from a wound in its torso. When it landed, it darted forward, but more slowly than before. He brought the gun butt up and around, caught the being under what passed for its chin, and it fell back, stunned.

Behind him Wakefield heard a weak cry, and turned to see Forster driving a knife into the flank of the smaller Interloper. Reloading, he fired, but this time the creature dodged easily and then charged at him. This time Wakefield summoned up blind rage, and swung the gun like a caveman swinging a club.

**

"There are no guards on your prize specimen?" asked Frankie, as Harriet Zoffany led her along the sub-basement corridor. The whole area seemed deserted. Frankie was using a basic GoPro to document the Romola Foundation's work. But, as Denny had pointed out, taking pictures of PCs and filing cabinets would not galvanize public opinion. They needed something truly graphic.

"Not today," the scientist replied, putting in her code. "We're short-handed, it seems. And Lucy has been inert for so long, I think they've become blasé."

There was a strong chemical smell in the room. Disinfectant mingled with another odor. It was one Frankie recalled from a visit to a funeral parlor owned by one of her many uncles in New Orleans.

Embalming fluid.

Frankie almost gagged at the sight of the Interloper. It resembled an illustration from some old anatomy textbook. The creature's ribs had been broken and peeled back, exposing the internal organs. As she looked on, a grayish-blue sac of tissue pulsed slowly. Zoffany stooped close to the Interloper's head while Frankie skirted the edge of the room, which suddenly seemed small, and cramped.

This could look so damn fake, Frankie thought, as she zoomed in on the un-dead being.

"Benson," Zoffany asked. "Tell us about Benson."

The rebels agreed that Lucy had to be filmed and conversed with. A conventional interview, though, made no sense. The creature would know exactly what they were doing. But the creature might still disclose information to suit its own ends. Frankie had asked how they would know if it was telling the truth. Gould and Denny had both argued that they wouldn't, but the more disturbing the revelation, the better it would sound.

"Tell me about Benson," croaked Lucy.

Smart gambit, Frankie thought. *Answer a question with a question.*

"He's an asshole," she said, "Grade-A, large."

The creature's head turned slowly to face her. Now that she could observe it full-on, Frankie saw signs of dissection with stitches across the inhuman features. There were only slight traces of scarring, though. The Interloper clearly had extraordinary powers of recuperation.

"How does he screen his thoughts from us?" Lucy asked. "When he was very close I heard nothing."

It took a moment for the question to sink in. While Frankie was struggling to grasp it, Zoffany answered.

"He has the talisman," she said. "He must be using it."

The creature again turned its head, and the muzzle-like mouth moved painfully.

"No," it rasped. "A talisman ... does not ... obstruct ... mind sight."

The two humans looked at one another.

"Then what the hell is Benson doing?" asked Frankie. "Does he have some cool gadget he's keeping to himself?"

Zoffany looked helpless and scared. Frankie decided to focus on the purpose of the 'interview'.

"Hey, Lucy," she said. "What's it all for? Why are you attacking us? What did we ever do?"

"You destroy the barriers between worlds," said Lucy.

"How?" Zoffany demanded, sounding frustrated. "You

keep saying that, but how do we do this? Is it by scientific experiments? Particle accelerators? Or nuclear testing?"

"By existing!" Lucy rasped, raising its head off the dissection table. "Swarming … vast numbers … psychic overload. Too many minds."

"What? That makes no sense!" Frankie protested.

"Maybe it does," Zoffany said quietly, holding up a hand. She leaned closer to the creature. "Do you mean that too much psychic energy breaks down the barriers?"

Lucy turned a hideous face toward the scientist. After a moment the Interloper's flesh rippled, the baboon-like muzzle retracted, eyes and other features softened. Now Lucy resembled the child whose place in the world it had tried to steal.

"Your swarming minds tear holes in the universe. All your stupid, loud thoughts!"

Zoffany nodded, stood up, and looked at Frankie.

"Gould suggested something like this," she said, her voice unsteady. "It's a quantum-mechanical thing. Perception alters reality, just as reality alters perception. So people are, to some extent, going around tinkering with reality just by perceiving it."

Great, we're back in quantum-land, Frankie thought. *Let's see what I can remember.*

"But all that stuff's happening on a really small scale," she said aloud. "We're talking about electrons. It doesn't apply on a human scale, or larger. Old-style cause and effect still applies. Galileo, Newton, all those guys. You can't just wish away the truck that's about to hit you!"

"No, but we're not just considering our reality, are we?" Zoffany countered. "We're talking about the effects all those over-complex human brains are having on other dimensions. Destabilizing them. So, indirectly, our minds are changing reality. And not in a fun way.

"People have been around a long time," Frankie protested.

"But only as scattered tribes, hunter gatherers, subsistence farmers," Zoffany pointed out. "Just a few million minds for most of our species' existence. Not enough to put a burden on the fabric of other realities. Just enough to weaken the boundary here and there, allow gateways to appear. Now there are billions of us. And from the Interlopers' perspective, it's all happened very suddenly. Time flows differently for them."

Frankie thought about her own experience in the Phantom Dimension. She had tried to grasp Interloper viewpoints when trapped with them in the Soul-Eater. She had not made much progress. But one overwhelming impression remained. There was a strong sense that the balance of 'nature' in the alien world was gone. The Soul-Eaters themselves had been evidence of that. Frankie had been surprised to learn that the beings had once been small and marginal, but had somehow grown vast and destructive.

"So it's like putting too much weight on a supporting wall in a house?" she suggested. "Or overloading a ship so that it breaks up in rough seas? I'm struggling to visualize all this cosmic chaos."

"The point is," Zoffany said, "that if their world is being destroyed, they have no choice but to come to ours. They're fleeing a reality that soon won't exist. It's far more drastic than humans going to Mars, say, to escape the destruction of our planet. They have to adapt to new natural laws. You could say they're the ultimate refugees. "

And even less welcome than the human kind, Frankie almost said aloud.

***

Davenport signed out of the Romola Foundation to find London still in the grip of February snows. The sidewalks were treacherous with frozen slush and another blizzard seemed set to descend from the low, gray clouds. He made his way to the nearest Tube station, dodging through the throng in the automatic way of the big city dweller. What he had seen and heard kept running through his mind, so that he bumped into a couple of people at the entrance to Wells Lane Underground. It was only then that he realized crowds were surging out of the station, in unusual numbers.

Bomb scare? Usually is.

Davenport's mind snapped back into focus. People were looking scared, confused, a few grinning in excitement. A single uniformed police officer was just visible inside the foyer. The man seemed to be trying, and failing, to get a response from his radio. The station lights were flickering ominously.

Davenport tapped a suited stockbroker-type on the shoulder and asked, "Hey, mate, what's going on?"

The man in the suit looked Davenport up and down, then snorted.

"The usual cock-up," he said. "The whole Thames Line. Absolute disgrace! Don't these bureaucrats know some of us have actual work to do? Whole country's going to the dogs!"

The businessman's tone suggested that the Tube had been sabotaged to inconvenience him personally. Davenport was about to ask for more detail but the man pushed past him, followed by another surge of travelers. This time there was a sense of genuine panic, and from inside the station Davenport heard a scream. It was hard to tell if it was from a man or a woman. He began to push through the mob, abandoning even the pretense of big city politeness.

The surge ended and Davenport found himself close to the ticket barrier. The policeman had given up trying to get orders or information and was helping an elderly woman outside. As Davenport hesitated, the lights flickered, then went out. More screams echoed up the escalators. With the sound came a whiff of putrefaction, a vile stench as if all of London's myriad sewers had somehow been re-routed into the tunnels below.

Davenport thought of the odor of decay when Interlopers died. This was far more pervasive. He looked around for signs of inhuman corpses, but could see none. The stench was definitely being wafted up from below ground.

There must be hundreds of them down there, he thought. *Killed by a train? Electrocuted?*

Training took over, and Davenport decided to investigate. He took out a handkerchief and held it over his nose, then pushed through the ticket barrier. The flickering lights went out, and Davenport hesitated. Someone collided with him in the dark, and he heard a faint scream

"Just keep going, head for the light," he snapped.

Davenport took out a torch and went to the top of the escalators. He could see other lights. People were holding up their phones as they fled the short, pedestrian tunnels that led to the platforms. As Davenport watched, a huge, dark mass lunged from one tunnel and slapped down a couple of screaming travelers. The stench increased. The rotting limb withdrew, dragging with it a man who was half-submerged in the bubbling protoplasm. The tentacle left behind a black smear of rotting organic matter.

Not a lot of them, he thought. *Just a single big one. Decaying, but evidently not fast enough.*

He retreated, fighting his panic, and in seconds found himself out in the cold winter air. People were milling around, shouting questions, not listening to answers, and inevitably filming on their cell-phones. He thought of his girlfriend, who would now be at their home in a distant North London suburb, then of his colleagues at the foundation. He decided to call them, and then go to her.

"What's happening in there, mate?" demanded a middle-aged man in a trench coat.

"Monsters from another dimension," Davenport responded.

"Oh, piss off!" responded the man.

Davenport worked his way out of the crowd then sent a message back to the foundation. Then he called his girlfriend and told her to buy plenty of tinned food, batteries, and candles.

"Just in case, love," he told her. "Better safe than sorry."

Chapter 8: Pre-emptive Strike

The Crazy Committee was poring over online maps when Frankie and Zoffany returned. There was a quick exchange of information, interrupted by a text message from Davenport.

"'SE - check the news'," Jim said, looking up from his phone. "That's all it says."

A few seconds later, they were watching a special BBC broadcast. The announcers seemed fairly clueless, but the crawler along the bottom of the screen spoke volumes. It mentioned a 'huge leakage of toxic waste' into the Thames Line.

"I'm guessing that it's living toxic waste, at least for now?" suggested Frankie.

"SE – Soul-Eater," Jim said, aghast.

"What can we do?" asked Zoffany. "Apart from wait for it to die?"

"We can take advantage of the chaos," replied Denny. "The Tube system will be shut down, right? So can we get in using your security clearance, Jim?"

Jim nodded, albeit hesitantly.

"We can get to Hobs Lane easily enough," he said. "But what exactly do we do when we get there?"

"Prove the gateway exists, film the Phantom Dimension," Denny said. "And let's be clear who 'we' are."

She looked around the group.

"Frankie and I have been through and know the score," she said. "We'll leave what footage we have with you guys, okay? Plus the password for my YouTube channel. Which is also the password for everything else – yeah, I know. Ted, Harriet, you put it out there. Leave 'em wanting more."

The others began to protest, but Denny held up a hand for silence.

"I'm pulling rank," she said. "I'm the expert on going over and coming back. And I've got this."

She held up the talisman.

"I think it can protect the two of us, at a stretch," she said, with a smile at Frankie. "But I reckon a third wheel would get picked off. So Jim, I'd like you to stay on this side of the gateway. Frankie, you up for this?"

"Sure, boss," Frankie replied, removing a memory card from her camera. She handed it to Gould. "Got any more of these, Ted?"

**

Denny and Frankie left the foundation with Jim. The roads seemed to be one big traffic jam, which they presumed had been caused by the incident at Wells Road. They headed away from the station until they found clearer streets and could hail a cab. The driver had the radio on, tuned to a London news channel.

"Nobody seems to know what's going," the cabbie remarked. "Makes you wonder what they're not telling us."

"Sure does!" replied Frankie in her most touristy voice.

By the time they got to Hobs Lane, a police cordon had been set up at the station entrance. Jim took a while to find an officer, senior enough to recognize his security clearance. In the meantime, Frankie took a few discreet shots of the crowd. Finally, they were admitted, and Jim led them down the stopped escalator onto the platform.

"If we're right," he said, gesturing at the gaping tunnel mouth, "the gateway is in there."

"We're sure the power's off?" asked Frankie, gazing dubiously at the tracks.

"If not we'll soon find out," said Jim.

He took out a coin and tossed it onto one of the two power rails. Denny flinched, half-expecting a flash and an explosion. But the coin just bounced with a dull ringing sound and came to rest on the dirty gravel under the tracks.

"Looks good," Jim said, and lowered himself carefully off the platform.

Denny was about to follow when her phone chimed. She hesitated, then checked the message. It was from Russell Wakefield. The message was titled 'Jedi Mind Trick'.

"What's up?" Frankie asked.

"Somebody we know," Denny replied, opening the message. The image that appeared was of a patch of brownish-gray matter in a field of snow. It only took her a moment to recognize the badly-decomposed body of an Interloper. Denny read the text underneath, then looked down at Jim.

"Some bad news from Machen," she said quietly. "Forster's guys got wiped out."

***

Sir Lionel Bartram's limousine pulled up outside the Romola Foundation.

"Can't guarantee your security inside that place, sir," the officer said dubiously. "Probably quite a few entrances. Old building like that. Don't you think we'd be better off back at the Home Office?"

"No," said Bartram, flatly, and opened the car door. "Wait here for me. I will be collecting a passenger."

Hang on, the bodyguard thought. *That's against protocol. You can't just shove random strangers into this car.*

But before the man could speak, Bartram turned to look at him with deep-set gray eyes.

"Don't argue," said the minister. "Your job is to follow orders."

The bodyguard was so surprised by this that the Daimler's door had slammed shut before he could think of a response.

"He just put you in your place, mate," drawled the driver, with a wry smile.

"Bollocks," retorted the bodyguard. "He thinks you're an Uber, how does that feel?"

"Hey, I'm getting paid," replied the driver. "If he wants to pick up another floozy, doesn't bother me."

"Doesn't it strike you that he's ... changed?" the bodyguard asked.

"Maybe he's sobered up," the driver suggested. "That'd make a change."

The bodyguard grunted noncommittally. The car's short-wave radio squawked, and the driver picked up the handset.

"Yeah? What?"

The driver's laconic manner vanished, and he glanced around at the bodyguard.

"Okay," he said, replacing the handset. "Seems our boy's needed back at the aitch-oh. Maybe you'd better–"

Before the driver had finished speaking, the bodyguard had clambered out of the limo and was dodging through the dense throng on the pavement. The Scotland Yard man was vaguely aware that the other pedestrians seemed panicky, excited, confused. He took out his own radio as he entered the atrium of the Romola Foundation.

"Is it a Code Black?" he asked, using the code for a terrorist attack.

"Negative," crackled the reply. "Possible Code Silver."

It took the officer a moment to recall what Code Silver was. It had been covered briefly during training when he had joined the ministerial protection unit. He paused just inside the door, frowning.

Chemical spillage? No, not that, he thought. *Oh yeah, hazardous outbreak, like Ebola or anthrax.*

"Okay," he snapped into the radio. "Will move cargo to safe haven."

The bodyguard strode over to the reception desk where a uniformed security man was sitting, looking oddly unconcerned. The Scotland Yard officer took out his ID, held it steady in front of the guard's face.

"Can I help you?" the security man asked.

"Yeah, Sir Lionel Bartram, I need to get to him. It's an emergency so I need to go straight through–"

The bodyguard paused. A group of people had approached quietly and formed a semi-circle around him. He glanced around the group. There seemed to be two young women in cleaners' overalls and another security guard. The latter's uniform looked a bit sloppy. A couple of buttons had been torn off.

"Yeah, what's up? I haven't got time for this."

One of the cleaners brought up a mop and drove the handle, hard, into the bodyguard's stomach. It was such an unexpected attack that he doubled over more in shock than in pain.

"You bitch!" he gasped, groping for his pistol.

He heard a creak and clatter as the guard behind the desk

jumped up. The other three were closing in, reaching for him with oddly long hands. The bodyguard backed against the desk, drove an elbow backwards into where he guessed the first guard's face would be. He felt a sharp pain as something lacerated his elbow. He looked up to see the cleaner who had attacked him start to crouch, and her mouth gape wide to reveal a circle of sharp, inhuman teeth.

What the – he thought, then stopped thinking forever.

***

"How long will it take?" asked Zoffany.

Gould shrugged.

They were looking at a PC screen on which a bar was filling up, showing how much content had uploaded. It was half an hour since the other members of the Crazy Committee had left.

"It's amazing how dull doing something rebellious can be," she said. "Maybe we could have a look at our special guest? While we wait?"

"Why?" he asked. "She can't have escaped."

"She did almost escape before by manipulating a guard," Zoffany pointed out. Then added, "Admittedly that was before we–"

"Nailed her to an operating table?" he cut in. "But I don't suppose it can hurt to check."

Gould smiled and moved to another computer, then tapped in his security password. This allowed him to bring up live camera footage from inside the building. Once the system was accessed, it showed an array of small screens. Gould was about to click on the image of Lucy's cell when he stopped, frowned.

"What's going on?" he exclaimed.

He selected the closed-circuit feed from the foyer, where some kind of fracas seemed to be going on. As they watched, they saw a foundation security guard and two cleaners reveal themselves to be Interlopers. They took down a young-looking man in a suit who managed to pull out a gun, but did not get to fire it.

"Jesus Christ!"

Gould checked the other security feeds. The building seemed to be deserted. Then Zoffany spotted a couple of bodies lying in a corridor just off the foyer.

"The actual human guards, I'm guessing?"

"Probably," Gould said, switching to another viewpoint. "At least they're not heading this way. They seem to be going downstairs, in fact."

"To the sub-basement?" Zoffany gasped. "But how will they get past the security?"

Gould gave her a quizzical look.

"Oh," she said. "They'll have taken a swipe card, and of course Lucy will have picked the code out of my mind."

Gould walked briskly to the door and locked it, shoved a chair up against the handle.

"Better safe than sorry," he observed, returning to the computer. "Now let's see what they get up to."

"Shouldn't we call someone?" Zoffany asked. "I mean, the police or, well ..."

"Message Jim," Gould suggested. "Let him know there's an incursion. Probably best if they don't come back, considering the numbers."

"If they get the message," Zoffany pointed out, taking out her phone.

After a few moments, they saw a familiar figure in a dark suit emerge from the elevator, accompanied by three Interlopers in non-human form. They watched the suited individual walk along to the secure unit and quickly open the door.

"That's that politician!" Zoffany exclaimed. "Do you think he was replaced before he visited or after?"

Gould shrugged.

"It hardly matters," he said. "They've clearly got access to high levels of government now. Not bad going. Perhaps we should be trying to report this. The trouble is, who could we trust?"

Zoffany did not reply. The two watched as the Interlopers entered Lucy's cell and began to free their comrade.

***

The gateway was only a few yards from Hobs Lane station. Their torches picked out the spherical shimmer of the portal. It was in the mouth of the disused tunnel Jim had located.

"You sure you want me to stay here?" he asked. "I might be a lot more use as backup if I've actually got your backs."

Denny hesitated, glanced at Frankie, who said, "He's got a point."

"Okay," Denny said, "compromise. You wait about three minutes – that's may be an hour over there, right? Then you come through. Because we just want to get some shots of the PD, not win awards."

"Fair enough," Jim said, still sounding unhappy.

"We need you here to cover our retreat," Denny explained again. "We've no idea how many of those things are loose in London. And remember what we discussed?"

"Wakefield's trick?" Jim asked. "Do you really think it can cloud their minds?"

Denny gestured at the gateway.

"Through there we're fighting on their terms, in their world," she said. She took out her key ring, held up the talisman. "We have one small advantage. Another one would be handy."

"Tick tock, guys," put in Frankie, hefting her camera. "I don't feel comfortable just standing here, knowing there's a Soul-Eater down that tunnel."

As if to underline the point, a whiff of foul air blew past them. Denny felt herself gagging. She tried not to imagine the rotting mass of alien protoplasm blocking the tunnel and spilling onto the platform at Wells Road.

But at least there were plenty of witnesses, she thought. *And there must be phone-camera footage.*

***

"What are they doing?" Zoffany whispered, leaning over Gould's shoulder.

"Some kind of – ritual?" he suggested. "You'd think they'd

just grab her and run if—"

He paused.

"You know, this makes no sense. If they just want the data she's gathered on us, they don't need to rescue her at all. We know they can share thoughts over short distances. So, what the hell are they doing?"

Four Interlopers had set Lucy free and then stepped back, heads bowed, as Lucy heaved itself painfully into a sitting position. Her ribs were still peeled back, internal organs hanging obscenely over its lap. A trickle of blood, black in the CCTV screen, ran down the short, skinny legs.

"Can we get sound?" Zoffany asked.

Gould fiddled with the settings, brought up the sound as high as he could. There was a slight hint of breathing just audible over the whir of an air-conditioning fan. But the Interlopers were saying nothing. Instead they moved closer, reached out their clawed hands, and placed them on the fake Lucy's ravaged body. As the humans watched, the gaping ribs began to fold in, covering the slow-pulsing organs. The four newcomers remained motionless, heads still bowed, as the rib cage began to heal itself.

"You learn something new every day," murmured Gould.

Within a couple of minutes, Lucy was physically intact. The creature got down from the surgical table and almost fell. Its movements were hesitant, suggestive of great pain and weakness. The others held it upright, helped it to the door.

"I never thought—" Gould began.

"About how much they might care for one another," Zoffany finished. "Me neither. And I suppose the information she's gathered is valuable. But still. This is a lot like compassion."

As if they had heard her, the five Interlopers stopped and stared straight up at the camera. The human flinched back from the small screen. The creatures said nothing, alien faces simply staring blankly with deep-sunken eyes. Then the rescue party turned its attention to the cell door, and took Lucy slowly toward the elevator.

"I've always hated them," Gould said, switching to a view of the corridor. "For what they did to my sister, and to all those other innocent people and children. I mean, I was fascinated by them, but the driving force was always that hatred."

"How do you feel now?" Zoffany asked.

"Confused, to be honest," he said. "If any intelligent species is desperate to survive, extreme measures must seem justified. We're in War of the Worlds territory, I suppose."

They watched in silence for a few moments as the rescuers took the freed captive to the elevator. Inside, one of them took off its cleaners' uniform and put it onto Lucy. When the rescue party emerged in the foyer, all the Interlopers had taken on human form. One had adopted the form of a naked young man. It calmly walked over and took the clothes from the stranger they had killed earlier.

"Do you think they'll take her home?" Zoffany asked.

"I suppose Bartram has clearance," Gould mused. "But that might not be their objective."

***

Denny went through the gateway first, expecting to land on something like the stone platform in the Interloper city. Instead, she tumbled onto a floor of compacted dirt. It was pitch dark. She moved quickly to one side just in time to avoid being struck by Frankie, who was holding her camera above her head. As a result, the other woman landed heavily with a yelp of pain and dismay.

"Either it's night or we're underground," Denny said, helping Frankie up.

She flicked on her flashlight and pointed it straight up. There was an irregular surface about ten feet above their heads, walls about fifteen feet apart. It was a tunnel, but much larger than the ones Denny had traversed during her first venture into this world.

"Big," commented Frankie, turning on her camera light and filming the scene. "Their version of Hobs Lane station, maybe?"

"Hate to see what passes for a train," Denny replied. "Or maybe the tunnels reflect the size of the creatures that use them?"

Frankie froze, lowered her camera.

"A Soul-Eater?" she whispered sharply.

They stared at each other for a moment, then both laughed nervously.

"Doubt it," Denny said, pointing at the ceiling. "This is way too small."

Frankie stepped back a few paces, resumed filming.

"Okay," said Denny, "we're in some kind of tunnel, and it could be anywhere on regular, boring old earth. So we need some proof we're in the Phantom Dimension. Let's go–" she pointed at random. "This way. Uphill, I think."

They set off, and after a couple of minutes, it was clear that the tunnel was sloping upwards as well as curving gently to the left. A faint light showed ahead what Denny hoped was the surface. She anticipated filming from the relative safety of a tunnel mouth, getting footage of the drifting Black Stars, perhaps even a passing Soul-Eater. But, as they got closer to the light, its quality seemed wrong.

"Turn off your light," she said, flicking off her own.

The radiance ahead was clearer, now. It did not have the colorless quality of the sky in the Phantom Dimension. It was a dull reddish glow, reminding Denny of the color of the dirt walls of the tunnel. She mentioned this to Frankie.

"Yeah," said the camerawoman, "but maybe the sky's different in different places. I mean, a British sky isn't the same as one in Hawaii, right? Could be the same over here."

Denny clung to the idea, but soon it was clear that Frankie was wrong. Without conferring, they both slowed down and pressed closer to the tunnel wall. The tunnel opened out into a large chamber illuminated by patches of what looked to Denny like glowing moss. The angle of the tunnel made it impossible for them to see the ground level without going right up to the entrance.

"Crap," hissed Frankie. "We've still got zero proof."

Denny crouched down and worked her way up to within a few feet of the entrance. As she did so, a figure appeared, shambling slowly past the tunnel mouth. It was an Interloper, but vastly bigger than any they had seen before, standing at least seven feet tall. While the smaller creatures had a baboon-like basic shape, this one resembled a gorilla in its broad, muscular form. The main difference was that its huge forelimbs terminated in taloned claws bigger than Denny's head.

Denny froze until the monster was out of sight, then turned to see if Frankie had got it on tape. Frankie raised a thumb. But Denny did not respond. Instead, she was staring past her friend at the two Interlopers behind Frankie.

"You are welcome," said an immense voice. It echoed around the chamber and down the tunnel. "Come closer."

Chapter 9: Survival

"I am the All-Mother."

"Yeah," Denny said quietly. "I get that."

Beside her, Frankie murmured something not quite audible as she focused on the vast creature at the far end of the oval chamber. There was no sign that the Interlopers wanted her to stop filming. In fact, the huge guards – all four of them – had ignored the humans. The 'Type One' creatures that had followed them along the tunnel had likewise stood looking on, instead of attacking.

The All-Mother was roughly humanoid in shape, but would have been about ten feet tall if she had been able to stand. To Denny, this seemed unlikely. The Interloper Queen lay on a kind of mattress of pale fibers, taking up about a quarter of the brood chamber. The creature's limbs, while even larger than those of her gorilla-like guards, seemed small and atrophied in comparison to the vast, bloated body. The creature's head was likewise dwarfed by the huge, swollen abdomen. The deep-set eyes, however, were alive with keen intelligence and restless energy.

But it was the other living creature that drew most of Denny's attention. A body was fastened to the Queen's massive belly. It was tiny in comparison, and at first Denny thought of deep-sea fish in which the male becomes a mere organ of the larger female. But after looking more closely, she realized that this was probably not a male Interloper. A few shreds of what had been a bright-colored dress still clung to the body, and untidy ropes of dark hair hung down over the pale gray alien flesh. Denny guessed it would be, if human, a girl of about six or seven.

The Queen's abdomen heaved and a dark gray object began to emerge slowly from between the stumpy legs. The All-Mother moaned, limbs thrashing, as the egg slid out. One of her giant attendants caught it, and rushed to insert it into a niche. There were several layers of these recesses around the oval chamber, and they fell into distinct size ranges.

The egg that had just been produced was of the most common sort, about a foot long and six inches wide. But there were a handful of larger cavities that contained glossy black eggs. And, Denny noticed, there was a single, huge niche that apparently contained nothing. Any egg that would fill that space would be enormous, at least three feet long. Denny flinched at the thought of the Queen producing it.

"That space was made for our daughter, the new All-Mother," the Queen boomed. "So that future generations may endure."

Okay, Denny thought, *I'm going to interview an alien monster while she squeezes out a few eggs. No biggie.*

"What do you mean?" she asked aloud, and pointed at the huge guards. "Aren't these all your daughters?"

The All-Mother gave a shuddering, deep bellow that might have been a laugh. Another egg began to emerge from between the creature's thighs.

"I mean," the creature said, "that there will be a mother to our people in their new homeland. So that the race can endure."

"Another fertile female?" Denny said. "But how will she survive? Oh, I get it. She's going to be one of the new types. She'll be able to live in our world indefinitely, right?"

The Queen did not reply, but finished producing a fresh egg. Again, one of the hulking attendants picked it up and placed it in a niche. As it did so, the egg in an adjacent niche split open. A small, white claw emerged, ripping the leathery shell in two. Then a perfectly-formed miniature Interloper dropped to the dirt floor. It began to lick off a layer of glistening slime.

"You're still ... producing regular Interlopers," said Denny, trying to quell the disgust in her voice. "Why is that? You can't build an army at this late stage. Your world is going down, you know that?"

This time the Queen's response was more emphatic. The All-Mother bellowed, thrashed her bloated limbs, and a flailing arm knocked a chunk of out of the brood chamber wall. Denny was hit by a blast of rage and frustration, far more intense than anything she had experienced before.

"I have no choice but to breed! It is the eternal way."

A mental image suddenly appeared in Denny's brain. She

saw a group of bizarre creatures that she knew, without being told, were male Interlopers. They were the ones that hatched from the larger eggs, she realized. The beings were all too obviously male, huge and aggressive, with far more vicious claws than the familiar sexless Interlopers.

Denny saw them from the Queen's viewpoint. The males were brutal, stupid creatures seeking to impregnate her. She looked on as they tore each other apart, until eventually only one survived. Physical excellence was all the males contributed, Denny realized. Intelligence and psychic ability were passed down the Queen's line.

Next, Denny experienced the mating ritual of another species. The prolonged coitus literally sucked the life out of the not-so-lucky partner, leaving him a dead, blackened husk. The twitching, near-dead 'husband' was carried off by an attendant and dumped, unceremoniously, on the surface. From the grotesque mating on the All-Mother, she was just that, the sole reproducer of a cloned tribe. And she would produce offspring every few minutes for as long as she lived.

Denny fell to her knees, retching, as the intense, alien memory washed over her. She looked up at Frankie, who was shaking her head in disbelief.

"I just got a whiff of that," Frankie confirmed. "I guess romance really is dead."

Denny, still on her knees, pointed at the child lying sprawled on the fleshy dome of the Queen's abdomen.

"What do you need her for?"

She thought she already knew the answer thanks to the human cells found in the body of the fake Lucy.

"The child was chosen," the Queen hissed. "Her flesh can become our flesh."

Monster logic, Denny thought. *All those child abductions down the centuries. To experiment on them, try and find a way to adapt to our world.*

"So your changelings spied on us," she said, slowly getting to her feet, "while you tested the children to see if they were compatible with your biology. And you captured adults, experimented on them, too. Centuries for us, decades-long project for you. If you rejected a captive, you gave them to the

Soul-Eaters. Win, win situation, right?"

"It is your way," the All-Mother replied. "You experiment on your own kind. You slaughter your own kind. Torture, maim, starve, destroy. We make war as you do. We are not human, and we owe you nothing."

Denny felt another blast of emotion, this one of disgust and revulsion. Again, she saw things from the Queen's viewpoint, but this time she was looking at herself and Frankie. What she saw were flabby, misshapen creatures with huge bulging eyes, weird flat faces, tiny pursed mouths, and mops of grotesque hair. The impression lasted only a split second, but it brought another wave of nausea.

"Good people," Denny gasped, "good people don't harm children. Everybody knows that–"

She paused, knowing she would condemn herself as a hypocrite if she went on. The Queen was skimming her mind, stirring up memories of school shootings, terrorist bombings, every atrocity she knew.

"Okay," Denny conceded, "we have some pretty shitty individual humans and some lousy ideologies back there. But two wrongs don't make a right!"

This time there was no response, in words or thoughts. Seconds passed, and the only sounds in the brood chamber were muffled creaks and rustles from the egg niches. Then the Queen's body began to buck and heave as her biological machinery continued its mindless, remorseless task.

"You wish to save this child? And your friend who carries the machine?" asked the Queen, after the fresh egg had been safely deposited. "Then we must make a new covenant."

***

Jim got the text from Zoffany just as he was preparing to go through the gateway. The time agreed had not elapsed, but he felt incapable of simply waiting. Besides, news updates suggested that the Soul-Eater on the Thames Line had perished. There were no reports of people being attacked, merely chatter about 'toxic waste' or 'sewage'. A new theory gaining traction was that a cache of chemical weapons, dumped sometime after 1945, had leaked into the water table.

"Crap," Jim growled, reading the message. "They got their tactics right."

He reasoned that, if Forster's squad had been wiped out, the Interlopers could give their full attention to other matters. This meant that he, Denny, and Frankie were the next obvious targets. He checked his pistol and Taser and prepared to enter the gateway, hoping that the others had not ventured far on the other side.

"Davison? That you?"

The voice was familiar. Jim turned to see Davenport clambering down off the platform. After him came another man in a security guard uniform. There were other people on the platform but Jim could not make them out, just see a few legs.

"Yeah," he replied. "What's up?"

"Bloody shambles mate," Davenport replied, moving into the tunnel and raising a flashlight. "You heard about the raid on headquarters?"

Jim nodded.

"Why are you here and not heading home?" he asked, holding up a hand to block the flashlight beam.

"Couldn't leave my old mate Jim," Davenport said heartily. "I rounded up a few survivors and brought them down here. Thought we could help out."

Jim frowned, still puzzled by his colleague's change of heart. Davenport lowered the flashlight, spoke more softly.

"Look, it's up to you, but I think we should get the girls back, pronto. Unite all our forces kind of thing. Then go back to headquarters, see what we can do there."

"Okay," Jim said, relieved to have some backup. "Who's that with you?"

"Some of the new guys," Davenport replied. "Not very experienced, but willing."

Jim nodded dubiously, hefted his gun. He knew that the most competent guards had all accompanied Forster.

So I've got the trainees and no-hopers as backup. Great.

"Okay, that's great," he said aloud. "So let's get going."

A few seconds later, Jim was in the large tunnel looking

around in vain for Denny and Frankie. As Davenport came through, Jim spotted small footprints in the dirt, leading uphill. He pointed these out.

"Yeah, they must have gone that way," Davenport agreed.

A security guard Jim didn't recognize appeared, then another. The second stranger was followed by a man in a suit, then a couple of young women in casual clothes and overalls.

"Hang on," said Jim, "You brought the contract cleaners? And who's this guy?"

Then another figure, far smaller than the rest, materialized and tumbled to the floor of the tunnel. It looked up as the others helped it to its feet, and Jim gaped in stunned horror. It was a little girl, dressed in adult clothes. It grinned up at Jim.

"I remember you!"

"Lucy!" he gasped.

The world seemed to tilt and reset itself as Jim realized that he was the only human present.

"Sorry, mate," said the fake Davenport, reaching out to take Jim's gun. Already the creature's visage was losing its familiar shape. "I said we were going back to headquarters. I just didn't say whose. It's right up this tunnel. Don't make a fuss. Killing you is not part of the plan."

***

The word covenant brought Denny up short. Then she remembered the diary of the British officer who had worn the original talisman during World War One.

"That was more than a hundred years ago," she protested. "If your world is dying, and you with it, what's the points of making treaties?"

To underline her point, she formed a powerful mental image of her own. She visualized a group of Interlopers being hunted down by humans. The creatures were outnumbered, spotted by the air with drones using infra-red cameras. Vastly outnumbered, the creatures were cornered in a bleak, industrial landscape, then shot by black-clad troops.

"No!" screamed the Queen. "We will not perish!"

A mental counterblast swamped Denny's imaginings. Interlopers in human guise moved across a desolate landscape. The perspective shifted and Denny saw that they were in a desert. Another image, this time of Interlopers on an island, again far from civilization. Again and again, the Queen offered Denny visions of her race surviving with little or no interaction with humans.

"Naive," murmured Frankie. "And can I just add, we're not getting any of this telepathic stuff on film."

"All we want is to be left alone," hissed the All-Mother. "We did not seek war."

"But you found it," Denny retorted. "And there's no way you could survive in our world without our agreement. You need our acceptance."

"A new covenant!" insisted the Queen. "A truce. We offer our powers to you in return for our survival."

"I can't negotiate for the world!" Denny responded.

There was no verbal reply. Instead, the All-Mother transmitted a bewildering series of images, all showing Interlopers co-operating with human beings in various contexts. Scientific experiments, military operations, espionage, crime-fighting. In a few moments, the end-game of the All-Mother's plan was outlined.

Denny felt the 'new covenant' as much as saw it, a blending of human and Interloper abilities to produce a kind of super-race. The first nation or alliance to achieve this, she realized, would have a huge advantage. Soldiers and spies with psychic powers, extraordinary strength and resilience, and the ability to assume any guise.

The original human race would be extinct within a few generations.

For a moment, the intensity of the Queen's vision almost overwhelmed Denny. She glimpsed a world without war, without crime, without oppression, without poverty. But it would also be a world without humanity as she knew it.

"No!" she shouted. "That's obscene. There has to be another way."

"You must agree!" insisted the Queen. "If you were linked mind to mind, as we are, all your petty conflict would cease.

See how we take care of our own."

The creature raised a huge, flabby hand to point. Denny turned to see Jim being escorted up the tunnel behind them. Among the group of Interlopers with him limped the tiny figure of the false Lucy, intact but still showing scars of her dissection.

"Sorry guys," Jim said. "Major back-up failure."

"Not your fault," Denny replied. "As you can see, we got more than we bargained for."

"There will be no more bargaining!" bellowed the Queen. "The new covenant must be. Our world will soon be torn apart!"

Denny felt the sheer mental pressure from the monstrous female becoming unbearable. At the same time, however, an idea began to form. It flitted across her mind, and she quickly suppressed it, leaving just the flavor of it. She took a few steps forward, holding up her hands in a placatory gesture.

"Let Lucy Gould go free," she said. "Let us look after our own. As a gesture of good faith."

She formed an image in her mind of the girl being severed from the Queen's bloated body by one of the attendants. Then she focused intently on another idea, trying to drive all other thoughts and feelings out of her mind. Denny kept thinking of a pink elephant, huge and absurd, a comical cartoon animal.

She was within a few yards of the All-Mother, now. The creature was silently squeezing out another huge egg. Denny reached into her jeans pocket and took out her key ring, holding up the talisman. The hulking attendants shambled forward, then hesitated. Seizing the moment, Denny ran forward, leaped onto one of the All-Mother's huge thighs, and plunged the stone into the creature's immense torso.

The Queen screamed, shuddering, as her flesh bubbled around the talisman. Denny yelled too, feeling a piercing pain in her own side. She had expected it, but the sensation was still startling and uncomfortable. This close to the All-Mother, the monster's psychic aura was almost overwhelming. But Denny also felt satisfaction that the creature's agony was being broadcast so strongly.

Denny scrambled along the paralyzed creature and took

hold of Lucy Gould. As expected, the girl was attached to the pale gray flesh of the All-Mother, and screamed as Denny pulled at her skinny body. But the destructive force of the talisman had already done some of the work, its effects spreading through the vast body and weakening its tissues.

With a sucking sound, the girl's body came free, leaving sticky trails of darkening tissue. Bright human blood splashed onto the Queen's body. Lucy squealed, fought Denny feebly, and then became still, clinging to her rescuer. Denny leaped down to the floor of the chamber. Her whole attack had taken a couple of seconds.

I was right, she thought, looking around at the other Interlopers. *Hit the boss and you hurt them all.*

The huge guards and the rest were thrashing wildly, some lashing out at each other, others simply lying prone, their limbs jerking. The Queen's suffering was theirs. The mental link that gave them such huge advantages was also a terrible weakness. As Denny dodged one of the Queen's hulking guards, she saw Jim grab a pistol from one of his captors and shoot the creature in the face.

Frankie had ducked into the largest of the niches and was filming the chaos, focusing on the All-Mother's agonized writhing. More gunshots sounded, along with pained screams from Jim's targets.

"Let's go before they recover!" Denny shouted. "Frankie, come on!"

She glanced back and saw that the All-Mother was plucking the talisman from her side. The huge guards were struggling to their feet, as were some of the regular Interlopers. Frankie lowered her camera and ran after Denny, dodging around the creatures that flailed at the humans. Jim was less agile, and less fortunate. A grasping claw caught his ankle and brought him down. Denny hesitated.

"Just go!" Jim yelled, firing at the Interloper to free himself. "Put the truth out there!"

One of the Queen's guards loomed over him, and Jim emptied his pistol into the massive being. The bullets seemed to have no effect. The colossal creature was still confused and in distress, but one of its flailing fists caught Jim with a glancing blow and smashed him against the tunnel wall. He fell to the floor like a rag doll, neck twisted at a sickening angle.

Denny turned and ran. As she followed Frankie along the curving tunnel she felt the pain and confusion radiating from the All-Mother dwindle. Soon the psychic link was broken, but not before Denny felt the Queen's hate. The feeling was just barely perceptible, like a glowing ember in the darkness. And there was another emotion, something Denny could not quite grasp.

"Crap!" she shouted, rounding a corner to almost collide with Frankie.

She did not need to ask what had stopped her friend from entering the gateway. The black globe was gone. In its place was a wall of darkness blocking the entire tunnel. Frankie looked back up the tunnel, her eyes wide with fear.

"Denny, what the hell?"

"It's breaking down," Denny replied. "This must be how the big critters break through into our world – the gateway goes unstable, grows bigger. We can still go through!"

But neither woman moved. The inky barrier was advancing then receding like a black ocean breaking on a beach. Now that she looked more closely, Denny could see flickers of silvery radiance inside the darkness. She felt a pain behind her eyes as she tried to focus on the weird lights.

Reality coming apart, she thought. *A whole universe collapsing.*

As if to confirm her suspicion, a seismic shock-wave ran through the tunnel floor and a chunk of roof fell, striking Denny on the shoulder. At the same moment, one of the All-Mother's guards shambled into view, loping along like an ape, huge mouth gaping. Seeing the circle of shark-like teeth decided the issue. Both women ran straight into the wall of darkness.

Denny felt a sickening lurch. She was buffeted up and sideways, and then felt a piercing shaft of pain in her head. Lucy Gould clung even more tightly to her. Green and orange lights played across her vision; a sudden migraine. Then she was collapsing onto the dirty gravel that lay between the tracks of the Thames Line. At the last moment, she rolled so as not to crush the child she still held.

They had emerged not far from the original gateway. Frankie was already getting to her feet, picking up her camera. What had been a black wall across the tunnel was, in this reality, a flickering veil of silver that ebbed and flowed. Denny ran towards the edge of the platform and tried to disengage Lucy Gould.

"You've got to get up sweetie!" she urged. But the girl stuck to her like a limpet, eyes wide, face expressionless.

The massive Interloper burst through, stumbling and collapsing onto the tracks. Both women were already running as it heaved itself upright and gazed around, disoriented. Then it caught sight of its prey and began to pursue them in bounding leaps. Denny realized that she and Frankie were stuck on the tracks, with no time to climb onto the platform. Frankie turned, and hurled her camera at their pursuer's face. The Interloper knocked the camera aside as if it had been a toy, hardly breaking its stride.

Sorry, Frankie, Denny thought. *I got you into this!*

There was a deafening explosion and the Interloper reeled, black blood spurting from one arm. The creature bellowed in fury and turned to look up at the platform, just as another blast caught it in the face. An eye socket exploded and the entity reeled backwards, its huge arms splayed out. It lay groaning against the curved wall, blood streaming over the steel rails. Denny looked up to see Gould, Zoffany, and Davenport on the platform, the latter reloading a shotgun. Gould was already reaching down to give Frankie a hand up off the tracks. Denny stared up at the security man.

"I thought you quit?" she asked.

"I changed my mind," he said. "It's not just a woman's privilege, you know."

Davenport nodded at the dying Interloper.

"Any more of them coming through?" he asked.

"I doubt it, because–"

Denny stopped talking at the shimmering wall began to fade. The migraine-inducing flickers of light vanished, and the gateway returned to its familiar globe. Then, after a few moments, the globe shrank to a point of blue light, which died out.

"... because the Phantom Dimension just died," Denny finished.

Finally, after much coaxing, she got Lucy to let go and handed the whimpering child up to Zoffany. Gould realized at that moment who the newcomer was. He seemed frozen in shock, then went over to Zoffany and began to talk softly to the child. Lucy seemed oblivious to her older brother, however. Denny picked up Frankie's camera, handed it up to her colleague.

"Sometimes you get the shot," Frankie said, examining the smashed casing and broken lens. "And sometimes you just get away."

Epilogue: End Game

While Zoffany and Gould tended to Lucy's injuries, the other survivors sat in the security control room watching news footage from around the world. In Brazil, a Black Star had appeared over Rio and crashed into the sea in front of stunned crowds. The remains of a Soul-Eater had been found at the end of a mile-long swathe of dead wheat in Kansas. Chinese state television had declared that several 'ape-like creatures' had been shot dead after appearing in Inner Mongolia.

The general tenor of reports was that some bizarre, worldwide disaster had somehow been averted, but nobody could be more specific. There was talk of experiments, propaganda, and of course, space aliens. Some serious commentators took the line that unrelated phenomena were being 'falsely blamed' on a single, paranormal cause.

"After all," said one, "a chemical leak on the London Underground doesn't have to be connected to dead crops in America or dead apes in China."

The committee searched the mainstream media in vain for the uploads they had put out earlier. It was only when they started looking at what Frankie called 'fringe fruitcakes' that they found some shares, re-tweets and the like.

Nobody – at least officially – was taking the Phantom Dimension seriously.

"Is there any point in uploading any more of this stuff?" Frankie asked, taking the memory card out of her camera. "Assuming we got anything usable."

"I don't think so," said Denny. "People believe what they want to believe, dwell in their little echo chambers."

"If the PD is gone and the Queen is dead," Davenport pointed out, "then it doesn't really matter, does it? I mean, the threat is gone."

"So will Benson give us a bonus?" Frankie asked. "Productivity, you know?"

The others looked at her, startled.

"Completely forgot about the old bugger," Davenport said.

"You mean Benson?" said Gould, stopping in the doorway. "No idea where he went. But he can't be in the building, he'd

428

show up on cameras. There's nobody else in the building, is there?"

Gould gestured at the screens.

"Unless he was in the conference room," Davenport corrected. "Top floor. No cameras in there."

Gould frowned.

"I didn't know that," he admitted. "Do you know why?"

The security man shrugged.

"Forster told me it was so nobody could eavesdrop on the trustees' meetings. All very hush-hush."

"Well," Denny said, "chances are the creep is long gone."

Gould looked pensive.

"It might be worth checking," he said, and left.

"Trying to keep himself busy," said Davenport. "Hell of a shock seeing your little sister after, what was it? Thirty years. And she's hardly aged."

Denny nodded.

"If Lucy was an adult we might've interviewed her," she said. "But the poor kid will need a specialist's help for years."

Frankie sighed as she inserted the camera's memory card into one of the office PCs.

"We know what we saw," she said. "Now it's done. Time to move on. No more nasties from other dimensions."

"Just that familiar, desperate need to get some kind of work," added Denny. "Any suggestions, guys?"

There was a long silence.

"Hey," said Frankie, "I did get something!"

On the PC monitor some low-quality footage of their escape from the Phantom Dimension appeared. The others gathered around as Frankie wound the video back and forth. The familiar interference with electronic devices had left much of the film useless. But Frankie managed to find a few clear still images here and there. One, in particular, showed the All-Mother in her brood chamber, Lucy still attached to the creature's body.

"Nobody will believe it," Davenport said flatly. "God, *I'm* having trouble believing it right now."

"Not show-reel material," Denny agreed, then something caught her eye. "Hey, stop! Wind back a couple of seconds!"

Frankie obliged, reversing a panning shot of the brood chamber.

"Stop there!" Denny said, pointing. "Can you clean up that part?"

Frankie tinkered with the software until the area indicated filled the screen. It showed the shadowy interior of the biggest of the dozens of niches. Denny pointed to a few dark patches.

"Could those be the remains of an eggshell?" she asked.

"Nah," responded Davenport. "Just a few rogue pixels. No real detail there."

The women exchanged a glance.

"He's probably right," said Frankie.

Denny recalled the last pulse of mental energy she had felt from the Queen. There had been rage at the attack Denny had inflicted on her, certainly. But there had been something else, a hint of a different emotion.

Was it triumph? Or am I being totally paranoid?

"Yeah," she said. "Maybe we'll never know."

***

The conference room was full of Bensons. They were not quite present, however, or at least not all the time. The Bensons were shimmering in and out of view, shadowy figures on the edge of perception. Every chair around the table was occupied by a ghostly figure that, if Gould looked directly at it, became invisible. Other Bensons stood around the walls, or stalked toward the intruder. Despite the insubstantial nature of the throng, Gould felt himself pressed back against the door. Twenty or more pairs of deep-sunken eyes turned to regard Gould.

"Who ... What?" He struggled to find a question, gave up, groped for the doorknob.

A looming, shadowy form glided toward him, grew more substantial, and reached out to touch him. Gould flinched but could not dodge the long, slender finger that flicked across his forehead. He felt a sudden, overwhelming sense of calm. He no longer wished to run away from the bizarre scene.

"Who are you?" he asked calmly.

"We are all Benson," said the nearest Benson. "You have spoken to most of us down the years."

"You're not human," Gould stated. "You're not Interlopers either."

There was no reply.

"Are you escaping your world, too?" he asked.

A few ghostly figures shimmered, almost vanished, returned.

"We are explorers, not refugees," said the nearest Benson. "And we prefer to operate discreetly. Through human intermediaries such as yourself."

"We knew some time ago that the Interlopers would cause problems," said a second Benson."

"They are primitive," said another. "Their powers are few, as are their numbers, and the time disparity meant that they had to improvise hastily. They concocted a few specimens that could survive in this world. No great matter. Humans are good at hunting down outsiders. They will not survive."

"What are you?" Gould demanded.

"You cannot understand our nature," said a third Benson. "We occupy a higher plane of existence."

"Did you come here because we eroded the barrier with your reality?" he demanded. "Are we a threat to your world, too?"

There was a chorus of gasps, a sound Gould assumed passed for laughter among the Benson-beings. His question was naive, apparently.

"What the Interlopers saw as a threat, we see as an opportunity," said one. "So many busy life-forms, a world ripe for – development, as you would say."

"But the Interlopers were a nuisance?" Gould asked. "A distraction?"

"Quite. You perceive the problem. The solution was to make it clear that the Interlopers were the only non-human beings in your world, that the Phantom Dimension was unique. We managed to guide your own research in that direction with little difficulty. You never really gave the many-worlds hypothesis enough attention. We have found it a most profitable area of study."

The nearest Benson stood up, unfolding himself from the chair until his head almost brushed the ceiling.

"You needed a failed invasion, a threat that we could withstand," Gould whispered. "So we would feel we had the measure of the problem. And now we humans can draw a line under it, and leave you free to do whatever you want."

"A virtue made from necessity."

More Bensons had arisen, and now two were striding languidly toward Gould. He backed to the door. Groping for the handle and found it was locked. He started to sidle around

"We have been experimenting much more carefully than the clumsy Interlopers," said the closet Benson. "You are very confusing creatures. But we think we have found a way to tame you."

A vast hand descended gently onto his head, fingers wrapping themselves effortlessly around his skull. He felt all emotion, all thought, begin to drain away. A rushing sound, like a great tide washing into a vast sea-cave, swamped his consciousness.

"No, please!" he shouted, pulling in vain at the arm above him.

Then he was standing in an empty room, winter sunlight slanting in through half-open blinds. A dozen chairs were pushed in under a long table. He walked over to the glossy expanse of pinewood, ran a finger over the surface. A thin film of dust obscured his fingerprint.

Empty for weeks, or months. I wonder where Benson's gone?

Gould shrugged, turned to leave. As he opened the door, he paused and glanced quickly round, half-expecting to see a silent cohort seated around the table. But of course, no one was there. The conference room retained its neglected air.

"We may never know," he murmured to himself, as he shut the door and set off to re-join the others downstairs.

***

A trucker had just spent ten minutes cursing the narrow roads of a small English town when he saw the hitchhiker. At first, he was not sure if it was a man or a woman. The dark-clad figure by the roadside was tall, and wearing some kind of black uniform. When he saw it was a young woman, and one with a very pretty face, he stopped and let her run up to the side door.

"Where you going, miss?" he asked. "I'm heading west, over the border."

The woman looked up at him, and smiled. The trucker felt an immense sense of well-being wash over him. It was as if he had been immersed in a warm bath of pure happiness. He realized that the hitchhiker was speaking, but found it impossible to concentrate on her words. He opened the door, and she climbed in.

"Sorry, where did you say you were going?" he asked.

"Up into the hills," she said. "A remote corner of Wales. A nice little village where I can live in peace. But anywhere to the west will do."

"Okay," he said cheerfully. "I'm heading for Cardiff but I can drop you anywhere."

As he steered the big ten-wheeler into the westbound lane he had a sudden vision of himself and the young woman having sex in the back of the truck. It was graphic, intense, and downright pornographic. It shocked him, not merely because it was against company rules, but because it was against his rules, too. He had a wife and kids at home and loved them. *Why would I do anything to endanger that?*

Rattled by the unwanted thought, he flicked on the radio. The news was still obsessing over the weird influx of so-called monsters. There was talk of alien invasions, parallel universes, and mad experiments in secret labs.

"None of them have a bloody clue, do they?" he remarked, re-tuning to a classic pop station. "I reckon it's all exaggerated." He glanced over at his passenger, and again he was struck by how lovely she was. Her face reminded him of someone, a girl he had once known. She had married another man, broke his heart. He had not thought about her for years.

"Take a picture, it'll last longer," said the woman, then smiled.

"Sorry," he said, smiling back. "It's just that you remind

me of someone I ... somebody I once knew."

"I get that a lot," she said. "Hey, do you think you could take me off the main highway, up into the hills?"

No. Of course I can't, I've got a load to deliver.

"Of course," he said. "We're coming up to a turn-off in a few minutes. Where do you want to go?"

The next morning a farmer found the truck at the end of a track, blocking the entrance to his field. He knocked on the side door, assuming the driver had gotten lost. When he got no reply, the farmer climbed up and tried the handle. When the door opened, a corpse tumbled out. Later the farmer recounted his shocking discovery to a local reporter as they stood near the scene.

"What I don't understand," he said, "is how such an old guy could be driving a truck in the first place. He was so dried up and wrinkled, he looked like he could be a hundred years old. And–" The farmer hesitated, looked around at a few curious bystanders, and lowered his voice.

"... maybe you shouldn't print this," he went on. "But he must have been a bit senile, or demented. You know? Because the poor guy had taken his pants off for some reason. Naked from the waist down. What a way to go!"

* * *

FREE Bonus Novel!

Wow, I hope you enjoyed this book as much as I did writing it! If you enjoyed the book, please leave a review. Your reviews inspire me to continue writing about the world of spooky and untold horrors!

To really show you my appreciation for purchasing this book, I'd love to send you a **free extra spooky full length novel.** This will surely leave you running scared!

Sign up for the mailing list on our site to download your full length horror novel, get free short stories, and receive future discounts: www.ScareStreet.com/DavidLonghorn

See you in the shadows,
David Longhorn

Made in the USA
Coppell, TX
13 June 2020